DID YOU EVER DREAM OF HAVING A HANDSOME, SUCCESSFUL HUSBAND THREE GREAT LOOKING KIDS, A BEAUTIFUL HOUSE WITH A POOL, AND A PURSE CRAMMED WITH CREDIT CARDS AND THE WORLD'S MOST GLITTERING BOUTIQUES TO USE THEM IN?

Cassie did—and got what she wanted.

DID YOU EVER DREAM OF BEING A COSMO GIRL, COMPLETE WITH A CREATIVE CAREER, SOPHISTICATED SEX, UNCHALLENGED INDEPENDENCE, AND ALL THE EXCITEMENT OF MANHATTAN?

Celia did—and got what she wanted.

Which left both twin sisters faced with the same question: *What do you do with a dream when it comes true?*

THE TWO OF US

"BOTH HILARIOUS AND DISTURBING . . . causes one to contemplate the twin sides of one's own nature."—*Newsday*

"DARING . . . DAZZLING . . . a triumph and a treasure . . . Nora Johnson has revitalized the American novel."—Garson Kanin

"WITTY, COMP[ ] WITH EMOTIO[ ] can only marvel [ ] her characters' e[ ] key dilemmas of [ ]

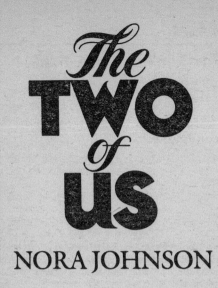

The TWO of US

NORA JOHNSON

A SIGNET BOOK

NEW AMERICAN LIBRARY

NAL BOOKS ARE AVAILABLE AT QUANTITY DISCOUNTS WHEN USED TO PROMOTE PRODUCTS OR SERVICES. FOR INFORMATION PLEASE WRITE TO PREMIUM MARKETING DIVISION, NEW AMERICAN LIBRARY, 1633 BROADWAY, NEW YORK, NEW YORK 10019.

SIGNET TRADEMARK REG. U.S. PAT. OFF. AND FOREIGN COUNTRIES
REGISTERED TRADEMARK—MARCA REGISTRADA
HECHO EN CHICAGO, U.S.A.

SIGNET, SIGNET CLASSIC, MENTOR, PLUME, MERIDIAN AND NAL BOOKS are published by New American Library, 1633 Broadway, New York, New York 10019

First Signet Printing, December, 1985

1 2 3 4 5 6 7 8 9

PRINTED IN THE UNITED STATES OF AMERICA

CASSIE
(At the Mountaintop Priory)

I may sound cruel and hard-hearted, but in the long run I'm not sorry any of it happened. It's no secret that life's best lessons are its most difficult, and it's only pain and suffering that enable us to rise above our blind, selfish lives and see beyond to a higher "purpose." I don't pretend to be as wise as some of the people here who are always talking about "the Word" and "the Way" and quoting chapter and verse and acting as though they had some kind of direct line to God. But as I sit here under the rose bower in the little garden, looking down over the valley, I'm beginning to understand that this is the place I was destined for all along.

I, of all people. Cassie Armstrong, outgoing pom-pom girl, Glee Club mezzo and Prom Queen. Cassie Cooper-smith, busy, involved, affluent California housewife, mother and media hostess. I was the last person you'd expect to end up leading a quiet, contemplative life in a remote community far from life's "hurly-burly."

But now I'm beginning to understand God's message. Even though I sensed His presence within me when I was a small child, I misused this precious gift in various ways. Closing my eyes to my calling, I was determined to be normal and lead a conventional life, which I now know was impossible. I was not always kind to those who were different from me or who didn't come up to my expectations. I "assumed" too many things, I was often closed-minded and sometimes snotty and superior. Instead of trying to help those who stumbled along on clay feet, I was scornful of their blindness and impatient with their inevitable faults and mistakes. So it was necessary for my eyes to be opened, which they could only be by some of the terrible things that happened to me and my family: and now I—the new Cassie—have risen like the Phoenix from the ashes.

So now I can tell my story as it happened, as though I were living it again: for only that way can it be fresh and true, and not full of "hindsight" and clever I-knew-it-all-along comments, which I personally find extremely annoying when nobody ever knew it all along, or could possibly guess what was going to happen. I know I can't tell it alone, but I don't mind that anymore, because I'm no longer afraid.

In only one short year I have been catapulted from the ordinary to the sublime. Just how far I realize only when I hear the voice of the woman I used to be.

CASSIE
(Santa Barbara)

I am an ordinary person who leads an ordinary life. I have a husband and three children, and we live in Santa Barbara, California. I'm forty-three years old, but thanks to the care I give my appearance I resemble a much younger woman, besides being fortunate enough to have excellent health and enough money to satisfy all my wants and needs. My life is in general quite happy and my problems are mostly those of an average housewife; for instance, whether we should put in a tennis court in the area beyond the pool, or whether the condition of the rose garden is worth arguing about with the gardener, who speaks English very badly and with an impossible accent.

Sam and I have discussed the tennis court without coming to any conclusion. I personally feel it might be a good source of exercise for Sammy, Stu and Shelli, who seem to spend a great deal of time lying around the pool or in their rooms, sometimes with earphones on their heads—though Shelli does go for a ride every day on her horse, Ginger, who is stabled just up the mountain. Sam says they are already spoiled rotten and "glutted" with possessions, such as stereos, tape decks, TV sets and expensive clothes, not to mention orthodontia, Vidal Sassoon haircuts and therapists—unlike the small number of possessions that he and I had at the same age. Besides, if we had a tennis court, he'd have to play too or else feel guilty, especially since, unlike me, Sam has a tendency to put on weight. I don't think either of us is really very much interested in this tennis court, but it's something to talk about.

Of course, no life is completely tranquil, and even in mine there are signs of the changing times. One example is my neighbor Angela's therapy and the new attitude it has given her. Before she started going to this Dr. Pui, or Piu, or Pew, or whatever his name is, her interests were very much like mine—shopping, household matters and care of her appearance, to name just a few. Now she's gotten very snippy and superior, and acts as though she were the only one who knows anything, which of course is not true at all. She'll come by for a swim and a glass of wine by the pool and in no time she starts in, all about her wonderful therapy and how it's given her a whole new purpose in life, and how I should do it too. Well, not only have I heard it all before, but I simply don't need a therapist. After all, Angela doesn't have a husband and I do. But she said that was beside the point. It wasn't, she explained, that she'd *failed* at her marriage, or that there was anything *wrong* with her. It was because she'd never understood herself at all. She'd gone through life half-blind. Now she could see a little more every day.

I don't want to see a little more every day, and I told Angela so.

"But Cassie," she said, "the unexamined life is not worth living."

"Maybe you mean that the husbandless life is not worth living, Angela."

"My God, you're like something from a time warp. The only reason you think you couldn't get along without Sam is because you were brought up believing yourself to be helplessly dependent on men."

"You're wrong, Angela. I was brought up to be quite independent. But I'm realistic enough to know that if I had to support myself, it would not be like this." I waved my arm to indicate the house and patio, with its lovely view, and the bottle of Chardonnay in the wine cooler.

"Is that all you can think of? Only money?"

We've had this discussion a dozen times. As Bernadette

Peters said to Steve Martin in that stupid movie—I can't recall the title—it isn't the money, really, it's the *stuff*. How I love all the stuff—buying it, bringing it home, admiring it, taking care of it. Wearing it. Driving it. Sitting on it. Showing it off. Eating off it and drinking out of it. Just having it around makes me feel good. I have a feeling that part of Angela's attitude has to do with the limited amount of her support money, which doesn't allow her to go shopping with me the way she used to. I feel sorry for her and don't want to rub it in. I'm glad she has her Dr. Piu and her new theories to help make up for the trips down to Rodeo Drive.

I have to admit that nothing gives me a kick like a shopping trip. I feel a lttle funny saying it these days, when we're all supposed to be so worried about inflation, unemployment and interest rates. Certainly I would be among the last to want the poor to become poorer. But also I would be less than honest if I didn't admit the joy I get out of a day in the shops, with maybe a trip to the hairdresser, a facial and then lunch at some nice restaurant with Angela or another of my girl friends. It's times like that I wish my mother lived here, instead of three thousand miles across the country. There's something so nice about the idea of a mother and daughter shopping together and then having lunch. There's a word for it, I can't think what, but it means that mothers and daughters have been doing the same thing for hundreds of years, or maybe even thousands. In a couple of years Shelli will be old enough to be interested in something besides her horse and will probably ask me for advice about clothes, boys and other female matters, and I look forward to giving her my opinions.

The last time Angela went shopping was before the judge set the final amount of her support payments, the day I got my purple Giorgio Armani jump suit with the green sash, and she bought that Chanel suit and sent the bill to Paul—or Pauline, as she was calling him by then. It was the last thing she charged, and she really wanted him to remember it.

"I can wear it anywhere," she said. It's true that there's nothing as practical as a Chanel suit. This one was jade-

and-gray kalimousse, fifteen hundred dollars. I asked her how she knew he'd pay for it, and she said he would because he was guilty as sin.

Surrounded as I am by catastrophes like Angela's marriage, and most of the marriages/liaisons on our side of the mountain, I feel extremely lucky to have Sam. And I do mean "lucky." I don't happen to be one of those people who think a good marriage is some kind of skill. I think it's a crapshoot right from the start. I could just as easily have drawn Paul, for instance. Angela thinks that something inside attracted her to Paul twenty-three years ago, some kind of evil eye that could see ahead and could tell he was going to turn out to be gay, and that she married him to destroy herself or something. Well, sometimes Angela is full of shit. Twenty-three years ago the man was as masculine as Sam, and in fact they weren't much different—two bright young TV guys like a million others in L.A. She got one and I got the other. She was unlucky, but it could just as easily have been me. The point is, it's not because I'm better than Angela or smarter or anything, though I am better-looking. Sometimes things just happen, as though God willed them to.

I suppose that's one reason I've never gone to Dr. Pui or any other shrink, because I think there are things God doesn't want you prying into. There are things you aren't supposed to know. I can see how if something goes wrong you might want to find out why, but as far as I'm concerned, I'm sure I'm better off not rocking the boat.

After all, look what I've got. I'm married to a handsome, successful television film producer. I have a lovely home on the side of a mountain in Santa Barbara and three wonderful children. Sam and I still get along fine. We have many friends and go to a lot of parties both here and in L.A. I believe I would be very foolish to tamper with all this.

It's true that Sam does screw around a little, but in his profession, who doesn't? I know, and he knows that I know, but we never talk about it. And once I had this really stupid affair with a man I met on the plane coming back from Honolulu. (Sam doesn't know, and don't tell him.) To this day I can't imagine why I did it, unless it was to get back at my husband. My "lover" was in Santa Barbara on business and was staying at the Biltmore, and I'd go down there to meet him. I always wore a raincoat and sunglasses, but even so I was recognized several times by people I know, who greeted me cheerfully. I'd hide out in the ladies' room and then sneak to his room, and we'd make love—which, frankly, was a disappointment. In fact, the whole thing just was not the "romantic affair" I'd expected. We never sat in the bar and had a bottle of champagne, we never went dancing, we never walked barefoot on the beach. I'd just go straight to his room and we'd undress and he'd pump away and then afterward we'd have a cigarette. Well, it didn't last long—all that I could have at home.

To tell the truth, I think sex is overrated. I'm not going to go into it, because I'm so tired of hearing Angela talk about orgasms, clitorises and vaginas that I could scream. Sometimes she uses dirty words just to shock and annoy me. Once she actually said that Sam and I should go to a sex clinic. I replied, "Angela, I'm your best friend, and I try to be understanding and charitable about your stage of life. But I honestly think that living without a man is making you soft in the head."

"Well, putting *that* little comment aside, can't you understand that I make these suggestions to help you? You could be getting real pleasure out of sex, Cassie, if you only knew how."

"Please, Angela. Pass me those nuts. I find this whole conversation embarrassing. What Sam and I do in bed is our business."

"You're the one who said sex was boring."

"So what if it's boring? So are a lot of things—it's not the worst thing in the world. It's like screenings—they're just something you have to sit through. It's like waiting at the pediatrician's office." I sat up and adjusted the top of my bikini. "Frankly, I don't mind boring things at all. They give me time to think."

I didn't say that if I wanted to get rid of all the boring things in my life, she would be among the first to go. But I love Angela and will stick with her until she settles down again. In the meantime I enjoy lying on my back beside the pool, sipping wine and listening to her drone on and on about the things she thinks I should be worrying about. If she's right, I'm grateful to her for carrying my share.

I probably sound as though I did nothing but lie around the pool all the time. I probably sound fat. Actually I'm not fat at all, being one of those people who can eat whatever they want without putting on weight, as long as no one tampers with my habits. Sam is not so lucky. If he let down his guard he'd swell up like a balloon, and it's hard for him to watch me eat a baked potato, for instance, with sour cream, chives, chopped parsley and freshly ground pepper, while he has to make do with alfalfa sprouts.

This has occasionally been a slight problem in our marriage. Once when we were sharing such an unbalanced meal he called me a cunt. I was deeply shocked. I couldn't believe he'd say that. I felt just terrible until I realized that his cruel word came out of pure starvation. I still felt bad, but with a little more understanding. He said he was sorry he'd said it, and then added that it would make him feel a lot better if I dieted along with him. Foolishly, I agreed. It was a dreadful experience. I was so hungry in the daytime that I couldn't stop picking things out of the refrigerator, and I put on twenty pounds, which made me so depressed I cried all the time. I'd think of that rotten little salad I'd planned for dinner, and the gazpacho or the jellied consommé first, and I'd go into the kitchen and make myself a grilled cheese-and-bacon sandwich. Then at dinner I'd look at those stupid little shredded carrots and sprouts and cherry tomatoes and broccoli "florets" and something inside me just sank like a ship going down. I'd pick at it, and my eyes would get teary. At first Sam said, "Cassie, baby, why are you crying? Is it because you feel sorry for me, having to diet?" His voice was tender.

"No," I said. "It's because I hate this crap."

"So, do you think *I* like it?"

"No, Sam, I do not. But there are some places I can't follow you, and this is one of them. Our bodies are separate."

"That's probably why I can't help noticing that those pants are too tight."

I said, "Sam, I have never been so cruel as to say such

a thing to you. This whole thing is wrong. I can't alter my entire eating pattern. God wants me to eat in a certain way and I tried to change it, and I'm very unhappy. I'll do almost anything for you, Sam, but there are limits. I can't abuse my body like this anymore.''

It's strange, but true, that very often in an argument I end up having the last word. I don't know why. Sam is certainly much smarter than I am. He went to college and majored in Literature, and he reads all the time and is very educated. At parties he has a great deal of witty repartee. He knows everything about the movie business and is also capable of having serious discussions about politics and world affairs. I only went to high school in the town where I grew up Back East, and then came straight to the Coast. I wanted to be a movie star, ha ha. Anyway, not to labor the subject of my short-lived career, there's no question that Sam is my intellectual superior—but there are times, in the middle of a conversation, when he just stops talking and can't think of anything to say. He stares at me with his mouth open, as though he'd never seen me before. This particular time, he said, ''Whenever you can't think of anything to say you drag God into it''—but the truth was, *he* was the one who couldn't think of anything to say. Very often he just sighs and says, ''Cassie, you're the limit.''

One big difference between Sam and me is that he doesn't believe in God, and I do. When the kids were small, I took them to church every Sunday. I think Sam was secretly glad I did it, though he wouldn't have been caught dead there himself. Deep in his heart he was glad his kids were getting some religion—he would have been just a little afraid if they weren't. So in that sense we agree. The way I see it, you have nothing to lose by believing in God and everything to gain. I don't mind admitting that in many ways I play it close to the vest. Safety First Cassie, you might say. I know people who don't believe in God and they have difficult lives. The two things might, of course, have nothing to do with each other. But you never know. I'd just as soon not take the chance, especially since I'm doing it for Sam and the children too, because now that they're older they seem to be following in their father's footsteps.

Anyway, since I believe in God, I also believe strongly that He wants things to happen in certain ways. He doesn't want me to stuff myself in the afternoon. He wants me to enjoy my dinner. If I go along with my body's natural needs, I am a happy, healthy person. But if I try to change them, I'm miserable.

It really is a shame when you think of it. Ten years ago, or even five years, one of the things Sam and I enjoyed most was to go out for dinner at El Paseo, a place here in town. We'd have a couple of martinis and then a whole platter of tostadas, tortillas, burritos, guacamole and enchiladas, and a big pitcher of Mexican beer. Sometimes we took the kids and sometimes we went alone. We'd eat ourselves blind, and laugh, and get a little high, and sing and hold hands in the car going home. Well, we must have had steel-lined stomachs. Gin. Salsa. Chilies. Hot peppers. And sometimes we'd stop on the way home for a frozen custard. We'd go home and sleep like babies. Well, if I ate a meal like that now I'd have to have my stomach pumped. Things are different after forty.

I don't really mind being my age, I suppose. Why should I? A lot of women are worse off than I am. I look very good, which I damn well should considering the time and effort I put into it. I've only had my eyes done so far, but as other parts of my body need attention over the passing years, I'll do whatever is necessary. Fanny. Bosoms. A nip here and a tuck there. I sincerely believe that this is part of my obligation to my marriage. Sylvia, just down the canyon, has thighs like wrinkled old silk. Her marriage, if you can call it that, is a joke. Her husband, Harold, no longer even tries to keep his cheating a secret. I've seen him downtown twice with his chippies and he doesn't even try to hide them. "Hi, Cassie," he calls, as though we were out walking our dogs. I'm almost sure it has something to do with the condition of Sylvia's legs, and her pendulous, crepelike breasts, and the flab on her upper arms, which gathers like the surface of very heavy cream. I certainly don't mean to criticize Sylvia for nature's marks, for she is, after all, almost sixty. But she could *try*. It's hard for me to understand people who don't give life their best efforts.

To tell the truth, I'm glad my thirties are over. A conscientious person like me puts everything into her home and the raising of her children, and now that all that's mostly finished, I'm looking forward to a more leisurely life. After what I've said about lying around the pool all the time, it probably sounds as though my life weren't exactly difficult. But this has been so only in the last year. Before that there was always something. Boy scouts. The orthodontist. Swimming and riding lessons. Travel and entertaining, which we did about once a week. Well, I needn't document the tasks of a busy housewife. Of course, I've heard that there are women who can do all these things and hold down a job too, though I'm not sure I believe it. I know if you're a perfectionist like me it's impossible. I'm not comfortable unless everything is just right.

And don't talk to me about help. I know about help. In the fifteen years we've lived in this house there has been a steady parade of ethnic people in and out of here who have been more trouble than assistance. I certainly don't mean to say anything against the Chicano race, which of course has many excellent qualities. But there does seem to be a certain native streak of laziness or carelessness in most of them. I always hoped to find a good, loyal, hardworking person who would stay with us for years and become part of our family—someone I trusted completely so that I could feel truly at rest in my own home. But instead we have had a string of Spanish drunks, thieves, drug addicts, whores, maniacs and just plain incompetents. Concepción has been here for a year and so far she seems to be adequate, except for a slight moroseness of character. But good Lord, that's nothing compared with what I've had before. I try to be sympathetic when I find her crying in the kitchen and I do my best to understand her problems, which is almost impossible since she speaks hardly any English. So I can't do much to help.

You might have heard the old expression "My home is my castle." Sometimes I think I love my home more than I love Sam and the children. After several experiments,

I've gotten it *just the way I want it*. Sam, being a typical husband, has hardly any interest in domestic arrangements, and was more than happy to turn the job entirely over to me. (I think this is one of the secrets of our successful marriage—neither of us interferes with the other's job.) His only requirement was that it be comfortable and luxurious, suitable for both a growing family and the home entertaining of media personalities. The present decoration is my favorite of them all and fulfills both these functions.

It isn't a grand house, compared with some of the mansions around here. It's a simple one-floor California-style ranch, halfway up the mountain behind the city, with a three-car garage, surrounded by eucalyptus and flame trees. In back are the pool, bathhouse and Jacuzzi. By the pool is a large patio, with comfortable outdoor furniture upholstered in peach canvas, and large glass sliding doors lead into the living room. In the afternoon sun pours in and floods the room with light.

In the center of the living room is a tree that grows straight up through the roof. The fireplace is of fieldstone, the largest rocks that could be found. (I copied it from a lodge in the Adirondacks where we went when I was a child.) Of course, we don't build actual fires in this mild Southern California climate. But we have a small gas unit inside with artificial logs that glow just like real ones. It gives a little warmth and is pleasant on damp, chilly evenings. In front of the fireplace is my ivory Naugahyde playpen, where I love to curl up in the evening and watch something on the big screen, or do my needlework (I'm making petit-point covers for the dining-room chairs, though it's taken me a year to do only one.) Recently I've been watching all the early *Dallas* shows that we Betamaxed when they first came on.

I wanted the room to look like the inside of a seashell, and on two walls are peach metallic foil, and on the other two, silver. The peach metallic motif is repeated in the coffee table in the middle of the playpen, which is covered in the same shiny paper. The lighting is indirect, and spotlights pick up the paintings that hang on the wall. Though my taste is, as you can see, quite modern, when it comes to art I'm pretty old-fashioned. I like scenic paintings and am even fond of religious subjects, though Sam objects strongly to those.

On the other side of the room is the bar—always fully stocked, of course—with the Lucite barstools. They're amusing because sometimes, after a drink or two in our rather dark living room, you can hardly see them, and a couple of times people have sat in the wrong place—right down on the floor! On the floor is wall-to-wall thick, furry shag carpeting in white. The poodle, Mimi, is such a similar color that sometimes, when she's lying on the living-room floor, you can't even see her, or couldn't except for her two brown eyes. Oh, and the ceiling is mirrored. Sam's idea.

There are four bedrooms in our house, one for each of the children and one for us. I won't dwell too much on the children's bedrooms except to say that we have been through various stages in respect to their maintenance, and at the moment I'm holding fast to the rule that Concepción may not *enter* them to clean unless the floors have been cleared, nor will any of their laundry be done unless it is put in the hamper. Let them rot in their own filth. If I sound cruel and uncaring, it's because I've been driven to it. Probably I am more particular than most people about personal habits. I respect my home enough to go to some trouble over its appearance, and have little patience with those who don't. I've been told that Sammy Junior and Stu, at twenty-three and seventeen, are typical of most young men in their complete obliviousness to their surroundings and their compulsion to live like pigs. It has something to do with rebellion. I must say, I don't understand what they're rebelling *against*. People rebel against things that make them unhappy, but as far as I can see, Sam and I have asked very little of our children and given them almost anything they wanted.

In our bedroom I allowed myself to give full expression to feminism, or do I mean femininity? The color scheme is pink and white and gold. Our white four-poster has pink ruffles cascading from the top. The lamps are golden cherubs. The bedspread is pink with golden sequins. There is a white leather kneehole desk where I sit and reply to invitations, and a white velvet chaise lounge sits by the sliding glass doors that lead out to our private hot tub, surrounded by oleander bushes. Our bathroom, which has black porcelain fixtures and dramatic gold-and-purple flocked wallpaper, has twin tubs and twin sinks. (The toilet is in a stall.) On the floor is a rug that Sam got somewhere which looks like many female breasts in three dimensions, all in flesh-colored foam rubber and each with a red dot on the tip. I think it's disgusting—but as always, we found a compromise. I will tolerate it when we have guests, for he enjoys showing it to his friends, but the rest of the time it stays rolled up in the closet. In return, the picture of Christ and Mary Magdalene that usually hangs on our bedroom wall is put away when company comes.

I believe our bedroom is my favorite room in the house. I love to put on one of my negligees or peignoirs and sit on the chaise lounge, reading a magazine or doing my nails. At such times I feel truly contented and at peace, which in this difficult world seems harder and harder to achieve.

Certainly I'm a lucky woman and have almost nothing to complain about. But even so there are problems these days that didn't exist when I was a child. Sam doesn't agree about this. He says things have always been difficult, and I just didn't notice because I was young. Or else, he says, I'm just noticing the difference between California and Connecticut, which is a hundred years behind the times. But no matter what he says, there were not, when I was a child, *drugs*. To me drugs are the main peril of modern-day life. I have never touched any, even marijuana, and never will. This fact, of which I am proud, has been a source of serious disagreement between Sam and me, and even between my children and me. I am not by any means a prude, and I ordinarily sip a glass of wine or a vodka-and-tonic, and have even gotten, on occasion, a little tipsy. But drugs I will never try, even at the risk of imperiling my marriage.

You may not believe it (I didn't at first, either), but drugs are a way of life in the entertainment business. It amazes me that these people manage to do their difficult, demanding work while taking them. Sam says that one has nothing to do with the other, but he hasn't convinced me. Even Sam smokes joints and occasionally takes cocaine.

He has "tripped" and taken " 'ludes." He says that the reason he occasionally spends an evening away from home is that I won't join him in this activity and he wants company while he gets "high."

Since Sam is an important network executive, naturally we entertain frequently, though less frequently than we used to. We have had parties in this house that made me sick. People falling-down stoned. People hiding in the powder room to "snort." Drugged-up people having sex all over the yard and once, even, in my ivory Naugahyde playpen! Naked people jumping into the pool. I've tried on these occasions to be good-natured about all this, but it gives me a disgusted feeling inside. It's hard for me to be a good hostess while all this is going on.

I've talked seriously to Sam about the children. I don't believe it does Sammy Junior, Stuart and Shelli any good to see adults behaving the way they do at our parties. Naturally, they take drugs too, and Sam doesn't see the connection. He says what we do has nothing to do with the children because we're adults and have earned the right. Or else he says everybody smokes pot, and even if we forbade it the children would smoke it anyway. Once he said that there was no contradiction between drugs and religion, and that many nations took certain drugs, such as peyote, for religious purposes.

There are two things I don't understand about people who take drugs. One is what happens to their ordinary logic, which in Sam's case is usually quite good. The other is why they can't let people like me alone. I don't bother them. I let them do what they like in my house (unfortunately) because I'm a good wife. Why do they keep offering me " 'ludes" and "tokes" and "uppers"? Even Angela does it. A famous television actress who has been here for dinner twice has a hole through the membrane that divides her nostrils from each other. When she showed it to me I thought I'd be sick to my stomach. She wasn't sure whether it would ever grow back together and she didn't even seem to care. I think a person like that is as good as dead.

Out of consideration for me, and because Sam secretly admires my beliefs, we now have very few parties at our house. Now we are more apt to entertain smaller groups at sit-down dinners, and at most they smoke pot after dinner. On the other hand, because people seem to have gotten so health-conscious, there is less drinking than there used to be.

Unfortunately, our dinner parties are usually boring. (I probably sound as though nothing satisfied me, complaining one minute about one thing and the next about something else, but in fact I am a fairly contented person and quite easy to please, which is one of the reasons Sam loves me.) I haven't mentioned this to Sam, because he and the guests, who are all in the entertainment business, seem to enjoy them well enough—which they damn well should, because it takes Concepción and me three days to get ready for one of them. I am a Gourmet Cook and everything is always elegant, tasty, nutritious and not too high in calories and cholesterol. We often eat on the patio. The shrubbery is indirectly lit and so is our free-form pool, which is a lovely shade of pale green. There are candles in hurricane lamps on the table, and the whole effect is lovely and romantic. The women are often beautiful and tastefully dressed in elegant caftans or evening pajamas.

And what is the conversation about? Deals. My God, I'm so sick of deals. It's not that I don't understand that they are crucial to the maintenance of my life-style. It's not that I begrudge Sam his dedication to his business. It isn't even that I object to the men talking over their daily affairs in a pleasant and leisurely atmosphere, for the truth is I have much more in common with the other women and always enjoy discussing domestic matters. But while the men talk about pitching stories and properties and pilots and distribution and going to series, the women try by any possible means to interrupt them and get their attention. They make jokes, they nudge them and poke at them, they often drink too much and once one even threw most of a salad, with cherry tomatoes, at her husband. It is truly sad to see these beautiful creatures behaving this way, and sadder still that the men continue to ignore them. Whatever our disagreements, Sam would never humiliate me. He never fails to catch my eye across the table, and either winks, smiles or puckers his lips in a little kiss. Sometime during the evening he always stops by my chair and says, "Babe, you're perfect." It takes very little effort on his part, and I believe many of these women are starved for this sort of affection.

Affection is an extremely important part of a relationship. Though I've said I'm not all that interested in sex, what I actually meant was the intercourse part. However, I love it when Sam puts his strong arms around me and holds me tightly to his manly chest. Hugging is what I need to feel truly fulfilled and complete as a woman. At the same time, I am never more aware than when we are in bed together of the profound differences between male and female. I don't mean biological differences. I mean what's in our minds. Sometimes it seems as though there is hardly any area in which we think alike about sex, though we discuss it very little if at all. We seem to be two people who want entirely different things.

I would rather keep the holy veil of privacy around our personal moments, but I will mention that there are times when Sam can't get it up. At those times he carries on as though this were some sort of failure rather than the blessed relief it is. "Cassie," he says, "I'm getting old," or, "I had too much to drink," or "Please forgive me," or else "It isn't you, baby. I love you like I always have." At such times he seems to need consolation, which of course I am happy to give, though I don't mention the real reason for my happiness, which is having a night of respite from that thing poking into me. I mention this only to demonstrate what seem to be very significant differences between men and women—not to bare my breast in public, so to speak, as so many people, including Angela, seem to do these days.

I met Sam Coopersmith a year or so after I came to Hollywood.

I'm not going to make much out of my so-called career. Needless to say, I did not become the movie star I dreamed of being. However, I'm glad I had that year to myself, because I grew up in several important ways.

I came from a small town in Connecticut, the child of two loving, old-fashioned parents, Caspar and Dorothy

Armstrong. We lived in a house on a quiet street lined with maple trees where my parents still live. We went to church on Sundays. My sister and I were raised with the old-fashioned values of duty, honor and self-respect that I still cling to today. I was a normal, well-adjusted child who gave her parents little or no trouble. I worked hard at school and usually passed all my courses. I won ribbons at girls' basketball and trampoline. I had the lead in the Senior Play (Emily in *Our Town*) and was a cheerleader and a pompon girl. I sang in the glee club and the church choir. I had many friends with whom I exchanged "charms," and my girlhood charm bracelet is among my most treasured possessions. I was often invited to parties and was nominated for class president. In my junior year I was "lavaliered" and in my senior year I was "pinned." Neither relationship worked out because I wouldn't "go all the way."

I always loved movies and spent many Saturday afternoons at the Rivertown Rialto, humming as Doris Day sang. When I was younger I had dreamed of waltzing away to happiness with Rock Hudson or sitting beside Charlton Heston in his chariot as he whipped his horses to a froth. I don't mean to suggest that I was one of those maladjusted children who escape into unreality. The movies were like a door to the outside world. Even then I had a taste for beauty, glamour and the things money can buy— none of which would ever come to me in Rivertown. I thought if I didn't find fame as a movie actress, I would at least find a man who wanted the same things I did.

I've sometimes thought about what my life would be like if I'd given in to Ron Burnside, the boy I was "pinned" to. It wasn't that he wanted to seduce me and then leave me afterward. He wanted us to become engaged so we could sleep together. In that respect his strategy was faulty, because he almost never talked about what it would be like when we were married; what he talked about was how he was dying to go to bed with me. However, I have no doubt that if I'd wanted to marry him, he couldn't have gotten out of it. We would have lived in a tiny house down near the railroad tracks or else with either his parents or mine. Ron would have gone to work at his father's hardware store. I would have been stuck at home with babies. I'd be wearing dowdy dresses and my hair would still be mousy brown, or by this time, streaked with gray. I'd look more like sixty than forty-three.

On Saturday nights we'd go out to the roadhouse with our friends, and Ron would get drunk and I'd have to drive home. I can imagine our home. Dotted Swiss curtains at the windows. Curly maple furniture. Hooked rugs. Home Sweet Home samplers on the wall. Polyester leisure suits in the closet. I could vomit when I think of it. The worst part is I wouldn't have known any better. I wouldn't ever have known how ignorant I was, how lacking in taste and sophistication, how dull and provincial. I tremble when I think what I narrowly missed. I remind myself of it when I feel like complaining about my life, which usually happens only the day before I get my period.

When I definitely decided that I wanted a career in the movies, I spoke to my parents. I pointed out that I had demonstrated some talent in *Our Town* and had a fairly good mezzo-soprano voice. I was pretty and had a good figure. I added that a college education would be wasted on me since I wasn't all that interested, and asked if they would give me one year's tuition for travel and living expenses while I got started and possibly voice lessons. (I'd planned to ask for all four years, but judging from the expressions on their faces, I decided not to.) Since they had always spoken of my going to college, I assumed they had the money put by. But they didn't. They had expected me to get through on loans, scholarships and part-time jobs. I was very disappointed—though not all that surprised when I thought about it later, because Daddy makes only a modest amount of money. (He owns a florist shop called The Bower of Flowers.) In the end, it turned out that all they could afford was a bus ticket.

How well I remember the evening all the plans were made. After dinner, while Mother and I were doing the dishes, I noticed her wiping her eyes, very quickly, when she thought I wasn't looking. She looked so pretty that night—she was wearing a pink blouse, a navy blue skirt and a frilly white apron. She had long brown hair which she always wore in a bun, and she had her half-glasses on

the end of her nose as she scraped the plates (we'd had
meat loaf for dinner, and mashed potatoes and corn on the
cob). She grabbed a Kleenex out of the pocket of her
apron and blew her nose. Then she said, "Are you sure
you want to go so far away, Cassie? You're only eighteen."

"I have to, Mama. I'm going to be a movie star."

"I'll miss you," she said, and a big tear fell down and
splashed into the sink. "I've always had a special love for
you."

Mama and I have always been close, but we've never
talked about it. She never says things like that—never.
She's strong and independent, besides doing most of the
talking, while Daddy is more quiet and retiring. I felt so
strange, I hardly knew what to do. I gave her a little hug,
which was unusual too, for she is not physically demonstrative. She gulped and blew her nose again.

"I love you too, Mama," I said.

"You've always been the calm, happy one. I'm afraid
our life at home hasn't been perfect. Lord knows I tried to
make it that way. I've done my best to make everything
right for you."

"Oh, Mama. I know you have."

"I suppose every family has a few problems. But you're
the one who could always smooth things down and make
everyone feel better." She sighed and fussed with my hair.
"I hope you're strong, Cassie. It won't be easy for you. It
won't be like life here on Maple Street."

"Oh, of course I am—I'm very strong. I'll be fine. I
can't wait to see California. And when I've gotten on my
feet, you and Daddy will come and visit me."

I feel a little guilty about that one. She's come only four
times in twenty years, though Sam and I have taken the
children there for a few visits. Sam has been generous
about sending her extra money. For a while she refused it,
but then I discovered that if I sent a check directly to her
bank, she simply used it and never mentioned it. It makes
me feel better to know she has enough, when my own life
is so comfortable and even luxurious.

A week later I left. I remember so well what I wore—a
seersucker suit, white pumps and a straw hat. I laugh when
I think of myself then. I was so cocky on the surface, and

underneath I was frightened to death. A bus ticket and a hundred dollars—fifty I'd saved from jobs and babysitting. And I'd never been much of anywhere—once to Boston and a few times to New York: that was all. A lot of girls have come to Hollywood to make their fortunes, but I don't think any of them have been as naive as I was. I didn't know anybody here. I didn't have a single letter of introduction. I had some idea about going to each of the big studios and asking for a job. If it didn't work out as quickly as I thought, I could take a job waiting on tables, at some place where the movie producers might notice me. God—was I *dumb!*

As I sat on the Greyhound bus that night speeding through Illinois or Ohio or whatever it was, I felt worse and worse every minute. I leaned my face against the window and looked out, and I was so homesick I thought I'd die. I thought of Mama and Daddy sitting by the fire, Mama knitting and Daddy reading the paper or listening to the radio. I saw that dear old room, with the worn rug and the wing chairs, and the firelight reflected on the polished brass fender, and the ticking of the mantel clock. I remembered how it looked at Christmas with the tree by the window, with its homemade decorations—paper chains and strings of popcorn and cranberries—filling the room with the scent of the pine forest. I thought of all the Christmases in that room from the time I was a little girl, with snow falling outside and the smell of roasting turkey and pumpkin pie, and I remembered how I had lain awake as long as I could listening for Santa to come down the chimney, and through the window I could hear the carolers outside, singing in front of all the houses on the street. I sat on that bus and cried and wondered if I were crazy to do what I was doing.

It wasn't just that I might never become a movie star. I might not even make it at all. I might starve or be raped or kidnapped or fall into depravity. If I didn't lose my life or my money—what little I had—I could lose my self-respect. I promised myself right then and there that no matter how difficult circumstances were, I would never do anything I didn't believe in in order to survive. It was a resolution that proved very difficult to keep, but from the moment I made it I felt a great deal better, as though I were armed with my own personal "bow of burning gold," as the old hymn says.

Well, God knows I needed it during that first year in Los Angeles. I can hardly overstate its difficulties. The first week I lived at a "Y" in a dreary part of town, and after that I alternated between cheap rooms, taken by the week, and "shares" with a series of roommates. I was a waitress in two sleazy restaurants and one fancy bar, and the only thing I did that made more than a small amount of money was a toothpaste commercial on TV. I had eight auditions, sang for two nights at a dive called the Ruby Heart, was offered a job as a topless dancer on the Strip, did some filing for a depraved producer, hung around and waited in places where there was supposed to be "action," worked for two weeks at a Laundromat in Marina Del Rey and was offered a thousand dollars for taking some dope to Mexico or bringing it back or something, which I turned down, though at that time I hadn't eaten in two days.

You may wonder why, if I was pretty and had a good figure and a pleasing mezzo-soprano voice, even if I failed to achieve stardom, I didn't at least manage to earn a respectable living in some lower echelon of show business, particularly since I was willing to work at almost anything—which was not true of most of the other girls I knew. But "respectable livings" didn't seem to exist in Hollywood. During the year I speak of, I was mauled, manhandled, "felt up," propositioned countless times and almost raped several others. The "respectable living" I would have been contented to make—even running the Laundromat, for instance, which I found fairly pleasant work, or singing at the Ruby Heart in East Hollywood, which in some ways was amusing—seemed to depend entirely on my willingness to "put out." The proprietor of the Laundromat unexpectedly took me into his office, locked the door, undid his fly and took out his cock, which he expected me to "eat." When I told him I would do no such thing, he fired me, even though his business had never been better run. As for my boss at the Ruby Heart, the only reason I didn't charge him with attempted rape was that he gave me

$200 to keep my mouth shut—which, all things considered, seemed the most sensible thing to do.

As for the producer (he's extremely famous; you'd recognize his name immediately), what I was filing was his "porn" collection, an enormous file of ten-by-twelve glossies of girls posing naked with their legs apart, which I was supposed to file according to color—an absurdity which made me immediately suspicious. At any rate, I did this for a couple of days to make a little money, which I desperately needed, and on the third day the producer, whose name starts with P., came in and began talking to me about "twats" and "cunts" and "split beavers" and other terms which I had never heard before. Now, if this had taken place in some sleazy office downtown, I would have left immediately. But I was working in his mansion in Bel Air, and he had brought me there in his Maserati. I had never seen such a beautiful and elegant house in my life—very modern, and full of built-in screens and fancy sound systems so that there was music wherever you were, and a huge pool and a patio with a view to the sea, surrounded by the most fabulous gardens I'd ever laid eyes on. For lunch I ate smoked salmon and caviar and sipped white wine brought in on a tray by a Japanese houseman.

You may think I was stupid not to be suspicious of such a setup. But for once it wasn't my being stupid, for I had a feeling I shouldn't stay there. It was *hunger*—not so much for the food, but for the sparkling pool, the thick towels piled in the bathhouse, the soft carpets, the music that thumped softly all day, the cool breeze and clear air that you got only up in the hills, the perfume of the flowers and the shaved green lawn that swept down to the entrance gates; oh, it was the *stuff*, and how I loved being there! It was like a dream, that house. Even though I sensed that there was something evil there, I felt as though if I just could be there for a few days and soak in all its beauty, I would be sustained through the next weeks or months of hardship, just by spending a little time in the Hollywood of my dreams. I suppose I was a little hypnotized by it all, and possibly a little drunk, because after lunch the Japanese houseman always left the bottle of wine there for me to finish.

Anyway, on the third afternoon in came P., my boss. I
told him I'd finished filing the pictures and was ready to
start on something else. P. just smiled and asked me if I'd
like to share a "reefer."

"No, thank you," I said. "I don't use drugs."

"Okay," he said. "You won't mind if *I* do."

"Mind? It's your house."

So I watched while he lit his flat litle cigarette and took
a couple of puffs. "Come on, Sissy, let's have a swim."

If there's anything that annoys me, it's a person who
doesn't listen to another person's name. I couldn't believe
this P. He stood there in the middle of the living room and
took off all his fancy silk clothes and left them in a pile on
the rug, and stood there in the nude looking at me. He was
short and fat and covered with black hair. The hair on his
head was long in back and bald on top, and he had a
mustache. He had loose, sloppy, depraved lips. He was no
beauty, but I had to hand it to the guy for his *cool*. Most
men, if they did this number, would be heavy-breathing
and jumping around, and I would have been out the door
and running down the hill. But P. acted as though taking
off his clothes in front of his "office temp" were the most
natural thing in the world (which for him it probably was)
and calmly said, "I'm going to take a dip. You're welcome to join me."

Somehow the way he said it made me feel that it would
be silly not to do it. He went out to the pool and jumped
in, and I followed him out and watched him as he splashed
around.

"I don't know if you're interested, but a dynamite
property came across my desk today," he said. Real soft-
spoken and low-key. "It's unusual, too. In my position
I'm offered an awful lot of crap. I'm always looking for
that special spark, that little surge that might be called
'talent.' " He dived down to the bottom, displaying his
not-so-impressive heinie, and came up again. He really
looked pathetic with his hair wet. But the guy had
something—I don't know what. He had these metal-gray
eyes I couldn't stop looking at. "Do you have talent,
Sissy?"

"My name is Cassie."

"I'm so sorry, Cassie. How thoughtless of me. Tell me your name again."

"Cassie Armstrong."

"Where are you from?"

"Rivertown, Connecticut."

"Aha. I was almost right—I guessed Massachusetts. I'm pretty good at detecting the source of an accent." He smiled, floating on his back. I tried not to look at what he was exhibiting, but it was hard, and I was also growing terribly tempted to get into the water. The afternoon sun was beating down, and I was wearing polyester pants and a long-sleeved, flowered nylon blouse—clothes I wouldn't wear now to take out the garbage—and I felt hot and sweaty. P. went swimming down to the other end of the pool, and on an impulse I took off my outer clothes, leaving my undies on, and stuck one foot in the pool. P. suddenly came swimming back.

"A New England girl," he said. "I can hear it in your voice."

He asked me about my life and I told him, slowly sinking into the delicious cool water. I don't think anything ever felt so good, it was like drifting around in melted emeralds. We swam around and talked for a while. He never came very near me, so I relaxed and chattered away. Then he told me about his "dynamite property" and how he was looking for the right girl for a certain part.

"I'll know her when I see her," he said.

"Have you seen her yet?" I asked, smiling.

"No, but I hope I will soon." His metal eyes were boring into me. "Cassie, I'm a funny guy. Visual, that's part of my business. It's the industry of the visual. You know that—I don't have to tell you. Sometimes the way we operate seems a little crazy, but then the movies have always been a crazy business. We look for talent in funny places. Do you know, I can sometimes spot talent by looking at a girl's cunt. That's what those pictures are about." Hearty laugh. "Those pictures are reminders—they tell me more than the faces. God, you'd be amazed at the number of styles and kinds there are. Soft and pink. Flappy and purple. Tight and white. All colors of hair."

I shouldn't even be telling this. I'm contributing to the

man's sickness and depravity by repeating his disgusting words. It was only at this point that I realized that it was time to leave—and fast. The temperature of the water seemed to drop about twenty degrees. By the time I got to the edge he was asking me if I would mind just stripping and sitting on the edge of the pool with my legs etcetera, etcetera. He wouldn't touch me, he just wanted to look. He had a certain specially built seat, which I suddenly recognized from the pictures. It had been there all along, of course, but I hadn't put two and two together, so to speak. It was a little metal thing, with foam-rubber padding, right at the edge of the pool. You straddled it, putting your feet in high stirrups the way you do at the gynecologist's, while this jerk-off floated around in the water and looked, I suppose snapping pictures with his Nikonos, and probably snapping himself at the same time.

What happened next is the hardest thing to confess. I don't know what was the matter with me that day, but I had to undress and sit in that seat. The truth is, God forgive me, I'd gotten very sexually excited. And P. was still splashing around and talking about twats and how they look and taste and everything. I'd been sipping the white wine that seemed to follow me around like magic. I felt unreal. Maybe I *was* hypnotized—by the hot afternoon sun, the cool green water, the whispering trees. That soft thump-thump of music. Anyway, to speed up this embarrassing episode, I took off my bra and pants and went over and sat on the seat, which was at a special place of honor at the head of the pool, like a throne. Oh, God, it felt good. I've never felt so *female*—so open and all-encompassing. (I wish I felt that way every time Sam and I go to bed.) P. and his putz came swimming over and treaded water right below. And something happened to me that never had before—a momentous sweep of feeling that shook me from head to foot. Again and again and again. Just from the sun, and the seat, and the place, because P. *never touched me*. He just pulled his putz and smiled. I never touched myself. I thought I'd gone crazy.

Finally my host groaned and practically drowned. I groaned and got off the stupid seat, lying in the sun till I recovered. "Cassie," cried P, "get back! I didn't get "your picture!"

"You creep," I said. "I'm leaving this place. I'll walk home if I have to. I thought this was a job and it's turned into another disgusting Hollywood experience."

P. came leaping out of the pool, at which point I grabbed my clothes and ran into the house. "Don't touch me!" I screamed. "Call me a cab!"

"Calm down, you silly bitch," said P. quietly. "I'll take you home whenever you're ready. I never make people do what they don't want to. There are plenty around who are eager and willing. And talented besides."

As I got into my clothes, and he did, I felt like crying. I've never felt so foolish and cheap. I kept thinking of that orgasm chair. What had happened to me was enormous and depressing, glorious and mortifying. I felt as lonely as I had on the Greyhound bus. Besides, now I had to leave this dreamland forever and go back to my current roommate, a large, noisy redhead named Lilyanne, and our lousy little apartment on Cahuenga where the radio played constantly and the hallway smelled of burned Crisco.

As P. and I got into the Maserati I acted huffy and insulted, though I wasn't sure what I really had to be insulted about. He, however, was perfectly calm and pleasant. He gave me a brown envelope. I opened it: a hundred and fifty dollars—fifty dollars a day; no more, no less. I almost wished he'd given me less, so I could yell at him for cheating me. Or more so I could throw the difference in his face. He was smart, P. And cool. He and his kind, they kept cool in their pools.

But downtown where I lived it was hot, hazy and dusty. The street was lined with cracked, mangy palm trees, and in front of my apartment were these crappy-looking century plants, or whatever they are, with big leaves that are always split and brown. I lived in a fleabag called the Xanadu Bungalow Colony, in one of several small pink huts, each of which had its name in script over the door. Ours was "The Cubby," which Lilyanne called "The Cruddy." I had been hoping she would be out, but unfortunately she was there when I got back, having been hanging out the window watching my arrival in the Maserati.

"Jee-sus," she said. "Who was that?"

I told her the story, with slight revision, making it sound as though P. had attacked me in a more conventional way, for I was still embarrassed about what had happened, and she probably wouldn't have believed it anyway, it was all so strange. Her response was exactly as I had expected.

"Do you mean to tell me that you were actually with Milton P., and that he was talking about a part, and you wouldn't put out? Cassie, are you *crazy?*"

In case you assume that Lilyanne was a simple slut, let me explain the circumstances that caused her apparent lack of morals. The two of us sat in a dreadful, dark little so-called living room furnished with three ugly chairs, two purple and one green-and-brown-flowered; small imitation-wood tables; tipping lamps and a cheap woven Mexican rug on the tile floor. On the wall hung two colored scenic prints of the Grand Canyon, one with a donkey. We slept in an even tinier room just beyond, both of us tossing and sweating in a bed that was too small for us, and cooked on a hot plate in the "kitchen," which was more like a hollow in the wall. The bathroom was so small you could sit on the toilet only with your knees splayed out (a terrible reminder of P.'s chair), and you showered in a rattling tin box. The whole place was a mess because the closet was about the size of a shoe box, and so there were piles of shoes in the living room and Lilyanne's curlers in the bathroom sink, and our good dresses hung on hooks on the living-room wall. The coffeepot and sticky cups were always on the floor by the kitchen because there was no other place to put them. The other people in the Xanadu were noisy and disreputable, and even if they were quiet after midnight, for a change, other drunks, whores and dope addicts screamed and yelled outside on the little paths that connected the bungalows, sometimes throwing bottles or beer cans into the shrubbery that was lit up by blue lights.

The only way out of this place, for Lilyanne even more than for me, was by "putting out." She came from some horrible little town in Arizona or Idaho or somewhere, and she *could never go home* because her father had raped her several times. The evening she told me, I was so shocked I

couldn't eat my dinner. I thought of helping my father at
The Bower of Flowers, arranging daffodils in vases and
wrapping roses in green tissue paper. I remembered him
working in the garden behind our house, trimming dead
twigs and pulling out weeds. He was a quiet man, kind
and sweet and gentle. I could hardly imagine him having
sex with my *mother*, though of course he must have at
least once. I thought how sad and horrified he would feel
if he knew the sort of thing I was being exposed to
here—P. and his depravity, for instance.

I could always go home, and Lilyanne couldn't. Her
mother was dead and her father sexually abused her. All
she could do was, if you'll excuse the expression, fuck up,
by which I mean put out to people who were in a position
to help her. And so she did, for dinners and auditions and
dresses and even for her car, an ancient Dodge Dart which
she let me use sometimes. Also, as she explained to me,
she was twenty-seven and more desperate. She was a
dancer, and dancers are finished at thirty. She didn't have
much more time to make it. In the meantime she smoked
two packs of cigarettes a day, which gave The Cruddy the
sour, repulsive smell of an old ashtray. In the beginning I
didn't like her at all, but as I got to know her better I felt
sorry for her and then began to be fond of her. One of the
signs of maturity is learning to like people who are different from you, which doesn't make them wrong, just
different.

Possibly the saddest thing about our pathetic lives during that period was that for all the feeling and fingering,
the smirking and grinning and hinting and unzipping and
sometimes actual violence (for I was knocked down once
and almost raped twice), none of these people ever wanted
to hug or just hold. There was no love and no gentleness,
and Lilyanne and I were both starved for love. Sometimes
at night we'd put our arms around each other and just lie in
bed holding each other out of pure loneliness. Mostly it
was too hot, but sometimes when there was a cool breeze
we even slept like that. You might think it was somewhat
perverted, but there was nothing sexual about it. Lilyanne
knew I was not interested in women in that way, and as for

her, she had so much sex all the time she was just plain worn out.

Lilyanne and I lived together for two months, and when she left one day with some guy who was going to take her to Vegas and get her a job dancing in a nightclub line, we both cried. She knew as well as I did that there probably wouldn't be any job, but he wasn't a bad guy and he drove a Mercedes and she thought she might at least have a good time out of it. She packed up her clothes and gave me her half of the last week's rent, and even left me the Dart. She was a nice person; she could have disappeared and left me holding the bag, the way the next one did. She stooped down (Lilyanne was five feet ten inches, and I am five feet five) and hugged me goodbye.

"Good luck, Cassie," she said. "I hope you get everything you want. I'll send a postcard from wherever I land."

I cried, and for the next few days I half missed her and half was glad to have the place all to myself, which didn't last long because I couldn't afford it, and I advertised and got Myrna. Myrna, who shaved her stomach, who passed gas in bed, who stole my money, who masturbated in the flowered chair in the living room after dinner. And she was stunningly beautiful, a swarthy, almond-eyed Mexican girl with long, curly black hair. Her men almost broke the door down, and she sent the ones she didn't want in my direction. That was when I became a blonde, to be more of a contrast to Myrna and get a few more dates. But there wasn't a single one who didn't either grow three extra, grabby hands or start pushing his bulging crotch at me. None of them came back.

Except Sam.

I didn't meet him through Myrna, but at a fancy party the two of us somehow got ourselves invited to. It was at Malibu, at the house of a medium-sized enchilada at one of the studios. There were hundreds of people there, and a band and "reefers" being passed around on the sneak—not openly, the way they are now—and the booze was really flowing. I was wearing a new flame-colored chiffon dress with beading around the neck from I. Magnin that I couldn't afford, even though I'd gotten it on sale. I had spike-heeled silver sandals to go with it, and I wore my new streaky-blond hair in a chignon.

I didn't really know anybody there. I did a little dancing, just by myself—I love to dance and don't really care if I have a partner or not—and then took off my shoes and went out on the beach for a walk. Near the house, couples were writhing around in the sand, and in one place about six or seven people with most of their clothes off were in a big pile together. I ignored them and went and sat down near the water.

Lord, how beautiful it was! The dark Pacific stretched away into the night. All up the beach the houses were lit, and you could see for miles in each direction, it was so clear. In the sky were a million stars. The sand was white and soft, and the air was so sweet and salty and gentle I understood why people in L.A. paid such huge amounts of money just to live where it smelled like that.

What I didn't understand was why, having done so, they ignored what had cost them millions of dollars. I was the only person, it seemed, enjoying the vast natural beauty that God had bestowed upon California with such a lavish hand. All the rest were either grunting and sweating and yelling in acts of so-called lovemaking or else were so stoned on liquor and marijuana that they wouldn't have noticed if an earthquake ripped them out into the sea. But this was part of my promise to myself, my "bow of burning gold." I had vowed never to close my eyes to the earth's beauty, which in the end will outlive us all. It's no secret that I love luxury, delicious food, expensive clothes and lovely surroundings as much as the next person, if not more. But I will *never* let these things replace my deep appreciation of natural things, which is truly the source of human religion in its deepest sense.

Anyway, as I sat there, along came Sam, whom, of course, I didn't know. He wore white pants, a purple shirt open to the waist and a silk ascot which was half off. He looked a little disheveled, and in retrospect I think he may have come from one of the piles of bodies on the beach. I sat facing the water, and he came up from behind me.

"Mind if I join you?" he asked, after a moment of

silence. Mind! I was grateful he didn't jump on me and
start ripping up my new outfit.

So he sat down, and we talked. Sam has a kind of
smart-ass party talk that he throws out when meeting
somebody new, and we threw one-liners back and forth like
people in a TV sitcom. To tell the truth, I wasn't paying
too much attention to him. There's no way it can be said
that bells rang or violins played when Sam and I met. I'd
met a hundred like him, even to the long, curly blondish
hair and the blue eyes (though sometimes they had dark
hair and beards). I'd had dates with about twenty, or
maybe it was forty—who knows? I'd turned down sex
with all the straight ones, and of course the gay ones didn't
try. I'd heard the same stupid network conversation, the
same babble about deals and shares and properties.

It was beginning to be clear to me what you have
probably already figured out: that I wasn't truly and deeply
ambitious. If I'd wanted to be a movie star as much as I'd
thought back in the Rivertown Rialto, or as much as the
other girls I knew did, I would have done anything with
anybody. I would have stayed up all night reading the
Hollywood Reporter and *Variety,* when in fact I preferred
romances, *Reader's Digest* or stories of an inspirational
nature. I would have hung on to every word spoken by
anybody in the "business" about matters which in fact
practically put me to sleep. It was just around the time I
met Sam that I was beginning to realize this and wonder
what I was doing in Hollywood at all. Truly I had reached
a crossroads, and that night when Sam and I sat on the
beach, I stood in the middle wondering what direction God
wanted me to go in. And during such moments of conflict
in my life I wait for Him to give me a sign.

"You know, Cassie, you're different from most girls,"
Sam said.

I'd heard that one before, though I appreciated his getting my name right. That meant he was going to tell me
his life story. He came from some small town in New
Mexico or Idaho or somewhere. His family had never
really understood him and in fact had preferred his older
brother to him. He had spent his early years at the movies
. . . so what else was new? Up to there it was a Xerox of

everybody else's. His parents had sent him to the state university and then the money had run out, so Sam had worked his way to Hollywood working on construction gangs and waiting on tables. He'd always wanted to be a writer, and if he'd been able to afford it he would have stuck with feature films and hoped to write a great one someday, but he needed the bucks, so he went into TV, and he had since decided that TV was where it was at anyway. Some people might say he'd sacrificed his artistic creativity for commercialism, but it really wasn't so, because blah, blah, blah—the usual excuses.

By now we'd taken off our shoes and were walking along the beach. By the time Sam had gone into Phase Three of the usual conversation—his therapist's opinions—I was beginning to enjoy myself. Not because of what he was saying, which I didn't pay any attention to, but because the whole setting was so romantic. Bare feet on the sand. The moonlight on the tip of each wave. Some old jazz tunes coming from somebody's stereo. The scent of mimosa and jasmine. "Manuel [the therapist] thinks my love of feature films is just a transfer of my Oedipal hostility onto a nonthreatening object." Whatever that meant. He sure liked to talk. That was all right with me, I prefer to listen anyway.

Then Sam put his arm around my shoulder. He didn't grab me but just put it there casually, like a brother, as we were walking along. "I've been trying to explain to Manuel that the film symbolism is more from my mother, because when I was little she taught me to take pictures with her Brownie." For just a minute I got tense, with his arm there, waiting for the grabby fingers to go sneaking down my front, or down my back to my behind, or whatever direction he'd plotted for his approach. *But his hand stayed where it was.* I sneaked a look at his crotch, which was outlined against the light of a house we were passing, and it was practically flat as a pancake.

Later Sam told me he couldn't have made love to me if he'd wanted to at that point, because he'd already done it three or four times that evening. Which had occurred to me, along with the possibility that he might be a fruit. But there was something so nice about just strolling along with his arm on my shoulder, something that hadn't happened the whole time I'd been in California.

He moved on to his soon-to-be-ex wife, from whom he was separated, but the psychotic bitch wouldn't give him a divorce. I pointed out that in this state, "irreversible breakdown" was ground enough, but the problem was, as usual, financial. The woman was demented about money—even her shrink admitted she had a problem about it. So what else was new? I've never understood why people in the middle of a divorce have to keep insisting the other person is crazy. Who cares? But there are a lot of things I don't understand. Sam's psychotic wife sounded like all the other psychotic wives, slugging martinis and rampaging through Rodeo Drive. (Since then I've met her, and she's not bad at all.) Babbling about Women's Rights. But, of course, beautiful and brilliant and capable of doing anything she put her hand to, if only she weren't certifiably insane. They're all like that.

Then we turned around and started back, and Sam asked if he could take me home. I said that would be fine but that I should check with my roommate, Myrna, because I had come with her. I found her in one of the bedrooms with two men and another girl, all of them shiny with some kind of scented oil and slithering around the floor with little or nothing on. She was so stoned she hardly recognized me, so I only said, "Myrna, I'm leaving," in a loud voice, and turned to leave the room. Sam was standing by the door.

"That's your roommate?" he asked.

"Yes, that's Myrna La Pinez. But I don't think there's much point in introducing you to her."

After that, Sam got rather quiet. We left the party and went out to the lot and got into his car, the usual Mercedes. I hated to tell him where I lived, but I had no choice, unless I wanted to walk a mile or so alone from some phony address in a decent neighborhood. So I gave him the address of the Xanadu Bungalows. Neither of us said much on the way—I because I was depressed, as usual, by going home. And I was feeling about Sam the way I hadn't felt in a long time. I wanted him to hold my hand, which I stuck in the middle between the seats, but he didn't touch it. I wanted him to ask me out for dinner the next night, but he didn't say anything. We tore along the Freeway in silence. I clicked on the radio and hummed a little.

"Do you sing, Cassie?"

"I'm a mezzo," I said.

"We're looking for girls for a shampoo commercial," he said. "Want to try for it?"

At the Xanadu Bungalows he looked out of the car and said, *"This* is where you live?"

"Home sweet home," I said.

He sighed and wrote something down: *"2 P.M. on Tuesday at CBS"* and a lot of complicated instructions. Impersonal and businesslike. Another queer, I thought, though he didn't seem like one. He gave me a kiss on the cheek. "I enjoyed talking to you."

The audition was put off a couple of times, so I didn't see Sam for about a month. It was a pretty rotten month, with the topless offer and the dope-smuggling offer; the only reason I didn't starve was that I had a couple of weeks of office work until the guy I was working for suddenly dropped dead of a coronary.

I didn't ever write home for money, the way some people did, for the simple reason that I never told my parents about the tribulations and hardships of my life. Instead, I told them I shared a garden apartment with a lovely girl from Philadelphia, and that though I would not subject them to the ups and downs of my new career, they could rest assured that I was going, generally, up, and that when something came along that they could see—a TV commercial or a small part in a feature film—I would immediately tell them. I believe any considerate child would do the same thing for middle-aged parents who lived quiet, protected lives and didn't know the half of what went on in the outside world.

It was the least I could do to thank them for their love, the stable home they had provided for me in my childhood and those old-fashioned values that had stood me in good stead—for there were moments, such as when I looked at Myrna lying face down on the floor, naked and oily, her drugged eyes flat and unfocused, when I thanked God for my upbringing. Still clearly in my mind was that quiet street in the fall, the red and golden leaves showering down on the lawns, the houses with their broad front porches, and on Sundays the church bells tolling, summoning the faithful to prayer. I had told hardly anyone in California about the picture in my mind—only Lilyanne, who laughed at first, then wanted to hear it again and again, and one bearded network fruit who wanted to use it for a sitcom.

Anyway, along came the audition, but I didn't get the part. I wasn't in too good voice, which had partly to do with the fact that I had never been able to afford lessons, and if I practiced at The Cruddy, even in the shower, our unfriendly neighbors banged rudely on the thin walls. Afterward, Sam came over to me as though he were trying to figure something out.

"You know, Cassie, you can't sing at *all*." He didn't say it in a nasty way—more amazed that anybody could be so bad, he told me later—and he kept his voice low, so nobody else could hear. "Did you really think you could do this?"

"I didn't know."

"Why did you come here?"

My heart beat so fast I almost fainted. What a coward I was, considering the things people said and did in this town. It took all my courage.

"To see you again," I said almost in a whisper.

Sam looked at me for a minute, then smiled. I'd taken an hour and a half to dress. I was only wearing shorts and a T-shirt, and my hair was loose. But let me tell you, it takes longer to look perfect when everything's showing than when everything's covered up. There wasn't a hair on either of my legs. Myrna had done my nails, both toes and fingers. My makeup would have been perfect under a microscope. I'd done my hair with hot rollers and tied a little blue ribbon in it. My T-shirt said HUG ME. Oh, how important this moment was! At the crossroads, a new sign said, "SAM."

The first time we went out, a couple of days after the audition, we went to a Chinese restaurant and then to a nightclub to hear this stupid comedian and then, against my wishes, to his apartment, where he came on in the usual way. I told him that I didn't mean to hurt his feelings, but I never "put out" on a first date and sometimes I didn't put out at all. I said I considered sex deeply important, almost holy, and I would never degrade it by indulging in it with someone I didn't love. Sam looked amazed at this unusual point of view, which he said he thought had been left behind in the last century. Then he began to laugh and joke, and it was clear that he didn't believe me. It was just too crazy.

Four dates later he believed me, at which time he said he loved and adored me, he hoped I loved him and let's go to bed. I told him that to me, sex should be an integral part of a permanent relationship. I knew there were many people who screwed around without even thinking about it, but that conflicted with the strong sense of values with which I had been raised. I was sorry if he was disappointed, but I would not be less than completely honest with him about my beliefs and the standards that guided my life.

After this, Sam stayed away for three weeks and then called up again. This time he took me to dinner at the Beverly Hills Hotel, and then we went out afterward and sat in that little park across Sunset. Twice while we were sitting there policemen came and asked us for our driver's licenses or other identification and wanted us to explain why we were sitting in the park. In between these tiresome interruptions, Sam asked me many questions about my life and background, all of which I answered honestly and openly. We talked for hours. He didn't touch me except once accidentally when he opened the door of the car. It was a strange evening, and I wished he would kiss me good-night, but he only dropped me at the Xanadu and left.

After that we saw each other once or twice a week. It was usually on weekends, and we went on picnics, to the Venice pier and to Disneyland. We went to movies and to a couple of concerts at the Bowl, and once we drove up to Santa Barbara and had lunch on the terrace of the Biltmore Hotel. It was such a beautiful place, I told Sam I loved it and never wanted to leave. Sometimes he held my hand in a jolly way as we ran along the beach, or put that friendly arm around my shoulder. Obviously I had become his "fun" date, the girl he did everything with but make love. The only time we had dinner was on a weekday evening before a screening.

However, nature will prevail, and one day after we'd had a picnic in the Malibu Canyon and a long walk, we ended up having a swim at Sam's (he lived in an apartment complex with a pool) and then had dinner at an Italian place in Westwood. By this time I was really crazy about him, and we both sat there staring into each other's eyes over the candle. Finally he said, "Cassie, my divorce from the psychotic bitch is final, and the financial settlement has been made. Let's live together. Leave the Xanadu and move in with me."

Oh, how happy I felt! I reached over and took his hand, his strong, brown hand with the turquoise-and-silver Indian ring he always wore. He picked up my slender brown hand and brought it to his lips and kissed it—four times, once on each knuckle. He poured us each another glass of Sebastiani.

"Sam, I love you more than I've ever loved anybody. I feel close to you, and when we're apart I count the hours until we're together. Our relationship is deep and meaningful to me."

Sam almost floated out of his seat with joy as I said this, which I did just as a little cushion for my next point. I explained that since our relationship *was* so special—far more special than I had ever dreamed it would become in the beginning—I had become convinced that it deserved nothing less than a legal bond. It wasn't that I had anything against people living together if they loved each other, but then what did the word "love" mean, most of the time? It meant sex, that was what. Myrna said she was in love every week, and by now the word had lost its meaning. Her shallow emotion had nothing to do with the deep feelings Sam and I had for each other. A love like ours needed a serious agreement.

Sam dropped my hand and looked grim, and I wondered if I'd gone too far.

"By the way," he snapped, "where did you find Myrna?"

"Through an ad in the paper," I said, surprised.

He explained that Myrna had confused him. What was a girl like me doing with her? As a matter of fact, what was I doing here at all? He couldn't believe I was real. Sometimes he got furious at me for being such a prude, and sometimes he was filled with admiration. He loved me, but I was driving him nuts. He *admired* me. The truth was he admired me so much I made him feel like a piece of shit for all the screwing around he did—or used to do, he rapidly corrected himself. My whole life was a statement that blew his mind.

"Cassie," he asked cautiously, "you aren't a virgin, are you?"

"I am," I replied, "and proud of it."

"Oh, my God," he said softly.

Sam and I were married a month or so later in San Juan Capistrano. Our witnesses were Paul Brookman (who later married Angela) and Lilyanne, who came back for the occasion. I invited Myrna, or would have, but she had disappeared, along with the twenty-five dollars I had hidden in my bedroom slipper. The four of us had dinner at a lovely dark, cool adobe restaurant, with lots of champagne, and then Sam and I went back to our motel by the sea (the Hibiscus Lodge) for our wedding night. While the waves boomed onto the sand outside, while the breeze softly ruffled the hibiscus growing outside our door, I gave myself to my new husband in the first lustful embrace of my life. We both drew redoubled tenderness and love from the knowledge that no man had ever "known" me before.

You may wonder why Sam and I didn't have an old-fashioned wedding in my hometown. The reason was that Sam's schedule was very hectic at the time, with a new margarine commercial and trying to start a series of his own. Besides, it was the second time for him; he said he'd feel funny doing the whole church-rice-bridesmaids number that he'd already done once and that hadn't turned out very well. He also said that he hoped it was the only time he would ever disappoint me and because of this he owed

me one. I told him that the thrill of becoming Mrs. Sam
Coopersmith far outweighed my girlish dream of a traditional wedding, and that somehow our gay, lighthearted
trip to San Juan Capistrano with friends was more suitable
to two wanderers such as we and to our easy, laid-back
California life-style. Even many years later when I thought
back on it I had no reason to regret that trip, including our
four blissful days and nights at the Hibiscus Lodge which
will remain in my mind forever even in the face of many
subsequent difficulties.

Afterward, we went back to Sam's and I became a
housewife. I had moved my possessions into his apartment
and now set about giving the place a woman's touch. I
cleaned thoroughly, placed fresh flowers around and set
about learning to cook. (I had learned simple home cooking from Mother, but now began to study Gourmet Cooking.) I promised myself I would never be slovenly or
careless, and that each evening when Sam came home I
would greet him in a fresh caftan or lounging pajamas,
with dinner simmering on the stove and wine chilling in
the refrigerator.

Unfortunately, this didn't work out too well, because of
Sam's hours, which were hard to predict, and because,
rather to my surprise, I found myself bored after so many
months as a busy career girl. There was not that much to
do around the apartment, which was, after all, already
furnished, and after I had cleaned out all the drawers and
closets (throwing away certain distasteful objects he had
hidden away) there was not much to do. On the evenings
Sam had to be out I looked at TV, knitted or continued my
reading of *Ulysses*, which Sam had suggested for my
self-education. Sometimes I went to the movies with
Lilyanne, who was back in town after a revolting experience in Vegas. She now had a waitress job at a classy bar
on Wilshire and could afford to share a small apartment in
West Hollywood with another girl, Angela, which is how I
met my present neighbor and close friend. Sometimes
when Sam was working late the three of us went out for
dinner at the Hamburger Hamlet on Sunset.

There are some unfortunate women who despise, or
have not yet discovered, the pleasures of spending time

with their own sex. I have even heard women speak with scorn of other women, and there are many who seem to regard their own sex with hatred. I believe such relationships to be both necessary and fruitful. I was far more content and interesting to Sam because of these contacts and was able to give vent to certain feelings that he, being a male, would never understand. Now that sex was a nightly episode in my life, I was eager to compare notes with my far more experienced friends, for Lilyanne was what some people might call "promiscuous" and Angela was not far behind. Without drawing aside the veil of discretion, I will say that Lilyanne and Angela were extremely helpful in telling me certain things that I didn't know about men and in giving me advice designed to improve our acts of love. He doesn't know, nor will I probably ever tell him, how much these girls have contributed to his happiness.

Both girls were amazed that I had kept my virginity until my wedding night and had no reason to regret my decision. I said I felt that Sam treated me with a certain tenderness and respect that he might not have otherwise, though of course I couldn't prove such a statement. I said that he had mentioned several times the thrill he got knowing that I was *all his,* and how masterful he felt instructing me in matters sexual. It gave extra excitement to our lovemaking to be "teacher and pupil." I had the feeling this groundwork would be an important part of our marriage.

Angela was particularly impressed by what I said, and after she met Paul Brookman at our house one day, she phoned me in the morning to tell me that he had asked her out for dinner and she was going to try the same thing.

"But Angela, I don't know how you can when you are not actually a virgin."

"So who's to know? Unless somebody tells. You won't, will you, Cassie?"

"Your secret is safe with me, Angela. But aren't you afraid he might find out sometime, and hate you for not telling the truth?"

"Good Lord, you're a worrywart. By then he'll be so crazy about me he won't care."

Leaving Angela to perpetrate this fraud, I set about

finding some sort of work suitable to my new life as a young matron. At first Sam seemed surprised, but when I explained that I was anxious not to become stagnant and boring, he seemed pleased and understood. It was just one of the many occasions when Sam's disapproval turned to support after I explained the situation to him—which, in fact, is one of the secrets of our long and happy relationship. I wonder how many wives "assume" their husbands know and understand certain things when in fact they need to have them explained in simple, direct terms. The world of men is so different from that of women—I truly believe even their natures are different—that the things women know in their hearts to be true and obvious may be invisible to men. This is why I have always felt the word "people" to be misleading. There are two kinds of people, and there is simply no point in pretending otherwise.

However, the subject of my career was not settled yet. After not too much time I found a job selling lingerie at Regina's, a fancy shop in Beverly Hills, which seemed convenient, respectable and not too difficult. To my surprise, Sam hated the whole idea. Why the hell did I want to sell bras? He'd find me something in "the media" if I wanted to keep from becoming stagnant. His wife, stuffing female asses into corsets? For God's sake, Cassie.

I carefully explained that even though he might see such work as menial, it was actually anything but. For one thing, none of these women wore bras or girdles anymore. The ones who came into this shop wore elegant hand-embroidered Victorian nightgowns, silk chemises and hand-hemmed chiffon panties. The picture he seemed to have of obese women struggling to fit into "foundation garments" was old-fashioned and inaccurate. This shop was patronized by Audrey Hepburn, Marilyn Monroe, Rita Gam and Kim Novak, to name only a few—not one of whom was fat by any stretch of the imagination! I welcomed the chance to work with such beautiful and talented women in a quiet, elegant atmosphere.

Sam then had a better idea, he said. Why didn't I go to college? It would be so easy to enroll at UCLA or UC and study in a leisurely way. Now that I didn't have to worry about where my next meal was coming from, I could have the education that circumstances had denied me before. He would be happy to pay for it, and could help me with my work in the evening. Forget the damn job—we didn't need the money. Didn't I want to study?

I thanked him, but declined. I had never enjoyed studying in high school, and quite frankly, I had been relieved when the whole thing was over. My talent and abilities lay, I felt, in my voice, a certain potential as a film personality because of my looks and my natural gregariousness and social poise. Selling lingerie sounded suitable because it would call upon these qualities, plus my interest in clothes and beautiful fabrics, and the innate taste which I had been told more than once that I possessed.

Part of the reason it appealed to me was that it reminded me of working at The Bower of Flowers, which I had done in the summers. Daddy had let me make the arrangements of mixed flowers that were sold in vases, and sometimes it had been my responsibility to do the window display. He told me that I definitely displayed a talent for color and arrangement, perhaps a deeply artistic bent that would someday be expressed to the fullest.

I'll have to admit that Sam and I had a serious disagreement about Regina's. He stood in the middle of the living room yelling about how it would look if his wife were a salesgirl; it would look as though he couldn't support me, wouldn't it? and for God's sake, what about my so-called acting career, which, now that I had a meal ticket, I was ready to drop like a hot potato? And if I wouldn't follow his wishes about that, why couldn't I take a few courses and get something into my head? How did I think he felt when he made certain literary references that I didn't recognize—or, if I didn't care how *he* felt, how it looked to his friends? After all, he worked among educated and scholarly people, and their wives were educated and scholarly too, and if I were as anxious to be the good wife as I was always saying I was, I'd hit the Great Books and American history and read the papers for a change (the news part) and about six other things Sam thought I should study.

I said to him, very slowly and clearly, "Sam, you can't make me what I am not. I am not one of your so-called scholars like all these other women, who, incidentally, I have met and talked to, and they aren't so goddamn scholarly at all. In fact, they are mostly a bunch of stupid bitches who I don't believe have any values or standards about themselves or their marriages. So don't tell *me* how educated they are. If that's education, you could have had one of *them*. But you married me, and you knew what I was like, because I never kept any secrets from you; I told you everything about myself because I thought it was my duty to.''

Sam, of course, couldn't think of an answer to that, so he slammed out of the apartment and stayed out for several hours, not coming back till four in the morning. The next day he apologized for his burst of anger and said I was right and he would never again try to make me into something I wasn't. He thought it had something to do with his converted Oedipal something-or-other, which meant it really didn't have anything to do with me, but with his mother, so that made it all right. He explained how his mother had done some kind of guilt trip on his father, and he had been doing Mom and I had been doing Dad—which didn't make any sense at all, because I'd never met either of them—but he seemed to think that explained everything. He loved me the way I was, though sometimes he forgot that I was the girl who had given him the gift of her innocence and therefore deserved special treatment. He took me in his strong arms and we made love with more tenderness than ever before.

I took the job at Regina's Lingerie Shop and spent many happy months there. I have mentioned my fondness for shopping, which even includes the experience of walking into and spending time in a fine store or boutique. I love the mirrors, the gilt, the carpeting, the racks of fine clothes, the cool air and hushed atmosphere. Before I married Sam, I used to drive to Beverly Hills in the Dart and park, and go into I. Magnin or Saks. Often the snooty personnel gave me dirty looks and asked nastily if they could help me in that tone which really was telling me I didn't belong in their store. Painful as it was, the experience of being poor taught me many things I would not otherwise have known, and I'm glad I went through it, because now I never take for granted what I have. I know that what God gives can be taken away just as easily, and it makes each purchase I can now make because of Sam's generosity twice as precious.

Maybe it sounds silly, and I never explained it to Sam for that reason, but working at Regina's somehow made up for that long year when I would go into those shops and wander around unable to buy, but just drinking in the atmosphere of wealth and luxury, to remember when I was back at The Cruddy. At last, one of those places was mine to go to everyday, to walk into every morning without shame. (I could also get lingerie at forty percent off.) I enjoyed the lighthearted give-and-take with the other salesgirls and shared their excitement when a Star came in for a big order—for instance, Kim Novak who came in regularly for her special Alençon lace nightgowns and chiffon teddies. I was privileged to wait on her and found her just as friendly and natural as a girl from my high school class.

Sam and I discussed Regina's, and he said his therapist had explained that women had to do their own thing in order to have their identity, and that he had to respect my means of self-expression. And at the suggestion of Sharon, one of the girls at work, after I modeled some of my new underthings for Sam and even let him take them off himself, his attitude improved a lot.

After I'd been working there a few months, I had reason to think that a big change might be coming into our lives in the form of a Little Stranger! I went to a doctor recommended by Sharon, and after examining me, he confirmed that I was pregnant! He said I was in excellent health and had no reason to worry, but could look forward only to pure joy and fulfillment. He gave me a prescription for vitamins and certain instructions about leading a healthy life, most of which, of course, I already knew, and I went home to tell Sam.

Sam's response was curious. "Are you sure, Cassie? I thought you were using your diaphragm."

"I was, Sam, but it isn't one hundred percent safe. I suppose something just sneaked past it." As he groped in the ice bucket to make a drink, I asked, "What's the matter, darling?"

"It's just sooner than we planned, that's all."

I hadn't remembered planning anything. "Aren't you happy?"

"Sure, baby. I'm happy. It's just a shock, that's all. I hadn't exactly been thinking about fatherhood. I've been up to my ears in Kayo's Margarine and The *Wimples*. What about you?" He came over to me, holding his drink and looking at me earnestly. "You'll have to give up your job at Regina's."

"Oh, not for a while."

"And another thing." His voice got heavier. "We'll have to move. They don't allow children in this apartment."

"Well," I said, "maybe it's time to look for our own home."

I had made ragout of veal for dinner, and gotten a bottle of Korbel champagne, but Sam hardly touched any of the food. He just kept drinking Scotch, and finally he staggered toward the door and said he had to be alone for a while. I shouldn't wait up for him. He might not even be back for a couple of days, which he was telling me so I wouldn't worry or think he'd been killed or kidnapped. It wasn't really personal (hic). It was just that I was laying a lot of stuff on him at once that he hadn't been prepared for. He'd assumed that we'd just stay here for a few more years and be the young career couple. He'd thought I was happy in our present life, working and eating out and enjoying our many interesting and talented friends. Now suddenly, for God's sake, we're going to have a baby.

"But Sam," I said, "didn't you know that I would, sometime, become pregnant?"

"Listen, baby. That innocent little egg that got fertilized in your womb is *the beginning of my middle age*. Now there'll be a kid. The kid needs clothes and shoes and the dentist and the shrink. We'll have to move and buy a house—for a fucking quarter of a million dollars I haven't got after being cleaned out by the psychotic bitch. And our whole life-style will change. Instead of little candlelit suppers and a good fuck, we'll be spooning oatmeal into Junior. Instead of going dancing with Paul and Angela and the gang, we'll be putting the little bastard on the potty. It's the beginning of the end. This kid's start puts my death *right on the horizon*. So that's why I'm going out for a couple of days and get drunk and stoned and get used to the idea. Then when I'm back, we'll talk.''

I had begun to cry. "Shall I get rid of it?"

"I don't know, Cassie. I'll let you know when I come home."

"Where are you going?"

"How the hell do I know? Maybe I'll sleep on the beach.''

I looked at Sam Coopersmith, tall, thin and good-looking, with his wavy blond hair and his sexy green eyes, his L.A. suntan and his Hawaiian shirt and his perfectly pressed white pants, the love of my life and the mate of my lifetime. I looked at the veal ragout cooling on the table and the flat champagne in the glasses, and at the room I'd redecorated and the fresh flowers that I always kept in big white china vases, at the cigarettes in the glass box that I kept there just so he could keep up his rotten unhealthy habit even though I hated it. In the bedroom was the king-size bed made up with fresh blue sheets and matching quilt, just waiting for him to get into it, and in the closet hung all his clothes, clean and brushed and pressed, and his shoes and his stupid cowboy boots, shined, waiting for him to put them on.

The tears dried up, and I said, "You lousy bastard, you can sleep in the ocean for all I care. I am pregnant with *our son* and all you can think of is your stupid middle age! You are selfish and cruel and irresponsible and you are failing in your duty as a husband. You've never thought about anybody in your life but yourself and your stupid Oedipal whatever-it-is and your sad and pathetic child-hood, which I am so tired of hearing about I could scream. Well, now you have a family whether you like it or not, and I don't care if you spend your two days doping or screwing or hanging by your toes, but when you come back here, Sam Coopersmith, you'd better be ready to act like a father or I never want to see you again!"

God, I was mad. I just stood there and yelled all the things that came into my head as if something had taken possession of me, and you know, I guess something had. All I knew was that there was a baby inside me and I was going to kill anything or anybody that threatened it. I must have been crazy when I suggested getting rid of it, because now I knew I would never get rid of it—or rather, him or her—if I had to bring it up myself and work for the next twenty years at Regina's to support it.

Sam yelled back, "Oh, you and your goddamn duty and responsibility, and now I suppose you're going to bring God into it, which you always do when you're against the wall. Have the damn baby or don't, I don't care. I don't want to discuss it anymore, because I'm very (hic) upset. I feel trapped and manipulated and shitty, if you want to know."

He left, banging the sliding glass door after him so hard I was afraid it would break, and took off across the patio. At the pool, which all the apartments backed up to, he teetered on the edge, and I thought for a moment he was going to fall in. But he didn't, and he leaped over the hedge that separated the pool area from the parking lot, got into his car and caromed out the driveway.

I cleared up the dinner dishes, washed them and put them into the rack to dry. I poured myself some flat champagne and put an ice cube in it and went into the bedroom and stood in front of the full-length mirror, turning so I could see myself from the side. I was wearing pink shorts and a white angora sweater and my gold high-heeled mules. I looked at myself carefully and it seemed that my tummy was sticking out just the slightest bit, even though I was only six weeks pregnant. Or maybe it wasn't, but my bosom was definitely larger and felt tender to the touch, which Dr. Fritz had said was one of the first signs.

I began to laugh happily and drank off the champagne. To hell with Sam; let him fall into the ocean. Let him *die* of middle age. But then I sat down on the bed and took off my mules and put on Sam's slippers, which were sitting there by the bed and were too big for me, and started to cry. I felt all mixed up, but Dr. Fritz had told me that mood swings caused by changing hormonal conditions were common, so I at least knew what was the matter with me.

Then I did something I don't do very often: I picked up the phone and called my mother.

As you have probably figured out, Sam came back in a couple of days with his tail between his legs, as the old saying goes. He was also a wreck and hung over. I didn't know where he'd been and frankly, I didn't want to know. There are many men who lead a "double life," and Sam was one of them. I wasn't crazy about it, but had decided after a great deal of thought that I'd accept his vices as long as he kept them separate from his life with me. Only let him wash his mind and his body before entering the door of our marriage.

He said he was sorry and begged me to forgive him, which, of course, I did. He explained that crossing life's hurdles could be difficult, especially for a person with an arrested neurotic something-or-other, and now the worst was over and he knew that with his therapist's guidance and my support, he'd be a wonderful father; in fact, he was beginning to look forward to the little bugger.

A day or so later, we got into the car and drove up the coast and had dinner at the Santa Barbara Biltmore. We sat on the terrace and watched the sun set slowly into the Pacific. There were little candles flickering on the tables, and inside, the band played old dance tunes. We had a bottle of champagne, and we held hands across the table, and the night air smelled of honeysuckle. Sam looked handsome in a seersucker jacket, and I was wearing my white cotton sun dress and my spike-heeled red sandals and a red bow in my hair, which was "teased" in the new way. We danced under the yellow moon, and we both felt so romantic we took a room for the night and stayed at the hotel, just because we felt so crazy. The truth is that Sam was feeling me up under the table, and we both got rather aroused and didn't want to make that long drive home before making love.

That night Sam tried something in bed I wasn't so sure I wanted to do, and when I explained that it might not be a good idea because of the Little Stranger he understood completely, and after making love in the usual tender, familiar way, we fell asleep in each other's arms.

Oh, how these twenty-four years have flown! The birth of Sammy Junior and then Stuart, six years later. Then Shelli three years after that. The little house we rented in Culver city, and then the move to Santa Barbara. Sam's success, including his own show, *The Wimples*. And our continuing marriage.

Once Angela said that the reason we were still together was that we complimented each other.

I said, "Not very often, we don't."

"Complement, with an *e*, you dope," she said. "It means go together."

It's certainly true that we have many similarities, but even truer that we have great differences. I am by nature a cheerful person, and Sam is on occasion quite depressed. He has what he calls "anxiety attacks"—periods when he lies on the bed with a ghastly grin on his face and takes Valium. And I may as well confess that on two occasions Sam has asked for a divorce, which of course he doesn't even have to bother to do in California because of "irretrievable breakdown," but there is the matter of money. Upon further discussion, and considering that by law I would have half of our assets and he would, of course, have to pay the expenses of the children, including college tuitions and psychiatrists' and orthodentists' bills, he has so far decided it isn't worth the trouble. Even though we appear to be rich, apparently we are not very "solvent." Sam says we spend too much and we don't save anything and we put nothing by for a rainy day. So while we have a lot of stuff—cars and clothes and jewels and furs and the house in Santa Barbara and a condo in Acapulco—we don't actually have much money.

You might wonder why I stay with somebody who wants a divorce. Well, it's not exactly the way it seems, because Sam always asks for a divorce in the middle of one of his anxiety attacks, not because he doesn't love me, but because he hates himself. It's hard for me to understand how a person can hate him- or herself, but Sam has explained that self-hatred goes back to childhood, and the people like me who have never experienced it find it hard to grasp. He says he isn't a good husband and he isn't a good father and we'd all be better off without him. Of course I told him how wrong he was, and that I had married him for life, no matter what he turned out to be like.

Even when he told me about that girl in L.A., I told him I was willing to wait it out, because she was only twenty, for God's sake, and he was only infatuated, and I knew he'd get over it and come back to me, and we'd be closer than ever. Even during the separation we had I wouldn't go near any lawyer, even though Angela told me I was crazy and I should protect my rights. But I knew Sam, and he didn't cut off any of the checking accounts or charge accounts, and I just went on as before and waited for him to come back.

And he did come back, and I never asked him about it, only prayed every day that it would all be all right, and somehow it *was* all right. I remember one night when we were all having dinner together by the pool, and the kids were talking and joking, and Sam was at one end and I at the other, and our eyes met over the table, and love was there again. And Sam got a new shrink, which he does every once in a while, and we took all three kids camping. This was a couple of years ago, up the coast to Cambria and Big Sur and the Monterey Peninsula. My Lord, it was so beautiful as we sat on the cliffs at night and had our dinner, fried fish and cold wine, and all around there were eucalyptus and Joshua trees and the dark live oaks on the yellow mountainside, and the air smelled so sweet with the jasmine, and the flowers were caught in the breeze that came with the sunset, and the sun dropped behind the dark purple ocean and made a path of gold right across to where we were. And I knew I'd been right and that God had helped, and so had my "bow of burning gold" and my "arrows of desire" that I never let out of my hand.

CELIA

She didn't even mention me, the bitch.

That's typical—I knew she'd do it. I hate knowing her so well, but that's part of it. That's why her not mentioning me, and pretending I don't exist, is so *sick*.

At some point Cassie decided it was disgusting, or stupid, or one of her other oh-so-original adjectives, to have an identical twin, which is like saying it's disgusting to have two hands or two ears. So from that time she pretended I *wasn't*. She was just sweet little Cassie from Rivertown, where she'd had a typical happy, healthy all-American youth. Probably by now she believes it, for Cassie's primary talent is her ability to stick her head in the sand like an ostrich. She thinks it makes her invisible, and forgets all about her cute little tail feathers hanging out.

Of course part of me envies her—that goes without saying. She got all the tranquillity and I got the grief. She got the blindness and I got the eyes. She sleeps and I lie awake counting my dollars, my hopes, my guilts, my regrets. She prays and I weep because I can't go back to the beginning and make everything different from the way it was.

One of the ways she avoids the truth is by never going home, or hardly ever, and I have to admit that such a plan has merit. I go home all the time, like a dog going after a bone just on the other side of the fence. Home to Rivertown to sniff and nose around Dorothy and Caspar, looking for the unreachable acceptance. To sit in the living room and look at it through half-closed eyes, trying to see it the way I remember it on Christmas or my birthday or a spring morning, with the old sounds and smells as they were thirty years ago: a fresh, bright room, a fire in the grate, all the surfaces polished and sparkling. To go up and lie on my bed in my old room and pretend I'm twelve or sixteen, to pretend the room looks the way it used to instead of faded and shabby and old-fashioned.

Bernard doesn't understand why I go at all, since I always come back depressed, but then there are a lot of things Bernard doesn't understand. It's not that he couldn't, it's that he doesn't want to bother. He's got enough on his mind, and he looks upon me as the relaxation in his life, not another ingredient in his boiling vat of problems. Though God knows why anybody should find me relaxing. Most of the time I'm a nervous wreck.

Let me explain myself. I'm a divorced woman living alone in Manhattan—the cliché of our time. We are legion. We are liberated. We have careers and affairs. We drink and smoke too much. We are lonely, but we avoid intimacy. We think we know everything, but that doesn't prevent us from making vast, irreparable mistakes. We pretend to be vital and alive, but we are very, very tired.

I am an aging *Cosmo* girl.

Survival in my world, from a practical point of view, depends on one's apartment. Mine is in the low Eighties near Second. Three flights up. Sunlight ten minutes a day. A no-more-than-average-crazed super. It consists of a small-ish living room, a smaller bedroom, a john, a miniature hallway and an amusing little kitchen. There is a fire escape by the kitchen window where I try and fail to grow tomatoes in the summer. As I chop my vegetables, I look out over many tar roofs. I've lived here for five years and will never leave it. Why? The rent is only four hundred a month. Most of the block isn't bad at all, though there's a creepy patch down at the end you have to watch late at night. There are a few trees where sparrows twitter in the spring, around whose bases the Block Association plants tulips and marigolds.

I love/hate my apartment with a terrible intensity. Each night as I climb the stairs, terrible images flash through my mind: broken glass, bent and misshapen window gates flung aside, drawers pulled out and overturned, lamps smashed, *FUCK* written on the wall in green spray paint. Jewelry gone, fur coat gone, the few pieces of silver I have wrenched from Dorothy's grasp gone, melted down. My little baby spoon being used to measure a junkie's heroin. Curtain rods askew, empty booze bottles on the floor. A fresh turd in the middle of my rug. The maniac inside, waiting to spring, knife glittering.

So far this has not happened. I have been burgled, of course, but by a very neat fellow. He took the television set and two pairs of earrings and half a pound of prosciutto. He never returned. I brooded for weeks about his choice of booty, but finally gave up and admitted that there are some things that can never be explained—a very difficult conclusion for me to come to, since I overanalyze everything. Still he haunts me. I see him coming in carefully past the picked lock, looking everything over, then rejecting all of it except those three things, which, afterward, took on a glow of importance, the dark throb of loss. No Sony was like mine. No earrings so beautiful. No prosciutto so delicious—and it was the prosciutto I thought about most.

So far, as I open my three locks and cautiously open the door, there has been no such scene. In the dark, on a winter evening, it even has a certain Belle Époque charm. Through the tall windows, falling snow lit up by the streetlight outside, black branches of the bare tree. The silhouettes of my sofa and chair against the violet night. It could be Paris, or some Baghdad of the imagination. But it's Eighty-third Street.

When I turn on the lights, all the warts show—the frayed slipcover, the junk-shop table, the armoire that I painted an unfortunate purple. Bernard likes it, and Dorothy, with her genius for entirely missing the point, says you shouldn't have purple in the living room. The holes in the rug, the pile of newspapers in the corner. My little pet roaches. If it's a no-Bernard night I put on a record he hates, like Gregorian chants or the Bach *B-Minor Mass*, and take off my clothes and put on a bathrobe and fix myself a drink. I lie on the floor with my feet higher than my head, which relaxes my legs. I chant with the Gregorians. I sip my gin or my Chardonnay. I talk to myself, which prevents madness.

I am, by profession, a photographer, a field in which some make vast amounts of money. This has not yet happened to me; and not only that, but there have been times when I couldn't pay the rent, or else had to choose between paying the rent and eating. At the moment I'm working for a magazine called *New Day*, where I've taken hundreds of pictures of models in business suits crossing Madison Avenue, their faces taut and shiny with ambition and the pursuit of power. The staff at *New Day* are somewhat different—either they talk about their last fuck or they wonder where the next one is coming from. Underneath all this hip talk are chords of loneliness. Many are divorced and live the way I do. We mirror each other. The younger ones, still in their thirties, are full of the *Angst* of overchoice. Where am I going? What does it all mean? Do I marry or not? Have a baby or not? And all that.

The ones in my generation are quieter and more practical. The future is as close to us as the movie screen from the first row. I am blinded by the future, that big, white, blank screen. For us the choices have been made, if not consciously, then by life's dicey processes. No baby. In all likelihood no fame and fortune. Probably we already know the next man, if there is to be one—it's unlikely that a new man will ride into our lives. I don't know if the screen is blank or crowded, like a faded, cluttered tapestry, with the trivia of my life today, and either way I don't like it. I want some mystery place, some Babylon I have never seen. I want whispers and promises, strange songs, dark eyes behind a bead curtain.

The *New Day* women are frightened both of losing their men, if they have them, and of losing their jobs. No wonder everybody's on Valium. Compared with them I'm lucky, because if *New Day* folds I can take my cameras and go someplace else, and it's not so easy for them. I am, besides, more inured to the termination of jobs that is part of the nature of free-lancing. I *know* things end. I've always paid for my own Blue Cross. It gives me scar tissue. And photography is bigger than editing. Who edits anymore? Who reads? The streets swarm with unemployed editors whose employers have gone out of business, cut back or been gobbled up by greedy oil companies. The people who used to read now look at pictures, and ho ho, that puts me on top.

I used to read voluminously, like a starving person. I don't do it anymore—I don't know why. My dim and tired eyes crave images, not words. Most of the time I turn on the tube, which emits more anxieties to fuel the ones I already have: Hemorrhoids. Cancer. The Holocaust. The Unthinkable. Children's suicide. Incest. Gray laundry. Baggy stockings. Bursting garbage bags. Bracket Creep. Trickle-Down. I worry about it all, and it was all conceived by minds like mine and produced for minds like mine. We all feed on each other.

I think it started with my divorce, five years ago.

My divorce. I still can't say it without feeling suddenly chilled, as though somebody had put me on ice. Let me immediately make clear that this is not because I wish I were still married to Richard the Raven-Hearted. Oh, God, no. From that point of view the divorce was a release from hell, a gateway into semihuman life. But that passage was as complex and frustrating as one of those series of locks through which boats go from one water level to another. Sometimes I even wondered if I'd be better off staying on the high water than going through those crazy gates.

The problem was that Richard, though he hated me, wanted to stay married. He recognized quite realistically that if he lost me he'd have to go to all the bother of finding another wife, so he tried to block the divorce. If Richard could have turned me in for a replacement, quickly and quietly and cheaply, he would have done so. As it was, it took him several months to find one. Some women are devastated by a divorce, emotionally cleaned out. For months they can't look at another man. For years they are frightened. But I've met men whose wives have left them and they're dying of misery and they can't stand it and the mother of their children and so forth. After half an evening, pop, up it goes again. You have to admire such resilience.

During our divorce, Richard took on a passion and purpose he hadn't shown me for years before. Sometimes I thought, during those nights of horror, that Richard's strange golden eyes were seeing me clearly for the first time. As the blow landed, the cuff, the slap, the push across the room, he looked particularly fucused, as though this were the scene he'd been waiting for all his life. He always loved a good fight and got exasperated with me because I was such a poor adversary—when he'd picked on me, I'd pout or sniffle or go cowering out of the room. What was he to do with his anger, which he called the normal anger of marriage? For years he restrained himself and then, when I said I was unhappy and wanted a divorce, it was as though a bell had rung, a light had switched on.

I didn't recognize it for what it was for a long time, our *danse macabre*. We'd sit down to talk, though our inability to do so was one reason I wanted a divorce. We'd open a bottle of Scotch. We'd start understandingly, muting our accusations and exaggerating our eagerness to try again. "Richard," I'd say, "it hurts me that you refuse to touch me when others are around. That you won't let me sleep close to you. That you never touch me at all except before sex." And Richard: "Celia, I'd appreciate it if you never served macaroni again. If you'd find a better laundry so my shirts are correctly ironed. If you wouldn't call Dorothy when I'm around—it makes you too bitchy. If you'd be tidier, more thoughtful, braver, more optimistic. If you'd remember to buy wholewheat bread. If you'd never again wear the red dress that shows your tits, particularly around my professional colleagues. If you'd never again cut your toenails in my presence." Me: "Talk to me when you walk into the house. Don't throw your dirty clothes on the floor. Stop insulting my cooking, my appearance and my profession. Occasionally fix something around the apartment. Help me with the dishes, the laundry, with sadness and disappointment. Hold my hand in the movies."

And Richard: "Come out of the darkroom. Cook my breakfast. Clean the fucking place up. What do you do all day? I come home to a mess. You can't do this and you don't have time for that. What kind of a wife are you? Straighten my drawers. Shine my shoes. Suck my cock. Change your hair—it looks like shit. Conceive a child.''

That I could not do, in spite of all the clinics and all the drugs and the sperm counts. I was barren, Richard said. He'd been gypped. Taken. Probably that was why we stayed married for so long: the project kept us busy for years.

Me: ''Oh, it's that again! Is that what's at the bottom of everything? No son to worship at your feet—you bastard! You think this will help? Insult me some more—maybe it'll make you fertile.''

Richard's eyes would gleam—probably mine did too. He panted with excitement. Even his skin seemed to change, to become brighter and shinier. ''Maybe it will. I'll insult you all I want. You're a cunt. An excuse for a woman, a depressed, dried-up, maladjusted creep. You're hung up on your mother and your clone sister. You don't know how to love a man or take care of him. You're lousy in bed and you can't start a baby. You're a rotten no-talent photographer, but I let you do it to keep you busy and out of trouble.''

Then I'd go for him, rush at him in some stupid flailing way, and he'd let me have it, the stunning blow. Never a real beating—that was too inelegant. A whack, a cuff that sent me spinning and screaming across the room. Then maybe a little *frisson* or two—like poking at my gritted teeth with an extended index finger, or hooking a leg around mine so I couldn't move and shoving his laughing face in mine, maybe sticking out his tongue. Sticking a finger in my ear, chanting, ''Cunt. Cunt. Twat. Stupid bitch. Twatty twatty,'' till I wrenched away from him and went and locked myself in the bathroom or the study. But usually he didn't follow me—one outburst was enough. From behind the door I'd hear him laughing in the living room, then the snap of the television and its mumbled sounds. I'd weep, rage, beat on the floor, almost go crazy. I wanted to take a scissors and cut up his Sulka pajamas, shoot spray paint at his rack of Brooks Brothers suits. I'd scream, ''I want a divorce!''

Richard would reply, "When I feel like it."

I was terrified of him. I went to three lawyers, and none of them believed me. "Mrs. Sterner, you must be exaggerating. Your husband is a reputable, well-known attorney, top of his field. You don't get where he is if you're crazy. It's hard to believe what you tell me. Even if it's true, you have no witnesses. It's your word against his."

Richard at a meeting with his lawyer and mine, after one finally listened to me:

"Celia, your stories are incredible. That you'd even make such things up says something about you." To his colleagues: "She's always had a vivid imagination. She's always been unstable. She's a twin, and you know how they are." To me: "Maybe when you think it over, Celia, your memory will clear up." Little smiles on the counselors' faces. Me frozen with hellish rage, then tears, female ploy of last resort. No, I couldn't help the tears. I was so angry and hopeless, so beaten.

How often did it happen? Half a dozen times in so many months. Then why, Mrs. Sterner, didn't you leave?

I was going to, but my lawyer advised me not to.

That was only partly true. I stayed out of incredulity. It couldn't have happened, I must have been imagining it. Richard and I didn't get along, but he wasn't a maniac. (But there, the next morning, were the bruises.) In the beginning he was so, so sorry. Abject apologies, dinner at Lutèce, new start. Fabulous sex. God, if only there hadn't been that good sex! It made me not understand anything. It kept up right through the divorce. After it was over, I'd cry into the pillow. Richard lay there snoring and satiated. I was full of the-semen-that-didn't-work. I'd go into the bathroom and douche it out, terrified that it might suddenly become activated.

Ten years of marriage. Four years of love, five trying to have a baby. One going through the crazy gates.

It's really hard to believe you, Mrs. Sterner, when your husband has tried and won cases involving child abuse. Your husband says he wants to reconcile. Why don't you go home and talk things over? It's cases like yours that break my heart. You two have everything. You're a perfect couple.

The judge didn't believe me either, and there was no alimony and no apartment, which I'd left and which was in Richard's name. There was a settlement of five thousand dollars to help me get on my feet as a photographer, and Richard agreed to that only because he didn't want to look chintzy in front of his friends.

Ah, God. Why do I go over it? Five years have passed. But maybe I'm too old, maybe I'll never really bury it. Probably I won't. I'm haunted and bored by it at the same time. I carry it like a birthmark. And yet never, since then, have I been so alive.

I came out of it a different person. For ages I couldn't drink, and I still can't read because I have trouble concentrating. Sometimes I can't sleep. The experience tore something in my very depths which exposed a great black sea of fear which had been there all along, but neatly sealed over. Of course it's perfectly possible that if I'd never laid eyes on Richard Sterner I'd be the same way, but that's one of those specious arguments. The fact is I did, and this is the way I am.

I told Dorothy about some of this, because I didn't know how not to tell her. I suppose that was my problem along with everything else. I could have simply avoided her during the whole period, but I wanted to go home too badly, just to sit on the porch and lick my wounds. When I told her what Richard had done to me, her reaction was characteristic.

"Honestly, Celia. You get in the worst messes. Well, I never liked Richard. [Lie—she loved him.] There was something about him, I don't know, I could tell. A cruelty around the mouth. I could always read faces, you know."

You think, Dorothy. You wish. In a family with twins that's a loaded remark. But I wouldn't dare contradict her, because I still need her—if not her, what she has and what she represents. The quiet street in the evening, the slap of the newspaper on the porch. The smell of whatever she's cooking. The outlines of home.

"Though I really don't understand why you stayed there. Never did your father lay a finger on me. If he ever had, just once, I would have been in Jack Brodsky's office within an hour. If there was a mark or bruise, he would

have taken a picture of it. He would have sent me straight
to Ol' Doc Schroeder. I would have signed an affidavit
that very day.''

Dorothy is very litigious, at least in her fantasies. For a
while she got off on my legalities, but basically she was
irritated at me for not living a perfect life (like Cassie) and
for not supplying her with ample success stories for her
bridge club. As usual, I threw her into a dilemma. What
she ended up with was something like, if *she* had handled
my case I would have come out a winner. Three no-trump.

I'm a disappointment to Dorothy. I have no husband, no
children, and I'm neither rich nor famous. But then, none
of this is surprising. She had to choose one of us, and she
chose Cassie. What the bridge club hears about till the
women are ready to pull out their hearing aids is her
fabulous trips to California to visit her wonderful daughter,
her rich and successful husband and her three adorable
children—a total of three in ten years. The fifty times
she's been invited for dinner at my apartment, and the ten
times she's come, lie forgotten.

"I just don't know why you *put up* with it, Celia. The
woman always makes the rules. Your father knows exactly
what I will put up with and where I draw the line. Every
wife should make this clear."

"I was afraid of him," I said, and my voice was small
and thin like a child's. "I couldn't believe it was happening. After all, this was the man I'd been so crazy about.
He was my first real love."

We were sitting in the kitchen, and I was dropping half
the hulls from the strawberries I was picking on her clean
floor. Whenever I'm in that house I become a klutz,
dropping things and breaking things. No wonder her face
sinks the way it does when I appear.

"Oh, Celia," she says. "Hello."

"You're stuck with me, Dorothy. I'm all you've got."

I don't say things like that very often, because she gets
tense and angry and starts banging things around the kitchen.
I don't even know if it's true. She's still pretty good-
looking at sixty-three, all things considered. Straight-backed,
of medium bulk and very pretty; plentiful white hair pulled
back in a fat knot. Strong features and green eyes; a long

and graceful neck. People called her, or used to call her, "stunning." She looks like a person who once did something remarkable—wrote a best-selling novel, or broke a swimming record, or married into royalty, or conducted an orchestra. Actually, she resembles the editor-in-chief of *New Day*. But Dorothy's life has been limited, like everyone's, by the capacity of her intellect, and in her case by the fact of multiple birth. By the nature of my father. By fate in general. There are some bitter weeds in her garden, but she has triumphed, by God, over adversity, to hear her tell it.

People call her "brave" and "wonderful." "Oh, Dorothy," they say. "Oh, Dorothy's just wonderful." God, to have a mother who is not wonderful. A little mother who ducks her head and is ignored by everybody but me. I'd protect and cherish her forever, tuck her in at night when she got old. Bring her toddies and sing to her. But Dorothy, the figurehead? Praise is what she needs by the gallon, by the paean. A little adversity to overcome. She was born to have one of those nineteenth-century sons who gambled and went through the family fortune and broke everybody's hearts. I say "son" because she wishes she'd had one to complete her destiny, instead of two matching daughters. Daughters just don't have the clout. They do what they can. They put up with things. But males—ah. They have the power and the glory. They can lift you up and smash you down.

Dorothy has been disappointed in her marriage to my father, but she hides it admirably. Not because he's a florist, which is perfectly okay with her. It's that she secretly thinks he's weak. (Don't ask me how I know these things; I just do.) Caspar is the kind of guy who hums absentmindedly, likes to play chess, loses his socks and gives candy to the little kids who come into the store with their Moms. My sweet Daddy. He'd gather both of us into his arms and kiss us without knowing which was which. He didn't care; he loved us equally. I suspect he's been cheating on Dorothy for years, but I don't know whether she knows it or not. Probably not, for even if it might not appear that way, he's smarter than she is. He's just less exigent. She was always torn between power and exhaustion, for she has made clear how exhausting we were to raise. And of course, that terrible birth, thirty-six hours of agony. And a complete surprise—the incompetents had heard only one heartbeat. And then she couldn't have any more children, as if that were bad news.

"Oh, Dorothy," her friends say. "It must have been so difficult. So terrible. Why, I think you're simply wonderful."

When I told Caspar all about Richard, he listened with sympathy and held my hand as we sat on the porch swing.

"It's terrible, sweetheart. Terrible. I don't understand how anybody could act like that."

Caspar is so innocent it was hard for him to take it in. His brand of marital crime is much more hidden, less overtly cruel. He thought what Dorothy didn't know wouldn't hurt her, and maybe he was right. My suspicions about him came from the tiniest things—an accidental word in a sentence, a certain expression on his face. I hated spying on him, but he was such a creature of habit that the tiniest deviations were noticeable. Somewhere, somehow he had another life. Things were happening to him that had nothing to do with his home or The Bower of Flowers. I didn't know when or how, and I didn't want to know, and I didn't want Dorothy to find out. I suspected that Dorothy remained unsuspicious because she couldn't imagine him attracting another woman. She was utterly and completely sure of him.

Caspar—about six feet tall, thin, bent, sixty-five years old. Bald as an egg, except for a crescent of gray-brown hair going around the back. Bright brown eyes. Big teeth in a frequent smile. A little goatee. A little potbelly. A pleasant tenor voice which he sometimes donated to the choir of St. Anthony's Church. He dresses in short-sleeved pastel sport shirts of dubious patterns, worn with wide tie. Brown trousers. Dorothy broke him of suspenders only with great difficulty. Socks with clocks, suspended by garters. Middle America shoes. Thin white shanks, hairless halfway up the calf. Beyond that I can't say.

Who'd want him? Somebody did, it appeared. Maybe somebody he met at the weekly flower market. Or another choir member; or a customer. Somewhere in Caspar's rutted, grooved life was passion—or at least, companionship.

"Richard is crazy," I told him. I felt very contented. It was a summer evening, and we were drinking lemonade on the porch. Fireflies flickered over the lawn. "But a subtle, hidden kind of crazy that I couldn't see before I married him. Maybe he did me a favor by acting it all out; I might have stayed married to him for years longer."

"Favor," said Caspar, puzzled. "But wouldn't that have been better, Cece?"

"Well, I don't know. Suppose I'd had a child, after all? Then it would have been worse."

"I'm just sorry to see you lonely and unhappy."

"But I'm all right, Dad. Everybody has a sad story, I guess. Everybody I meet in New York does, anyway."

"Oh, Lord," he sighed. "How things change."

"Well, they certainly do," said Dorothy, coming out onto the porch. She can't stand not being included. "There's never been a divorce in the family." So she'd been listening.

"How about Cousin Barbara?" I said. "And Stanley's son Willy."

"Oh, well. Them."

"Cece's right," Caspar said. "And my crazy Uncle Anthony, he had a child out of wedlock and he brought it home and made Aunt Jane bring it up." Dorothy and I made little sounds of surprise and interest. "It grew up to eighteen, a smart, pretty girl, Minnie, and then she ran off with some guy and lives in Canada somewhere. He's a logger or some damn thing. Uncle Anthony called Minnie his 'ward' and said she was the child of a distant relative.'Course, the relative wasn't so distant." He laughed, his huge white teeth gleaming.

"That wasn't divorce," Dorothy said.

"Well, you're right, Dorothy. Dead right. It was Anthony's conscience, is all." The crickets chirped for a minute.

"I'm getting eaten alive," Dorothy said, slapping her arm.

"I'm going over to Nat's for a while," Caspar said, standing up. "Then by the shop to look at those accounts."

"Lord," Dorothy said. "Haven't you got those things finished yet?"

"Not quite," he said. "A coupla more nights."

His eye met mine, and I looked down. I know nothing, Daddy; I'm the monkey who covers his eyes. I see no evil. Besides, I'm your friend. When I looked up, he was walking over to his car, his sweater over his shoulder. How long it must have been going on. Same old green sweater—he didn't even go in to get a jacket, saying it was getting colder. Same old pants. Did he glance into the car mirror, smooth his six hairs into place? The car's motor started and we watched it roll down the driveway. Just like that. What a hardened adulterer.

"He's worried about you," Dorothy said. "It's not so easy for a woman your age, living alone in the city."

"Manhattan is at least two-thirds divorced women, many a lot older than I am."

"And I don't like that street of yours, Celia. It's rough, I don't know why you live there."

"You know why I live there." I closed my eyes. "It's cheap. And anyway, I like it."

Dorothy drummed on her glass for a moment. "Do you think you'll marry again."

I didn't tell my parents about Bernard till we'd been going out together for two years. Now it's three. I told them that Bernard was free of past encumbrances, when the truth is I am again the cliché of all clichés—I am having an affair with a married man. If my divorce was out of *Gaslight* or Kafka, his is in the manner of Proust or Joseph Heller—endless, circuitous, repetitive, nonprogressive, hopeless, boring. Maria (his wife) thinks. She's decided. She refuses. She's away; she's back again. She's run up a five-hundred-dollar bill at Gristede's. She wasn't home when the process server came. The bitch had a date! She's willing, she's not willing, she's eager, she's recalcitrant.

It's not just Maria, Bernard has explained to me fifty times. It's his daughters, Joanne and Sarah, a pair of unprincipled tarts if I've ever seen any. At sixteen and fourteen they are corrupt. I've met them, of course, only briefly, because I am not supposed to exist. Our encounter was in the hall of Maria's co-op building on Sixty-sixth Street, which apartment she is, of course, fighting to keep, while Bernard is fighting for half of it. Bernard was delivering them back, and I was meeting him. The little bitches gave me searing looks from head to toe—probably learned at Chapin, where Bernard spends fortunes to send them. "Hoyee," they whined, which I assumed was a greeting. After getting some money out of their father, which seems to be their main occupation, they went up in the elevator, long Alice in Wonderland hair flopping behind them.

Next time all four of us went to dinner at Top of the Sixes. Bernard introduced me as his Friend, whom he was working with. How—working? Well, Bernard is a stockbroker and I, it seemed, was doing a photographic essay on the interior of the New York Stock Exchange—not a bad idea at all. We'd been snapping and clicking around in there, said Bernard, and it was getting late, and he'd just asked me to come along to dinner with him and his girls. The two little Balzac belles turned their eyes to me. There I read knowledge and disgust with their poor father's guilty lie. They exchanged a smile and ordered Lobster Thermidor and Filet Mignon. Bernard, with my feeble help, tried to make conversation, but it was difficult in the loaded atmosphere—cathected, as my therapist would say. The girls' game was to shoot out references to Mummy, like BBs, and see what Daddy would do. Mummy was thinking of buying the most beautiful mink coat. She'd been to the Hamptons with—yum—such a nice man. She'd been out for *the night*. She was thinking of moving, with Joanne and Sarah, to Cuernavaca. Her life was so difficult she'd decided she needed therapy.

While Daddy reacted to everything, the cute kids kept their beady eyes on me, practically taking notes. Later Maria would hear it all: sunken eyes, dark straggly hair, discount clothes. My coat, from Bolton's, had the tag carefully cut out. Fake pearls—jewelers might not be able to tell, but those kids could. Scuffed boots, a hole in the finger of one glove. The three of them would laugh; poor Daddy.

What was this man, that I endured all this?

Around my age, a year or so older. Large; hunched over; weary, hooded eyes. Actually a little strange-looking, like Donald Sutherland. I like his mysterious looks. Odd sandy, grayish, gravel-colored hair, a brownish mustache— I hate the mustache. Big, gentle hands, a gentle soul. A sweet smile. A long, slow stride, one step of his to two of mine. A way of humming tunelessly. A way of pulling me to him and kissing me on the head. A good cook, and he cleans up after himself, which his mother made him do. There is something about Bernard. Sometimes we just sit together, at my apartment or his, on the West Side. One of us reads; the other watches the tube turned down softly. I fiddle with slides. He fiddles with his plants. One of us goes and makes some tea. It's the simplicity of battle-scarred warriors. We're both tired. I could live my life with him this way.

I might add that though Bernard appears to be so calm and tranquil, his behavior, is at times, maniacal. It can't be just goodness of heart and tender loving kindness that have taken him three years to get a divorce that he still doesn't have. Possibly—anyone but me would say—he doesn't really want one. But I can't bear to think that way. I have to feel that we are making some sort of progress, some wormlike motion through the sands of time. There must be something ahead, something on my white screen. I can't believe that Bernard is happy to go in endless circles . . . but the truth is, not much progress has been made since I met him.

It's true that the effort toward divorce has not been consistent. There were two terrible halts while Maria and Bernard "reconciled"—in other words, fucked. Both times Bernard, all honesty, told me. Both times I screamed and yelled, cried and threw up, happily alarming him to death and throwing him into insupportable conflict, though not enough to lay off Maria. *That* happened only when she began abusing him again, which she did after a couple of weeks: the limit of her ability to be human. I couldn't avoid the grim truth—that only Maria really mattered, that I could hang by my heels from the roof and while Bernard would be deeply upset, he wouldn't make a move to save me if Maria, the cunt, told him not to. He is married as I never was; married, really, to the grave. He is one of those people who can do it only once.

That I accept these humiliating things, things I never would have accepted twenty years ago, is a sign of age and defeat. The truth is I'm lucky to have him. He is in essence a good man. He's not gay. He's basically sane, and he's only half-married. We like to be together. Besides, if I got rid of him he'd find another woman in about two days and like her just as much as he likes me. So we lead a half-life together and possibly always will, though I would really like, someday, to be married to him. In spite of their contradictory behavior, I believe that someday Maria and Bernard will be divorced. The passage through those gates takes on a momentum of its own—once started, it's hard to go back. After the three years and the fortunes they've spent on lawyers, they'd feel like fools turning around. Anyway, they hate each other. Maria, who is short, fat and Spanish, considers Bernard lumpish and unexciting. Bernard says she's a bitch but somehow she still turns him on.

I'm obsessed by Maria in the sickest possible way. I've seen her a couple of times, *en passant,* accidentally. Getting into a cab in front of Bernard's. She trotted across the sidewalk on her fat little legs, in four-inch heels, waving arms loaded with boxes and shopping bags. Black designer suit. Black gloves. Little red hat on black hair. Blood-red lips and overloaded eyelashes. Eyes like bullets. Big tits and big behind, which led as she got into the cab. She didn't see me. As the cab left, Bernard appeared on the steps of his brownstone, white-faced. "Did you see her? That's Maria." This bloated broad is what Bernard considers beautiful. And brilliant, he says.

Another time Bernard and I went into a restaurant, and there was Maria. She was wearing cut-to-the-nipples silver satin at a simple neighborhood Italian restaurant—giving the lie to Bernard's conviction that she has perfect taste in clothes. Three of us caught sight at the same time. She couldn't have known her Don Juan that well; he stared stupidly across the room wondering why she was twanging with awareness. Maria's and my eyes locked. Every curl of her hair and those blood-red fingernails went into my permanent consciousness. I was sure she knew what I'd paid for my Orchard Street dress and that my makeup was from Lamston's. She knew whether my eyebrows were plucked, what I had in my wallet, what was in my heart. After this hot moment I looked at Bernard, who was frozen into immobility. Finally he pulled himself together and he and Maria mumbled greetings. I started toward a table and Bernard grabbed my arm and pulled me out the door.

"Celia, I don't want to sit in there, for God's sake. We'll get into a cab and go down to the Village."

"The *Village*?"

"I don't want to run into her later on the street."

I sat in the cab and sniffled. "I wanted their linguine with clam sauce. I was thinking about it all day." Tears turned to sobs. "She always gets there first. I don't dress as well as she does. I'm not as rich. I can't afford a hairdresser. I don't wear ten dollars' worth of makeup. I even have a run in my stocking."

"Shut up, Celia," said Bernard frantically, half hugging me and half trying to jump out the window. "You're different. You're you. Stop trying to make comparisons." He lit a cigarette. He'd stop smoking for a week or so and then something like this would happen. "Anyway, she won't be so rich after the divorce. The big-spender phase is over."

"There's nothing left to buy."

"Celia. It's all a legal ploy. Anyway, you should feel sorry for her. You don't need to be a compulsive shopper—you're creative, you don't need such things. This poor bitch has nothing."

Oh, God—I'm creative. I'd heard that one before: You artists are used to starving—you'd throw up if you were fed decent food. You're made to give out, not to take in. You're not supposed to care about the Four Seasons and Fendi furs. You're above all that, up there in your rags. You're above all of us.

"She has everything," I wept. "And she has you."

"Grand Ticino," Bernard screamed to the driver. "Thompson Street."

I don't do this to Bernard often. There are many things I can't be really honest about, and I have accepted this. I'm a little wary of honesty anyway. Why should he want to hear what I really think of Joanne and Sarah? Usually I was discreet. "They'll be better," he'd say. "They're very threatened by everything now." Threatened—if those minxes were threatened by anything, I'd eat my knitted hat. Nor could I question his basic taste in marrying the Spanish Fly in the first place. God, how difficult divorce was. In the same way there were some criticisms of Richard I would accept and some I would not. Granted—certifiably insane. Cruel, sadistic, psychotic. But handsome. Brilliant. Witty. A seed of goodness buried under the garbage, which I, in my innocence, had thought I could bring to fruition. I was eager to agree that he was a maniac, but God forbid anybody say he wasn't *quality*. In the same way, Maria was basically sweet, adorable, smart, etcetera, but had suffered from "you know, women's problems."

It's hard to keep a straight face at that one. When the women's movement came along, Maria was in a dressing room at Bergdorf's. Bernard chooses to beat himself, call himself a terrible male chauvinist pig. A typical unenlightened male of his generation whose eyes had since been opened. The poor little thing had to ask him for money before he realized how degrading it was and put everything into their joint names—a decision he has since had reason to regret. Never did he help her with the dishes or the children; never did he take her collages seriously. How blind he had been. But the truth, which Bernard cannot see, is that Maria wants liberation the way I want cancer. What she wants is every buck she can wring out of him. She's tired of Bernard and wants another, richer husband. Maybe she has one lined up—who knows? The collages stink. I suspect she started them because all her friends were doing "something." But I say nothing. If this is the way Bernard's consciousness got raised, so be it.

"Of course you'll never marry if you keep on with that Bernard," said Dorothy on the porch.

"Oh, he'll be divorced someday. Maybe we'll marry. Maybe we'll live together." Sharp intake of breath from Dorothy. "Maybe we'll just do what we're doing now. After all we both have rent-controlled apartments."

I was afraid of getting married. Dorothy was afraid of my not getting married. People belonged in couples; she didn't understand the half-lives that my friends and I led. I'd worn my voice out arguing with her, and now I was secretly beginning to agree with her. There was a persistent picture on my screen:

A house in Connecticut—not this house, but another, my own. (Connecticut, place of happy endings in old movies.) My house is next to a wood, near a stream. At night I can hear the clear dark waters rush over the white stones, hear the willows rustle. There are a big lawn and a vegetable garden. The house is long and low, all on one floor, for we are, after all, old. There Bernard and I sit by the fire, like Darby and Joan. He wears dungarees and a plaid shirt. I wear a country cotton dress. Our old feet rest on footstools. Everything is spotlessly clean. The cat is curled up on the hearthrug, the dog near the door to warn us if a stranger comes down our road. The clock ticks. We read or I do needlework. We talk a little, doze a little. At ten o'clock we get into our bed, make love in whatever fashion we can in our decrepitude and go to sleep with our arms around each other.

I block out illness, ambulances, bad eyes, boredom, poverty, plague and pestilence, winter storms and failing heat, abusive visits from Goneril and Regan. Or I accept it all—just let me be old with Bernard in Connecticut. Let us die at the same moment so neither of us need ever be alone. Let us breathe each other's last breath. Is it love or loneliness? Possibly they are inseparable.

Dorothy stretched and yawned. I could see her mound of white hair, bright against the dark shrubbery behind. The swing squeaked—imagine still having a swing—as she stood up, smoothing down her wrinkled skirt.

"Well, you were always the one we worried about," she said.

"There had to be some way to tell us apart." I felt my gut tighten.

"*I* could always tell you apart." She sighed. "Sometimes I wish we could all be together here again. The years go by so fast." She walked to the steps, peered down the street. The leaves of the trees looked pale green and milky

in the light from the streetlamp. From out in the dark
somewhere came the whistle of a child calling a dog.
"Well, I see Caspar's late again. Guess I'll go to bed."

The unsuspicious woman went indoors, banging the
screen door behind her. I heard her walking around the
living room, then climbing the stairs to the bedroom. I
knew just what she was doing—turning on the light in the
upstairs hall, taking off her shoes, opening the closet door.
There to the bathroom—plumbing sounds. Scrabble scrabble, Andy the Yorkie on the wood floor. And outside the
wind sighing in the trees, the put-put-grumble of a car
motor up the street.

I leaned back in the swing and closed my eyes. I told
myself I came home to rest, but really I was here for the
grief. Not only did I have chronic visions of the maniac in
my apartment, chopping up my armoire, stealing my clothes
and drinking my gin, then setting the whole place on fire,
but Dorothy's slightest, most casual words throbbed through
me like tom-toms. She wishes we could all be together.
What a twisted idea. Anyway, she didn't wish—she only
thought so. What she really wished was that it were forty
years ago when she was on top of things. And Cassie and I
were her two little prisoners. The ornaments that made her
special. *That* was what she wanted—the two of us. Her
two eyes, her two hands. Her two proud and uplifted
breasts. Yet what an ordinary woman she was, and how
quiet and dull her life. It was only I that made her into this
feral goddess.

How secret are my memories of my family. In this, I'm
not like everybody else at the deli or in the crosstown
bus—I'm unable to let it all hang out. Edith, my therapist,
says I face nothing but hide behind a veil of "assumed
uniqueness" when I should be learning why I am just like
everybody else. For this I pay her fifty dollars a week . . .
well, no, it's rather *because* she's fifty dollars a week that
I go to her. You get what you pay for, and as things are
these days, Edith is cheap. I suspect it irritates Edith that I
am *not* like most other people, and she doesn't quite know
how to handle it. Possibly she wishes she had a twin
herself, or some other buried hate or fear suggested by my
particular anomaly. Like many others I have known, she

wants to make me ordinary, for she envies what she can never have, my special experience with closeness. I carry it like a jewel, though a fiery one that has been known to burn.

As though to please her and fend off resentment, I lead an ordinary life and have come to see my parents as unremarkable people. As Bernard says, just look at the other mothers. His is an ancient Jewish matriarch who was once known as the ugliest woman in Warsaw. Her two front teeth are gold, her eyes deep and smoky with ancient wisdom and modern loathing. Though she totters around with a cane, everyone listens to her, Bernard most of all, for she is brilliant and crazy. He has promised to sprinkle her ashes over Jerusalem. Leah her name is. When she met me, she gave me a long look and sighed deeply, then promptly forgot about me. When from time to time she noticed me, at the evening tea we were attending, she'd kind of snap up with a slightly surprised look, as though to say, "Oh, *her*, I'd forgotten *her*. Now what am I supposed to do about her?" I'd far rather she hated me as she did Maria, for some good solid reason like not being Jewish, or for stealing away her son. But to Leah I'm just another damn thing to worry about, though not much. But to Bernard she's the old Mother, fount of chicken soup and noodle pudding, source of God and the guilt and misery to which he is addicted.

And Richard's mother, with her hard topaz eyes and her two-pack-a-day habit, her varnished blond hair and gravel voice. She was always saying, "Cece, you and I understand each other." Once she told me all men were pricks, Richard included. It was pretty early on, and I was a little shocked. I looked at her through the trails of smoke that were always rising in front of her face from the Virginia Slim in her twisted mouth. "Pricks, Cece. I *know*." I gently protested. "They can't help it," she said. "I feel sorry for, 'em." Lydia Sterner had pouchy textured skin, thick with Clinique, and eyes like little yellow marbles. "You let me know," she said, "if you have a problem. Any kind." At the time I didn't know what she meant. At the time I didn't know she was alcoholic, very guarded and secret. She admitted to only two drinks a day, Glenlivet if possible. She was tall, and at fifty-five her body was still beautiful. She always wore brown and gold, though, wisely, with something white around the face like a Colette heroine. For someone so hard and knowing, she seemed to have been grievously wounded by her divorce. "Fifteen years, Cece. Then one day he just walked out. 'I can't take it anymore, Lydia,' he said. *Take* it, for God's sake. Richard was ten. I went to work because I had to. The bastard never gave me a cent. He moved to Louisiana."

Richard and I had gone to New Orleans and looked him up. While I waited at the hotel, Richard went to see him, and he never told me about it. When he came back he'd been crying. What pain there was in that family, and how they hid it! *"Tell* me," I said to Richard. "What do you think I'm *for*? Why do you have to live with it alone?" "Because I'm ashamed," Richard said between clenched teeth. "Can you understand that? *Ashamed.*" He never told me. "I can't stand your secrecy," I said to him. "It puts up walls between us."

"It has nothing to do with us. It has to do with me and my self-respect. You wouldn't understand."

And yet, "Cece, would you take Lydia to lunch? You're good with her. She likes you."

"She doesn't. She thinks she does, but she doesn't."

"Oh, stop splitting hairs."

"Sure I'll take her. Actually, I like her a lot."

Lydia and I would go to some fancy place, which gave her pleasure, and after her Glenlivets she'd stop sulking that Richard hadn't come and take my hand across the table. "You're good for him, Cece. He needs you. God, what a lovely child he was! People stopped on the street to look at him. He had a perfect disposition; he never cried. Whenever I looked at him I knew everything was justified, it was all worth it. I knew I'd done something wonderful. I think you feel his specialness even if he's difficult sometimes. I pray the two of you have a child."

Of course, she accepted me only after she knew I was not only inevitable, but her channel to Richard. He would forget about her for weeks; it was I who thought of her in the apartment hotel in Chelsea where she'd lived for years on a spare, mysterious income. The place was dirty, dangerous and falling-apart, but she wouldn't move. It was on the third floor, and the traffic sounds were deafening. But if she closed the windows she'd swelter in the summer. I worried about her and thought of gifts to give her that at first she wouldn't accept—an air conditioner, a new coat, a toaster-oven for her tiny kitchenette. Each time she was insulted—such gifts implied neediness. The Pringle cashmere cardigan was graciously accepted, and so was a little golden clock—even though her fur coat was old and tatty and she made toast by spearing a piece of bread on a fork and holding it over her gas jet. Later, as she drank more, she did accept things. It was because she was spending more money on booze, but I pretended to myself that it was because she was needier, and my heart warmed to her. There she was—and there would I be, possibly, in another twenty or thirty years, but worse off because I had no child and would never have one. I would never have her dreams and delusions.

I liked her for the vulnerability that Dorothy didn't seem to have. Sometimes I even envied the *New Day* women who talked of their mad, broke or broken-down mothers—mothers who phoned them to beg for money or attention or some fantasy of a happy future, who hung on them for details of their lives. And those few to whom I described my family envied me. "A mother who bakes blueberry pies and plays bridge . . . who puts up preserves . . . who lives in a house with a porch! A mother who's still married to a father! Celia, how incredible! I'll trade you—mine just came out of the closet, and she's in love with my *au pair*," a senior editor told me. My mouth began to curl with laughter till I saw her eyes. "My *au pair* from Sweden, that we brought over for the kids," she whispered. "They are *in love* with each other."

It was strange how desirable Dorothy's ordinariness had become, how her cliché life had begun to seem unique. What had always seemed to me drab and stifling now appeared to others as a sort of warranty of mental health. "You, a shrink? Nonsense. Save your money." "But I'm crazy," I told people. "I'm very nervous and I don't sleep well." "You can't be crazy. Let me tell you about *me*.

I'm on my third stepfather . . ." and so on. People cuddled up to me as though some of it might rub off. "You see?" I said to Edith. "I'm extraordinary in my ordinariness." "You're full of shit," Edith said. "You bandy words around. You won't look at the situation." For this I pay her fifty dollars an hour.

Even Bernard fell prey to this—in it lay the sources of his early enchantment, when we met at my "local," a watering-hole for the middle-aged called The Gibbon's Head. It was fairly late. Bernard was drinking himself into a stupor and I had drifted over for a glass of wine with Meg, a clinical psychologist who lives in my building. In accordance with a frequent agreement among females in such a situation, we would not necessarily leave together. Not that The Gibbon's Head, I hasten to add, is a meat rack. Its tone is older, darker and distinctly low-key. People drop in for a drink after work or for a nightcap, as Meg and I sometimes did. It was assumed that you might just want to talk. You could do what you wanted.

Anyway, Bernard and I met in the dark. "You're so pretty and pure," Bernard said. "You look like Miss America." "I'm old and crazy," I said. "No, you're fresh and alive and American." I'd just hit Bernard at the moment when he felt what he really needed to be happy was a shiksa. I was the WASP he'd been looking for all his life, he said, though of course he hadn't. We had a long, inane conversation, as Bernard was, as we say in Rivertown, three sheets to the wind. But still living with Maria. I knew his kind; I'd encountered his racked and conflicted heart before. He couldn't stand it anymore. But the kids. Twenty years down the drain. Last week she'd closed the bedroom door to him. That was all right—he didn't want anybody who didn't want him. She wanted him to move out, but he wouldn't. His daughters needed him. (The fuck they did.) Maria ate in the dining room, he in the kitchen. She made furtive phone calls, clicking off as he came into the room. The thought of a lover made him crazy. He was afraid he might kill her.

I hummed and picked at the edge of the bar and nibbled potato chips. Such *déjà vu*. Everybody's stories were the same, and yet one's own misery felt unique, as though no one had ever suffered before. And what had he for me, if I sat through his expiation about his wife, if I endured his guilt, his obsession, his stops and starts? Was he a man or a shell? There was no way to find out—for most relationships started with this penance, this pay-in-advance about the previous mate. You listened; it was all you could do. And I would tell him about Richard too. We would spill blood before we even started. In a sense, it had nothing to do with each other—we could have been talking to stones. And yet it was so very intimate, the way we talked. It was exciting. Will you be better than this? he asked. Could you love me more than he did? was my not-so-secret message.

So when Meg signaled that she was leaving, I shook my head. She looked at Bernard, who was weaving, and made a little *moue*. She thought I was silly and weak, strong psychological woman that she was. Never mind. I stayed a while longer. I liked his eyebrows, after all. And those hooded green eyes with their heavy lids. The thick, sensuous mouth and big teeth. The mix of strange and gentle and strong. We walked out together.

"I have to stay for the kids," Bernard said for the third time as we walked along Second Avenue.

"It wouldn't be too good for your kids if you got mad and killed her, like you said."

But such wisdom was wasted on him as he went staggering off into the night. Or so I thought—but he was back at The Gibbon's Head the following week. Sober and charming. Would I have dinner with him some night? Not in the neighborhood, of course. The neighborhood turned out to include the entire East Side, and we ate at a place in SoHo. He kept looking at his watch. He talked continuously and then apologized halfway through the meal.

"I'm a man possessed," he said, "and yet I find you so attractive. Fresh and bright. Now tell me about yourself for a change."

Instead of laying my ex-marriage on the table, like a rotten piece of meat next to his rotten piece of meat, I told him about Dorothy and Caspar. I laid on the normal-Main Street atmosphere with a trowel. Bernard was enchanted.

"They go to church? "They have a vegetable garden? Do you mean it?" He begged to be invited for dinner.

"Honestly, Bernard. It's not what you think. They have fake paneling on the walls, and my father wears a vest with a satin back."

Even better. "You don't understand Jews," he said.

So Bernard came, and we all sat in the dining room while Caspar carved the roast chicken. Bernard did his best, but he couldn't know that while Caspar's mind wandered and Dorothy grew ever more rigid and hostile (she had liked Richard, and couldn't like a second time), I watched her in silent agony, waiting for some sign of approval and not getting it. In my mind was some loving, tender Dorothy, giving me a hug in the kitchen: "Darling, I just love your new gentleman friend. Why, he's charming, and it's obvious he's crazy about you." But this was what she could not do. And Caspar was elsewhere, though he neatly laid pieces of chicken on the platter. Bernard looked at them expectantly—he wanted something too, though what he probably didn't know. Probably some functioning, encapsulated life form, a family that worked. When I wasn't watching Dorothy, I watched Bernard and tried to see us, with all our flaws, through his eyes.

"What's your line of work, sir?" Caspar asked.

How old-fashioned he sounded, my adulterous father. He wore a green short-sleeved shirt and a yellow tie. While Bernard talked about being a stockbroker, he hummed, glancing out the window. And Dorothy, when Bernard turned to her to finish what he had started saying. Tall and straight in her chair, she wore a brilliant blue blouse. A brilliant, frozen smile. Her white hair was a magnificent snowdrift.

"My, that sounds interesting. I've never understood too much about how the stock market works."

She said it as though the whole thing were unworthy of her consideration. They were provincial, my parents, which I had once loathed but now had come to like. The stock market was for rich people. For ordinary people there was nothing wrong with the savings bank. Though of course, Mr. Armstrong's and her assets were just about all in the house and the business. Then Bernard looked at me, probably wondering what he was doing here. Me in my gray sweater and my brown hair, careful not to steal any of Dorothy's glory. How silly this was—after all I was forty. But he had wanted to come, though now he looked as though he couldn't remember why. When I brought in the dessert he looked deeply, incurably sad, even when I told him it was apple crisp which I had made, with whipped cream.

As soon as possible, Caspar excused himself, saying he had to "go by the store and see to a couple of things." He made it clear he wasn't coming back, and shook hands with Bernard.

As he started toward the door, I said, "You never stay. You always run away." My voice sounded like a small child's, and they all looked startled.

"Honestly, Celia. Your father has things to do." Dorothy sounded annoyed, as she always did at the slightest trace of a human feeling.

"It's true, Dad. I grew up looking at your retreating back." I think I was doing it for Bernard, to try to break the plastic artificiality of the afternoon. But I frightened myself, trying to say these true things in this familiar quiet room, brightly lit by the ceiling fixture, at this highly polished table. It was not a place for such expressions, and as I spoke I waited for some terrible retribution for violating our tribal laws.

Caspar looked pained and turned to Dorothy, who said, "Well, this is hardly the time or place to start these recriminations of yours. We never did anything right, it seems." She turned to Bernard. "Ever since she started with this psychiatrist."

"It has nothing to do with her. And I didn't say you never did anything right. I just said—"

"I had to work, Cece," Caspar said from the doorway. "What you say isn't fair. Times were hard when you were growing up. There was the time I almost lost the store. It was during the war, and maybe people didn't feel a lot of flowers was right."

Dorothy said, "You always rise to her bait. Don't pay any attention to her."

"That's it," I sang with terrible triumph. "Don't pay

any attention to her. That's the watchword.'' I glanced at
Bernard, who was beginning to look entertained for the
first time in the entire day.

"You told him to pretend I wasn't there, and he did," I
said to Dorothy, who was on her feet, furiously stacking
plates.

"Ridiculous," she said, "to go into all this. To embarrass me."

"That's not why I brought it up. It has nothing to do
with you. Why don't you let me talk to Dad? You've
always gotten in between us."

"You're lying," blazed Dorothy, while Caspar looked
increasingly miserable. I saw him dart a look at his watch.
No wonder I was attracted to Bernard, who not only
looked at his watch all the time but shook his whole wrist
to make sure it was going. Richard had done it too, but in
a slower, more arrogant way. I made men long to flee;
time crawled when they were with me. But Bernard looked
rapt at our Chekhovian exchange. Grabbing up the meat
platter, Dorothy said, "Cassie would never do this to
me."

"Who's Cassie?" Bernard asked.

"She didn't tell you," Dorothy snapped. "Well, I don't
know why I should be so surprised. Celia has a twin, and
she's always hated her. She drove her away with her
jealousy."

"That isn't true," I said. "And that's what you can't
stand, Dorothy. In the beginning, you weren't first with
either of us."

There was a slight scuffle, during which Bernard suddenly got up and picked up the picture of Cassie from the
buffet—the surfaces of our house are extensively covered
with framed photographs—and Caspar managed to disap-
pear. Dorothy and I quivered and twitched as Bernard
examined the picture, a big, glossy one in a silver frame,
all face and golden curls. She looked like a Maybelline ad.
Black, evenly spaced eyelashes. A simpering smile, the
curve of a bare shoulder. Like an old movie still. Across
the bottom was written in sixth-grade script, *"To my
darling parents, love, your daughter Cassie."* Then he
picked up a picture of her and her family. Her husband, all

gleaming teeth and hairy chest and Marlboro stance. Cassie in an off-the-shoulder peasant blouse, leaning coyly against his shoulder. Three kids—two moronic-looking boys and a cross-eyed daughter. My nephews. My niece.

Bernard looked at me. "You're alike," he said. "Except for the cosmetics and the bleached hair."

"Well, of course," I said, annoyed.

"Why didn't you tell me about her?" he asked.

"Because she's jealous," Dorothy said. "She's always been jealous."

"I haven't told you everything about myself, Bernard. After all we've only been seeing each other for a couple of months. There are probably plenty of things you haven't told me either just because you haven't thought of them."

"But I've told you everything about my family."

I groped desperately, then said, inspired, "Hardly anything about your father."

"He died in the war," Bernard said, turning pale. "I told you. It isn't a secret."

"I don't mean to cause you pain, Bernard," I said. "But you see some things hurt."

"You were never hurt," said Dorothy loudly, annoyed that she was being left out of the conversation. "You had everything a child could want. I made sure you and Cassie had a perfect childhood. But somewhere along the line, Celia, you developed a terrible ingratitude."

"Mrs. Armstrong, surely you don't think children are ordinarily grateful to their parents."

While Bernard and I eyed each other in a stragely excited way, Dorothy treated us to a lecture about *her* parents, Grandma and Grandpa Stevens, and how thankful she was to them for a lifetime of sacrifice for her and her brothers. She waxed eloquent about her own perfect devotion. Said Bernard, when she was out: "How soon can we politely leave?" Said I: "I'll get us out in twenty minutes."

We gulped down coffee and I rinsed off a few dishes in the kitchen, and then Bernard and I fled in our rented car. First we drove toward the parkway and got on it for about ten minutes; then Bernard said, "Let's pretend we're kids," and got off at the first exit. We wound round and round, always choosing the road that seemed to point toward darkness and obscurity—which, in fact, was where we felt the most comfortable. We were still far enough out to find woods and dirt roads; the sun had just set, and dusk lingered moodily over the countryside. As we passed and dismissed one spot after another, I felt my body fairly gushing, as though my three places had become fuuntains with which I could water the earth. Under my hand, Bernard's hardness strained against the fabric of his pants, which I didn't dare open because like many New Yorkers, he was a terrible driver, and I was afraid I'd distract him so he'd run into a tree.

At last we stopped in a dead end surrounded by trees. There was a house across the way, but it seemed dark, and the only sound was the intermittent coo of a dove or owl. It wasn't perfect, but we no longer cared, and with my mouth and hands I freed Bernard's cock from its Sunday-afternoon containment. Quietly and rather fiercely we made love. Usually we are rather elaborate lovers, full of new tricks to whip up our middle-aged appetites; but that day he slipped directly inside me with litle premliminary, and frightened as we had been by those glimpses of our own and each other's abysses, we clung and dug into each other and cried out in unison, our voices echoing in the dark woods.

Afterward, as usual, I cried—from sadness that it was over, and because it was never, no matter how lovely, how tender, how well orchestrated, as good as I expected it to be; and because I knew that it never could, nor would anything, be; because I couldn't drown my own hope, and I didn't think I could bear it.

It's time to go back.

Nineteen forty-eight. Cassie and I are six. It's our first day of school, and Dorothy has dressed us accordingly in matching white blouses, navy skirts with suspenders, knee socks and brown oxfords. The blouses have little bunches of three plastic cherries for buttons. Our brown hair is parted in the middle and braided, and on the end of each braid is a red hair ribbon. Dorothy is joyous over what she has wrought. She takes each of us by one hand and we set off toward the Rivertown Elementary School. Down Maple, over to Waterside, into Main Street. Past the bakery and the coffee shop, past The Bower of Flowers, Burnside's Hardware, the fish store, the pharmacy. Now it seems that in each shop was a smiling face, a nodding head, as in a Disney movie, admiring our personae. There go the Armstrong twins. Isn't it amazing?—you simply can't tell them apart.

Cassie and I, being six and stupid, think this admiration has something to do with our beauty or charm or accomplishment, rather than the fact that we are freaks. Not that we could have made such an analysis. Let's put it differently—we *liked* everybody staring at us rather than hating it, as we should have. And there's Dorothy beaming away. ("Oh, Dorothy. You're wonderful.") We smile adorably. Up the steps of the school, down the hall to the first-grade room. But now there are fewer smiles, more stares. Children are more honest. Into the classroom. We're a little late, Dorothy having planned our entrance. A roomful of gimlet eyes bore into us. Dorothy marches up to the teacher, Miss Lenahan, who looks stunned, then twists her face into a gargoyle smile.

"Oh, *twins*. Look, class. Twins." They all stare while Dorothy enjoys her finest hour, as though she'd had anything to do with it, which she really believes she did. Somehow God touched her. Like the Virgin Mary she's a holy vessel. While she stands there with a heavenly beam of light on her, Miss Lenahan says, "Now, how am I going to tell you apart?"

As Cassie and I look momentarily perplexed, Dorothy says, "Cassie will always wear a little bracelet," and so saying, raises Cassie's small arm with a little charm bracelet on it. Cassie stands there like the Statue of Liberty.

"Oh, good." Miss Lenahan claps her hands. "Class, the one with the bracelet is Cassie. The one without is . . ."

"Celia," I blurt, before Dorothy can say something wrong.

"Celia. Cassie and Celia. Now, twins, will you please sit in those two desks over by the window?"

We sit in the two desks while the gimlet eyes follow us. The children all twist around in their seats and stare.

Cassie's eyes meet mine, and we smile. Dorothy gives us one last blessing before departing. Another milestone passed.

All morning Miss Lenahan has to fight to keep the attention of the class, whose gaze keeps turning back to the phenomenon in its midst. Finally she puts us in the front row. It's one of many devices—together, apart, front, back—to try to lessen our impact. In the schoolyard at lunchtime, as we open our lunch boxes and take out our identical ham sandwiches, the stares continue, along with the questions:

"Can your parents tell you apart? Do you get sick at the same time? Do you have the same dreams? Do you both go pee-pee at the same time?" and so forth. But the worst thing was one small girl who wandered over, looked at us for a few seconds, and began to cry.

"I hate you," she screamed. "You're freaks. You belong in the circus."

"We do not, you jerk," I yelled. And as the little creep stood there screaming and pointing till a teacher took her away, Cassie put her arm up in the air—the arm with the bracelet—as though identification would make peace.

"That's Pamela Graham, and she's crazy," said a dark, glossy boy from our class, our first friend. "Never mind her. You can't help it. Hey, do you go to sleep and wake up at the same time?"

It was endless, that first day at school. It was boring, for one thing. And frightening in a way. We had been stared at enough, but never with such penetrating disapproval. And there were hints of what would go on later. Someone pulled one of Cassie's braids. Somebody else threw a ball at me, then bumped me going after it. "Oh, *sorry*," he intoned, as a group of friends laughed. "I'm so *sorry*. I only have one ball." It's hard to believe now, but in those innocent days no reference was intended to male genitalia. And yet everyone laughed anyway. In the playground they found it hilarious when we seesawed. And the teachers rolled us together into one. "Twins, sit here. Twins, please go up to the board and write the addition problems. Will the twins please lead the class down to the assembly." There was a certain hostility, easily explained by the fact that they couldn't tell us apart. Cassie kept raising her small white arm, like a white flag.

At the end of the day we ran all the way home, buoyant with joy at being back together and alone again in our little world. It would, that day and every day, last until eight-thirty in the morning, when we went back to school. But to children of six, those few hours were forever. Dorothy stood on the corner and watched as we came up the street. She gave us identical pats and smiles—hugs were not in her repertoire—and took us home to lemonade and cookies. She said she wanted to know every detail, though when we started to tell her, she interrupted with what she really wanted to know: "Well? Could they tell you apart?"

For the first years of my life there was only Cassie and me.

How carefully I approach the memory of those years, as though by thinking about them I might shatter their fragile warmth. How far off they are now, those tiny lights at the end of the tunnel. I save them, just as I used to save the bite of cake with the icing for last, or the small, perfect package under the Christmas tree. I'm afraid if I return to them too often, I might spoil their purity—start remembering my memories rather than what actually was, or start decorating those small bright rooms with details that were not there in my urgent need to keep them alive. For I'm afraid that if they fade, I will start to die, as though they are in fact the light that keeps me alive.

During our early years (which started to end when we went to school) our twin-ness was like a warm little house we lived in, accessible to no one else. In it we shared every experience. We were two bodies who shared a mind, the way lovers are supposed to. And we made our parents happy that way, though Caspar couldn't tell us apart. On Sundays we went driving around town in our convertible Packard as they showed us off. We were always invited to tree-planting ceremonies, cornerstone-layings and parades, and to be in Chamber of Commerce pictures, as though something in the local air bred the likes of us. And there would be Dorothy with that triumphant smile, as though we proved something about her—when really we proved nothing; we were as accidental as a broken plate or a litter of puppies.

When I was small—when we were small—it was like always living before a mirror. If I wanted to know anything about myself, I looked at Cassie. The way her hair grew behind her ears, so did mine. The way her knees looked from the back, the way her eyes moved when she was excited. The rabbity look she got when she cried. The sound of her voice was the sound of mine—far different than I would have thought. If she looked ugly when she sulked, so did I. And so she looked at me.

Even though to others we may have appeared to be one large unit with two moving parts, there was never any doubt in our minds that we were two separate beings. What isolated us was our ignorance of the fact that others did not have our closeness, a togetherness we regarded as natural. We never had a friend we didn't share (and not many of them), and we sometimes did each other's homework. If a teacher found out and told us we shouldn't, we really didn't understand such a concept, because we didn't understand why it should make any difference. There it sat on the dining-room table. Cassie would do the subtraction, then get tired of the number work and go do something else. I'd wander over and do some multiplication, or read a story in the reader and tell her what it was about. Our marks were an amalgam of the two of us. In the same way, we ate each other's meals (if nobody was around, for we soon learned that this bothered other people), took each other's baths, said each other's prayers at night, kneeling on our little prayer rugs. When Dorothy, who controlled what went in and what came out, wanted to know about our poo-poo, we said whatever we thought would please her. We even took each other's praise and blame indiscriminately.

I could see through her—and she through me—as though we were made of glass. When I felt laughter bubble up, her face would break into a smile; when I felt the cold hand of fear in my guts, her hand would reach for mine. We slept in the same bed—which Dorothy, who wanted us equal but separate, didn't approve of—curled together like two little animals. I still remember the warmth and peacefulness of it, of waking in the morning with her arm across my back, with our legs entangled. We'd lie in the one of the two beds where we'd secretly slept as the pale early sunlight sifted through the trees outside and the gently fluttering organdy curtains, and listened to the sounds of our parents' moving around. I don't remember that we talked much, though sometimes we told our dreams, and sometimes we just made a few of the sounds that nobody else understood.

Then Dorothy's steps would come along the hall, as one of us scuffled into the other bed, and she would appear in the doorway in a fresh zippered "housedress," her hair, then brown like ours, tied back in a ponytail, her color and spirits high. "Good morning, girls. Cassie, what's that on your face? You couldn't have washed very well last night. Celia, pick your clothes up from the floor and put them in the hamper." I would rush around obediently—at that time we were both driven to try to please Dorothy. Then down to breakfast, where Cassie got to fry the bacon, I to make the pancakes. Dorothy, the genius, made sure her attention was equal. Cassie's clean face would be admired as well as my excellence at not spilling. We took turns feeding the dog and watering the plants.

Then Caspar would appear and sit down at the breakfast table—ours was a traditional household. A big toothy smile. "Hey there, Casselia." We'd both run to him and he'd put one on each knee. How clean he was, how deliciously redolent of Bay Rum. In those days his jaw was smooth, his hair reddish and well over the top of his head. A shirt freshly ironed by Dorothy—the goddess was also a servant. His smooth, domelike forehead shone in the overhead light. Dorothy couldn't stand it—"Stop messing your father up"—as though he were her creation, which in a sense he was. "He has to look respectable when he goes to work. What will the customers think?"

"Now, Dot. Never mind! These two are my flowers—my two roses, my two daffodils. Or maybe two . . . snap-dragons!"

"Nooo!" I'd shriek blissfully. "We're daisies!"

"Hollyhocks!" sang Cassie.

"No, much too big," said Caspar. "How about tulips?"

"Forget-me-nots!"

"Morning glories!"

And so forth, on into the delightful nonsense that was as foreign to Dorothy as Chinese. As she served the pancakes, her lip would stiffen, and Caspar would succumb.

"Okay, girls, let's have breakfast. Here, Cassie, sit right here."

And then she would pounce: "That's Celia. I should think you could tell by this time."

It bothered us less that he made the mistake than the strange tone that came into their voices on the subject. Caspar had various methods of dealing with it. "Oh, Lord. How could I? I must be going blind," in a joking tone. Or, "I *meant* Cassie. You're trying to mislead me," which we all knew wasn't true. Or to us: "I'm sorry, sweetheart. You know I love you both the same."

Of course he did—we did know it. At that age we didn't care what he called us, though later, of course, we did. But sitting on his knees, we'd feel him stiffen. He had to please her too. He had been guilty of some kind of inattention or abstraction, a certain stupidity. It would happen only once, because once he knew, he used some other means of identification—I was the one in the union suit this morning, Cassie still in her nightie. Once he knew, he'd relax. And once he knew, Dorothy would get naggier and pickier than ever, because of course his not being able to tell was her triumph.

To the bridge table: "I probably shouldn't complain, for Caspar is an excellent husband in every way. A good provider. Good to me and the children. Doesn't stray [A lot you know, Dorothy]. But, my Lord, he still can't tell the twins apart."

South: "But Dorothy, nobody can but you."

North: "And particularly since you always dress them so nice, and just alike. I saw them the other day in those little pink jumpers, and I just wanted to hug them both."

The Dummy: "I'm sure he loves them, Dorothy."

Dorothy: "Oh, I've no doubt he does. But my heavens, he should be able to tell which is which. His own children." And she would sit up a little straighter, stick her chest out a bit, give her head a little shake.

North: "Well, maybe you should dress one a little differently. Maybe give one a pink hair ribbon and the other blue. That would be nice."

Dorothy: "Oh, they wouldn't stand for it. They want everything exactly the same. If they don't have it that way, they fight."

A lie, Dorothy. A bald-faced lie. We never fought—what was there to fight about? If by some miscalculation there was an inequality, we resolved it between us. We were expert negotiators, probably because we had no real sense of possession. We both owned everything anyway. We were truly impregnable, stronger than we have ever been, and certainly happier.

Imagine, if you can, our enviable existence. Imagine having someone whose heart beats in rhythm with yours, who has the same dreams, who understands you without even thinking about it. Imagine always having somebody there to reach out to: somebody who knows when you're cold and lends you her sweater; who finishes the food you can't eat, the sentences you can't end. Imagine always having with you the most interesting person in the world, your own double: and having her love you back. And stretch your mind, if you can, to some never-never land where there is no competition, and where you have never heard of abandonment or rejection, so you don't know that this enchanted state could end. That's what everybody in the world wants, and we had it.

That such things don't last was our hard lesson.

"You're creepy," Pamela Graham screamed in the schoolyard. "You're *unnatural*. My mother says."

That didn't matter—let her scream. But it did that we were starting to separate out. Such things bothered Cassie more than they did me—she would cry and I would comfort her. Or she would be upset by Dorothy's pursed lips or Caspar's loving, indiscriminate smile. And then: I would have a nightmare, and if I crawled into Cassie's bed I would find her sleeping peacefully. And she got measles and I didn't, even though I drank out of her glass to try to get it, and slept in the same bed after Dorothy was asleep, and she even spat in my mouth, very tenderly and carefully: "There—now you have to get it." But I didn't, and oh, such guilt did I feel, putting a cloth on her head and looking at her poor flushed body with its ugly rash. I took a crayon and put red dots all over my own body. But I never got the measles.

When we started to separate we were both terribly frightened. We clung together more tightly than ever to inhibit the inevitable process, and in so doing irritated everybody at school more than ever. We were, around nine or ten, strange and unsocialized creatures, hanging together out of fear rather than the previous happy inevitability. We'd start to relax a little, to play with other children, and then some tiny difference would surface—something almost invisible to the naked eye, but to us evidence of our outward drift—and we would cling together tighter than ever, and drive the other kids away.

Then a particularly shrewd teacher, a Miss Larkin, got hold of Dorothy. There were no school psychologists in those days, but other teachers fulfilled the same function. Miss Larkin was the science teacher, and she called Dorothy in and told her we had problems she'd better pay attention to. (We listened through the register when she told Caspar that night.) She said we shouldn't be dressed alike and we shouldn't have identical lunch boxes and meat-loaf sandwiches, nor should we always do the same things. We didn't really know we were two different people, and if we didn't find out soon we'd probably end up in a lunatic asylum. She must have been an early Freudian, because she used terms like "introvert" and "inferiority complex" which are by now as quaint as horsehair sofas.

Dorothy was stunned—and only Miss Larkin could have done it to her. Most other teachers Dorothy would simply have mowed down with her vast understanding and superiority. But Miss Larkin was even more old-fashioned and confident than she was. She clomped into the chemistry lab in her oxfords and her green crepe dress and her little tufts of hair with scarcely a smile on her flat, round face. By God, we were there to learn, and she was going to make sure we did. She couldn't abide laziness or sloppiness. She wouldn't tolerate lateness. If we didn't do the work in the proper way, we'd flunk and be back in the same class with her the next year, and next time around she'd be tougher and meaner than ever. The result was that all the children except the complete morons worked themselves to death in her class out of pure terror, fueled by the sight of an occasional unfortunate who was there the second time around, and to whom Miss Larkin was merciless. No one had ever been there three times, and everybody ended up knowing quite a lot of chemistry.

Miss Larkin was the first person in four years who'd seen through us and taken the time and trouble to do something about it. She seated us on opposite sides of the room and made us answer separately, no matter what we did to try to get back together—sneak over, go to the bathroom, cry and anything else we could think of. She started by keeping us alternately after school to do homework, alone, but like everybody else she couldn't always tell us apart, so we began tricking her, pretending to be each other, a prime technique of rebellious twins; when we did that, she kept us both after school and made us do our homework in separate rooms, while she posted herself outside to prevent any switching. When once we managed to change places by climbing out the windows and back in again, she gave us fifty extra problems to do.

Why did she bother, when all the other teachers had taken the easy way out, and let us slither back and forth into each other's personalities? Maybe she was bored. She had no husband, children or relatives of her own to call her home at the end of the day. Probably she had little life other than the school, and little money to spend—the green crepe dress was shabby. She must have been one of those remarkable people who, when they see something wrong, do something about it. And she was one up on Dorothy. Miss Larkin didn't give a damn what we, or anybody else, thought of her, and Dorothy cared deeply and passionately.

So if we carried on, and I wore Cassie's bracelet, or if one of us feigned illness or sleepiness or an urgent need to go to the bathroom, Miss Larkin simply said, "Get back in there and finish your work; you can leave afterward." And once, when we pulled a double tantrum, screaming, crying phony tears and calling her terrible names, she rose up to her full height of five feet three or so and said, "If I see one more minute of this disgusting performance, you will both fail and I'll have you back again next year,'' and that was the end of that.

Of course we told Dorothy about this terrible woman who was, we said, trying to "separate" us. And so when Dorothy went to call her onto the carpet, and tell her how she was damaging her little darlings and she was only there to warn her that she was on her way to speak to the principal, Miss Larkin threw the book at her, and told her that if she didn't start separating out our identities, she, Dorothy, would have a couple of maniacs on her hands. Since Miss Larkin was so smart, she picked Dorothy's most vulnerable point. If we went mad and had to be locked up in twin cells in the state lunatic asylum, Dorothy would no longer be so admirable.

It's hard to pinpoint the moment at which the delicately balanced Calder mobile that was our family began to change its weights and motion. It wasn't only Miss Larkin—we were already changing ourselves and trying to hide it. Miss Larkin was the first one, except Pamela Graham and her ilk, who questioned the absolute goodness of our twinness. Not only that, but she was the first person who not only wasn't cowed by Dorothy, but actually established herself as more powerful. So by the time Dorothy sat us down for The Speech, we already knew, from eavesdropping, that Dorothy was acting not from her own powerful integrity, but because somebody else had scared the hell out of her.

"Girls," said Dorothy one evening before the fire, "as you know, your father and I are concerned about every facet of your upbringing, and we talk often about our plans for raising you. Naturally, we agree completely on certain basic standards of child-raising, which were those of our own parents and their parents before them. By this we mean the general expectations we have of you about courtesy, respect for your elders, academic accomplishment and general cooperation, besides such qualities as honesty; kindness to others, especially those who are less fortunate; ladylike deportment . . . [What a bore Dorothy could be]. But because you are twins, you are not quite like other people, and perhaps your father and I have emphasized your similarities a little too much rather than encouraging your differences. Maybe it's too hard on other people and not really courteous for you to be so alike they can't tell which is which, as though you're trying to play a trick on them. So." She folded her hands in her lap and looked at our two identical faces rising out of matching red flannel bathrobes. "Maybe you should start dressing a little differently—just to help out your friends at school, your teachers and even your relatives who sometimes can't tell you apart."

"And your father," said Caspar, who was chairing this meeting.

"Yes, sometimes even your father can't tell," Dorothy said, after giving Caspar a superior look. "So, tomorrow why don't you wear your red sweater, Celia, and you, Cassie, wear your blue."

Please note the terms in which Dorothy couched this new policy. It was all to be out of politeness and consideration for others, though Miss Larkin had put it in terms of survival. This added to Cassie's and my confusion, and fused our terror. We drew closer together until we were touching, head, shoulders and hips, on the hearthrug. We knew Dorothy was lying—twisting, as it might be somewhat more kindly put: to ten-year-olds it wasn't even clear how. But for the first time there was an off note in Dorothy's orchestra; some of her sounds weren't pure. And she was asking us to do the thing we dreaded most. How frightening was this intrusion of what would now be called "reality testing" into the contained pathology of our family! Our hands reached for each other at the same time. How frightening was Dorothy's fall from power, for she had no idea she was lighting her own fuse. She thought she could pull this off and stay in the seat of the goddess. But from that moment on we didn't trust her.

We both looked at Caspar, but he'd retired behind his newspaper.

Now I wonder if it happened to both of us. *I* knew—and *I* didn't trust her. I knew for the first time that she didn't always ring true, but I don't know if Cassie did. I looked at Cassie as she sat there in the firelight, and an instant later she looked at me. That tiny gap in time frightened me, as did any of our minute differences, almost without my being aware of it. I suppose I was experiencing the first anxiety of my life.

"But we don't *want* to be different," I said.

Dorothy frowned. "Now, Celia, you know you and Cassie can't always be alike. It's babyish. How many adult twins do you see walking around dressed exactly the same? You're getting to be big girls now. You should make your own friends. In a few years you'll have beaux. [She really says beaux]. Perhaps one or both of you will go to college. Whatever happens, you'll have to separate. I see little differences in you already."

Cassie and I began to cry, almost simultaneously, and Caspar said, "Oh, now, Dot, I think we've talked about this enough. I can't stand to see my Cassélia unhappy. Come here, girls. Come to Daddy." As we wound our arms around him, snuffling, crunching the evening paper as we clambered up onto his lap, he said, "Tell you what. Come by after school tomorrow and you can trim the window."

This was a thrilling project which Caspar gave us from time to time. We got to choose which blooms would go into the special "Mixed Garden Flower Bouquet." We got to arrange them however we wanted, or almost, and Caspar would put our sign in the window: ARRANGED BY CASSÉLIA. Passive as Caspar was, inattentive in his perceptions, no prize dreamed up by Dorothy could equal this for its theatrical quality and aesthetic exposure. Caspar invited us to create.

Later on, we clung to each other and promised each other that even if we must be different, we would never separate: that we would spend our lives together, always live in the same house, marry twin men and have matching children. I don't know whether it was that night or another that I first felt sexual excitement when I was close to Cassie—a strangely delicious and alarming feeling between my legs that wouldn't go away, that even seemed to take over my mind. Possibly I had felt it before without being aware of it. Nor do I know whether Cassie felt the same thing. Certainly I couldn't imagine mentioning it—it was the first completely private thing that had ever happened to me, and the first thing I never told her about. It represented another difference between us, for I assumed without thinking much about it that the feeling was unique to me—some strange disease, possibly, or some early manifestation of the madness that Miss Larkin had said would probably claim us.

Our sexual education had been, of course, minimal—either in terms of pistils and stamens, from Caspar, or in Dorothy's verbal tracts heavily larded with duty, devotion, the rewards of motherhood and so on, none of which seemed to have anything to do with the way my body flamed so unexpectedly, nor the vivid and disturbing pictures that crowded into my mind about my body and Cassie's—about touching her small nipples that were, like mine, just starting to stick up, or even of touching her *there* to see if she felt as I did. I felt warned about these feelings. I sensed danger as one does in an empty house, without there being any clear reason for it. And we had at other times touched each other everywhere to see what it was like, making each other giggle with surprise, thinking it was like tickling. But this time it was different—far darker and deeper—and I wanted to cry at the inevitability of our separation, which seemed to progress by itself with or without Dorothy, as well as at the fear of encountering these new feelings alone without Cassie.

In the morning, Dorothy came marching in as usual and got out the sweaters—what not long ago would have been a simple enough procedure, but oh, how complicated things were becoming! The blue one for Cassie. The red one for me. Dorothy talking all the time about how glad she was that "we" had decided to dress differently, that the little bracelet had never shown up enough and oh, how relieved our teachers were going to be—as though she had not, for almost eleven years, gone to incredible lengths to make us indistinguishable. But now, the blue sweater was new and pretty, with a white ruffled collar and white buttons, and the red one, mine, was old and stretched—or so it seemed to me, anyway; and Cassie put on hers without a word. She also glanced at herself in the mirror, first with a little smile, then with alarm as she caught my reflection too and saw us different for the first time. And then, as we went into the kitchen for breakfast, Dorothy looked at us and

said, "Oh, my goodness. Well, you both look very nice."
But she looked at Cassie. "I like the little white collar on
that," she said.

She said nothing to me, only went on stirring the oatmeal. And for the first time in my life, I looked at Cassie
with hatred—a feeling as strong and disturbing as what I
had felt in bed, different but curiously similar. I watched
her as she packed her books in her book bag. She had the
good sweater and I had the lousy one. Then she looked up,
a little surprised. "Oh, Cece. Would you rather wear the
blue one?" Which was worse, in a way, than saying
nothing, because it meant she knew about my envy. How
dreadful everything was getting; now we knew some things
about each other but not others, and had no way of telling
which were which.

Years later when I thought about it, I wondered why
Dorothy so easily relinquished her X-ray vision, in spite of
threats of madness, humiliation before the bridge club and
so on. But I realized that of course she hadn't relinquished
anything—no matter what we wore, Dorothy could tell us
apart. Stark naked she could tell us apart. It was the others
who couldn't—it was the rest of the world that needed
assistance, not Dorothy, whose superiority had long been
proved.

When we marched into school in our red/blue sweaters
that morning, we clung closer than ever at the prospect of
being distinguished—to us a terrifying idea. Silly as we
were, we really thought the sweaters would identify us;
and we were amazed when they did not, because, of
course, nobody knew which of us was wearing what color
sweater. Some learned, of course, by the end of the day,
and during lunchtime, I had the unfamiliar experience of
being called by my name by somebody other than Dorothy. And on the way home, Cassie said, with an air of
wonderment, "Miss Tyson knew *who I was* in math today.
She knew I was Cassie."

If all this sounds incredible, we did not, of course, go
through ten years of our lives without ever being told apart
by anybody. And the school did its best to put us in
separate classes. But the school was small, as Rivertown
was, and there were not always two history classes, or two

music classes. More important, we were always trying to be together, sometimes sneaking into each other's classrooms; and until the pronouncements of Miss Larkin it was thought that there would be grave psychological danger in separating us. We were thought of, truly, as one entity in two parts, and splitting us would be like splitting an atom—great amounts of destructive energy might be released; God knew what would happen. Some strange, unnatural force held us together. And so most adults were rather careful of us, and some even a little frightened, the way people are frightened of the supernatural. It gave us a peculiar feeling of superiority to everyone except Dorothy, who, we had always believed, was frightened of nothing, us least of all.

Gradually over the next couple of years, a pattern emerged. By the time we were twelve, you could have told us apart, and so could anybody else in town. It was, we found, more than just the color of a sweater, though those two little sweaters had turned out to symbolize what we became.

Two years later, here's what we would have been doing at about four in the afternoon:

Cassie, in a polka-dotted dress, is being escorted to the baseball field to watch practice. Some local hulk is carrying her books, while three others are falling over each other to pay for her Saturday movie, hoping to get a feel or two in the dark as she goes into transports over Rock Hudson.

I, Celia, am either in the library reading *The Catcher in the Rye* or flaked out in my room loudly playing Bartok or The Weavers, dreaming of passion, power and success, in no particular order, or nursing self-destructive fantasies (suicide while they all weep over the grave, or simple disappearance from the face of the earth while they all suffer torments of guilt wondering what they have done wrong—"they" being, of course, my family). For my agony I wear blue jeans and an old stretched red sweater.

It's never easy to be thirteen. But I seemed to have all the misery for the two of us. We still, of course, looked the same. But somehow Cassie eased into feminine prettiness while I was stalemated in some limbo of the soul.

While she chose which hulk got to buy her popcorn, I moaned and hated her and jerked off, which in those days was called "self-abuse." Though our bodies grew apace—same number of pimples, same-size tits and we even started to menstruate on the same day—somehow Cassie's hips had a gentle and graceful swing as she walked, while mine remained rigid with self-denial; somehow her eyelashes batted and mine cast a defiant shadow over dark and staring eyes. *Her* gaze was inviting and mine was alienated.

Somehow I knew everything and she knew nothing. And somehow she had everything and I had nothing.

Cassie—Cassie the unthinking, Cassie the oblivious—had led the move toward differentiation. Cassie was the one who reached first into the closet for the flowery skirt, who chose the pink hair ribbon for her hair. She was the one who mused more at her single image in the mirror, who tried Dorothy's lipstick and rouge, who begged for nylon stockings. Truly it was Cassie who moved out from the two of us, while I followed. It's impossible to say now whether I would have put on that flouncy flowered skirt if I had been the one to choose. But in the new pattern we were establishing, somehow Cassie had been designated to lead and I to react to her.

It could be said that Dorothy designated our roles for us by giving Cassie the prettier sweater that first morning. As a matter of fact, I *know* Edith, my therapist, would pounce on that if I ever told her about any of this—superficial, go-by-the-book, cut-rate shrink that she is. But Edith, for one thing, is an only child. And for another, I'm tired to death of hearing everybody blame his or her parents for everything. I hear it at work, at the deli, at cocktail parties. I see the twisted, tortured, self-pitying look, the dark sick stare. "My father never worked out his own Oedipal so he's doing his trip on me, the prick." Or, "It's become obvious in therapy that my mother has an acute character disorder and she rejected me from the minute I was born." Then a series of boring stories about rejection—the kid brought home a crappy picture from school and she didn't frame it and hang it on the wall. Or he shitted (shat?) in the middle of the kitchen floor and she swatted (swit?) him one, which ruined his life. I always sympathize with the mother, having to bring up this creep; and yet I understand the feelings too well myself: within me is a baby wail crying out exactly the same things. In a sense I envy these wounded infants for their complete self-centeredness and self-pity, while in my head there are always two or three voices arguing, a cacophony of reasonable opinions in eternal disagreement.

How hard I try to be fair, though deep in my heart I am as bad as the party anxiety disorders: I blame Dorothy for everything. But truthfully, things just sort of evolved, with all of us falling into the places on the mobile where our weights balanced. Cassie, tying pink bows on her two pigtails, pleased Dorothy's orderliness, her superficial piety, her narrow view of female life. Cassie was the one who learned to cook, carefully basting the turkey at recommended intervals; who went to church with Dorothy and on shopping expeditions with her—where they were both capable of spending hours in delicious torments of indecision about which gloves to buy or what blouse to go with last year's suit—for though we were comfortable enough, there was no extra money for clothes that went beyond need into desire. In their tiresome and trivial world, there was no room for me and my existentialist gloom. So I closed myself in my room and wrote bad verse, or else hung around with one or two other depressed friends, and might have gotten through those difficult years in one way or another if—oh, God, only if—we had not been twins.

For it was not as though I lived with and watched another person, from whom I could be separate and apart while admiring or condemning her behavior, while going my own way. Cassie was *me*—a part of myself that was spinning off in an alien direction; and I couldn't stand it.

When she went into the kitchen and baked a heart-shaped cake for Dorothy on Valentine's Day, I could not, as I could have had our bond been different, laugh it off. Instead I hung around the kitchen, tasted the batter, told her how lousy it was and picked on her till she yelled, "You never do anything for Mother. All you do is make her miserable and make fun of her, because you're jealous, that's what; you think you're so smart and everything and you're just a bad-tempered and evil person."

When I remember some of the things I did, I shrink with shame. I took things from Cassie—a little mirror she liked, and a ridiculous and filthy stuffed cat she took to bed every night. When she cried, I admitted about the cat and returned it, but the mirror is to this day buried in the backyard under the rhododendron. I took her clothes; I lied to her boyfriends when they asked if she was around; I ruined her homework, unhitched the chain on her bicycle, cut holes in one of her dresses. Once I . . . oh, I can't. I had determined to tell everything, but I can't. At least, not yet. The humiliation is too terrible. But oh, what a damn prune she was. A Goody Two-Shoes, pious and superior. Going off to church every Sunday with Dorothy, the creep, while Caspar and I stayed home and mowed the lawn or put in the roast.

Oh, God, how I hated her. And Dorothy too. Somehow in this terrible shift, I had lost. And Caspar was as kind as he knew how, but he didn't really know what was going on. It was hard to tell how unperceptive he actually was and how much he faked. Anyway, he was remote. "Oh, I can't help you with these girls' problems, honey. Ask your mother." Maybe he was just lazy—I suspect that was part of it. His attention was elsewhere. His heart was elsewhere.

In the tenth grade, when I was fourteen, I went away to boarding school.

It was a solution that on the face of it suited everybody. Dorothy and Cassie were longing to be rid of me. I was full of the thrill of adventure, besides the satisfaction of knowing that Dorothy and Caspar had to dig deep to find the money. Caspar too felt a slight relief at my departure, for still there were times he couldn't tell us apart.

On a brilliant September day they all drove me to the train station to go off to the Pine Hill School, in Vermont— far enough so that I couldn't come running home every weekend. Caspar parked the old Packard and dug out my trunk, which was to go by Railway Express. Dorothy and Cassie got out slowly, feigning sadness, while I hopped out and skipped around the platform. Cassie wore one of her little flowered dresses. I wore a new suit of vivid tweed, stockings and black calf walking shoes. I had a leather bag with a shoulder strap, and leather gloves.

I was as thrilled as if I were about to board the Orient Express. I loved trains; perhaps I would meet a handsome, somewhat older boy on this one, hopefully one who smoked and who gazed out the window with his collar and tie loosened. I loved it when the engine chugged in, sending up jets of steam. How nervy I was—much more than I am now. And how dumb—I believed this to be a journey toward freedom and glamour. I was at the age when anything strange was better than anything familiar—for me it came early. I shoved my suitcase on board, grabbed the new polo coat (Cassie was wearing last year's) and kissed my parents goodbye—a tentative, dutiful kiss for Dorothy, and a hug for Caspar.

"Goodbye, Cece," he said, and his voice broke just the slightest bit. "I want a letter every week. You hear? And you work hard, sweetheart, and make me proud of you."

Something moved inside me, changed its texture. The excitement turned darker, and I felt a surprised sadness. My Daddy.

"I'll make you proud." There was a lump in my throat, and the conductor was waving his arm. Then I looked at Cassie in her old dress and her old coat, standing there watching me. She wore her flowered dress, her hair was curled . . . we looked at each other across fourteen years and then suddenly, in a single gesture, threw our arms around each other. I felt a terrible, wrenching dread. How could I leave her? Was I crazy, to think that it was possible? I clung to her, my eyes filling and spilling over, while Dorothy said, "Well, for heaven's sake, after all the fighting. Hurry up, Celia, or you'll miss the train."

"Cassie," I wept, "I'm so sorry. I can't go; it's all a mistake."

"Yes, you can, Cece," she whispered. "It's all right. Don't be sorry."

"But I've been so cruel and I've said such dreadful things. I didn't mean to hurt you. It's just that everything changed."

"I know, Cece. But it's all right. It's better this way. I'm sure God wants you to go. Don't be so guilty, I still love you."

Somehow they got me, weeping and protesting, onto the

train, where I sat with my nose pressed against the window like a child in a Disney movie. Tears streaming down. Hat askew, hair tangled. Nose running. Oh, God, I would die. I would weep myself to death without her, mourn for her; they would find me in my room at the Pine Hill School starved with grief; they would bury me on some wind-swept Vermont hill in a lone and single grave. On the platform the three of them stood—Dorothy tight-lipped because something was going on that she didn't quite understand; Caspar wiping his eyes with his big, clean handkerchief, his glasses steaming. And Cassie, trying not to cry—Cassie, if you want to call her that. Really, it was I, and I was being torn in half for my own folly, my own foolishness; I was starting my own long, slow suicide.

And I kept my face there until they were three tiny dolls behind me, and then three dots, and then nothing. When they were gone my heart broke again, as though it had swollen up with sorrow and then burst. I thought I would die from sadness, from the pain that seemed knotted around my bones.

CASSIE
(Aboard American Airlines
11 A.M. flight to Kennedy)

You won't believe the things that have been going on in the last twenty-four hours. Suddenly my whole life, which was previously calm and full of contentment—the kind of life others might well envy—has turned into what Sam calls a "maelstrom." I hadn't heard the word before, and when he used it I looked it up, as usual, in the dictionary—to find that a maelstrom is some kind of Norwegian whirlpool. Well, I don't know what's so Norwegian about it, but certainly things are storming and whirling around. The thing I don't like about it is that whirlpools *suck* everything down into their depths, and I don't like the idea of being sucked into somebody else's problems at all. Though maybe you can't really call your parents "somebody else."

It started around five yesterday just as I got home from shopping. I'd wandered through a couple of dress shops, not looking very hard because I don't really need anything unless we put in a whole new closet. So then I priced clothes dryers because ours is breaking down, and looked at some Mexican tile flooring I'm thinking of having installed in the kitchen. All I bought the whole afternoon was six pairs of panty hose (three plum, three raspberry) and some jeans for Stu, and two coffee cakes from the bakery, the kind Sam likes, though from the looks of his waistline he shouldn't be eating them at all. I drove up the mountain slowly, taking as long as I could, because . . .

well, Sam has been in one of his moods recently and unfortunately has been talking again about divorce. I try to ignore it, because he has explained to me about self-hatred and guilt and how he will always come back to me in the end, but honestly, it's difficult to listen to a person telling you he doesn't love you anymore and he doesn't want to see you ever again and telling you to call a lawyer without taking it a little seriously. To tell the truth, I didn't know what to do; which was why I had gone shopping, because shopping clears my head the way swimming does for some people, or meditation, or therapy, or sex. Invariably after a couple of hours in the stores I feel my self-confidence return and my mind starts working again in the usual way. It's really amazing what a reliable trick this is. In my handbag is the little folder of credit cards, and if I reach in there and feel them, each in its own plastic slot, I feel fresh and courageous, as though a cool wind had blown over me.

Anyway, it's a nice feeling to look around some shop and to know that I could buy almost anything in it, but the truth is, it didn't make the problem of Sam go away. It even made it worse, because I thought of Angela and the last Chanel suit before she was forced to start going to the discount places, and I realized that I would be a fool if I didn't admit to myself that the same thing could happen to me.

This was a very difficult thing for me to do, which I finally did in the parking lot on Anacapa Street, and by the time I was in the car and on the way out I was feeling pretty upset. After all, I've been married to Sam for twenty-five years and have gotten used to a certain way of life, by which I mean partly from a material point of view and partly from having a strong man to lean on, and even though I think of myself as a fairly strong and sensible person, the idea of being alone frightens me. I mean, look at Angela. Ever since her divorce, she's been chasing one thing after another—Dr. Piu is only one of a series that includes est training, Primal Scream, Hindu contemplation, assertiveness training and several other silly therapies, including an awful Guru she found somewhere who comes down the mountain wearing a brown blanket. It's hard to tell if any of these have done Angela any good; but even if they have, I doubt if they would do *me* any good, because I'm a different kind of person entirely, possibly because I came originally from Back East. And I doubt if any of it would make up for not having a husband. I know I'm old-fashioned, but that's the way I am and I won't apologize for it.

So I came up our steep mountain road, and was about to turn into the driveway when I spotted Angela waving to me from her front yard. Honestly, she looked awful—but then, that isn't unusual these days. She was wearing a bikini which showed all her pregnancy scars and her cellulite. She has stringy breasts, and the area above, just below her collarbone, is a permanent, awful shade of purple, and all shriveled up like a prune. She used to have a good figure, but now her fat is all pooling in her lower half, so that her collarbone and ribs stick out as if she were somebody from a concentration camp, but down below, her behind sticks out, her stomach sticks out and her legs, which were once rather attractive, are swollen at the ankles and riddled with varicose veins. Please don't think I blame Angela for any of this, for of course the aging of a person's body is out of his or her control. But poor Angela can't afford to do anything about it. I'd have those veins stripped in a minute—in fact, I've had mine done twice—and I'd never let my chest get so burned that it looks like a piece of carbon paper. And for Christ's sake, I would do something about my hair—hers looks like old straw. On the other hand, I do blame Angela for this to a certain extent, because the money she's spent on all these stupid witch doctors could have been put to far better use on the only body that God gave her. Her mind she should be able to take care of by herself.

Anyway, when I saw Angela waving I drove into her driveway instead, and decided to have just one glass of wine with her before going home and coping with Sam, and to try to cheer up a little. I was going to make some remark about the way she looked, but she came over to the car and said, "Oh, Cassie, what a pretty outfit," referring to my white pants, jade-green silk shirt and navy blazer, and I changed my mind. "Now that you're here, what the fuck's the matter with Sam? Does he trip like this often?"

"What do you mean?" I asked nervously.

"Well, he was over here saying all sorts of strange things. I mean he sounded kind of crazy. Is he serious about divorce?"

"Oh, God. Oh, Angela." Tears came into my eyes. "Sometimes he talks that way."

"I didn't think you guys had problems."

"We don't, Angela. That's what's so awful. He just gets in these moods." She was leading me toward the patio. "First his eyes start to sink into his head in this peculiar way, usually after dinner, until they're very small and dark, and they don't blink." I was sniffling. "I'm sorry. But it's such a relief to talk about it."

"Go on," said Angela eagerly. "You poor kid."

"He stops talking and stares into space. He seems distracted, as though he's thinking about something, and I can't get his attention. Then after an hour or so he gets agitated, and he begins to pace around like a caged animal. Then he tells a lot of boring stories about his childhood which I've heard a thousand times. Then he starts on me and tells me everything that's wrong with me." I gulped. "I know I'm not a perfect person, Angela, but I have sincerely tried to be a good wife for Sam. I bore him three children. I run his home. . . ."

"You're terrific, Cassie. He couldn't find a better woman. You aren't the problem—*he* is. Does he take anything to make him act like this?"

"I don't know. Not that I can tell, except some Valium to calm down."

"When does he do that?"

"That's when he throws himself on the bed and tells me he really means it this time, he wants a divorce. He says I just make him feel rotten somehow, and other women don't. Sometimes he says it isn't even my fault for being the way I am, we're just a bad combination and he hates himself for not leaving me sooner. How can we be a bad combination after all this time? Then he starts drinking."

"After the Valium?"

"Well—sometimes. He says it would be just as well if

he were dead; then I'd be rid of him, and have the house and all the money and everything. And sometimes I say, 'Sam, never mind the money. I want you alive.' And he says—"

"He's here," Angela said, looking past me. "Hello again, Sam."

I slowly turned around, and we stood there watching him come up the driveway. Just to see him like that broke my heart. I suppose in my mind I still see the Sam Coopersmith I used to know, the one I met on the beach in his white pants and purple shirt, so young, handsome and hopeful. Now in his place is this fifty-year-old wreck—his face puffy, his eyes slits. A stubble of a beard, his long hair falling in his face. Shirttail out over his paunch, barefoot—my impeccable Sam.

"I'm drunk," he said. "How's about something in a glass, Angela?"

"No," I said.

He turned to me with that expression I've learned to dread. "Cunt," he said. "I wasn't even talking to you."

"Shut up, Sam," said Angela rather crossly. "Don't talk to her like that."

"Get me a drink," said Sam, "or I'll break your neck."

Angela said, "I guess I'd better give him something, Cassie. Then, maybe we could all talk a little. Maybe I can help."

"I doubt it," I said in a low voice.

"Now, now. What would you like, Sam? A little vodka?"

"Terrific. Actually, I'm just here to deliver a message to my lawfully wedded wife, with whom I am trapped in holy matrimony till the day I die."

"That's crap," said Angela.

"It isn't," Sam sad. "I'm trapped in a community-property state. Cassie has half of everything I own, including one of my balls. Here, Cassie. Want it now? Cut it off."

Suddenly I was furious. "Sam Coopersmith, stop this disgusting performance. For one thing, you can have a divorce *tomorrow* if you really want one. You're goddamn right I'll take half and anything else I can get, because that's the law of the state of California, where you've

earned all your money in television which you could have
earned nowhere else. You have—or *we* have—plenty of
money, and the truth is you are so greedy that if you were
as miserable as you say you wouldn't even think about
money, you'd pay to get rid of me.''

"Right on," said Angela, handing Sam his drink, which
she'd made from the bottle of watered-down vodka she
keeps around for such occasions. There's a tiny, almost
invisible mark on it that differentiates it from the regular
vodka. "Good girl. It's not so bad out here. There are a
lot of us."

But I didn't know whether I meant it—I didn't want to
be like Angela. "I don't understand," I said to Sam.
"What made you like this? What happened to us? We
used to have everything."

"You'd never understand," said Sam, "in a thousand
years. You're too fucking perfect." He turned to Angela.
"I'm married to perfection," he said.

"Well, I never had that problem," said Angela. One
reason I didn't want to be like her was that I had a feeling
that this discussion was the most interesting thing that had
happened to her all day. She was sitting on the edge of a
lounge chair, almost panting with interest. "Paul had a
million faults right from the start."

"Well, Cassie has *none*," Sam said. "And she tells me
frequently how wonderful she is. She's a great wife. A
terrific mother. She's kept her figure and she's bucking for
best-dressed. Blah blah blah. And you know, Cassie, every time you tell me how great you are, by God, I start to
believe you. I start thinking I'm crazy to want to leave
you. And the honest truth is no matter how many twenty-
year-olds I screw they all end up like gumdrops, sticky
little nothings you can't get rid of. You're *something*,
Cassie—and that's just the trouble."

Possibly the worst part of this is that Sam is basically a
good man. Probably one middle-aged guy in a thousand
would admit that. And that's what broke my heart. It
seemed so wasteful, all this, and I've always hated waste.
I still insist that Concepción save all useful leftovers to
make nutritious soups and salads. I suspect she thinks I'm
a little crazy to save little bits of meat and onion that even

the Mexicans would throw out. But somehow it makes me feel I'm doing my duty. In the same way, I can't bear the thought of so easily tossing out twenty-five years of marriage, any more than I'd throw out half a fresh rib roast.

Even Angela looked impressed. "She is something. I'm glad you see it. So it really has nothing to do with money, of course—it never does. That's just an excuse."

"It's God," Sam said. "Cassie, either God goes or I do."

I said, "God will never go. You might do better to get to know Him."

Sam was sitting on Angela's low stone wall, staring into his drink. He really looked terribly unhappy. "Ah, God," he said. "Maybe it's this therapist."

"Why don't you try Dr. Pew?" Angela suggested.

"The truth is I don't think there's a therapist alive who could get rid of this self-hatred of mine. It's turned into a sort of contest. If I leave Cassie I'm strong. If I stay with her I'm weak. It has to do with control and my whole relationship with my mother."

While he and Angela pursued this uninteresting subject, I wandered around the terrace and picked withered blooms off the hibiscus and the fuchsia, which were half-dead. Angela can't afford a gardener, and the place is really a disgrace. In fact, she can't afford a house at all, and I've suggested to her more than once that she sell it and live in one of those apartments near the beach. She says she would have to give half the house money to Paul, which she says she couldn't bear to do, which sounds like Sam. So she sits here among the tangled weeds and broken appliances. But it's more than that. She says I'm her best friend and she gets lonely and it's important to her to have me across the street.

Sam was saying, " . . . and so the whole relationship with my mother became a sexual power struggle, which could only be broken by my marriage. And now I'm doing the same thing again, and I know it. Christ, I feel like a wimp—and now more so than ever. I can't even do what Caspar Armstrong is doing."

"What?" I said, turning around.

"Oh, fuck. I forgot what I came here to tell you. Your father wants a divorce."

"Sam," I said, "I've been patient about your drinking and your dope. I've done so because I trusted your judgment about what your own body could take. And also because you are my husband. But if you are starting to have hallucinations you'd better stop right now and never touch either again, or you'll end up a human wreck."

"I mean it, Cassie. Dorothy called. She almost shrieked my ear off. Caspar wants out. He's in love with somebody else."

I looked hard at Sam, and I knew it was the truth. His eyes were bleary and he sat hunched over as though his spine had caved in, but he wasn't drunk anymore, or not drunk enough to make up something like that. As I realized it was true, I felt the most awful cold terror within me, a chill like death. When I thought of it later, I didn't really understand why I felt so terrified, as though the earth had opened up beneath my feet, or as though I had faced the jaws of Hell. For of course, distressing as it was, divorce happened all the time. But, I'd supposed, not to my parents. Strangely enough, even the thought of Sam's leaving me was not as bad as this. Oh, not my precious parents.

"Oh, Cassie," Angela said, coming over and putting her arms around me. "Are you all right?"

"It's not true," I said to Sam.

"It is, Cassie, I swear it. Jesus. Would I make up something like that?"

"What else did she say?"

"She was raving, I swear to God. Caspar had told her he was in love with this other broad and wanted to marry her. And he's been having an affair with her for years. He wants to behave 'honorably.' " Sam gave a hollow laugh. "And Dorothy was half-crying and half-yelling. You'd better call her back."

"Oh, my God. It's horrible. Oh, I can't believe it. You promise, Sam—you wouldn't joke." My eyes filled with tears. "Oh, I know you're not. Angela, would you fix me a vodka-and-tonic?"

"Darling, of course." She made one with the real vodka.

"How terrible. I can't believe it. I don't want to believe it—I've always thought of your family as perfect, the last of the perfect families. Maybe he'll change his mind. He'll see that the really honorable thing to do is stay with his wife."

Sam gave another hollow laugh. He'd reached his cynical phase. "God. Poor Caspar."

"Stop it," I said. "Don't 'Poor Caspar' me. He's been untrue to Mother for all these years. That's terrible—terrible. Her whole life has been a farce—cooking for him, washing and mending his clothes, keeping his home. I can't believe he would do this to her." I looked at them. "For the last forty-five years she has centered her life entirely around him. She has nothing herself—no money, no skills, nothing. Only her bridge club. I don't know what's going to become of her."

"Cassie," Sam said, "Dorothy is a . . ." He stopped, and hiccuped, taking a sip of his watery drink. "She's rather strong-minded. She always led Caspar around by the nose."

"Well, so what? He let her do it. And now look what he's done to her. My poor, poor Mama." I stood up. "I've got to go call her. If she needs me, I'll go home."

"Poor darling Dorothy," Angela said. "Please tell me if there's anything I can do, anything at all."

"God," said Sam, closing his eyes, "I'll bet I end up paying for her lawyer."

"Very possibly you will," I said, "unless you'd rather support her for the rest of her life because she didn't have adequate representation."

"She's fast, that Cassie," Sam said to Angela. "Some girl. She knows how to play dumb, but when it comes to the bucks, she's shrewd."

I planted myself in front of him and said, "Now, listen to me, Sam Coopersmith. Hold up your head and look at me while I'm talking to you." I tried to grab his hair to pull his head up, but there wasn't much there. "I am going to ask you just once to pull yourself together and control your little digs and insults because I now have a family crisis. My parents are old and of modest means and they are in a very difficult situation. Probably I'll have to take

some responsibility, both emotional and financial, for my
poor mother, who is doubtless beside herself with grief
over this treachery. For the next few weeks I will simply
not have the time, nor the patience, nor the emotional
ability to cope with your endless feelings of being rejected
or your talk of divorce or your dope or your liquor.
Frankly, at this time in my life, all that sort of thing drags
me down beyond my strength. So I'm asking you, Sam, to
just try for one last time to use a little self-control for my
sake. It might be the last favor I ever ask of you. After my
family situation is settled we will talk about a divorce, if
you like. But if you are the decent human being I know
you are at heart, you will try, for once, to think about
somebody but yourself for a few weeks. Perhaps if you
think about poor Dorothy and Caspar it will take your
mind off your own stupid little problems, like having a
perfect wife who loves you and two houses and three cars
and three wonderful children and an adorable poodle.''
Angela began to clap. "Will you do this for me, Sam?
Just this one last thing.''

Sam looked stunned at this speech, which turned out
much better than I had expected. But I think there are
times when emotion gives us "the tongues of angels,'' and
this was one of them. Perhaps God was speaking through
my mouth; but whether or not He was, Sam was impressed
into silence, and so was Angela. There are times when the
truth shines through, and when it does, it touches all who
hear it. Anyway, after these words I went back down the
driveway to put my car in the garage and to go and call
Dorothy.

Inside, my house was cool and silent, and the light came
through the skylight onto the ficus trees in the front hall. I
went through the dining room and into the kitchen, where
Concepción, who is small and dark, was weeping over an
onion, or over something else, I don't know which. She
seemed to be preparing the shrimps as I had directed, and
after a small exchange in Spanish, which I have never
mastered, I went back through the inner hall and into the
bedroom wing.

A familiar smell came from the bedroom of Stuart, my
eighteen-year-old son—a slightly sweet, spicy, almost Ori-

ental odor which ordinarily I found annoying but now, at this time of great crisis, I found infuriating. I rapped sharply on the door several times, and finally, after an interminable wait, a voice mumbled, "Yah, wazzit?"

"Open the door, Stuart," I said sharply.

There was a silence and some scuffling noises and the murmur of voices, and eventually the door was opened by Stu. He is ordinarily—maybe I should say occasionally—a nice-looking young man, with brown hair, clear eyes and even features, and when he was young, a sweet disposition. But he is now in some hell of adolescence. He wore a twisted scarf tied around his head, a pair of "cut-offs" and a black T-shirt with glitter pictures on it advertising some rock group. He had a strange "Mohawk" haircut—*has* I should say, for it certainly couldn't have grown out in the last twenty-four hours—and is attempting—not very successfully, in my opinion—to grow a beard.

Even though, as I have said, my life affords me great satisfaction, I admit to feeling almost desperate sometimes in the presence of my children. Sometimes it seems that they have actually plotted and planned in some devilish way to be everything and do everything that I cannot bear. Since I am a very neat and orderly person, they must be messy and completely disorganized, always losing things and then expecting me to find them, howling "Mom—I can't find my . . ." whatever it is they have misplaced. Since I am very clean they must be dirty, though this has varied at different ages, and I'm not sure that it counts that Stu is cleaner than he used to be, anyway, since he dresses so peculiarly that you can't believe he doesn't smell, even if he doesn't. I like peace and quiet, and they seem to go to great lengths to surround themselves with earsplitting noise of a sort that makes me want to scream—in fact, I hardly ever exchange a word with any of them, in the course of a day, without the background noise of stereo, TV, "ghetto blaster" or Sony Walkman, which surrounds the face of the wearer with muffled sound. And while I am a strong believer in being responsible, and realistic, and coping with whatever comes along life's path, they fill themselves with dope to zonk out their minds and reduce their motivation to zero. Perhaps I'm being hard on them, for most of their friends aren't much different. But as I've explained to them so often, I have my values and they are not, at this time of my life or any other, going to change.

"I smell marijuana," I said, looking around Stu's room, which he seemed to be trying to prevent me from doing by moving back and forth in front of the door. The place was about the same as usual—black posters on the wall, the thump-thump of electronic music.

"Not here, Mom. You're imagining things. Christ, man, you smell it in your sleep."

"If I do, there's good reason for it." Something moved over on the bed, and then I saw Shelli, apparently asleep. "What's the matter with her? Get out of my way, Stuart." I shoved him aside and went in, where the smell of pot was stronger than ever, or else it was the smell from the little incense burner on Stu's desk, which was smoking. Of course, I know they do that to confuse the adults, because the smells are very similar.

Shelli was lying face down on the bed, and I shook her. "Shelli? Wake up, honey." She didn't stir, and I slowly turned to my younger son, who was looking more nervous by the minute. In fact, he seemed to be shrinking before my eyes back into the little boy he was at heart.

"What's the matter with her?" I asked him. "Stuart. You didn't give her anything, did you?"

"Oh, Mom. She's had it plenty of times before."

"She what? She's only fourteen!"

"You always say that. You know she does dope."

"But that doesn't explain the way she looks now. What's the matter with her?"

"I guess it made her sleepy."

"Did you give her anything else? Pills or anything?"

I have had similar conversations with my children on other occasions, and each time I find myself watching a little Cassie up on the ceiling looking down on the sickening scene, wondering how in the name of God the road of life has led to this. But because it wasn't the first time, I'd developed a little "hide." I grabbed Stu by the arm and looked him straight in his red-rimmed eyes. "Answer me, and tell me the truth."

"Nothing else, Mom. I promise."

I don't trust the promises of a person who takes drugs, and I said, "Stuart, listen to me. I hope you wouldn't risk your sister's life or health out of your own fear and guilt. If something is really wrong with her, I promise you, you'll be guilty for the rest of your life, and I will probably never forgive you." He looked nervously at me, then over at Shelli, who seemed to stir a little, and I went over and shook her. "Shelli, wake up. It's Mother. Speak to me, Shelli."

Suddenly she rolled over and opened her eyes. The pupils were so large they almost filled her brown eyes, and my heart made a sickening thump. She gave a strange half-smile, half-grimace and flopped over again on her stomach, where she lay still as death.

"She's tripping," Stu finally gasped. "It's acid." He looked rather strange himself. I felt like strangling him, and possibly would have if he hadn't been my son and if he hadn't looked so frightened. "Oh, God. I wish I hadn't done it."

"I suggest you lie down on the other bed," I said, "and while I hope you suffer no permanent harm, I'll say frankly that I hope your experience is bad enough to scare the shit out of you. How long ago did she take it?"

"Around lunchtime." We looked at Shelli, who now began to shiver, groping for the quilt that lay bunched up on the bed. "She'll be okay. I mean the worst is over, like." She lay there trembling and making strange sounds like an animal in pain.

"I'm going to phone Dr. Battaglia. And I'm going to get your father, Stuart. He's going to hear about this." How hollow the words sounded as my eyes met his.

"Big deal," said Stu, as he lurched toward the other twin bed. As he collapsed, I said,

"Stuart Coopersmith, don't you dare speak of your father with disrespect. He is the head of this family, besides holding a position of tremendous responsibility. When the rules of this house are broken, he is the one who dispenses discipline. . . ." Stu's eyelids fluttered, then closed. "Shit," I said. "Shit."

I went into the study to call Dr. Battaglia. I will not

bore you or myself with the tedium of getting the doctor
off his boat and out of his scuba suit, but when at last I
talked to him he sounded neither too concerned nor too
interested about Shelli's "tripping." Probably in a couple
of hours she would be herself again, and if not I should
call him at the following number. This might teach her a
lesson. When his son did it, etcetera etcetera. Right then
and there I decided to get another doctor, one who showed
some concern about stoned children, if there was such a
thing.

I hung up the phone. I thought of going over and telling
Sam, but the sad truth was it probably wouldn't accom-
plish anything in the condition he was in. Probably by now
he was crying all over Angela, or had fallen asleep in one
of her tattered lounge chairs. When Angela got tired of
him she would throw him out. I had occasionally wondered over the years whether Angela and Sam had ever
slept together, or whether either of them had wanted to or
thought about it for more than a moment, for she is always
hanging around in her bikini or even topless. But I couldn't
believe that Sam, who, after all, spends a good deal of
time chasing female children, would be attracted by those
beanbag breasts of Angela's. And not only that, but when
I once hinted around about it to Angela, she looked me
straight in the eye and said, "Cassie, *never.*" And though
there seem to be fewer and fewer things in my life that I
can count on, I believe I can count on Angela's friendship
and her promise.

I went back to Stu's bedroom, where both children
seemed to be fast asleep—Shelli tangled up in the quilt,
and Stu splayed out on his back with bare feet hanging
over the end of the bed. In spite of my anger and despair at
them and their foolishness and self-destructive tendencies,
I loved them and couldn't help noticing, as always, how
lovely Shelli's skin was on her cheek and neck, how pure
she looked; and how strong and slender were Stu's arms
and hands, and how soft and white those hands had been
when he was small enough to want me to hold one; and I
wanted desperately to turn back the clock to those years
when they were small and the world was so much simpler
and better, or else it seemed so. Certainly I had gotten

tired and impatient during those years, but I had had hope, and now there were times, like this one, when I had none at all, and even felt a kind of despair I had never known in my life before.

Then I went into our bedroom to call Mother. That, strangely enough, was the worst of all: I believe that one thing that gave me strength to cope with some of the difficulties of my life had been the knowledge that they were there together, strong and steadfast, for me to fall back on. But now my poor dear mother would expect me to be a tower of strength for her, just at a time when I felt helpless and sorely tried by my husband's problems and my children's adolescent monkeyshines. I suppose I am not the first woman approaching middle age who has realized that it is she, and she only, who is expected to shoulder the load and bear the brunt and be the source of strength to her entire family of three generations.

So I sat for a few minutes on the white velvet chaise, just looking out at the greenery and trying to compose myself. I reminded myself that it was always the people like me who were chosen to take the responsibilities, and if God didn't think I could do it, he wouldn't have sent all these things my way. And I reminded myself, too, that if worse came to worst with Sam, we lived in a community-property state and I had him by the short hairs, and in fact he had been such a lousy husband that I almost wished we did not live in a community-property state so I could go into court and testify to every kind of cruelty that he had perpetrated on me, and so the judge would punish him and teach him the lesson of his life. But it wasn't the time to worry about Sam; it was the time to take my own advice and see what I could do for my tragedy-stricken parents. So I gathered up all my courage, recited a small prayer, then picked up the phone and pushed the eleven digits.

After several rings Mother answered. Her voice sounded strange.

"Mama, it's Cassie."

"Oh, Cassie, dear. Sam must have spoken to you."

"Oh, Mom. Are you all right? Is it true about Daddy?"

"It certainly is. After forty-five years of marriage. He walked into the house two nights ago and said, 'Dorothy,

would you please sit down. I want to talk to you.' We
were in the kitchen. We sat down at the table, that dear old
kitchen table where we all had so many happy breakfasts
together. Oh, it's such a shame. So I sat down and said,
'Yes, Caspar. What is it?' 'Dorothy,' he said, 'I'm telling
you this because I respect you and I can no longer live
with the shame of my life. If you were any less of a
woman maybe I could go on this way, but I know how
important honesty is to you, so I'm going to take you at
your word.' Well, I didn't know what he was talking
about. I mean it never occurred to me—not once. I have
always fulfilled my . . . marital responsibilities. I never
did refuse him, or hardly ever— only when I was very
tired, or when I had my monthly period, or during my
pregnancy, or on the anniversary of my dear parents'
death, when it wouldn't have been right. Though I suppose
I am an innocent woman, compared with the way people
seem to be now, I was brought up to believe that if a man
was kept happy at home—''

"So Mama, what happened?'' She sounded a little
strange. I had never heard her talk so much at once.

"So Caspar said, 'Dorothy, I have come to ask you for
a divorce because I have fallen in love with another woman,
and I can no longer continue to be a hypocrite like this. It
isn't fair to you or to Yoland, the person I—' And at that I
screamed, 'Not Yolanda Simpson!' Because Yolanda Simpson, if you recall, is one of the women I play bridge with
every single week! And how many Yolandas can there be
in a town the size of Rivertown? And to think that I have
sat and looked at that woman over the dummy for seventeen years! To think that she looked me straight in the eye,
and drank my tea and ate my cookies and accepted my
hospitality!''

"I don't think I remember her,'' I said.

"Well, of course you don't, because it wasn't Yolanda
Simpson at all. It's Yolande Devereaux, a woman from
Danbury of French abstraction, a widow with a son of
eighteen, which he calls a 'grown' son. Which your father
thinks is just wonderful, as though having a grown son, or
a grown anything, is some proof of good character.''

She stopped for breath, or for something—she gave a

kind of gulp, and it occurred to me that it was possible that Mother was drunk, or at least, had been drinking. It seemed unlikely, but then it was the only thing I could think of that would explain the way she was rambling on and on and not sticking to the point.

"It seems this person, this Yolande Devereaux, works as a sort of matron or guard at the prison to earn enough money to support this son—"

"At the prison?"

"Yes, Cassie. [Pause—gulp.] Now, of course, I don't know too much about it, but I have never thought of prison personnel as the sort of people I would much care to know. They would have to be very sour and unpleasant, I should think, and even depraved, to choose to work among the miserable people society has put away. And your father has always had a cheerful disposition. I couldn't imagine what he saw in her. Sees in her, rather, for he will not give her up."

"Poor Mama." I began working on my nails with an emery board, for I could see that this was going to take a long time.

"Well, when I was over the shock of hearing your father's confession, I gave him the chance to apologize and mend his ways, after which I would consider whether our marriage could go on under the circumstances. I pretended he had never mentioned divorce, and I gave him the chance to vindicate himself. I decided that after all these years it was the least I could do. So I told him that, and he said, 'Dorothy, I don't think you understand. I will not give up Yolande. I will always be fond of you and respect you and will never forget that you are the mother of my children. But I love Yolande and want to marry her.'"

"Where is Daddy now?" I asked.

"Well, how should I know? I imagine he's with her. Now I know that all those nights when I was stupid enough to believe him, when I thought he was working late at the store, he was with her." For the first time, her voice broke. "You can imagine how I feel, Cassie. Goodness knows in all the years I was bringing you up I never imagined that such a thing could happen to me. I suppose I thought that if you were loyal, and if you worked hard, and if you were sympathetic to others and demonstrated Christian qualities, that somehow things would come out all right. And I guess that's what's so hard to accept, Cassie—that there really isn't any justice, that sometimes things just happen according to chance. And sometimes the good get punished and the bad rewarded. I know it sounds terrible, but sometimes I wonder if God really knows what He's doing, and if He does, why He let this terrible thing happen to Caspar.''

"Mother, would you like me to come home for a while?'' I really felt sorry for her now, for she was saying things I'd felt myself. I felt close to her, now that we were both adult women in very similar circumstances.

"Well, I hate to ask you to leave your dear husband and my wonderful grandchildren and your happy home. I'm no longer a girl, and for all my adult life I've been a capable person. . . . I haven't told your sister yet, but I just know she's going to find some way to criticize me, with all her psychiatry and her smart talk. She always does. She's always hated me and she's always been jealous of you. Of course she's my daughter, and I love her as I love you, but I don't believe she is going to be much help to me right now. I guess I need somebody I can just talk to from the heart, and you've always been the closer child. I don't mean for it to sound as though I don't love Celia, because of course I do, but there's always one who means more, you can't help it. You must know that from your own children.''

"Okay, Mama. I'll try and come tomorrow night.''

"Well, you mustn't do it if it disturbs Sam the slightest bit, because of course your first duty is to him. And it would just be a few days till we . . .'' Her voice trailed off. "Anyway, Cassie, it would be a relief for me to discuss this with somebody who has sense, which Celia doesn't.''

"Is Daddy still living there, or has he moved out?''

Stunned silence. "Why, of course he's still here. I mean your father isn't the kind of man who would just . . . he has respect enough to wait until we've arranged . . . well, of course he's here, Cassie. He wouldn't just *leave* me.''

She sounded as though she hadn't even thought of that possibility. "And he certainly won't when I tell him you're coming. And it's not that I made a scene or anything. I mean of course I was upset, but I would never behave in such a way as to drive him—"

"Mother, I've got to go. I'll try to get on the eleven A.M. flight tomorrow. I'll call you from the airport."

"Oh, dear. That would be wonderful. We might be able to straighten things out. Well, I certainly look forward to seeing you. I'd better look into your room; there are still all those old clothes in there I've been meaning to take to the thrift shop . . ."

By the time I got off the phone I felt absolutely exhausted. I could smell the shrimp, but wondered if I could even move to get to the table—not to mention the rest of the family, who were in even worse condition than I. I lay back on the chaise lounge with my eyes closed, kicking off my shoes, and tried to rest, but I felt a terrible cold worry that I was the one who had to take care of everything and maybe I couldn't do it. Then I got hold of myself. Cassie, I said to myself, you have to do it, that's all. Remain calm, think before you act and make lists. You can do it because you *have* to.

Well. My mind whirling with questions about Yolande Devereaux, Sam's demented behavior and a thousand practical details, I went back into the children's room, where Stu and Shelli seemed to be recovering from their latest prank. Not the least of my annoyances about them was that they didn't, either of them, have much to occupy them during the summer and so one reason for their self-destructive behavior was pure boredom. Stu had one more year at Santa Barbara High and was spending the summer "hanging out." And Shelli, at fourteen, had arrived at the age where she was too old for camp, or so she thought, and too young for anything else. So she too was in a "limbo," and had been spending her days on the beach or wandering aimlessly around town with her friends. In fact, the only one who's doing anything useful at all, if you can call it that, is Sammy Junior, who at twenty-three plays a guitar and sings at a restaurant down near the marina for ten dollars a night and all the beer he can drink.

As Stuart and Shelli came to, I let them have it. I told them they were ruining their health and their bodies and their brains. I told them their lives would be worthless unless they developed moral values and that they'd better not continue to ignore God, because He would certainly punish them for their irresponsible ways. I said many other things, too, and not for the first time, while they sat and listened to me without saying a word; or else they didn't listen to me, for their attention seemed to wander; and then Shelli suddenly said, "Oh, man, what time is it?" and when I told her it was almost seven she dashed out to feed Ginger, the horse, whom she had completely forgotten about while she was "tripping." The poor thing must have been going mad with hunger, thirst and lack of exercise, and I pointed out to Stu how irresponsibility hurt not only the person and those around him or her, but even dumb innocent creatures who had done nothing to deserve ill treatment. When Stu put on his Sony Walkman while I was talking to him, I snatched those stupid earphones off him and told him I expected him at dinner in half an hour, because I had something important to say to all of them and the only time was right now.

Rather to my surprise, everybody appeared at dinner, including Sam, who looked terrible and acted subdued and depressed, and Shelli, who came in just as we were starting. It's rather unusual to have everybody there at once. Sam often is away or works late (That's what he says, anyway), and over the years the children have had various projects, some of which extended through the dinner hour or started early in the evening. There have been music lessons and sports practice and beach picnics, though in recent years the gatherings have sounded less "healthy and normal" and more sinister, such as Guru Group or Punk Parade or the 666 Club or other activities which I can't honestly say I understand but which my children have assured me are the "in thing." Often Concepción and I have divided dinner into five individual earthenware casseroles which I bought at the Pottery Barn for exactly this purpose, for each person to eat as he or she had the time.

Anyway, in spite of all the tribulations of the day there was something pleasant about all of us gathering at the table for dinner in the dining room, which I have done in grape and dead-white (grape carpet; fabric walls in muted tones of grape, salmon and celery; French antique table and chairs; green-and-celery pottery tableware; outsized linen napkins in shocking pink; purple Mexican glassware and always either azaleas with fern, roses or sprays of bougainvillea in glass bowls). The glass doors open onto our patio, and as we eat we can smell the scent of the trees in the mountains or, as the night goes on, the jasmine and honeysuckle. I'll have to admit that nobody seemed either to appreciate all this or even be aware of the lovely setting we were in. In fact, they all looked like unshaven, unwashed bums, grunting and saying "Pass this" and "Pass that." Sammy Junior looked the healthiest, since he spends a lot of time surfing, and Shelli, except for a slight pallor, looked much the way she always does, for at her age one never looks better or worse. After the entrée, as Concepción was bringing in the dessert (an excellent pineapple mousse she makes very well), I said, "I have something to say to all of you." Something in the tone of my voice must have sounded unusual, for they all slowly turned and looked at me. Stu and Shelli exchanged glances. "As Dad may have mentioned, there is a crisis in my family. Grandpa is leaving Grandma for another woman after forty-five years of marriage." There were sounds of amazement and low whistles. "As you can imagine, poor Grandma is very upset at Grandpa's treachery. . . ."

"Aren't you loading the dice a little, Cassie?" Sam asked.

"No, Sam. I'm simply telling what happened. My father is the one abandoning the marriage."

"Did it ever occur to you," said Sam, between his teeth, "that she might have *driven* him out?"

"I don't really know, Sam and neither do you. To the objective observer, it seems to me that Grandpa is behaving *very* peculiarly." Sam rolled up his eyes in that dreadful way he does when he wants to appear amazed at my stupidity. "Anyway, what I want to say tonight is that I must go home to be with her, and I'm leaving tomorrow for a stay of a few weeks. I know it might be difficult for you, but I simply have no choice. I don't believe I have

ever before deserted my post here. You're all old enough
to get along without me. Concepción will be here, except,
of course, for her days off, and everything will go on as
usual. You're all going to have to get along. Somebody
will have to do the marketing.''

"Who's supposed to do that?" asked Sam unpleasantly.

I poured myself another glass of wine. "That's up to
you. You are all adults, and there are four cars." I gave
Sam my most serious and disapproving look. For all our
troubles, we have always agreed to keep a united front
before the children.

"We'll take turns," Sam said, recovering. "Each week
one of us will plan and shop."

"I don't have time," said Shelli, who has nothing in the
world but time.

"Oh, come on, cats," Sammy Junior said. "It might be
fun here without Ma. Give her a break; she needs a
vacation." He gave me his most charming smile. My elder
son has considerable charm, but truthfully, he seems to
have little ambition, and sometimes I wonder if he is very
bright. However, even though I don't really approve of the
life he leads, at least he has a cheerful disposition—unlike
the others, who all seem perpetually depressed. He is
bronzed from the sun, and he was wearing a T-shirt with
"HANG TEN" on it.

"I'm going to count on all of you," said Sam, trying to
appear fatherly—which was difficult considering his red
eyes, uncombed hair and hangdog manner—"because I'll
have to be in L.A. two or three nights a week."

"That's all right, Dad," said Stu. "We'll be just fine."

In fact, they all began to perk up so at the thought of my
leaving that I said, "I want to add one thing. I've been
deeply distressed today by some of the things that have
been going on around here. You all know how I feel about
drugs. In case you are planning to get stoned every day
when I'm gone, all I can say is that I'm glad I won't be
around to know about it."

This was greeted by an elaborate yawn from Stuart and
a conciliatory grin from Sammy—"Oh, come off it, Mom.
God, you're square"—but Shelli dropped her eyes and
frowned, as did Sam, who helped himself to more pineap-

ple mousse. I was so exhausted my eyes were starting to close, and conversation lagged. The whole dinner was unusual not just because everybody was present and because there was a general topic of conversation, led by me, but because there was any conversation at all. Usually there was either silence or a lot of joking and nudging between the children, or else Sam told boring stories about the television and movie world. Sometimes I attempted to bring up subjects of general interest, such as politics or world affairs, but usually none of them were very much interested, nor were they when I attempted to tell them the plot of a best-seller I was reading or any interesting gossip I had heard downtown. We seemed to be very much split apart as a family, with few common interests, and sometimes I felt so nostalgic for the better times when we had gone together to Disneyland or for drives up into the mountains for picnics that I could have cried.

But there was no time for self-pity, and I spent the rest of the evening packing, talking to Concepción and making lists for Sam about running the house. Sam lay in bed like an invalid, and in fact he did seem to have a terrible cold, for his nose kept running and he kept blowing it, and he took two or three antihistamines and propped himself up on three pillows looking miserable.

"God, Cassie. Aren't you finished yet?"

"Now, listen, Sam. On the blue sheet are names and phone numbers of the laundress who does your shirts, the dry cleaner, the gardener, the vet, the spring-water man, the plumber, the pool man and Dr. Battaglia. On the pink sheet are the stores I usually use so you'll know where to get your coffee cake and vegetables and the best meat. Now, all the local bills have been paid—"

"Hey, honey. Let's fuck."

"I haven't got time." I looked at him. "I'm sorry, Sam. On top of everything that's happened today I really don't feel particularly affectionate. Besides, I don't want to catch your cold."

"That's not a cold, baby. That's . . . allergies."

It was dope, then. "Were you sitting here this afternoon smoking pot? Aren't you afraid you're going to get fired?"

"Cassie, *I* fire people. They don't fire me. And I can

take care of my career, thanks." He slammed his book down on the bedside table. "You're going away for God knows how long and you don't even want to fuck."

"I hate that word."

"All right. Make love."

"I don't understand you, Sam. Only this afternoon you were telling me you wanted a divorce, and now this."

It isn't only Sam. I've noticed this before in my limited experience with other men, and my friends have told me they have too. They simply do not connect sex with anything else in their lives, and usually they don't even care whom they have it with. The main thing is to get it in. It doesn't even matter whom they get it into. Possibly this is the thing about them that upsets women the most, for women build their lives around one man and one relationship, and the act of physical love is the expression of that relationship. But men's lives center around their sexual organ.

"I'm ambivalent, Cassie. I've told you that. Marriage is tough. But now that you're going to leave, I miss you already."

I was looking at our appointment calendar. "Oh, Sam. There's that dinner party on the seventeenth." I had forgotten all about it: two moguls and three enchiladas and their tamales were coming for dinner.

Sam sat up slowly. "Do you mean to tell me you're going to be *away* for our dinner party on the seventeenth?"

"Yes, Sam. But it doesn't matter. It's all planned, and I'll make out the list, and all you have to do is tell Concep—"

"That dinner party is crucial to my career. There are three deals pending with these people. You have to be here."

"I *can't*."

He looked angry. "Do you mean to tell me that you're going to put your parents' little problem ahead of the most crucial deal of my life—the one that will affect your life-style for the next twenty years? This deal is for reruns of *The Wimples*. Do you understand what that means?"

"Yes, I do; but Sam, reruns have nothing to do with me. Either take them to a nice restaurant or have it catered or do whatever you want. Tell them I had to go home. They don't care.''

''*I* care, Cassie. You're the one who makes these parties work. Without you it'll be flat as a pancake. Of course the deals don't have anything directly to do with you, but you know how people are, and if they leave here having had a wonderful evening, fabulous food and a charming hostess—''

''They don't have *me*.''

''—they're human, they're going to feel much more eager to make a deal with me. You *have* to be here, Cassie.''

I screamed, ''Jesus Christ! Can't you do anything for yourself? I'm *leaving*. I don't know when I'm coming back. Hire a hostess. Ask Angela. Get one of your chippies. Stop piling things on me. I'm so upset and tired I'm ready to crack. And I don't care whether you agree or not, but my obligation right now is to my poor dear mother, and if more people thought the way I do, the country would be in better shape and there would be less divorce and war and everything else. I feel like I'm the only person left on earth who has any family loyalty and is willing to take any responsibility or carry any weight or anything. I am asking you, Sam, to *please* try and take responsibility for this family while I'm gone, and then if you want you can have your fucking divorce, I don't care, but *I can't stand any more*.''

Well, I began crying out of sheer exhaustion, and Sam comforted me, and we ended up making love after all. It was the first time in a long time, and strangely enough, it was very exciting, probably because Sam seemed tender, and it was something gentle and almost sad.

So Sam and I slept close together last night, which we hadn't done in a long time, and then in the morning he asked me if I were still going to go, and I said of course, and he began to sulk, and we were more or less back to where we were yesterday. I guess he thought that if we made love I wouldn't be able to bear to leave him; but if that's what he thought, he doesn't understand me very well, and it's a pretty silly thing to assume anyway. At least, he'd pulled himself together and was going down to L.A. to the office instead of staying home and getting drunk, which he occasionally did. So I told him how nice he looked and that I'd miss him, and we kissed goodbye. He tried to get me to change my mind again, which I suppose I should be glad of: if he were really through with the marriage, he'd be dying to get rid of me so he could chase his little girls without explanation. In fact, even after all these years I still don't understand Sam or what he wants or why he's so unhappy or a lot of other things either.

So I continued my preparations, and Sammy Junior said he'd drive me to L.A. Airport because he wanted to talk to me on the way. In the meantime, he, Stuart and Shelli all kept coming to me with problems they would have after I was gone that they couldn't solve themselves, just like their father. Even Concepción was weeping mysteriously over her tea, and I had to sit with her for fifteen minutes and pat her on the head and hug her and tell her everything would be all right—though maybe it won't, for God's sake. Then I went over and told Angela that I was leaving and would she just keep a general eye on everything. I think if Angela and Sam were sleeping together or at least had it in mind, Angela would have looked at least a little pleased when I told her I would be gone for several weeks, but instead she seemed sad and hugged me and said I was her best friend and she would miss me terribly because there was nobody else she could really talk to from the heart, and would I please write her, and she would do anything I wanted her to do, including fucking Sam if I wanted, though the thought didn't really thrill her that much. I said I didn't care whether she did or didn't, and she laughed, and we hugged each other goodbye. I am really very fond of her, and I don't think she would have said such a thing if that was what she had in mind, or else she is a much better actress than I think.

So finally everything seemed to be done, and I kissed the younger children goodbye—and Concepción too, which made her smile for a change—and Sammy loaded my things into his Toyota and off we went. It was so beautiful this morning, and the mountains were golden, and each green live oak stood out vividly on the hillsides in that way that happens only in California. As we drove down the San

Diego Freeway, I felt relaxed and free for the first time in days and realized how badly I needed to get away from my family and the numerous difficulties and problems presented by a middle-aged husband and teen-aged children. I leaned back in the seat and enjoyed the beautiful scenery, which even included some glimpses of the sparkling silver Pacific off to the west beyond the hills.

"Ma," Sammy Junior said, "one reason I wanted to take you to the airport is because it would give us a chance to talk. I mean not the *only* reason, of course, but at home everything's always so wild. Anyway, it's about Eleanor."

Eleanor? "Well, Sammy, you've mentioned many of your girlfriends to me and I honestly can't remember which one she is."

"We've been going together for almost three months now. She's a little older than me—forty, in fact. And she's gay. She's really terrific. She wants to get married, and I'm wondering if it's a good idea."

At that very moment I think if he hadn't been driving I would have pushed him out of the car. It's not that I don't love Sammy. He is my first son and will always have a special place in my heart. Besides, he is good-natured and sweet, which is clearly demonstrated by his willingness to even listen to such twaddle from this woman.

"Is that a serious question?"

He looked surprised. "Sure is."

"Have you really thought about what marriage is, Sammy?"

"Well, I guess so."

"It's years and years of living with another person, of putting up with their faults and making the best of things. Sometimes it means children, and if there are children the idea of divorce gets much more difficult."

"Who's talking about divorce, man? I'm talking about *marriage*."

Suddenly I thought of something. "Is she rich?"

He laughed. "Not exactly. She does charcoal portraits in one of the shops in the Paseo."

"May I ask why you want to marry her?"

"Well, I'm not even sure if I do. It was her idea."

"The answer to your question is no."

"How come?" He didn't seem disappointed—just mildly interested.

"Because she's too old, she's too poor and she's homosexual, for God's sake. And even if she were young, beautiful and straight, you can't even support yourself, much less a wife. Unless you plan to live on a surfboard."

"You really think so?"

By now I was counting the minutes till I got on the plane. I told Sammy that I thought he would regret marriage to a forty-year-old lesbian with no money. I suggested for the five-hundredth time that he think seriously about entering some work or profession, because he was twenty-three and not getting any younger—if not law school or medical school, which I suspected were beyond him, then possibly some local job or business or even craft in which we could help him get started. He was good with his hands, and there are many useful services he could be trained for, such as plumbing or electronics or carpentry. Or if he wished to pursue his music, he might do better in L.A., where the rock world was. Sammy listened with a big smile and said he'd think over all the things I'd said to him.

At the airport, I checked in and put my suitcases on the conveyer belt. Sammy walked with me over to the place where they X-ray you, and we hugged and kissed goodbye. He was so tall and good-looking, so brown and healthy-looking, and he has such a beautiful smile. I wanted to tell him to watch over the family while I was gone, but after hearing about Eleanor decided not to say it. But I loved him anyway, even if his judgment wasn't very good, and I hoped that life wouldn't treat him too cruelly. He seemed unprotected, like a kitten in the jungle, and I prayed that God would watch over him.

I'm contented sitting here on American's Flight 32, relaxed if rather tired. Possibly it's the vodka and the Valium I took after boarding, which I always take before a flight. Before long we'll land at Kennedy Airport in New York, where I haven't been for five years, and then of course there will be Mother's problems, but until I must face them I am blessedly alone.

In the next seat—I always travel first class—is a handsome, silver-haired, suntanned man in an expensive-looking suit. He looks like the chairman of the board of something or a famous retired director, and he has smiled at me a couple of times to see if I will respond. There's nothing wrong or unusual about that; in fact, it would be funny if he didn't, because I must say I am looking very well. I'm wearing my white linen pant suit and a silk sweater in blackberry, and my Bogie hat and some high-heeled purple sandals that are not as uncomfortable as they look. My outfit isn't fancy, but very comfortable and casual, and I believe that a person's whole behavior changes if she's wearing clothes she doesn't feel right in. It's not exactly that I'm vain, but for some reason if I look less than my best I start feeling very depressed.

Anyway, in time the silver-haired man, whose name is Fred, and I exchanged pleasantries, He is one of those lawyers who defend studio crooks, as far as I can figure out, though rather than crooks he calls them "misunderstood geniuses." Instead of saying "stealing" he says "reappropriation of designated funds." But according to Fred, the crooks' problem is not that they have done something wrong, it's that their pictures have not made money. In fact, said Fred, "Cassie, *there is no right or wrong*. There is only what works." There is only business ethics. There is only what they can get away with. The only right is making money at the box office.

I said, "Fred, you have just made a very immoral and unethical statement. I am a churchgoing person. I deeply believe that there are Christian ethics and that those who don't accept them are going to get into some kind of terrible trouble. Since my husband is in the entertainment business, I have heard your point of view before and have never approved of it. In fact, I have had this boring discussion many times previously and wouldn't even bother with it except here we are a mile up in the air with an hour to kill before we get to New York. We all have to earn money, and besides, being a citizen, I certainly agree that criminals need adequate representation as well as anybody else. But I think you make a mistake, Fred, in pretending that your criminals are not *wrong*. It's one thing to say to yourself, 'He's wrong, but I'll try to help him.' It's another to say, 'There *is* no wrong.' If you can't tell the difference between the two things, I believe you have a serious defect of character.''

Fred looked stunned at this speech and sat there staring into his drink, while I went back to reading *Cosmo*. So, basically, that was the end of our conversation. He had mentioned possibly getting together in the city and had given me his card, on which he wrote ''*St. Regis*.'' But he didn't bring it up again. Actually, I felt a little sorry I'd said it, and I glanced over at him occasionally, but he was always looking in another direction.

I've found people are almost always annoyed when I talk about ethical principles, and I've learned not to say these things when I notice them, particularly since Sam has forbidden me ever under any circumstances to mention these things, or even my beliefs, to anybody he works with. So probably the only reason I said what I did was that I was not with Sam and all my pent-up principles could come out instead of being choked back, and because I had had two vodka martinis. And not very surprisingly, Fred didn't react very well, for it's obvious that he's guilty as sin about the means by which he gets his first-class seat, his snappy Italian suit and his hair transplants, which I could detect in the overhead light, plus his Bel Air mansion and his Cézanne and his Picasso and his London flat, which he mentioned to me along with whatever else he didn't mention.

So I sat back and looked out the window. I love being on a plane and had arrived at a state of contentment and well-being I hadn't felt in a long time. Such is the effect of even this small amount of time and distance that now the children's problems seem less serious, if they could even be called problems at all. Though the foibles of adolescence are distressing, my children are no different from others I know and have heard about. They all take drugs. They all ''trip.'' They all dress strangely and have periods of great laziness. Angela's children are far worse than mine. One is a disciple of ''The Reverend Moon,'' and the twenty-one-year-old, Ginny, is gay. It isn't that I disapprove of people being gay, and Ginny is certainly a nice girl and thoughtful of her mother, thank God. And Angela says it's perfectly all right with her, but I don't think it really is. Perhaps it is biological and Ginny might have gotten it from her father. But poor Angela is grateful for Ginny because the other one, Peter, won't even speak to her because The Reverend Moon says he mustn't. So as far as that's concerned, Angela has only one child.

The pilot has just announced that we are approaching Kennedy, and I can see the city spread out below. Certainly there is a special excitement about Manhattan that exists nowhere else in the world. I don't think I would like to live there, because I am now a Californian at heart and much prefer our "laid-back" pace, wonderful weather and easy life-style. To tell the truth, I am just a little nervous about coping with everything I'll have to cope with in the next two hours, just for a start. I must see to my luggage, pick up my rented car and drive to Rivertown and prepare to provide poor Mother with a strong shoulder to lean on. Of course I know I can do all this easily, but the anticipation is always the worst, as I used to tell my children before they had to have a shot.

Now the plane has landed and we are gathering up our things to leave. Fred trails behind me, looking down and clearing his throat. I know that he will dart off the minute we are inside the terminal, and so he does with a brief "Goodbye, nice to talk." Among the mob I feel a little bewildered and so set out to follow the others to the luggage carousels, where I will then have to find a porter. I have brought several pieces of luggage in preparation for what may be a long stay, and if I have forgotten to bring something I don't want to waste time shopping when Mother might need me at her side.

But suddenly my name is called. I hadn't expected her to meet me, but she has anyway—there is Mother right on the other side of the rope. Possibly I mentioned the time of my flight to her—I've forgotten; but anyway, she is here. But the voice is not hers. And oh, what a strange feeling, a plunge into the past, such a combination of fear and excitement which turns into unbearable dread, when I look over to see whom that voice belongs to, and realize who is standing next to her.

CELIA

After I left for Pine Hill we grew more apart than ever. Cassie became the belle of Rivertown High. I became a preppie snot. I would come home at Thanksgiving or Christmas wearing my new identity—an artistic soul forced to live among peons—which only alienated us further. At first, I tagged around after her. She would ask me what I wanted. What a question—I always wanted whatever she had. I wanted her to love me again. But now I had new phrasing. How could she stand this dull town, this oppressive family, those boring boyfriends? Was this all she aspired to? Would this be her life—marriage to the local boy, clothes from the department store downtown, church with Dorothy on Sundays? "Be quiet," she'd say. "Let me alone. Just because you got to go away to school." (It never occurred to me then that she might envy *me*.) I'd try being friendly in the Pine Hill way. "Cassie, would you like to come into my room and talk?" But she didn't—the gap between us, which I interpreted as hatred of me, was simply too wide. "I'm busy. I told Mother I'd take the car down and get gas." The car. She drove and I didn't, and she'd never let me forget it. Sometimes I ignored her, hoping she'd come begging to me, but she never did, and sometimes I was able to really ignore her and live my own life, which was taking place more and more in New York.

I had discovered the city's lights and its shadowy seductions, which were still very innocent. Museums. Old bookshops. The Cherry Lane Theater; the jazz spots of Fifty-second Street; an occasional meal at a cheap French restaurant, Larré's or the Champlain. An occasional party when somebody picked open the lock on the liquor closet. Lots of feeling, fingery sex. Strangely enough, Pine Hill was more closely connected to the city than Rivertown was (Cassie wasn't interested in the city—it was too dirty and dangerous), which had something to do with the vast difference between public and private education. Now a cultural gap separated us as well. Sometimes I tried again. "Cassie, let's talk. Come to the city with me. Let's go on a double date. Bring what's-his-face and come along with me and so-and-so to Jimmy Ryan's tonight."

Once she did come along, she and Stan somebody, me and Pete somebody from Groton. Although I was in black and she in flowered nylon, although her hair was permanented and mine straight, Pete kept saying, "My *God*, you two look alike," and Stan got the jitters for some reason and drank too much beer and went outside and threw up.

"I'm sorry," I kept saying to Cassie, as though this were all my fault.

"It was a terrible idea, Celia. We have simply gotten too different. It's not that I don't respect your life and your values, but they aren't mine and never will be." She'd gotten this funny preachy way of talking.

"I don't expect you to have my goddamn values. I don't even *have* any values. I just thought we could go out together." All this standing in front of Jimmy Ryan's or Bill's Gay Nineties or whatever on Fifty-second Street. Stan was hanging over a car fender; Pete was running up the street trying to hail a taxi. "Why do you take everything so seriously? Can't we even have fun anymore? Why do we have to be enemies?"

"We aren't enemies." She took out Kleenex and dabbed ever so delicately at a spot of Stan's vomit on the nylon ruffle of her dress. "It's just that we've grown apart."

"Cassie, we are sisters. Doesn't that mean anything? Can't we even have a conversation?"

"Of course, Celia. We can have one anytime you like. But I don't think this is a very good one."

"Why not? We're both a little drunk."

She looked me straight in the eye, for the first time in years—the first time since the day I left for Pine Hill. It was almost too much for both of us, and I suddenly understood why perhaps it was better that it hardly ever happened. There on Fifty-second Street I looked into myself, my own soul—into that uncanny mirror which reflected not a hundred images but one so deep and true that it went beyond words or any prospective conversation. I wondered, not for the first time, why this had happened to us, why we weren't like other people. Then Stan retched again, and she said, "Well, Celia, I suppose one of the problems is our places in the family. I feel responsible for Mother, Daddy not being as attentive to her as he might be."

"But she steps all over him—can't you see that?"

Cassie sighed. "I was afraid we wouldn't agree. You see why this isn't a good idea."

"All right, let's try another subject. What are these values you keep talking about?"

"My values have partly to do with my religion and partly with some very personal convictions I've developed in the course of my life. Possibly they sound square and silly to you, which is one reason I'm not anxious to talk about them."

"I won't laugh, I promise."

"All right. Well, for instance, I've resolved never to have sexual relations with a man until I am legally his wife."

I wanted to laugh, she said it so earnestly. But I didn't. Pete was yelling, "Taxi! Hey, cabbie!"

I said, "So what?"

"Well, with your sophisticated life, you probably think such an idea is very small-town and silly."

"But I don't. It's just the way you say it, somehow. It's not silly. Most of the girls at Pine Hill feel the same—"

"Pine Hill!" she screamed suddenly. "Pine Hill! I'm so tired of hearing about your goddamn stupid boarding school! There is no way we can talk to each other anymore—no way at all!'' And she ran over to poor green-faced Stan and began shaking him. "Stan, wake up. I want to go home, do you hear? We can still get the twelve-twenty train. Wake up!''

The task seemed hopeless, and I stood there staring at her, wondering why she had said such a strange thing. Then I realized she must have thought I screwed everybody who came down the track or across the football field. And even if I did, still, so what? Why should she care?

"I don't understand you,'' I said. "Once we knew what went on in each other's heads without a word. Now nothing you say makes sense to me.''

She whirled around. "Don't ever say such a thing again. I never understood you—never. You *thought* you understood me, that's all. But you never really did, and I never understood you *one single bit.*''

As I stood shivering at this one, Pete blessedly came along with a taxi. We got poor Stan inside, and then Cassie and I got in.

"Grand Central,'' Cassie said to the driver.

"Oh, come on, Cass. We're going to the Village,'' said Pete. "Village Vanguard,'' he said to the driver.

"Stan and I are going home,'' said Cassie with an edge to her voice. "This evening has gone far enough.''

"Hey, listen. It's only midnight. You can all stay at my place. My parents are in the Hamptons.'' He was fairly drunk. "There's the couch in the living room and the—''

"Grand Central,'' Cassie repeated.

"How are you going to get him onto the train?'' I asked her. "He doesn't look as though he can walk.''

"He'll walk,'' she said in steely tones, "or else I'll drag him.''

"If you want to go back to Pete's,'' I said, "I promise not to open my mouth about anything for the rest of the night. I promise to be invisible.''

"That's not necessary, Celia. I prefer to get Stan home.''

"Of course, Cassie dear. Whatever you say.''

When the taxi stopped, she tweaked him till he was more or less ambulatory. They got out and went into the station, and that was the end of our double date.

After this, Cassie avoided me even more. It wasn't too

difficult, since we both worked that summer—she in a shoe shop and I as a menial assistant in a law office downtown. Weekends she spent at the movies. Later Dorothy told me that Cassie said I "wouldn't let her alone." True, if letting her alone meant ignoring her. I found it impossible not to talk to Cassie. I thought—I think now—I wasn't malicious, but only curious. If criticisms leaped to my tongue, I swallowed them, though it wasn't easy. I mean the B movies. The Main Street clothes. But I wanted to understand, and worse, I wanted to break her shell. So I suppose I tagged after her a lot. I must have pestered her. But I couldn't bear her cool integrity, her wholeness. How had she gotten like this, and I come out so frayed and wanting?

Then Cassie announced that she was going to Hollywood to be a movie star. I would stay home and go to the State U. The impending changes made Dorothy irritable, and a couple of times I found her crying at her immaculate white kitchen table. When I appeared, she blew her nose and tried to hide her tearfulness.

"Mom, you're crying." I was touched to see that Dorothy had some humanity.

"No, I'm not. I have a little cold."

"Is it because Cassie's leaving?"

"Of course not. She's perfectly able to be on her own. She'll be much better off." She wiped her nose and pushed back her hair. "In fact, I wouldn't be surprised if she were a big success. She's really beautiful."

"Yes. Aren't we?" I said, sitting down and helping myself to some grapes from the bowl of fruit. Dorothy looked faintly surprised. To her we looked different. "I mean, if she's beautiful, so am I."

"Well, I suppose so. But her looks are more feminine somehow. Softer. Yours are more . . . stylish." She groped for the word.

"But we look exactly alike."

"Not to me you don't." She frowned, clearing her throat. "I hear the climate is bad out there. The smog and all."

"Oh, she'll survive." I was dropping grape stems and seeds on the table. "She's tough."

"I suppose that's some kind of *remark* of the kind you're always making. Well, I don't know what it means. I would say Cassie is very *strong* and capable."

"It was supposed to be a compliment, for God's sake."

"Will you please clean up that mess?" She banged her head so hard on the metal tabletop that I jumped. "Can't you do anything without making a mess?"

At times like these I felt as though my blood had turned into an evil, poisonous fluid. "I graduated from a fancy prep school with a B average. I got three prizes—one for art, one for history and one for basketball. I made friends. I was vice president of the Senior Class. I was named for—"

"I know what you got. You did very well. I'm talking about the mess on the table."

"No, you're not, Dorothy. You're talking about me."

"That's ridiculous. You twist things, just as Cassie says. It's impossible to have a normal conversation with you. You have to make trouble. There's something about you, Celia—you see evil everywhere. You always have to have a problem."

"Am I like that?" I asked, surprised.

"You are not a cheerful person, Celia. And you try to impose your peculiarities on others."

"*What* peculiarities?"

"You know perfectly well. Your original ways. In fact, you might as well know that one of the main reasons Cassie is leaving is because of you. You simply can't let her alone. I've noticed it and your father has too."

I don't remember how this particular conversation finished. Probably I tried to make some sense out of whatever she was talking about and ended up either yelling at her or bursting into tears. Possibly I told her she was the one who was driving Cassie out, though I knew it wasn't true. Nor can I really separate this conversation out from many others, all similar, we had over the years. It didn't matter. I'd always be the one who dropped the grapes.

We all took Cassie to the bus station. She looked touching somehow, in her neat little suit and hat, her church clothes. She had a steamer trunk they put in the back, as though she were going off to camp. She looked scared, too. I wanted to put my arms around her; but as far as I was concerned she was surrounded by an icy wall. Or maybe by that time she'd actually convinced herself I didn't exist and didn't even see me. But tears gathered in my eyes anyway; I suffered again, though not as badly, as I had when I had left for Pine Hill. And this time alone. We all stood around in the bus station. It was hot, and Caspar bought everybody an ice cream cone. His seersucker jacket was damp across his back, and he had some chocolate stuck between two teeth. He said,

"Aw, you're awful young to be doing this, sweetheart."

"I'll be fine, Daddy." Her voice was thin and shaky.

"Now, the minute you decide to come home, you telephone collect, and I'll send you a bus ticket."

"I won't come home," Cassie said, "until I have something to be proud of."

"I'm proud of you, dear," Dorothy sniffled. Her thick brown hair, with a few gray streaks, was damp with the heat. She was eating a strawberry cone. "Oh, this is so sad. It's like the end of your childhood."

Well, finally she left, her little white face framed by the bus window. She looked so young. I looked so young. We were eighteen. I wept shamelessly. Another Rivertown family stopped by and said, "Well, they all have to leave the nest. I'll miss seeing the twins.

The twins—nobody had called us that for years. How completely it had gone.

Edith says I have "an obsession to be specifically perceived." Now, that alone is worth $241.95—a fancy explanation of why I pick on Dorothy.

I'd periodically go home from the State University and deposit my successes at the feet of Dorothy and Caspar—high marks, a painting in the college exhibition hall, a particularly suitable and appetizing male, whatever I had worked hard for. When that didn't get a response—or rather, anything near the response I wanted—I tried getting into trouble. I flunked a couple of courses and managed to be caught drunk at the wrong time and place, which brought a phone call from the Dean, and I was put on probation. Said Dorothy: "Well, I hope you don't do *that* again, Celia. Honestly. You're smarter than that."

"Do you really think I'm smart?" I asked.

"Certainly you are."

"Smarter than Cassie?"

"Of course not. You are both . . . exactly . . . the . . . same. As you are so fond of telling me."

"I take it back. We aren't. I'm smarter."

We were sitting as usual at the kitchen table, drinking coffee. "I've never understood why you *care* so much whether you're better or worse than her. She doesn't care anything about you. Why, Celia, can't you simply live your life?"

"Mom, tell me about when you were my age." A fast change of subject, like Novocain.

"At your age I was engaged to your father."

"Were you happy? Were you in love?"

"Well, naturally." It was warm in the kitchen, and she gently patted her upper lip with a paper napkin. "We got along well. We had many things in common."

"Did you sleep together?" I hadn't really meant to ask it: it just happened. She drew herself up.

"I can't imagine why you ask that. Things were entirely different then. Marriage was still a sacred institution, and as far as your father and I were concerned, it still is. It was still considered a fulfilling career for women. . . . No, we did not sleep together."

"Why do you get so angry? I'm a woman. Don't mothers and daughters talk about these things?"

"There are some things that are meant to be private."

"Well, maybe they shouldn't be."

"Celia, please don't try to provoke me. It's too hot and I don't feel like arguing." She looked a little frayed, unusual for Dorothy. "I'm a little out of sorts, anyway. And your father has been working too hard. I'm going to try to persuade him to take a little vacation in the Adirondacks."

"Mom, do you and Daddy really talk about things?"

"How could we have gotten through twenty-three years of marriage without talking? Of course we do. Of course . . ." She appeared to soften a little. "Sometimes we disagree. That's perfectly natural in a marriage. Sometimes I find your father a little . . . remote. I suppose that's the word. He's sitting there in the chair, but really I wonder where he is. And so I feel I have to carry all the responsibility. Not that he isn't a good husband,'' she added hastily. "He's always supported his family. He's very loving to his children, as you know. But sometimes . . . Lord, it's hot. I think I'll just make a salad for supper. Potato salad and some of the sliced ham.''

It was the September before my senior year, and I still thought it was possible to understand men. "Mom, forget the supper. Go on about Daddy.''

"I'll just put the potatoes on.'' She pushed back some stray strands of hair and began peeling the potatoes. "I suppose every once in a while I feel his life is not centered around his family.''

"Maybe it's centered around the shop.''

"Well, it shouldn't be.'' She sighed. "Now you've started me thinking about the old days. You know your father spent the whole war trying to enlist and they wouldn't take him because of his eyes. Finally he got a desk job in Washington, and that was when we lived there for two years. I thought we were lucky, but he wanted to shoot Nazis and Japs. He dreamed about being a tail gunner or a bombardier. Just what he could never possibly be.'' She looked over at me. "I swear I don't understand why men want to do such things. Why they aren't satisfied at home.''

"What was Washington like during the war?''

"Oh . . . it was exciting. Of course, you and Cassie were just babies. We had an apartment on P Street we were lucky to get. We knew so many interesting people, and everybody wanted to talk about the war. And of course, the town was full of rumors, and Caspar would hear things at the War Department where he worked. He'd come home every day with the evening papers and tell me whatever had happened that day. And I wasn't so confined as I was when we moved back here after the war. We had a black girl, Beulah, and she was wonderful and not snippy like some of the help I had later. She cooked and cleaned and took you two to the park every day. It wasn't like here, where all the women stayed home and took care of their houses. Because during the war everybody did something. If you didn't, you were considered unpatriotic. I worked for the Red Cross. I drove a car for them, and sometimes I picked up important generals at Washington Airport and took them to the Pentagon. Oh, how I knew my way around that town. I could find any single place in the District that anybody wanted to go to.'' She put the pot on, and her eyes were bright. ''And everybody was so proud of the country. It wasn't like it is now, when there doesn't seem to be much patriotism in the young. It's a shame, Cassie, for patriotism is a fine thing.''

''I'll pretend I didn't hear that,'' I said.

''What did you say?''

''Never mind.'' She had never made that mistake before, and I put it down to her unusual mood.

''Well, I guess that's about all. I suppose it sounds strange that I enjoyed so much such a time of trial for our country. But there was something in the air—that's what it was. The excitement. Almost every night there were people at our apartment, and I'd make chili or spaghetti or something, and we'd talk half the night. Or sometimes we'd go out to one of the bars, and there were always people around telling the latest stories and rumors. There was always a radio going. And there was respect for our leaders, too. We always said ''Mr. Roosevelt'' and ''Mr. Churchill.'' We knew all the military brass, or we knew them by sight. They were like our friends, or the heroes who were going to save us. And when Roosevelt died, I cried, Celia. I saw that headline on a newspaper on the street and I burst into tears right there. I didn't think we could go on without him.''

I had never heard Dorothy talk so much, nor had she ever, in my memory, looked so beautiful. Her eyes glowed, her cheeks were flushed. ''Did Dad like it too?''

''Oh, he loved it. Even though he was always complaining about how they wouldn't let him bomb the Krauts. He used to laugh so much—his big, hearty laugh you don't hear much anymore. And we were happy together, too. Very much in love.'' Her eyes dropped. ''There was an atmosphere . . . I don't know. You never knew what was going to happen. We had air-raid drills all the time, and

Caspar was a warden. Of course it would have been Washington and New York they hit, we knew that. And because there was danger, I think people held more tightly to each other. Some even had . . . affairs. And friends just looked the other way. If a man was going overseas, he and his fiancée were forgiven for not waiting. And it was the same for your father and me. It probably sounds silly now, but each embrace might have been the last.''

How I loved Dorothy for telling me all this, and how careful I was not to let her know she had given me a treasure. But when Caspar walked in a little while later, saying, "What are you girls talking about?" I said, "Mom has been telling me about Washington during the war."

"Oh, that. Oh, boy. Shortages, rationing, blackouts. You couldn't get on a train, and if you did you could be bumped anywhere along the line. Everything was scarce or inconvenient. And they wouldn't let your old Daddy see any action, just stuck me in a desk job somewhere in the Pentagon. Not much of a job, either. I was glad when those years were over."

After graduation, I went to Europe with my friend and lover, Jerry Fogelquist. Jerry was as poor and as deluded as I was. A journalism major at State U., he and I were going off to seek culture together, to put behind us the confinements of our middle-class backgrounds. By the most agonizing scrimping, we had managed to save up passage money and very little more, and counted on finding jobs when we got there.

We spent most of the trip over (on a decrepit old freighter called the *Marine Splasher*, or *Thrasher*, or something) fucking. It was probably just as well, for it distracted us from the bad food, the cramped and dirty quarters, the perpetual pitch and roll that had most of the other passengers violently seasick. During the fifteen days of our crossing, the food went from barely edible to actively revolting; the water ran out (fortunately, only a day before we landed); the toilets backed up; the Captain, who had been a quiet drunk in the beginning, became noisier and noisier, finally verging on dangerous incompetence, and mutiny threatened; a mysterious redheaded woman traveling alone went mad and paced up and down the deck raving about invasions of Martians, who, she said, were poisoning us all with lethal gases from the engines; and the ship's doctor, who supplied everybody with marijuana, was discovered to be, and subsequently arrested for being, part of an international drug ring.

For all the impression any of this made on Jerry or me, we need never have left Newark. Now, years later, I am horrified at what seems to me a terrible waste and stupidity—not only for myself but for Jerry, the budding journalist. Not often, I have found, does life deposit before one's eyes such a rich handful of human experience, and certainly never in my provincial life had so many crazies paraded before me in such a small space. We noticed but we did not really see, and only months later did I really grasp the import of what had been going on.

We traveled around some and then settled in Rome in a sleazy room in the Trastevere quarter. Our dreams died quickly—Jerry's of being immediately hired by the Rome *Daily American,* and mine of studying with a Famous Painter who turned out to be dead. We were, in fact, lucky to get jobs at all, his at a pasta factory and mine as waitress at a place called the "Arizona Bar," and what had been planned as a long, leisurely cultural wallow turned into a struggle to survive and, even harder, to get along with each other, for we were closed into a domestic situation that had no love to sweeten it. It wasn't good enough, in that hot little room with the magenta wallpaper, that Jerry was my so-called "best friend," particularly after he started fucking a German girl we'd met at a café. As I peeled away his feeble lies and excuses, I watched myself turn into a jealous monster—helplessly, with neither the urge nor the ability to stop myself. And though Jerry seemed quite able to juggle two women and art at the same time, the black clouds behind my eyes blotted out Michelangelo, St. Peter's, the Borghese Gardens—this place I might never see again.

Jerry and I finally terminated our arrangement, and I took up with a handsome advertising man from Milan I'd picked up at Doney's. He soon tired of me, for so arrogant was I, or so unrealistic, that I'd hardly taken the trouble to learn Italian beyond a restaurant and store vocabulary, and it wasn't long till he lost interest in my talk about art and my pretenses of ambition. But before he left, he bought me a camera—probably out of guilt, for he was married and the father of several *bambini*.

"You try this, *cara*," he said one day in the Via Sistina, where he had bought me my Nikon. "Forget about painting. Take real pictures. You'll make a fortune."

After Giorgio, I took my camera and my knapsack and went home to face my life.

Richard, as has been said before, was different.

His hair, for one thing. No human male I had ever seen had such hair—dark, dark brown, and fine, and plentiful, almost like fur. He cut it about three inches long all over, and it blew around in bright dark swirls. He didn't put any goo on it, nor did he spray, and it looked soft and shiny. I longed to touch it and loved it when I finally did.

Then his voice, soft, almost musical. Gentle, no rough edges. Classy. Insinuatingly sexy. None of this "Hey, babe" stuff. When he called me by my name, it was like a stroke of his hand.

And his neck. A lot of men have short red necks that bulge out over their collars, and some have long white chicken ones. Richard's was a honey-colored column whose cords rippled subtly under the skin when he turned his head, which he had a way of doing ever so slowly, with a sort of incredulity.

His nose, stolen in the night from some Greek statue. The line of his jaw. His topaz eyes, sometimes almost golden, with their dark lashes.

Lest anyone think I am still in love with Richard, let me say that if the bastard walked in here tomorrow, I'd call the police. Never have I trusted anyone less—I'd feel safer at 3 A.M. in the subway with three ethnic adolescents swinging chains at me. But Richard jammed my airwaves, stalled me back in that marriage in a way I don't quite understand. I persist in regarding him as my destiny, the great unsolved puzzle of my life.

Appropriately enough, I first saw him on the courthouse steps, where I was assisting a famous fashion photographer in taking pictures of models in black robes that might, if you were of that turn of mind, suggest the robes of Supreme Court Justices. (In *Vogue*, the caption for the picture was "He'll Judge You Right.") The black robes were silk evening cloaks and capes that retailed at two thousand dollars. I held the fan that made them flap around on that hot, still August day, the sky a blistered blue, my head full of vague depressing thoughts about compromise and commercialism, artistic integrity and lost ideals. I was full of the self-loathing of idealists who discover how successfully money can sweeten compromise; for there was the most profound comfort, right through to my soul, at being able to pay the rent and feed myself, and I hated myself for even caring.

Richard had long since decided that without money he could not express himself and be powerful, so he had no conflict about the dough he was making. He believed, correctly, that he could push people around more successfully in an elegant three-piece Italian suit than in an ill-fitting bag from some discount store. So Richard that day, as always, was custom-cut, confident, dazzling as he came down the marble steps with a couple of colleagues. Our eyes met, and his skittered away—I couldn't match him, not with old shorts and a T-shirt, even with my pretty hair and cute knees. As he went by, I could smell Knize Ten. I saw those shadowed hollows in his cheeks, his small, well-cut ears, the honey column, and marveled. A perfect male. Perfect, perfect.

The famous fashion photographer got him and his chums in some of the pictures. Wanted to use them. The young counselors objected. There was a lot of silly brouhaha, during which Richard and I kept running into each other. Then one day we had a drink at a bar downstairs from the lawyers' offices, one of those pitch-dark holes so beloved of the Wall Street Establishment.

"I don't see why not," I said. "You look wonderful in the pictures."

Richard smiled—I think; I could hardly see him—and said, "Celia. You look wonderful too, but that's not the point."

"What's the point?"

"It's not appropriate for my young barrister's image."

"But you're very handsome. You must have been told that before."

"Bless your little heart. But I don't want to be in *Vogue*."

At first I thought it was the money—they would give in when the famous photographer met their price. But though the other two buckled, Richard didn't. He meant it. So I thought, Oh, he has standards. He can't be bought. How wonderful and admirable.

Richard and I started to see each other—slowly. In retrospect, I don't think he was especially impressed by me at first, but he was disarmed by my admiration. I mean how could he not be? But when we met, his eyes would flicker over me in a way that was not entirely approving. A thoughtful little smile: Now, what can we do with this? I found myself looking more and more often into the mirror. However I'd been looking wasn't good enough. I'd been hanging around too long with the blue jeans crowd, and I'd picked up the look that was coming in at the time— long straight hair, no makeup, granny gowns, sandals; a lost flower child. Now I strove to improve.

"Oh, Celia. That's beautiful. Turn around. Perfect. The way it falls over the seat, I love it. Don't sit down." He'd marched around me in a circle. "Your behind is a work of art."

"But the dress. Do you like it?"

"I love it." Then the thoughtful look again, and he'd push back a strand of hair. "How about this—just up a little? Out of your face."

I'd watch his eyes and try to see myself through them. They were, most of the time, opaque, almost like golden coins; I found myself trying to see into them, or rather, make them see me—really see me.

"You aren't looking at me, Richard. You're miles away."

"I'm not, my dear girl. I'm right here."

"I know, but you aren't seeing me."

His tawny eyes aimed at me. "Celia Armstrong. Ravishing female, brilliant photographer. Five foot whatever. Silken hair, sea-green eyes. A body that drives men wild. A red dress brand-new from Bloomingdale's. What the hell am I supposed to see that I don't? Come here, *Liebchen*." But the eyes were golden velvet, and I wanted them to be deep, amber pools that I could see to the bottom of.

People said we made a stunning couple. I'd catch a glimpse of us in mirrors from the street or in restaurants, and catch Richard's eye looking too. We'd both smile. He was perfect already, and I was working on it.

It took more time than I expected. I went to the hairdresser every week and spent a lot of time shopping, and when I wasn't actually shopping, I was thinking about what sort of blouse I should get to go with a certain skirt, or peering into the windows of shoe shops. Or, if maybe that jacket would look right with the new black dress. And things like fingernails. Early on, Richard picked up my hands from where they rested on the table. "Good hardworking hands," he said with that thoughtful expression. Which I, correctly or not, interpreted as a criticism, and so started having manicures. I learned about makeup and spent half an hour in the bathroom every morning carefully applying foundation; eye liner and shadow from my little pots; lip liner; mascara.

I had lived with Helen Koch, a placid, good-natured singer, on Thompson Street for two years, having lost a previous roommate to matrimony. Together we'd been broke and lonely, broken bread and shared wine, grappled with all aspects of the human condition. We'd gone to a few peace marches and protest meetings, for the times were humming loud in our ears—louder in Helen's, for I was not very political, but even such as I could not ignore the sounds of the sixties. Now Helen watched me struggle into panty hose and put my feet into high-heeled pumps.

"You're getting so Uptown," she said.

"Well, that's where my heart lies."

"But Celia, it seems so irrelevant. Particularly after Selma and Watts."

I was teasing my hair into its new bubble shape. "My feelings aren't irrelevant."

"Oh, I don't mean that. I mean *this*." She gestured at my bureau top covered with its array of cosmetics. "Does he want you to be different than you are?"

"Not different. My *best*." I was not crazy about this conversation. I didn't really know whether Richard was nudging me into this new image or whether I was doing it myself. At the time I saw it simply as similar values, a beautiful agreement-by-two about how I should look.

"But Celia, you know what I mean. Richard is very Establishment and you aren't. It could be dangerous."

"But I honestly don't know what I am. Even at twenty-five. I don't have your integrity. I'm still in search of a self. Anyway, I'm not sure Richard's so Establishment. He's doing some civil rights cases."

The truth was I didn't know *what* Richard was, which was one of the reasons he fascinated me. I was tired of the earnest pot-smoking young men whom Helen and I hung around with, as well as the driven crazies of the world of photography who had so far remained blind to my talent. And I was getting a little world-weary—life was proving to be more difficult than otherwise, and a lot of the glitter was off Manhattan. Cynical explanations rose easily to my lips—so-and-so was gay, your typical just-out-of-the-closet type. Somebody else was just another psych major still being supported by parents. There was nothing new under the sun—in fact, I was talking like any other twenty-five-year-old who has not yet found her man. But Richard was a puzzle, elusive as quicksilver—first one thing, then another: unpredictable, given to mysterious moods that flitted inexplicably across his landscape. Marrying him—for he began to talk of this after a few months—would never be dull as my parents' marriage was. I would spend the rest of my life solving his mysteries.

I didn't really know what he wanted with me. Since I believed him perfect, I thought he could have had anyone. Why not someone more beautiful, richer, more charming, more successful? Why not a ravishing *contessa,* a movie star or at least an heiress? A female executive or brilliant research scientist? For I knew I was unspectacular, a bright and pretty young woman in a town that overflowed with them.

"You're the most interesting woman *I've* ever met," he said, which I took for an answer. "Besides, there's something about you, Cece. I don't know what. Maybe it has something to do with your being a twin. I feel we can cross over into each other. I feel you understand me so well I don't have to explain things. We can be closer than any other two people in the world.''

If I had put this down to the excesses of pillow talk, which it was, I would have been a saint. We were at his apartment. He lay on his back in splendid nakedness. I traced his outlines with my fingertip—over the chest, down the ribs, a dip into the smooth hollow below, up onto the hipbone, down the thigh—with a slight detour over *there*. This perfect creature was mine.

He loved to be photographed—which I did constantly, often in the nude. Sometimes in sunlight, sometimes in the dark—just the barest outline of light tracing his body. Sometimes I did time exposures of the two of us together. Some of them were good.

"Maybe I'll make my fortune from these."

His eyes deepened. "Please don't ever use these commercially, Cece. For God's sake. I'd be thrown out of court.''

He had a point, but I persisted. "Maybe just the ones where you're unrecognizable. Look, this could be anybody."

"*None* of them. Suppose the prosecuting attorney got hold of them? Exhibit A, nude photos of the attorney for the defense. 'Your Honor, I move for a mistrial.' '' I still didn't smile. "These are for us and nobody else. They're like acts of love in themselves.''

So I put them away—I still have them—and swallowed down the lump of anger. How silly I was being. Weren't they more important as acts of love? Weren't *we* the most important, and wasn't life—or my life at present, anyway—more interesting than art?

"All right, Richard. For your eyes only. But now I'm longing to do more male body photography. Maybe I'll—''

"You will not," Richard said.

"What?''

"You will not close yourself up in a room with a naked man, other than me, and take pictures of him.''

"Why?'' I was astonished.

"Because I'd probably kill him.''

"Oh, Richard. Now, honestly.''

"Well, of course I can't stop you, Celia. You have to do what you have to do. But I'd be very, very angry, I promise you."

He was jealous. I leaned over and kissed him gently. "How, Richard? With your bare hands?"

"I don't know. But you're right to want to know, because I might kill you too."

He really loves me, I thought.

We had a small, stylish city wedding, with a strange assortment of guests. My Village/Hippie/Fem/Radical friends, a few (mostly gay) photographers and Richard's cronies, who were all sort of like Richard, handsome and somehow puzzling. Most had wives, grandly got-up women who made me feel hopeless. Caspar and Dorothy looking more provincial than ever, along with a few relatives. Lydia Sterner pulled together and propped up for the occasion—how much I didn't know till later. At the time, I thought she looked elegant, an older wife-of-Richard's-friends. She had been cool to me before, but now, since I was apparently inevitable, she sighed and seemed to accept me. She and Dorothy, predictably, loathed each other. Everyone remarked on Cassie's absence, though she had sent a telegram, or her husband had. It said: "OUR VERY BEST WISHES ON THIS HAPPY OCCASION. LOVE CASSIE AND SAM COOPERSMITH."

Said Richard as we danced:

"Our lives are going to be perfect, Celia. We're going to be the kind of people everybody else looks at and envies. We'll show them what style is. No compromises for us."

And later:

"The trouble with most people is that they give up their dreams too easily. Dreams are the only thing that separate us from the animals, and I will always fight for mine."

Richard's dreams, which I had listened to idly and indulgently, were specific and detailed. When we exchanged fantasies—a favorite game of his, and one that occupied a lot of our conversation—I dropped out after the first lap. I saw the future as a gauzy extension of our present life, with a child or two added. We would work. We would be closer than any other two people on earth. We would live elegantly. We would travel and have fun. But Richard had furnished the apartment, named the children (Ian and Jessica), planned the trips and ordered the meals. He dressed us and put us on stage: Me, of a winter's eve, rushing home from my darkroom to put dinner on, looking cute in a fur coat; him coming along a little later, picking up the wine and the flowers, coming in to delicious smells just in time to wash up before the guests arrived. Us dashing off to the theater with friends. Me at Bloomingdale's choosing fabric for slipcovers. Him carving the roast at Christmas. Me nursing Ian and Jessica. Us going off to the country for the summer . . . Connecticut or Fire Island, he hadn't decided. Us in bed drinking champagne. Us consumed by passion, making love in the john at somebody's dinner party. Us in Menton at a *pension* he knew, in Rapallo eating dinner at a certain restaurant overlooking the sea, in Paris at the George V. Us on the China Wall, strolling up the Ginza, sipping pink gins in Bombay, dancing the hora in Jerusalem, playing tag with antelope in Kenya, scuba-diving in Barbados, skiing at St. Moritz . . .

Us in Scotland.

Scotland, for reasons I have yet to understand, was Richard's spiritual home. He had been there once and had never forgotten it. He had fallen in love with the salmon leaping in the streams, the shepherds and their sheep, those brown moors covered with gorse, or else peat, or is it heather? The Loch Ness monster. He would wring his brain to figure out some way that we could spend a year there—maybe he could teach at the law school of the University of Edinburgh and we could live in a wonderful thatched-roof cottage in the highlands, cuddling together by our peat fire. And outside the wild emptiness, the windswept moors, those dumb fluffy white animals looking toward the sea. A metaphor of life (How? Beats me). He could actually see retiring to such a place and living out the rest of his life as a sheep farmer, and it might be something we should think about . . . though the expression of alarm on my face blew that one away for a while.

Richard had some Scottish blood from somewhere, all mixed up with the Irish, French, Russian and Jewish, and was a direct descendant and legal member of the Clan MacDougal. He even had a kilt, which I didn't know till

after we were married. Then one evening he got out his
treasure and showed it to me, carefully removing it from
the tissue paper. He was apologetic about it. Probably it
was a little crazy—he didn't really have that much Scottish
blood at all; but he hadn't been able to resist it. Did he
ever wear it? Well . . . He looked down.

"Cece, I have a guilty secret. I suppose I should have
told you before."

My heart lurched into my mouth. "What is it?"

"Sometimes I go to the Clan dances in Queens."

It seemed that twice a year the MacDougals met somewhere in Queens and played their bagpipes and did the
Highland Fling. Richard had gone twice and would go
again if it was all right with me. I could go along if I liked;
in fact, he'd like it if I did. But since I wasn't a MacDougal,
I couldn't join in the activities. He would be *very unhappy*
if I ever told anybody about this. The other MacDougals
were sworn to silence, and if they told they'd get piped out
of the corps or something. He thought his friends and
colleagues would think it strange. I said people did a lot
stranger things in this town than dancing to the bagpipes in
Queens (thought at that moment I couldn't think what), but
if it was really important to him I'd never mention it to
anybody. He said it was proof of his love that he'd told me
at all, and besides, I might find the whole rig in the closet
boxes I had indeed wondered about—because not only had
he a kilt, but a jacket and hat and stockings and "flashes"
and a horsehair sporran and everything.

Richard stood there in the middle of our white-on-white
living room looking at me and I actually felt him *will* my
next words: "Richard, please put it all on for me." He
gave me that long, slow smile of his and retired to the
bedroom. In a few minutes he reappeared in full regalia—it
was Bonnie Prince Charlie before me. Slowly he turned
around for my inspection: black velvet jacket, pleated
tartan, knee socks. A tam-o'shanter, a misty expression.
He did look magnificent. He walked around the room in a
slow circle, humming one of those Scottish tunes—"Ta-
Dum! Ta-DUM! Ta-Dum Dum Dum!" Then he did a little
dance, a sort of heel-toe business. At just the moment I

thought he had entirely taken leave of his senses, he laughed.

"Celia, don't look at me like that. It's just a game I play with myself. I'm a mongrel who longs for pure blood. And don't tell me you don't have any little secrets. Everybody does."

"Well, of course they do."

"You owe me one," he said.

"My God, Richard. You know everything about me." But I thought hard. "Let's see. Okay. There are three hairs growing out of my chin that I always have to pull out with a tweezer."

"Oh, darling." He pulled me to him and kissed me, holding me against the black velvet jacket.

"I've never told that to anybody in my life."

"I'm very touched."

"But it's terrible!"

"No, it isn't." He kissed me. "Don't you want to know what people always want to know about Scotsmen?"

"What's that?"

"Whether they wear anything underneath their kilts." He took my hand and slowly guided it up under the skirt. There was no underwear, only Richard's penis—not only erect, but engorged and pulsating.

"How did you get like this?" I asked.

"From you, foolish girl. This is what you do to me."

"If I did this to you every time we had an ordinary conversation, we'd never work or eat or sleep or anything."

"Cece, take off your pants."

"Okay. Done. To bed?"

"No, darling. Right here. Right now. Come here—I'm going to pick you up. Like this. Hold on around my neck." He began to walk slowly around the room again. "Ta-Dum! Ta-Dum!" It was quite an accomplishment— singing, fucking and being a MacDougal all at once. And we almost got all the way around the room, almost, until my spasms knocked him off balance and we both kind of keeled over onto the couch, coming together with cries like the sound of bagpipes.

(I never told anybody about Richard's Scottish seizures

until during our divorce, when I trotted it out for my lawyer, who said, "The judge wouldn't be interested.")

The day after this curious scene, I was worried that Richard's Scottishness would come bursting all over our marriage like the pus from some terrible blister. But to my relief, it remained quite contained. Twice a year he went a-dancing in Queens. Usually he came home turned on, which was fine with me. The difficulties were more diffuse, so shaded and hidden that I didn't recognize them as difficulties. Well, of course, because if I had, I might have realized I was unhappy. Which I didn't.

Ever so subtly, Richard nudged us toward his dreams, which seemed self-propagating and insatiable. We had the fancy apartment on the East Side where he wanted it, the decor, the maid, the intimate little parties. I had my darkroom, and I rushed home in my fur coat on winter evenings. We traveled to the places he wanted and stayed at the hotels he chose. We ordered the meals he had always dreamed about. Our life, in fact, was modeled on what was in Richard's head, and if I tried to steer us in some other direction, he either refused to go or sulked. He approved of my photography, but not if it took one moment away from him or our home. After dinner (the maid left at four), I washed the dishes and Richard sat down to read. Though I earned my own money and we pooled what we made, he expected me to ask his permission to spend it. After we started trying to have Ian or Jessica and nothing happened, we both assumed from the start that it was my eggs that were no good, not his faultless sperm.

In a thousand tiny ways our marriage could have been a case history in the feminist literature of the decade, full of those little clicks and pings that ring in the downtrodden female consciousness. And indeed I read the books and went to a few rap groups, rushing home through the night drunk on revelation: I was not alone; my sisters knew it too. And though it was true that though Richard's and my consciousnesses were unexamined, that we both had rigid ideas about the roles of wife and husband that we had gotten from our parents, that I began clamoring for equality and he was unwilling to listen, and it was all this which explained to me, and eventually to the lawyers, what was wrong with my marriage, and that for years it was what I believed . . . I know now that there was something else going on that bit far deeper, a terrible disappointment for both of us in the marriage that neither of us understood. And that was about *distance*.

I wanted, for instance, to sleep all tangled up with Richard, limbs intertwined. I wanted, when I woke up in the middle of the night, to be able to easily reach out and touch his hair or press my lips into his beautiful brown back. I even wanted to sleep with his cock in my mouth, or at least go to sleep that way before it fell out. I wanted to open my eyes and see some part of Richard, any part, before I saw anything else. And indeed, so we had done before that fall ceremony, marriage; but slowly it evolved —or not really so slowly—that Richard preferred to sleep alone, remote, still as a corpse, untouched by human hands. It turned out, in fact, that when I touched him during his sleep, he woke up as though he'd been shot, glared at me and went to sleep again, while I lay alone and forlorn. Then in the morning he said he didn't remember, but "It's true, Cece, I prefer to sleep alone and untangled. It's just habit; I can't help it."

I would have loved to go shopping with Richard. I was deeply touched by old couples in supermarkets, comparing melons and discussing their dinner. But Richard hated supermarkets, didn't enjoy dithering over the price of beans or eggs and was bored by the whole idea. It wasn't, he said, that he was trying to make me do something I hated—I should just order from Gristede's. As for cooking, well, he was just terrible in the kitchen, except for his spaghetti sauce and his special tossed green salad. If I got tired of preparing meals I should just pick up dinner at one of those take-home food places, or else we'd go out more. "But Richard, you don't see my point. The idea is to do it together." "My God," Richard said, "we live together, don't we? Won't that do, ma bonnie lass?"

I wanted us to be as close as he had said we would be—to have one of us reach for the phone to call just as it rang, and to hear the other one say, "I was just thinking about you." I wanted him to call, just before I left the house, and say, "Don't forget your raincoat." I wanted us to say the same thing at the same time and laugh. I wanted to catch his eye at a party when somebody said something ridiculous and know he was hiding laughter as I was. And sometimes I thought he was, but afterward when I said, "Wasn't that an idiotic idea of Bill's?" he'd say, "What idea?" And I'd feel alone and disappointed.

I wanted us to agree on everything, which I now know was unreasonable—on where we went and what we did. And since this was more important to me, really, than my feminist consciousness, I thought I could achieve the closeness I wanted by always going along with Richard even if I disagreed. If he wanted Fire Island it would be Fire Island, or the Savoy, or veal scallopini, or a yellow dress. But this didn't work, because then Richard began complaining that I was a wimp. I used to have opinions, he said; they were what had made me interesting. What had happened to them? Anyway, he needed "space." People needed different amounts, and obviously he needed more than I did. In fact, sometimes he felt as though I were smothering him. The last thing he had thought I'd turn into was a clinger.

I tried to back off and regain my dwindling identity by putting more effort into my work. But then *he* felt rejected. He did not, it turned out, really like Stouffer's frozen dinners, and he didn't really like going out to restaurants every night. He loved our apartment and liked to spend time in it. Was it so difficult to pick up a steak on the way home? Was it so much trouble to make those nice *au gratin* potatoes he liked, even if they were a little extra work? To him such efforts were expressions of love, and if he came home to a messy apartment and TV dinners, it meant I didn't care. Anyway, maybe he was a male-chauvinist pig, but wives were supposed to, and so on. After all, he was earning all this money to support us in the style in which we lived. And by the way, Cece, I know you don't dress up when you go out on shoots, but honestly, when we met in the lobby this evening coming home, you looked like something out of Dogpatch. Would it violate your artistic integrity to comb your hair and wear a clean shirt? Those people from the tenth floor, the ones who are giving me such grief on the co-op board, were looking at you as though you had just crept out of a drain.

"Take me shopping," I'd say with the desperation of the obsessed.

"Celia, I *hate* shopping with women. I can't stand it. Go by yourself. Buy anything you want. I mean it. Just don't make me go along."

It was a sort of Catch-22. I should keep my distance, but do what he wanted. We should be together but separate, and I should be interesting yet the embodiment of Richard's fantasies.

The project of trying to start Ian and Jessica diverted us from the puzzle of our marriage for some years. Like many deluded couples, we really thought a baby would solve our problems, though if anybody had asked me what our problems actually were, I couldn't have said. (Was it really so bad that Richard hated me to use his toothbrush, would not give me a bite from his fork?) To begin with, Richard wanted to conceive him or her, of course, in Scotland. So while Richard went out looking for Mac-Dougals, I crept around the dreary streets of Edinburgh, damp, cold and bored. While Richard ran around the firths or heaths or whatever they are looking at those dumb, fluffy white metaphors, I drank beer at the local. While Richard fished for salmon in the lochs and streams, I sat under a tree with a book, wrapped in sweaters.

He had, of course, brought his whole Highland costume and was dying to join the local MacDougals. But when he found them, after days and days of searching, they seriously questioned his credentials. What was acceptable in Queens didn't go here on the bonnie braes. It had to be direct male line, see, and look at the French grandfather and the Irish uncle and the Jewish cousin—for of course, Richard had brought his family tree too. It was just too polyglot. I was with Richard when he finally got the pronouncement from the head MacDougal, or whatever he was, who looked as though he thought Richard was crazy. While I imagined reaching up under the kilt, Richard looked stunned with disappointment. O' course, Mr. Sterner, ye doo wat ye will in Queens. But nivver here wi' the original Clan. An' by the way, the tartan is noo correct.

With life's illusions falling around us like rain, we fucked at all the designated times, arranging our lives around my menstrual cycle as though in its mystic circle lay salvation. And so perhaps it did, but not of the sort that we were ever to know. Nothing happened for months, and then years. I cried into my pillow at night for the baby I was afraid I would never have. Richard sighed over my bad eggs, was forbearing, patient, alternately hopeful and desperate. Sometimes he grew solicitous, calling Lydia over to take care of me—Lydia who only minimally took care of herself.

"Celia you don't eat enough meat. And I've always heard artichokes, one a day. They create a welcoming environment for conception." Sip—slurp. "How wonderful for Richard this will be. You know how important it is for him to carry on the family lines. Every time I think of that Scotch bastard I get forious. He must be an impostor. Our descent is pure, I know it."

"He said it was anything but pure, Lydia."

"Well, he was wrong." Clouds of smoke. We were sitting in the white-on-white living room. "Mother was always very specific about the MacDougals. She kept track of things like that. Sometimes she made haggis."

"Please don't make me eat *that*."

"Cece, after you and Richard make love, do you immediately lie with your feet up?"

"Of course."

"God. If I could only give you some of my fertility. I mean the fertility I once had." A curtain of smoke. "I started Richard the very first try. I had never been late in my life, so when that day passed and there was no blood, I *knew*. And do you know what That Prick said?"

"No."

"He said it was nerves. Can you imagine? His own flesh and blood, he wouldn't recognize."

"Was he really so bad, Lydia?"

"Well, of course not. I wouldn't have married him if he was."

Abandon logic, all ye who enter this family. Or abandon the ordinary kind. Lydia went in strange spirals of free association, while Richard was able to grasp multiple conflicting concepts with no trouble at all. And I, what was I doing? Pretending it all made sense. By then I'd stopped trying to figure anything out, I'd just handed responsibility over to my body. It was the perfect cop-out. But not really so perfect, because I really wanted a baby very badly, and nothing seemed to work.

"Are you sure your temperature is up?"

"Yes, Richard. You can look yourself."

"You aren't looking at it right. Hold it in the light. Maybe you've misread it before."

"I'm sure I haven't."

Then one month I was late. Incredible excitement. It makes me sad to think now of the dinner at Barbetta's, the bottle of champagne we took to bed afterward. Richard swelled with the importance of coming fatherhood. I preened over the holy vessel that was my body, with its new tenant. We were loving but careful, and we slept entwined.

Then it all bled away, and I picked the biggest gobbet of blood out of the toilet, as directed by the doctor, and put it into a jar of alcohol to take to him. In the jar it emerged—a little purple sea horse.

Then the whole thing happened again. The second time I decided not to tell Richard until I was sure, which was a mistake.

"What are you holding?" He had a new manner now—tense, abrupt, suspicious.

"Just a paper bag."

"What's in it?"

"Something I'm taking back to Bloomingdale's."

"What is it, Celia?"

We were in the living room. "Richard, I wish you wouldn't ask me about this. It's just something . . ." I faltered. Oh, God. "It's not important."

Richard said, "If you tease people, they get curious."

"I didn't tease." I moved toward the door, but Richard suddenly came over and grabbed the bag and started to open it. "Richard, please—don't—do—that."

He was holding the jar in his hand. "It's not important. If this isn't important, what is?" His face was livid. "So you were taking it back to Bloomingdale's. Our son.

Why—were you going to exchange him for another, or just get your money back?''

"Stop it. I lied to spare you pain. Which you know very well.''

"You bitch," Richard said, enraged. "How dare you not tell me? What other secrets do you have you're not telling me about?" He was clutching the jar to his chest, its contents bobbling around, and I was afraid he'd break it, which I could not have borne. "You cunt. You were going to actually try to sneak this out of the house. Jesus Christ. You who are always talking about being 'close.' You're lying and deceitful. Who'd want to be close to you? *I don't trust you.*''

I said, "The reason I didn't tell you about this pregnancy is exactly this. Because the last time you sulked and fussed and behaved as though it were my fault, and because I can't take it. And because frankly, Richard, we have *problems*, and I don't even understand what's wrong, but it's not me, it's *you*. To tell you the truth, *I'm very unhappy.*'' I was yelling and began to feel a lot better. "I feel rejected and pushed around and dragged into your unreality. God, I knew you'd act like this. I'm sick of your little tantrums.''

His golden eyes cleared and deepened, until I felt he could see right into my soul. And his voice was soft as honey. "Oh, Mrs. Sterner. I'm *so* sorry your marriage isn't perfect. I'm *so* sorry you can't produce a child and that everything is not turning out the way you dreamed. That life is real and difficult and not as wonderful as it was with you and Caspar and Dorothy and Cassie. That life is real and difficult, you pampered bitch. You can't always take what you don't want back to Bloomingdale's.''

I stared at him. His face was the same but different— clearer somehow. "I don't believe you said that," I said. He was still holding the jar.

"I did, and I'll say more. What did you use, a knitting needle?''

I don't remember too well what happened after that. I mean I do, but not in any exact way. I got hysterical—I suppose I was hysterical. I began screaming and went for him—I remember going for his eyes, to scatch them out, I suppose. Richard held the jar over his head and laughed. "Don't touch, Celia. Can't have. Ah-ah, hands down. Now, try to control yourself." Then I began to cry, and ran out of the living room into the bedroom. "Poor Cece. Poor baby. Here's our son—see? Bobbling around in a jar. Isn't he cute? Much more convenient this way. He won't disturb your career at all." He stood over the bed grinning weirdly. And I said, with awful composure, "Get away, Richard. Get the fuck out. Go put your kilt on or something."

Mistake, one of many, for he reached over and slapped me in the face, hard enough to snap my head back. Once, then twice—and there would have been a third except I got a pillow in the way and his hand landed with a heavy thump. Then a ghastly silence, while both of us stared at each other. My face throbbed and my brain was whirling. Then Richard put the jar down on the bedside table and turned and walked out of the room, then out of the apartment. I heard the front door click softly.

That was the start. A couple of hours later he called, ashamed, appalled at himself. How could he? Would I ever forgive him? Now he understood temporary insanity. It was the disappointment. He'd do anything to make things all right. He talked on and on, but I was struck dumb. I couldn't think of anything to say. He came back a-courtin'. Flowers, champagne and so on. We got drunk and cried together. We made love; my face was still red from his hand.

Richard didn't want to adopt—it had to be the fruit of his loins. His son, his features. Going to the schools Lydia hadn't been able to afford to send him to. To the right college. Being the father he had never had, making up for it all. "You can't get American ones. And I don't want some Chinese kid." Nor did I. One night I told him, furiously, that I was sick of hearing about His Son when what I wanted was My Daughter. Surprise—I could be closer to a girl. He shook his head—Cece, that's sick. We'd better discuss it with Billhorn (our marriage counselor). That's from being twins.

"It's not. It's from no longer believing in the master race."

Richard sighed. "I know it's hard for you to maintain a mature relationship. From what you tell me about your childhood, I'd say you have a severe homosexual problem."

"Oh, shut up, Richard. If I do it's none of your business."

"What did you say? Whose if not mine? Are we working on our problems or not?"

"Please, Richard. I'm tired of fighting. I have no strength. Yes. No. Whatever you say."

"You passive cunt. You won't face anything. You make me sick."

Again we'd start—Richard getting steadily crazier. He'd follow me around saying "Cunt-cunt-cunt-cunt" in a low voice, poking at me with his finger, or giving me little kicks in the legs. He'd laugh. He'd pull strands of my hair. Once he bit my nose hard. Once he spat at me. Once I was in the bathtub and he pushed my head under. . . .

The marriage counselor thought it all sounded a little funny and wondered why I couldn't see the humor in such ridiculous behavior. Why, really, was I so upset? Had I ever actually been hurt, besides those few bruises I said I had? The reason I was such a wimp wasn't just Richard, it was my own aggression I was so afraid of. Did I ever hit him back?

Just once, and that was the time he gave me a bloody nose and kicked me in the stomach.

Again we'd try. "Richard, is there any hope? Are we both sick? Crazy? Do we love or hate?"

"Oh, Celia. I don't know. I'm so broken. Wounded. I strike out because I hurt. I hurt when you aren't here to greet me. It sounds stupid, but if you forget to do something I've asked you to do, to me it means you don't love me. Just something like going a little out of your way to pick up my whole-wheat bread."

Why did it take me so long to leave him? Because I believed I was as crazy as he was, and maybe I was, and so didn't have the right. Richard, protesting the divorce up to the end, hung on to the scraps of the marriage, or the scraps of whatever he had last said—for in his mind there was no truth, no center, no ballast, and that was what he needed me for. To have something to protest against, to blame, to point at and say, "See? She's the reason I'm unhappy." And perhaps I stayed too for the same reason, because I was afraid that bad as things were, nothing else would be any better. That without him there would be nothing, just nothing. Who would invent the future? Or, as a matter of fact, the past?

As it ended, I cried about many things. But one of the hardest losses was Richard's pictures of us and how our lives were going to be. Imagine us, Cece, at Vassar graduation. Jessica, of course, will be summa cum laude and queen of the daisy chain. We'll wear our country tweeds. I'll smoke a pipe. . . . Ah, I can see the exhibit now: Photographs by Celia Armstrong-Sterner. Fifty-seventh Street at night, The reception. The man from the *Times*, the girl from *New York* magazine. I'll be so proud. . . . Darling, you're going to love being a shepherd's wife. . . . It's not just sex, Cece, it's that we've always been able to talk. At seventy we'll still be talking, rocking away on our porch in our elastic stockings, two babbling old fools. . . . When Lydia goes, we'll strew her ashes over the Palatine Hill; she says it's her favorite place on earth. . . . Let's choose the hilltop to be buried on when we go. In the shade, don't you think?—how about a sort of clearing in the wood? The gravestone will say: Here lie two people who wanted to be perfect.

Fantasies, that was what he had given me—pictures of the future. A sense of what I was. Foolish hope, and when he left he took it with him.

The shop looked dark, but I could see a light in the back in what Caspar called his "office," and I rang the bell again. In the window were ghostly gladiolas, reflecting a shadowy red, and gloxinias in pots, large Disney monsters on stems. There were daisies and ferns and the seasonal "Mixed Bouquet," which was now mums and asters and sprays of golden and red leaves for the season of sadness and parental divorce.

I'd walked over from the house, after listening to Dorothy for an hour. Then I gave her a Valium and steered her toward bed, where she climbed in and sat ramrod-stiff in her pink bathrobe.

"I can't sleep. Everything is spinning around in my head."

"It works in about twenty minutes. Then you'll relax."

"Where are you going?"

"To talk to Dad." I'd decided on the direct approach.

"I'd better warn you, Celia. I think your father is having mental problems. He sounds very strange. Please be careful."

"Careful of what?"

"You never know what he might do."

"Dorothy, Caspar is gentle as a lamb."

She pulled the pins out of her hair and it fell down, white and shining. "Yes, but he is not acting rationally, Celia. This woman has turned his head."

"Please, Mom, *lie down*. I'll see you later."

I loved Rivertown at night—or perhaps it was just that I loved to walk around somewhere at night without constantly scanning doorways for creeps or listening for approaching footsteps on the pavement. It was so dark and quiet, and the lit-up shop windows looked so inviting. Rivertown had been prettied up, and there were big concrete planters, which now contained slightly weary geraniums and leggy petunias. There was the same cool sharpness in the air that had once meant school and still meant new starts. Of all the shops that had come and gone, The Bower of Flowers was one of the few that had existed, almost unchanged, since my childhood. There were better, fancier flower shops in town, but people still came to this one because they trusted Caspar. Or rather, the old-fashioned people still came.

I rang again, and finally Caspar came out of his office toward the door. Bald and a little stooped, he didn't look like a man with a mid-life crisis; nor did he look, as Dorothy had suggested, at all insane. He smiled a little nervously when he saw me standing there and opened the door.

"Hello, Casselia."

"It's Celia, Daddy," I said automatically.

"Oh, I know it is, sweetheart. I just used the old name." He kissed me in the formal way we did in our family. "It makes me think of the old days."

"Yes. Well."

"Let's go back and sit in the office. I made some coffee."

The office was in a sort of alcove to one side, with a curtain, now drawn, that pulled over it. The light from within made a golden pool in the dark shop and lit up a small jungle of baby's breath, fern and camellias. In the alcove was Caspar's desk, covered with the clutter of decades—all manner of clippings, lists, ads under the glass and carefully taped on top. Piles of catalogues, packets of seeds, a flowerpot with pencils in it. Some children's art—a lumpy yellow ashtray and a clay figure of a cat— made by Cassie and me. Notebooks and ledgers. The old green-shaded lamp. A glass ashtray with a truly horren- dous encrustation of ash. On the other side, an old file cabinet and a lumpy, spotted old sofa, with sprung springs, which once had graced our living room. The window, with its dusty venetian blind, looked out at the alley behind the hardware store. There was more of my father here than there was at home: his own ordered disorder.

He turned to an electric coffeepot plugged in behind the desk and poured us coffee. "How's your mother?"

"She's in bed with a Valium."

I knew he didn't know what to do. He looked at me cautiously as he handed me the envelopes of sugar and the artificial cream. Then he looked down as he stirred with an old spoon. Then he looked at me again.

"I guess she's pretty upset."

I sat down on the least lumpy part of the sofa, which I had picked out years ago. "Well, she is, sort of." I looked around. "Are you sleeping here, Dad?"

"No, Cece. I'm still sleeping at home, in the downstairs study." He leaned back in his spring chair and lit his pipe. "I suppose you have some questions to ask, and I'll do my best to answer them." His hand was trembling.

"Okay. The first is, why are you getting a divorce from Dorothy?"

"Well, I thought your mother explained, Cece. Because I'm in love with another woman."

"I know. I've known for years." He looked startled. "I don't really know how. I just knew there was somebody else. I knew every time you went out after dinner to go over your ledgers."

"Oh, Lord," Caspar said. "Oh, God." The cup clicked in the saucer, and I got up and put my hand on his shoulder. "Oh, that you should know!"

"Please don't feel bad. I didn't mind. I don't mind. I just don't understand why you had to tell Dorothy."

"What do you mean, Cece?"

"Well. You'd gone on for years this way. And maybe Dorothy knew with one part of her mind, without admitting it to herself. You probably could have gone on forever this way. I mean unless your . . . fiancée objected. Did she want to get married?"

"Oh, no." He sat up straight in his chair. "What I mean is that Yo has never put the slightest pressure on me. She understands the serious nature of matrimony and family obligations. She is truly a woman of character, and has a sense of what's right and what's wrong. I don't know if Dorothy mentioned it, but Yo has brought up her son all by herself after her husband died in a terrible accident and left no insurance. He was riding a bicycle and was hit by a truck."

"I believe she said something about it."

"She's turned that boy into an exemplary person. He's eighteen and headed for Harvard."

"How wonderful." I don't smoke much, but I was beginning to have a deep craving for a cigarette, which I found in the depths of my handbag. Smoking to me is like a tiny lifesaver for when life's waters get turbulent. Most of the time I might hate, I might grieve, I might laugh, but basically I understand, for I've found that most of life's mysteries and miseries repeat themselves. But Caspar was leading me onto strange shoals.

"He's a fine, handsome boy with a brilliant mathematical mind."

I wasn't too interested in Yo's son. "That's nice," I said.

"And of course, Yo continues to work at the Correctional Institute, where she does extremely delicate and important work. Do you know, she is schooled in the arts of submission and she once brought a violent two-hundred-pound convicted murderer to his senses after nobody else could get near him?"

I puffed harder. "Do you mean verbally or physically?"

"Oh, verbally, of course. She can be very persuasive. But she also has three Black Belts and is an expert in the martial arts."

"Do you mean she does karate?"

"Yes, Cece. She's remarkable." He looked a little stunned at the wonder of it all; but then, my Dad often looks stunned, whether from the enigma of life or because of the way the light glitters off his glasses, I've never been sure. "But she never resorts to the physical until the verbal has been completely exhausted, and honest, that girl can charm the birds out of the trees. I can't wait for you to meet her." He smiled his big, broad toothy grin—the one that was left behind in the genes, for Cassie and I had Dorothy's curly little smile. "She's of French extraction and she has just the slightest charming French inflection in her voice—not accent, mind you, but inflection. Her mother insisted she learn two languages when she was growing up. Her mother was born and brought up in Paris, France. I believe it was the Eleventh Arrondissement. Were you ever there?"

"I don't know." I lit another—the last, and I began to wonder frantically how I could get to a cigarette machine without stopping Caspar. But then, to judge by the way he was going, nothing would stop him. "Is she a large woman?"

"No, quite small. You see, size has nothing to do with success in the martial arts; in fact, small people do better at them. She's, well . . . smaller than you. But not *tiny*. I'd say she's about five foot two or three. She just comes up to here on me"—indicating his collarbone, then looking embarrassed. "Now, Cece, you asked me a question before, and I'm going to answer it. I'm not avoiding what you said. You see, it's partly because of Yo's fine character that I feel obliged—or *want* to make her an honest woman. I think if she were a pushy sort of person, I would not be doing what I'm doing. Or I might even break off the relationship." He gave a small smile. "She's a different sort of person than Dorothy. She's had a difficult life. She was"—he looked at me in preparation—"illegitimate. She never knew her father. That's a terrible thing, Cece."

"I'm sure." I stood up, to prevent the walls from closing in and crushing me to death. "Dad, would you like to go out and walk around a little?"

"I was just going to suggest that." He pulled out the plug of the coffeemaker and put our cups in a little sink in the corner. Then he turned out the light. We walked out through the damp, fragrant shop. "I'd even thought of taking you by Yo's tonight"—he cleared his throat as my heart did a double thud—"but I don't think it's a good idea so soon." He carefully locked the front door of The Bower of Flowers.

I thought of Dorothy sitting up ramrod-straight in her quilted pink bathrobe. "You're right, Dad. I wouldn't have felt comfortable at all. I'd rather meet Yo when I can. . . [When?] When I can appreciate her more." We were walking slowly down the street. "If you don't mind, I'm just going to dash in here for cigarettes."

When I came out of the East Side Tavern, a drab and grimy place where I had spent many hours of my youth, Caspar was standing on the corner with his hands shoved into his pockets, a little smile on his face. It was a clear, cool night, and the trees moved slowly in the wind.

"You know, Cece, I've never really known what it was like to be happy in this way. Your mother and I were married when we were quite young. You and Cassie were born when I was only twenty-one. For many years it never occurred to me to be unfaithful to my wife—something which, I've discovered, most men are at one time or another. I thought it was wrong to fool around. But you know, Cece, things change even in a place like Rivertown. When I grew up during the Depression, life was nothing but struggle. My parents lost the grocery store, and half the time we didn't have enough to eat." I listened with respectful silence, lighting another Slim. "The bottom line is getting food on the table, Cece. Only when that's accomplished does a man have the leisure to look beyond the table, so to speak."

"True."

"You know, you were always the smarter one."

"Was I?" Ridiculous pleasure.

"Your mother used to give it to me because I couldn't tell you apart. But even if I sometimes got your faces mixed up, I knew the two of you. You were the deep one, you were the one who asked the questions and tried to figure things out. And you figured something else out. For all Dorthy's shock, I think she did know that there was somebody else. She's not a stupid woman. And she looked the other way as long as things looked all right on the surface. What she's shook up about now is that I want to change the status quo, so to speak. I'm no longer willing to be a hypocrite."

"But why?" I asked. We were walking up Old Mill Road behind the Episcopal church. "If Dorothy would go along with it, and Yo would, why wouldn't you?"

"Well that's the end of a long process of thinking on my part. And watching times change, which started back during the war. Now people seem to be thinking less about duty and obligation to others and more about their own satisfactions. I even read something about how it's bad for you if you don't fulfill your own needs. Like if you go on for years in some situation that makes you unhappy, you might even get sick or go crazy or something. I never thought of things that way, that a person has certain needs and it's unhealthy to deny them. When I was growing up, it was the other way around. Certain kinds of fooling around could *make* you sick or crazy." He cleared his throat. "Anyway, I guess the thing that clinched it for me was *your* divorce. Not that I did anything about it right away. It took me five years to—"

"Dad. Did you say *my* divorce?" We were on top of Old Mill Road now. It was dark, and I began steering him down the other side—not from any sense of danger, but because I wanted to get him under a streetlight where I could see his face. "*My* divorce? *Mine?*"

"Well, you know there haven't been very many in the family, Cece. And I guess it was sort of a shock to your mother and me when you and Richard broke up. But in time I began to see that you were right not to settle for unhappiness. And I thought, Well, if Cece can do it, why not I?"

I said, "But Dad. But Dad. You can't compare the two situations at all. I was married to a raving maniac. I don't mean that I'm so perfectly sane, but I'd never do the things to anybody that Richard did to me. I never told you half of them, beause . . . because they were too weird and because I didn't want to upset you. Most people wouldn't believe they happened but I knew you and Mom would because you're my parents. I mean he'd knock me down on the floor and stand there laughing."

Even talking about it made me break out in sweat from head to foot, unless I was starting to have hot flashes. By this time we were back down to where the streetlights were, and I saw Caspar looking at me with a gentle smile. God, didn't they believe me? It had never occurred to me before.

"I'm sure it was terrible, sweetheart. I believe you. Of course it was awful. Now, I've always been against a man hitting a woman under any circumstances, but you'd be surprised at some of the people in this town who don't agree with me. Big, important people, too. I'll tell you one—Tomaselli, the ex-mayor. He used to knock that poor woman around once a month or so and then laugh about it at the Rotary Club. Just to keep her in line, he said. And there were those who laughed with him. But I was never one. I said, 'Tom, you really shouldn't do that.' And I heard once that Joe Larkin beat the bejesus out of Millie because he heard she was fooling around with some bastard."

"Dad, I don't give a damn about these people. I don't care if every man in Rivertown beats up his wife every night. It doesn't make it all right. It means the women are all nuts to hang around and take it."

"Well, Cece. Probably you're right. But there are a lot of griefs in marriage. There are a lot of ways people can beat each other up."

Score one for Caspar. "Sure. Of course. And if you can't take it, you get . . ." I stopped.

"That's right. You get out. And you showed me the example and made me realize I didn't have to be unhappy for the rest of my life."

I hated his logic—hated it. "It's different. Physical

abuse is different. *Insanity* is different. Dorothy isn't crazy. I mean she's pushy and bossy. I know that.'' I stopped under a tree. "I mean, I can see *me* divorcing Dorothy, because she's never loved me the way she loves Cassie. Which you know is true." Caspar said nothing, looked down at his shoes. "So in a sense she always tortures me. Not that I even blame her much anymore; she can't help the way she feels. But nothing I do is ever good enough, so if I had any sense I'd divorce her. But I don't have any sense.'' I fished for the Virginia Slims. "But not you. She never talks against you. She'd die rather than say anything about you behind your back, except that you're crazy to leave her. She respects you. She loves you. And she's sixty-three. And now what's going to become of her?"

We turned down Maple Street "I'll provide for her. You know that. She'll stay in the house and I'll send her enough each week to live on. I'd never rest if I didn't take responsibility for Dorothy.''

"But what's really going to become of her?" I was filled with an unfamiliar sympathy for Dorothy. "She can't do anything. She can't think without a husband. All she can do is cook and play bridge.''

"She's good at belittlement." We'd reached the house, and as we started up the path our voices dropped. "I'm in love with Yo. Crazy about her. It's not good enough just to sneak over to her house the way I've been doing for years. I want to be with her all the time. We get along so well. We even think alike.'' As we went up onto the porch, his voice dropped to a whisper. "Have you ever had that experience? Maybe with your husband in the beginning.''

"Yes," I whispered.

"Should I give her up? Should I wait another ten years, when I can hardly wait till tomorrow?"

We went inside the house and he went into the downstairs study, closing the door behind him.

Dorothy came down the next morning as I was sitting at the kitchen table, still in the pink bathrobe. She looked haggard.

"Is he gone?"

"Yes, Mom. Here, sit down. Here's some coffee."

"Oh, Lord. What a night. I slept well at first, thanks to whatever that pill was you gave me. But I woke up very early in the morning and couldn't go back to sleep. When I finally did, I had the most awful dreams."

"Tell me about them," I said soothingly, cutting a piece of Danish and putting it in front of her.

"Oh, well. One was about being in my grandmother's house, in the attic. I was searching and searching for something—I think a book. Perhaps a diary. I knew I had put it in a certain place and I couldn't find it. Then I was aware that there was something wrong with the house. Part of the roof was missing . . ."

As Dorothy talked away and drank her coffee I looked at her. Her hair was falling around her shoulders, and she had her glasses-on-a-chain around her neck, a particular *chatchka* of which I am fond. It made her look sensible and competent. I suppose if I'd had one wish that morning, it would have been 'Please let Dorothy continue to be sensible and competent.' But she seemed a little *distrait,* and I watched with slow-growing horror as she spilled the tiniest drop of coffee on her pink quilted lapel, then another and another.

"Mom, you're dripping."

"Oh, so I am." An aimless dab with a napkin. God, why didn't she run to the sink, wet a paper towel and rub, as she would have done only a week ago? "Then I began thinking about the summer spent on the Cape. I had a little yellow pail with a red duck on it." Another drip, this time in her lap, and I reached over and dabbed at it before putting a folded napkin under her cup. A fine beginning this.

"Dorothy, do you want me to stay here with you for a few days? I think I can manage it if you like."

"Oh. Why, that would be fine. Of course, Cassie is coming in this afternoon."

Cassie. How could I have not thought of it?

"What time?"

"Shortly before five. I told her we'd meet her at the airport." How normal—how right that she should want her daughters to be with her. How strange and fearful the corridors of my mind, like a dark old house through which winds blew and doors slammed. "I hope you don't mind my saying *we*, Celia. I feel so nervous I wouldn't trust myself at the wheel of a car. I thought you could do the driving, and we could go get her at Kennedy and bring her back here." I said nothing. "Celia, did you talk to your father last night?"

"Uh, yes."

"And what do you think of his mental condition?"

"Oh, it's terrific," I said, without really paying much attention to what she was saying. "He's fine."

Pause. Click click as Dorothy stirred her coffee. "So you thought he was fine."

"Oh. Yes, well, I mean, I don't know if I agree with him. But I don't think he's crazy or anything."

"You don't. I see."

"How do you know Cassie is coming?"

"Well, because she said so on the phone. And it doesn't help me at this painful and tragic time of my life to hear *that* tone of voice from you, which I mercifully haven't heard in many years. You are an adult, and I hope there will be no more of that cruel and senseless picking on her that used to go on. I shouldn't have to say it or even think about it. There are far more serious problems in this family than your little childhood spats and jealousies."

She sounded like her old self. "Don't worry, Mom." I would hide it all, stuff the feelings under the floorboards and nail them back down. Close the doors, turn out the lights. "I'll be fine. I'm sure she will too. After all, you are our main concern." A halo floated over my head.

"Yes. Well. I'm probably inconveniencing both of you. I know you have your job. And Cassie has her lovely family. But there are times in any family when—"

"Dorothy, we'll both be here with you. Have you had enough to eat? I'll make you some scrambled eggs."

"No, thank you. I can hardly eat. I would prefer to talk, and I'm surprised to hear you say that your father appears perfectly normal."

"Well, he does. It's just that he's in love with Yo." When she looked stricken, I knew I wasn't choosing my words very thoughtfully.

"Please don't mention her name. I can't imagine what sort of person this is. That in itself is a sign that the man must be experiencing a 'senile psychosis,' which I was reading about last night in *Good Housekeeping*. Many men Caspar's age start to get the idea that they're, well, a lot younger than they are. I've been thinking things over for half the night, as you may imagine, Celia. There are many decisions to be made. And I've decided I will forgive Caspar for everything if he starts immediately with a psychiatrist."

I almost choked on my Danish. "But Dorothy. He doesn't need a psychiatrist."

"Doesn't need! And who does need one, then, if not a man who after forty-five years of marriage chooses to leave his devoted wife, his pleasant home and rewarding life for some sort of prison matron! I don't know, Celia, if you have any idea what those people are like. I have had cause to visit the Correctional Institute on occasion and *I have seen them.* They are truly inferior female creatures chosen for their ruthlessness and animal appearance. I was once told of the way they routinely examine female prisoners. And not only murderesses and thieves, but perfectly ordinary women who forgot to pay a few parking tickets. *They commit insults on the body's orifices.* They are the ones who should be imprisoned, not the others." Dorothy's color was coming back, along with her appetite—she took another piece of Danish and spread butter on it. "It's not as though he had taken up with some little hatcheck girl. Or some semiprofessional floozy. As much as I would deplore it, I would be better able to understand women like that than the sort of person he seems to have chosen. A *prison matron.* Of course he needs a psychiatrist. He probably should go three times a week for several years."

Looking pleased, she poured more coffee. "Honestly, Celia, I feel much better having made this decision. As far as I'm concerned, Caspar may stay here and sleep in the study so that life at least appears to go on normally. I'm willing to go on cooking his food, which I'll leave on the stove for him. He'll have to do his own laundry, of course. I'm willing to be perfectly polite to him, but of course he may not share my bed."

The trouble with contradicting Dorothy was that she'd start dribbling coffee again and I couldn't stand it. "Are you going to suggest that to him?"

"Of course. It's only fair. I have no intention of treating Caspar badly. I have never believed in vengeful behavior." She got up and went to the back door, opening it and looking out at the garden and the lawn with its drift of dry leaves. "It's a lovely day. Clear and cool. I think I'll put on a sweater."

After she'd gone up to dress, I dialed Bernard's number. No answer. I tried his office. Not there, but expected shortly. Oh, Lord, I needed a friend. I called my boss at *New Day*, Gretchen. Told her family crisis of grave proportions. The last project finished, nothing really doing till Thursday. She grudgingly gave permission. Then I went and sat on the back steps.

Cassie and I here in this house again.

I'd seen her only twice since she'd left for California. She'd been very cool—cold, in fact. And I'd been too embroiled in my own life to be concerned, for the first time had been when Richard and I were starting to go out together, and the second when we were getting divorced. I'd come home and there she was. Why, hello, Celia. How nice to see you. You look well. I'm so glad to hear. I'm so sorry to hear. The children send their regards. Sam sends his regards. And I hadn't stayed long, but left her and Dorothy to their little snuggles and murmurs. I had other knives in my heart. But this was different.

I tried Bernard again, but he was in a meeting. I was supposed to leave messages only with a certain secretary, because the other one was on Maria's team, taping phone calls and such.

"Is this Sandy?"

"No. This is Deirdre. Can I take a message?"

"No way." I slapped down the phone. Deirdre was the one who stuck the little suction cup on the receiver. Then gave the tape to Maria for her by now massive collection.

"Why don't you fire her?" I'd asked Bernard.

"For one thing, I can't, she's the company's. For another, she's terrific."

"Bernard, don't you ever get the feeling that life is short? That the years are whipping by faster and faster?"

"I do. It's awful."

"Don't you ever get the feeling you want to get your life in order so you can enjoy the time you have left?"

"Sure I do, Cece. It's hard. It's complicated. Things are simpler for you."

"Nothing is ever simple for me, Bernard."

"Oh, yes, it is. You don't have the guilt. You have that WASP thing, everything's going to turn out fine. You don't have kids."

"That's not fair, Bernard. That hurt."

"I'm sorry, Celia. I didn't mean it to. I just meant that if you don't have them, you don't really understand the conflicts. I'm sorry, darling."

"I wish I did."

"I know. I know. Maybe . . . if everything turns out the way I want, you can share mine."

Oh, great. Thanks a lot. By that time we'll be old and doddering, the two tarts will be middle-aged. Maybe they'll be in jail. Maybe Yo will be their Correctional Officer. She'll fix 'em, Yo will. No mercy. I'd better stay on her good side.

Dorothy's spirits were so restored by her refusal to face facts that she was more or less her old self until it was time to leave for the airport. She baked a chocolate walnut cake and made a veal-and-noodle casserole for our dinner, an old family favorite. By three she was ready, looking handsome and sporty in her green tweed skirt and matching sweater. Her white hair was pulled back into a chignon, and her color was ruddy. She bustled—did she need a coat? Was it going to rain? Would we park far from the terminal? By three-thirty we were in the car and gliding down the street, and I still hadn't talked to Bernard.

"What are we going to do tonight, Dorothy?" I asked as we swung onto the Hutchinson River Parkway. "You, me and Cassie are all sitting around lovingly together. In walks Caspar from work. Then what?"

Poor Dorothy looked bewildered, and I rescued her. How slow I was at understanding that now she was the child, I was in charge. "We'd better all eat together tonight. It's simpler. Then you can have your talk with him later.''

''I suppose you're right, Celia. It will show my willingness to forgive and corp . . . cooperate. After forty-five years I can't hate your father. In fact, I'm still very fond of him in a way. Verrrry . . . fond.''

What was the matter with her? If it had been anybody else, I would have thought . . . but it wasn't anybody else, and my mother smelled rather strongly of booze. She gave a delicate *hic*, covering her mouth discreetly. No wonder she looked so good. Pink cheeks, sparkling eyes.

''Did you have a drink, Mom?'' Keep calm.

''Well, Celia, I've just been keeping a little gin in my room. I find it helps, though sometimes it seems to affect my speech for some reason.''

''You have to be careful of that stuff, you know. A little is fine. But you have to keep your wits about you.'' What for I really didn't know—there was nothing that could be retrieved from the situation. Probably for me. ''And it's better to drink with other people, not alone in your room. It's kind of sleazy.''

''Are you saying I'm . . . sleazy?''

''No, but you will be if you keep nipping on the sly like that.''

By the time we got to JFK, I was on the verge of an anxiety attack. How I wanted to be home in my apartment, curled up in front of the TV. In bed with a riveting book. Or swinging down to the corner deli for a corned-beef-on-rye. Exchanging jokes with Milton as he sliced the meat, stroking Raymond the tabby. Or wandering over to The Gibbon's Head for a beer on a fall evening. My simple, homey life—I felt as though I would never see it again.

Having parked the car, Dorothy and I went into the American Airlines terminal. We had a few minutes to wait, and I left her in the waiting room while I went to try Bernard again.

''He's tied up with a client,'' said the merciless Deirdre. ''Who's calling?''

''This is the nurse speaking. It's about his mother.''

There was a slight gasp, and Bernard was on the phone in about half a second.

"What nurse? What's wrong?"

"Your mother is fine, Bernard. Or I suppose she is."

"Is this Celia?" he asked, infuriated.

"It's the nurse. The mother, the universal tit. Bernard, dear. I'm sorry I lied, but sometimes it's difficult to invade your borders."

"What is it? I'm busy as hell."

"I'm desperate as hell. Cassie's coming."

Bernard had never really gotten it. Though maybe I had never really explained. "Celia, did you really call me to tell me your sister is arriving?"

"I did."

"Now, look, Cece. Honest to God, if it was something serious, you could interrupt me anywhere. If somebody died. If somebody was sick. But your *sister* is coming?"

"It's serious to me. I'm frightened to death."

Hand over the phone, muffled tones. " . . . a few minutes. Be right there." Hand off the phone. "Cece, just what are you frightened of?"

"I don't know. I'm frightened of her the way you are of Maria."

"I'm not frightened of Maria! What a ridiculous comparison. I'm tense and conflicted over the breakup of half my life and the traumatic effect on my children. And the matter of money is upsetting. Now Maria wants the co-op in its entirety. And almost everything I've got is in that apartment. The legal bills have practically wiped me out."

"Bernard—*my* turn. I don't know why I'm frightened. Never mind. Maybe I'll call you tonight. Will you be home?"

Split second. I hated those split seconds. "I'm not sure."

"Is the phone safe?"

After a pause Bernard said, "Son-of-a-bitch." Crackle snap crunch. "I think we were being taped."

"You think. You know Deirdre does it."

"Good Lord. Well, I've got it out."

"I love you, Bernard. Love—you."

"Well, I love you too, Celia."

As I hung up, his lying tones went through me like a chill. That's what I got for phoning. It wasn't even that he didn't love me, exactly. It was just that I'd called to drag it out of him and had only annoyed him. And left him wondering whether to fire Deirdre, the best secretary in the place.

I looked over at Dorothy's straight back on the red vinyl sofa and realized that the public-address system was announcing the arrival of Cassie's plane. Dorothy stood up and waved, and we walked together over to the barrier where the passengers disembarked. There were only a few greeters—flying had become commonplace; people didn't meet planes the way they used to. In fact, I began to wonder why we were doing it. There was something old-fashioned about it. Nice, really, as though people went back to old habits during a crisis, like taking one another to trains and meeting arriving planes. Except that I kept forgetting which crisis I was supposed to be worrying about. Dorothy was in better shape than I, in her Connecticut tweeds. I wore pants and an old raincoat. A black sweater. Cassie always made me aware of what I was wearing. Half the people were out of the plane. Maybe she'd missed it. Maybe she wasn't coming. Maybe Dorothy had gotten it wrong. Maybe . . .

I looked up and there she was, coming out of the tunnel that leads from the plane. She looked very snappy. White suit, nifty fedora at just the right angle. Sunglasses, of course. Suntan. And the blond hair. God, she was right off Sunset or Rodeo or whatever those streets were. Big, fancy Gucci bag. And what I could have sworn was a makeup case, as in an old movie. Was she really bringing her pots and potions to Rivertown? Her electric curlers? The glitter of gold chains, the glint of golden bangles.

She turned her head so that the shadow of her hat brim fell behind, and I saw her face.

"Cassie," I said. At the same moment, Dorothy waved and said, "Here we are, dear."

She looked first at Dorothy, and then suddenly at me. Absolutely stunned. White. As though she might faint. Standing still in the middle of the runway. Then, to my amazement, she turned around and went back toward the plane. Pushing desperately past the people coming the other way. Push, shove. Then disappeared into the tunnel.

"But where did she go?" Dorothy asked.

"She took a look at me and decided to go back."

"Celia, please don't start. We'll go find her. Let's talk to that one in the uniform."

A brief explanation convinced the airlines official that it would be all right for Dorothy and me to go back into the plane, since there was no way we could sneak aboard without tickets and go somewhere for nothing because the plane wasn't going anywhere anyway. But he wanted to know why. Well, our daughter/sister wasn't well and needed our help. Or maybe she had forgotten something. Well, if she forgot something she'd be back in a minute. What made us think she was sick? Ten minutes of pointless conversation. Finally we went back, the official lurking behind.

Cassie was standing in the middle of the empty 747, quite composed, immaculately groomed. A nice warm smile.

"Mama," she said, embracing Dorothy. "I'm so glad to see you. And Celia." A hug for me. "I forgot my bag and had to run back. Anyway, I have everything now."

"You look lovely, dear."

"But Mama, how are you? Are you all right? I want to hear about everything."

They walked ahead, arm in arm, off the plane, while I tagged behind.

CASSIE

Two weeks have passed since I arrived in Rivertown, and I hardly know where to begin. Everything here is so complicated that I go to bed every night exhausted just from trying to cope with the day-to-day life in this house. I now know beyond a doubt that we Southern Californians are much simpler and more "laid-back" than Easterners and our lives much more normal and calm, and it's hard to believe that I once not only lived here but fitted in. Or perhaps I didn't really fit in, and that was why I moved to California.

Part of this is due to the terrible crisis in my parents' lives, which didn't exist during my happy and peaceful childhood. Of course it's perfectly possible, as Angela says, that I may have "idealized" my childhood, which many people do, and that I remember it as better than it really was. Well, I don't know what difference it makes what something really was, if you remember it in a certain way.

Anyway, to start with the one I like least—advice given often by Sam, always so sensible. *Celia*. Well, I'd forgotten all about her, would you believe it? Not entirely, of course. It was really that I preferred not to think about her, and so every time she came into my head I simply looked the other way. And after a while she stopped appearing at all. So naturally, that moment at the airport, when I first saw her, was a terrible shock. It was like seeing a dead person come alive, and as far as I was concerned Celia was dead.

Possibly this sounds like a rather extreme and brutal view to take of a person's own twin sister. But considering her character, I had to do it to save myself from being destroyed. She has always hated me from the time we were small children. She was always jealous and envious of everything I had or did. She took my clothes. She stole my toys. She played my records and scratched them; she read my books and tore the pages or spilled food on them. She would watch me with an evil expression, then deny she was doing it. She told Mama and Daddy lies about me—that I hated her or was rude or cold or cruel to her, none of which was true. When I was older she tried to steal my boyfriends, but was unsuccessful, because they quickly saw what she was really like and wanted to have nothing to do with her.

And she would not let me alone. It seems only common sense that if a person hates another person, she would try very hard to avoid him or her. But even though Celia thought I was stupid and "square" and provincial, which she told me in her own words, she followed me around and nagged me and tried to start conversations. She would come into my room at night and ask why we couldn't be friends, when both of us knew very well the reason was that she hated me and only wanted to fool me into trusting her so she could do one of her evil, hurtful things.

I have read and heard many times that identical twins, such as Celia and I, are supposed to have great similarities in character and personality as well as looks, besides having a mysterious and close relationship, a secret language and strange psychic powers. Well, no two people could be more different than we were, in every way except our basic appearance. I was shy and she was noisy and hoydenish. I was quiet and homeloving and she was always rebellious, constantly complaining that her life was boring and her family didn't understand her and that most things, in fact, were not perfect. I remained pure until my marriage and she slept with anybody and everybody. I was contented and she always seemed to be angry and ungrateful to Mama and Daddy, even though they worked so hard to give her everything a young girl could want. She never even thanked them for the sacrifices they made to send her off to that expensive boarding school where she got so many fancy ideas about herself and how she was superior to everybody else—she thought.

I will say that Celia is a smart person and got good marks at school and college. But though I used to have quite a bit of respect for brains—they were, in fact, one of the things that attracted me to Sam—I have discovered that they don't necessarily lead to success or even much of an ability for a person to lead his or her life, and so I am not easily impressed anymore if I hear that a person is supposed to be so smart. And Celia hasn't exactly set the world on fire. She's a photographer for one of those "Women's Lib" magazines, which I must say sounds like just the sort of thing I would expect her to be doing. She looks a little sloppy, almost shabby—though it's hard to tell here Back East, where there are people who try to be shabby *on purpose*, as though it proved something not to take care of your appearance. Her sweaters are stretched, and she usually has a button or two missing and sometimes even a run in her stocking. She was wearing some boots the other day that are so run-down at the heels I almost suggested she take them over for repair, but she might have taken it the wrong way, and for Mama's sake I'm trying to be agreeable to her.

Celia's reappearance, when I had managed to put her completely out of my mind, left me in a state of shock. On the way to the car, when Mother was walking a little ahead, she said, "Cassie, we haven't really been friends, but we certainly aren't strangers, and I think we should try our best to get along as best we can to get Dorothy through this."

I found this perfectly acceptable, except for the hint that I had ever done anything but my best to get along with her. And I wish she wouldn't call Mother Dorothy—it seems so chummy and disrespectful. Also, thinking it over later, I wondered how she could even say such a thing when as far as I'm concerned I have no interest in her at all and so have no particular reason *not* to get along with her. But rather than splitting hairs I decided to take her statement as well meant, for I agreed that Mother's welfare comes first and foremost and all other matters should be put aside.

So we arrived at the car, a filthy old green Ford that reminded me of Lillyanne's Dart. I don't mean to be snobbish, because I know Mother and Dad don't have the money to buy fancy cars, and also that Back East they don't have the interest in cars that we do in California. But they could clean this one up and take seriously all the noises it makes instead of ignoring them or joking about them. Once during the drive home Celia said, "Mom, this door doesn't close tight." And Mother replied, "Oh, I know—it's been like that for weeks." I've suggested three times taking it to be fixed, but nobody bothers.

Celia suggested I get in the back. I took one look and said I wouldn't think of it, not only because of the generally filthy appearance of the back seat but because I knew just by looking that either there was no air conditioning or else it was broken, and I would be blown to bits because the windows would have to be left open. Then Mother said that *she* certainly couldn't sit in the back, and she couldn't drive either, because of being so nervous, so we all ended up in the front—Mother in the middle and me next to the window, after taking the precaution of putting a Kleenex down on the seat. My white pant suit is new and cost a fortune, and I don't feel like ruining it. Celia banged one of my suitcases against the bumper when she was putting it into the trunk, and now it has a big black mark on it that won't come off. I don't mean to be critical, but everything here is a little dirtier than at home, and since I have nice things, I have to be extra careful of them.

In the car on the way to Rivertown, Mother said that she had decided to forgive Daddy if he promised to go to Ol' Doc Schroeder and follow his recommendation for a psychiatrist. "There's no reason our home of forty-five years should be disrupted because of one indiscretion, and most men do the same thing from time to time," she said.

I was glad Mother was sounding so sensible and rational, far more than she had on the phone. "You're right, Mother. I'm sure there's a way this whole thing can be settled quietly. Dad probably needs time to think, that's all.''

"He's already thought," Celia said. "He's in love with somebody else." That's Celia—always making things difficult.

"Well, we'll see what the psychiatrist says about this so-called love," Mother said. "It should be pointed out to Caspar that love isn't seemly for a man of sixty-three. In fact, there are a lot of things that had better be mentiond. Your father is a victim of senile psychosis and needs intensive treatment starting immediately. And I'm certainly not going to run out on him, any more than I would if he had cancer or a heart attack. From what I was reading in *Good Housekeeping*, mental illness is as serious as physical illness, and in some ways it's harder on the other members of the family. But we have plenty of medical insurance—"

"Don't even think about money, Mama," I said. "I can let you have whatever you need."

"Well, thank you, dear. But it won't be necessary, even if Caspar has to be hospitalized or have shock treatments or intensive drug therapy. All those things are covered; I was looking at the policy today."

Celia went tearing past three cars and said, "This is really very silly. Caspar isn't crazy. In fact, he's saner than he's been in years."

Poor Mother said, "Why, Celia, that's a terrible thing to say."

"No, it's not. It's true."

Mother began to cry, and the remains of my patience disappeared. "I must say, Celia, you are as cruel and thoughtless as ever. Thank God I came. Poor Mother needs somebody to sympathize with her, not to make her feel worse." I put my arm around Mother, and gradually her tears stopped. None of us said anything for a while— till we got to Rivertown, as a matter of fact. I was absolutely furious at this so-called sister of mine. Now perhaps you can see why I haven't had any contact with her in years, and why I purposely put her out of my head.

It's strange to be back here. I've been back since my marriage, of course, with Sam and the children. But this is the first time I've been here alone. I'd forgotten how different it is. The air smells different here, damper and sharper. The trees are bigger and more plentiful, and the leaves are starting to turn yellow and bright red and purple. I'd forgotten about the seasons and how they dominate people's lives here and give them something to do. For instance, as we turned into the driveway, Mother said, "Well, it's certainly starting to get cool. Caspar will have to check the insulation in the attic—now that fuel is so high we have to be careful"—just as though life were perfectly normal.

I thought the house looked a little shabby. The paint is peeling off the shutters, and there are weeds in the driveway. The bushes need pruning, and the lawn needs mowing. Inside, the rugs look old and worn, and the wallpaper is starting to peel at the edges. Not that anybody except me even notices these things. I'm a little surprised at Mother, for as I remember she was always an impeccable housekeeper. She made us keep our rooms neat and taught us good habits from an early age, though I doubt that Celia has kept any of them up. Then, the living room always smelled faintly of lemon oil and of the wood from last night's fire, and there were always delicious odors coming from the kitchen. Though my taste is more modern than my parents', I know I have always tried to maintain that same atmosphere of serenity in my own home, though it has sometimes been difficult considering the attitudes of the other people in it.

Celia helped me with my luggage and I went up to my old room, which has hardly changed at all. I think when the day comes, if it ever does, that Sammy, Stu and Shelli move out and start their own lives, I will immediately remodel their wing of the house and turn it into either guest rooms or else a gym, or a solarium with sauna. But of course, my parents wouldn't be interested in such things, and I suppose they just left the rooms as they were to remind them of the happy days when we were living at home. The bed was made with the same old quilt I remember so well, and there were even some of my old stuffed animals on the shelf, and some books—*Little Women*, *The Wind in the Willows* and some of the Bobbsey Twins books, of which I once had every single one. Fortunately, the room looked fairly clean and the closet usable, after I pushed some old boxes and blankets aside, so I hung up my clothes and put my lingerie, nighties and panty hose in the bureau drawers, as well as my sweaters and a couple of knits that should not be hung on hangers.

My old record player was there, with some old 78 records. I put on Patti Page's "How Much Is That Doggie in the Window?" and was surprised that it still worked, even if it did sound a little tinny. I was humming as I combed my hair when Celia poked her head into the room (without knocking—typical) and said, "My God, I haven't heard that in twenty years. And it hasn't gotten any better."

I said, "I happen to like it, and if you don't mind, I'll play what I want in the privacy of my room."

She looked at me for a minute and said, "Of *course*, Cassie. I wouldn't dream of disturbing you." And she left without another word. It's sad that Celia and I can't get along, but probably she can't get along with anybody because she is such a sarcastic, critical and nasty person.

Anyway, I finished unpacking and changed into my gray pants and a white silk blouse. I set up my makeup mirror on the desk and plugged it in, and I repaired my shadow and mascara and put on a little blusher. I selected a sweater, my watermelon cashmere cardigan, in case it was chilly, and went downstairs, where delicious smells reminded me again of the good old days. Celia was setting the table with a surly expression on her face, so I went into the kitchen to help Mother, and she gave me the job of making the salad. I smelled something burning and opened the oven, to see several black circles lying on a pan.

"Oh, Lord, the biscuits," said Mother. "Celia! You've burned the biscuits."

Celia came in from the dining room. "Save them for ammunition."

"Well, I don't know what that remark means. Throw them out and Cassie will make some more." She gave me the box of Bisquick.

"Just a little joke, Dorothy. An attempt to make you smile. After all, we're all here together, aren't we?"

I mixed up another batch and rolled it out. "Mother

isn't in a mood to be amused," I said. "Nor would I be in the same situation."

"My tongue hurts from biting it," Celia said.

"It's amazing, isn't it," I said, "how differently we see things." I cut up the biscuits and put them on the cookie sheet.

"Oh, God," Celia said. "It's not a funeral. Do we have to be so serious?"

At this point, fortunately, the back door opened and my father came in, slamming the screen door behind him. When he saw us all standing there, he looked startled, though he has a naturally startled expression and sometimes it's a little hard to tell whether he really is. He looked at us one at a time as though he were seeing three ghosts. Then he held out his arms to embrace me.

"Cassie," he said. "I'm so glad to see you. How beautiful you look, with your suntan and all."

I started toward him and then hesitated. Though he is my father and of course I love him, I didn't want him to get the idea that I approved in any way of what he was doing. At the same time, I knew both Mother and Celia were watching me. So I didn't exactly hug him, but I leaned over and kissed him in an affectionate but cool way, so he could not misinterpret my attitude, and told him he looked well, when in fact he looked exactly the same except possibly a little grayer and a little heavier around the middle.

"We'll all be having dinner together tonight," Mother said, "in honor of Cassie's arrival. Everything will be ready in about ten minutes. Shouldn't you wash up?"

Daddy gave her a thoughtful look and went into the study, where he sleeps, and stayed there rather a long time. Mother went upstairs to comb her hair, and I waited with the biscuits while Celia sat at the kitchen table picking at the salad and drinking a glass of wine, which I had refused because I wanted to remain clearheaded. Eventually we all sat down at the table, and Mother put on her veal casserole and served the plates. Celia put the bottle of wine on the table and poured a glass for everybody, which I thought was rather tasteless under the circumstances. Mother turned her glass upside down.

''We haven't been together for a long time,'' Daddy said. ''It's nice having my Casselia at the table.''

How I hated that name! It was strange that Celia didn't seem to mind it and never had. She only smiled at him, but I said, ''Please, Daddy, don't call us that.''

''Sorry, honey. It just came out.'' He smiled. Nobody said anything. ''Well, Cassie. How's the family?''

''Everyone is just fine, thank you, Dad.''

''Sam all right?''

''He's very well and just got another raise. He's almost definitely made a deal for reruns of *The Wimples*. And if he gets that going, he's considering starting his own production company.''

''He must be making lots of money. I've heard those reruns make a fortune.''

''Well, we certainly have a comfortable income.'' I told him about some of the children's activities. Then there was a silence except for my father chewing and Celia tossing the salad, which she did onto the table. ''Ooops. Sorry.''

Mother said, ''I never understood why you couldn't tell the girls apart, Caspar. Celia was the one who was always dropping things.''

Celia said, ''Oh, Dorothy, let me up.''

''You could talk to her a little more gently,'' I said. ''You know she's upset about what's going on.''

''Cassie, I swear to God I'm trying to be patient. But any more of these little digs of yours and I'm going to tell you exactly what I think, and you're not going to like it.''

Celia slugged down the rest of her wine and poured some more. It was an Almadén, one of the worst Californias.

I said, ''That would be very stupid. Anyway, I unfortunately know what you think and have no desire to hear it again. The problem is between them, not us. I didn't come here to argue with you but to lend support to my mother, because you're obviously incapable of doing so.''

Mother said, ''Thank you, Cassie. I appreciate that. You've always been the peacemaker in the family. Celia, I do think this is the wrong time to pick a fight with your sister. After all, she's just flown three thousand miles, left her dear husband and her lovely children and come here to help in a family crisis and the least you could do—''

"I'm not picking a fight with anybody. I'm killing myself being agreeable. None of you want to hear the truth; you just avoid—"

"Celia." My father's voice was strong and unexpected. "Dorothy and Cassie. I have something to say to all of you." We all turned to look at him. I had never heard him sound so serious. He had pushed his chair back a little and put down his fork. "I'm tired of your goddamn arguing. I've been listening to it for forty years. I thought I could last another month or two weeks, just to make things look respectable and out of consideration for Dorothy. But I can't even get through one meal without the three of you starting again."

I reached over and took Mother's hand. She said, "Caspar, as long as you've brought The Problem up, I have something to say to you. I had planned to say this in private, but since you have dragged the children into our fight, it might be better for all if we got some things out in the open. I believe it's worse to pretend that everything's fine when they are witness to disturbed behavior on your part. Which must be very confusing to them. But anyway, as I've told the girls, I'm willing to forgive you, Caspar, if you will go to Ol' Doc Schroeder immediately and let him recommend a psychiatrist to treat you."

My father stared at Mother in amazement for several minutes, and then, to my horror, he began to laugh—a loud sort of braying laugh. He kept it up while Mother looked at him in an alarmed way. Then she said, "None of us are ignorant enough to think that there is anything bad or wrong about going to a psychiatrist. You'd be amazed at some of the people I know—lovely people right here in Rivertown—who take their mental illness to a psychiatrist. Why, Regina Lewis was telling me the other day that she had been going to one for six months and she felt better than she ever had in her life. And she told me that even the ex-mayor, Tomaselli, was in treatment with an excellent doctor in Hartford. Going to a psychiatrist simply doesn't have the stigma it once did. And of course, right here in our family, as we all know, Celia—"

"I'm *not* going to any psychiatrist," Caspar said. "I'm not nuts."

"That's exactly what I was saying, Caspar. Celia wasn't 'nuts' either. She was in a difficult period and she needed some straightening out. Why, you're still going, aren't you, Celia?''

"Yes, but with me it hasn't worked, as we all know."

"Celia, don't start. Honestly, sometimes I've wondered if it's your sarcasm and nastiness that's driving your father away. I hope you talk about your jealous nature with that so-called therapist of yours. Though I must say I've never thought a woman would be very good at it; it takes a man's strength to really point out—''

"Dorothy," said Dad, "I'm not going to a therapist. The only place I'm going is out of here tonight. I just don't think there's anything left to talk about." He stood up. "Cece has nothing to do with it. Neither does Cassie, except I'm just tired of hearing all your goddamn women's voices whining and bickering all the time. A man can't find a moment's peace in this house."

I said, "Daddy, that's not fair. I haven't been here for years. And Celia isn't here much either. And frankly, I resent being blamed for your problems, which have nothing to do with me at all, but only with your irresponsibility to your marriage. I'm sorry to speak so frankly and I don't mean any disrespect, but I know that if Sam and I had any marital problems, which of course we don't, we would never involve the children in them or even let them suspect there was anything wrong at all." I happened to catch Celia's eye, and she was watching me with an unpleasant know-it-all smile, which was not nice after I was kind enough to defend her. "The only reason I speak up at all is because I am an adult woman and no longer innocent about the ways of men. If you are going to try to make me responsible for your abandoning Mother, perhaps I should go upstairs and start packing immediately, and go straight back to California." I looked at him defiantly, and Mother patted my hand.

"Don't fall into his trap," she said in a low voice. "The article in *Good Housekeeping* said the mentally ill often try to blame others for their faults. Don't you dare let him force you out of your first home. You have every right to be here." She glared at Daddy. "How dare you blame your children for your own irresponsibility? How can you, Caspar?''

"I'm not blaming them for anything," he said, "except their whiny voices. In fact, I'm not blaming anybody for anything. And now if you'll all excuse me, I'm going to go pack."

As he stood up, Mother's eyes became wide with fright. "Caspar, I said I'd forgive you. Didn't you hear me? You can stay."

"I don't want to stay."

"Just a few sessions with a psychiatrist, then. Ten sessions. That isn't very many." Her voice was low and pleading. Celia was leaning on her elbows, covering her face with her hands. I couldn't help noticing how badly cut her hair is. Probably she can't afford a decent haircut.

Daddy said in a gentler voice, "Dorothy, we've talked about this before. You'd better face the truth. We've been strangers in our marriage for years. It's time to stop going through the motions. Don't make me say any more." I glanced at Celia, who stared at him as he said it.

"Everybody has difficulties," Mother said, her voice rising sharply. "But responsible people stay and try to solve them."

"I've stayed for forty-five years, for God's sake. Isn't that enough?"

"It's that woman!" Mother yelled. "That dreadful woman has turned your head. I know about her. Don't think I don't. Everyone knows who she is. And what she is."

Celia said, "Dorothy, you'd better stop right there."

"It's time somebody told the truth. She's a whore. She's a disgusting, immoral person. She's leading you by the nose. She wants your money, and you're too foolish to see it."

"That's enough," said my father angrily. "I don't want to hear another word about Yo. Do you understand?"

"Don't mention her name again in this house!" Mother shrieked. "How dare you even name her? I'll never be able to eat another bite of food in this room. Yo indeed!"

Daddy looked so furious I wondered if he was going to hit her, but of course he wouldn't do such a thing. He turned and left the room. We heard his steps going into the study, then up the back stairs to the bedroom. When Mother heard his steps in the upstairs hall, tears began streaming down her face. I was astonished, because I had never seen her cry before. All my life Mother was the strong one who could always cope with life's difficulties and bring things back to order. It was frightening to see her on the brink of hysteria. I got an enormous lump in my throat that wouldn't go down, no matter how hard I swallowed.

Then she got up and started up the stairs, not quite at a run, but quickly for a woman of her age, calling my father. "Caspar! Caspar! Don't leave, please don't leave me! I'm afraid to be without you! You don't have to go to anybody—I don't care. You can be as mentally ill as you want. Just don't bring her here." I felt tears in my eyes that started spilling down my cheeks, which I knew must be making trails of mascara. Both Celia and I got up and went out into the hall toward the stairs. "Caspar . . . Caspar! I can't live without you! Please—have some mercy on me. I'll kill myself, I swear I will. That's what I'll do. I've saved forty sleeping pills. I can't live alone—I'm too old."

Celia and I went toward her and Celia got there first. "Mother, stop it. You don't have any pills. You're not going to kill yourself. Let him go. You'll be all right."

My father was in the bedroom packing a suitcase. "Of course you will, Dorothy. I'm not leaving you destitute. You'll live right here in this house and I'll send you money every week. The girls are here to help you. Now please stop this scene."

I was furious at both of them. "How can you be so cruel?" I screamed at Caspar. "She's threatened suicide! How can you not take her seriously? A woman of her age, expected to survive alone! And all you talk about is money! As if money could make up for the rejection, the loneliness and the hopelessness! The empty years ahead! Her life is on your head, Dad—yours! If anything happens to Mother you are entirely responsible, and don't you forget it!"

"Bullshit," Celia said. "Mother, where are these so-called pills?"

"You'll never find them," Mother sobbed. "They're hidden. I've been saving them for years. What a comfort it's been, knowing they're there during those lonely years."

"What lonely years?" Celia asked.

"For all the years he's been visiting her two nights a week. I always knew, Caspar. Don't think I didn't."

Father closed the suitcase, and Mother began crying again. I put my arm around her. "Mother, you must be strong. As far as I can see, the marriage is over. There is a point at which things are beyond retrieving, even if you could get him to a doctor or a marriage counselor. Even if he got rid of this woman, the basic trust between you is gone. You'd never believe him again." As Daddy started down the hall to the stairs, I said, "I hope you're satisfied."

He said, "I'm not satisfied at all, Cassie. I'm sorry things have to be like this. But they are."

"Suppose *she* had a lover—*then* would you be so calm and unfeeling?"

"Of course not," said Daddy, opening the front door. Mother began screaming again. "Don't leave! You can't! I'll call the police! You're abandoning your marital home. I read it in the *Ladies' Home Journal*!"

"Jesus Christ" were my father's last words as he closed the door.

As soon as he had done so, Mother collapsed completely, and Celia and I put her to bed, where she lay with her white hair streaming out over the blue pillow. Then she reached under the mattress and brought out a silver flask. She took a good slug, sighed deeply and shortly seemed to be asleep. Celia and I left her, leaving the door open. As I went into my room, Celia said, "Welcome home."

I sleep very badly here. The room is not air-conditioned, so if the window is open, all the noises from outside can be clearly heard. The birds twitter and screech and even peck at the window screen, which has holes in it, so of course there are mosquitoes. Cars start up early and trucks go by, and there is the most awful tooting and whistling from something down the street. And children scream and chatter as they go by on their way to school. How amazing it is that all these things were once part of my life, and now I long for the silence of mornings in Santa Barbara.

I always suffer from jet lag, so it has taken time for me to adjust to the local time. It's difficult to get up early and go to bed before midnight. So I have time on my hands in the evening. Sometimes we look at Mother's small black-and-white television, which she seems to enjoy, but I miss my large-screen video terribly. In fact, I miss many things. My hairdresser, Carlos, along with my manicurist and Zelda, the girl who gives me facials. My oversized bathtub and outdoor whirlpool bath. My new BMW. My best friend Angela, always there for support and sympathy and problems worse than mine. My house—my kitchen, my bed, my satin sheets. My Naugahyde playpen and my Betamax.

Celia's job requires her to be in the city every day, and so for the most part I am here with my poor, unhappy mother. Certainly I have every sympathy for her plight and agree that my father has been cruel, sadistic and neglectful of her. But God, I get sick of her endless moaning, groaning and complaining. What will she do? How will she live? How can she bear it? Honestly, how the hell should *I* know? And I can't help wondering how she'd feel if she had *my* problems. Not, of course, that Sam is any worse than any other man, and he's a lot better than some. But Mother has been fortunate—or unfortunate, I'm not sure which—in knowing more happiness and security than most women.

Now she mopes around all day in a dirty pink quilted bathrobe, taking an occasional slug from the flask she keeps in her pocket. She doesn't do her hair, and it hangs down her back in white strings. She has pouches under her eyes, and her expression is dull, defeated and miserable. Sometimes she cries, and sometimes she gets angry and threatens to get a gun from somewhere and to go and shoot Daddy and Yo. Sometimes she is overcome by despair and says she is going to take her forty sleeping pills and put an end to everything. Fortunately, I brought along some of Sam's Valium, and when she becomes impossible I give her half a little yellow pill, which relaxes her—an effect Sam could get only with two or three of the blue ones.

After a few days of this I took her to Ol' Doc Schroeder, our General Practitioner from childhood. And I mean old. He shakes and can hardly see a thing, and I wouldn't go to him with a head cold, but he's the only one Mother trusts.

"Dorothy," he said, "I've known you for thirty-five years, and you're tough as nails. Now stop all this a-maunderin' and a-palaverin' and pull yourself together. Caspar is gone and there isn't a doggone thing you can do about it. Now get dressed and do your hair and get to work on your house."

"I can't, Jonas," Mother sniffled. "I miss my husband too much."

"Maybe she should have a few sessions with a psychiatrist, Doc Schroeder," I said.

"I don't hold no truck with any dad-blasted psychiatrists. They're all witch doctors, preyin' on people's natural misery, and Dorothy can't afford 'em anyhow. Dorothy, now you get home and put up some green-tomato pickle and do your storm windows and rake your front yard—it looks like hell. And if I hear any more bellyachin', you're gonna hear from me good."

For this Ol' Doc Schroeder gave Mother a bill for ten dollars, which I couldn't help comparing with the seventy-five dollars Dr. Battaglia charges me whenever I walk into his office, not counting the three hundred dollars' worth of unnecessary tests he gives to protect himself from malpractice suits. I also can't help noticing that even though it seems ridiculous, this backcountry codger with his seasonal activities did Mother more good than Dr. Battaglia ever does me. She went home and said, "Well, probably Jonas is right," and she put on her overalls and got the rake and began raking up the leaves on the front lawn—to my tremendous relief, because frankly, I'm exhausted from the cooking, cleaning and laundry I've been doing since I've been here, with very little help from anyone. I mentioned to Ol' Doc Schroeder that I was trying to find a maid, whom of course I would pay for myself, but he said, "Cassie, the best thing for Dorothy would be doin' all that work herself; best cure in the world. Don't give me no truck with no maid."

My father turned up three nights ago with a check for

Mother for two hundred dollars. He was there for only a few minutes, but that was long enough to send Mother back into hysterics and out of her clothes and back into the pink bathrobe. Celia was here at the time, and she got him out while I tried to console Mother and gave her half a Valium. "Remember what Doc Schroeder said, Mother. Pull yourself together."

"I can't believe he walked into this house and then walked out again. I was sure that once he came in and saw the dear familiar place, he would never want to leave again. And even with the apple pie cooling on the kitchen windowsill."

"He never got into the kitchen, Mama."

"But he could *smell* it," Mother wailed. Then she grabbed the check. "How long is this supposed to last?"

Celia, lurking around as usual, said, "He's going to give you a percent of his profits, Mom. It will be different from week to week according to how business is."

"Well, I don't know if I like that or not."

"Frankly, Mama, I think you should see a lawyer," I said. "This arrangement, if it is an arrangement, is too insecure. You need much more money than this, and it should be in a legal agreement. Besides, he's abandoned you and you should have a share of the business—at least half."

"You're right, Cassie." She took a slug of whatever she keeps in the silver flask, which, from the way she smells, must be gin. "I'll make an appointment with Jack Brodsky."

"Who's that?" I asked.

"He's Dorothy's legal guru," Celia said with her pointless wit.

"Well, I think she should have superior representation. Perhaps Louis Nizer or F. Lee Bailey."

Celia said, "Aren't we getting a little carried away?"

"I told Sam before I left that I was prepared to pay anything so that Mother would be adequately represented. You don't know what Daddy has in mind. He might leave the state or try to escape to South America. He might change his will and leave everything to That Woman. Even if you don't have the sense to look out not only for your mother's security but your own as well, I intend to look out for mine. Someday this valuable house will be ours.''

''Already we're killing Caspar off.''

''Celia, you seem to forget that we are dealing with a man with serious mental problems.''

''He doesn't *have* mental problems!'' Celia yelled.

''Well, maybe he doesn't. But Celia, I know from the experience of friends, and you should know from your own unhappy experience, that people can behave very strangely during a divorce. Even the nicest, most considerate husband can start acting like a disgusting prick and try to avenge himself on a helpless, dependent female. And on the other hand, I've seen the most charming, sweet women turn into shrews and harridans when their marriages start to break up. And please recall that a large percentage of so-called family crimes involving rape, assault and murder take place between separated but not divorced couples. So there is not only the danger of Mother starving or ending up on Welfare, but of possibly being raped or murdered in her own home. And I see nothing wrong with anticipating the worst because that is usually what happens.''

Celia looked at me with the same astonished expression I have sometimes seen on the faces of Sam, Angela and others when I make a sincere effort to express the truth in a straightforward way. Then she began to laugh. ''You're right,'' she said. ''You're absolutely right.''

''Well, I'm going to Jack Brodsky,'' Mother said. ''If Caspar is going to come back here with a gun to rape me, I'd rather have somebody right here in town than one of those Fancy Dans from the city.''

I didn't argue, because I had seen how helpful Ol' Doc Schroeder was and saw that Mother would be better off with somebody she knew, even though God knew what this local shyster would be like. So she got dressed the next day and went off to her appointment, looking very nice in her navy blue crepe with the white collar and a navy blue pillbox hat that we both decided would be attractive yet appropriate. It never fails to interest me the way women dress for their divorces. When Angela went to court with Paul, she wore rags and dyed her hair gray.

And Sam told me that his ex, the Psychotic Bitch, was always elegantly turned out to show that she expected to be supported in the style to which she had become accustomed. Considering the way things turned out, the Psychotic Bitch came out a lot better, so I advised Dorothy not to try to look poor, or the lawyer and the judge might decide that she might as well stay that way—which I sometimes suspect is what happened to Angela. (In the same position, I would wear my simplest, but most expensive clothes.) With my help, Dorothy added a pair of navy blue pumps, white gloves and a single strand of pearls—in other words, her usual small-town, ladylike self, with a composed but grieving manner.

Please don't think that with all the taxing demands of Mother I have forgotten my own family back home. I phone them every other day, and until a week ago nothing seemed to have changed. Then on a Sunday night, Sam phoned me sounding absolutely terrible.

"You'd better sit down, Cassie. This is rough. Sammy Junior has married a forty-year-old dyke."

My legs went right out from under me. The phone here is on a little table in the hall, next to the stairs, and I collapsed onto the bottom step, though I was careful of my oatmeal tweed skirt, which shows every spot. "Oh, Sam. I *told* him not to."

"Well, when the cat's away the mice will play, and all that. They got married in Las Vegas Thursday, and he phoned me and told me to prepare to welcome Eleanor Coopersmith to the bosom of the family. Then this basso voice got on the phone and said, 'Hi, Dad. I'm your new daughter.' God, I thought I'd pass out! I tried to be polite. I said, Hi, El. I'm your new patriarch.'"

"I don't know why you even tried to be polite. I wouldn't exchange a word with the bitch. She has duped Sammy Junior into marriage because she's after his money."

"Well, he doesn't *have* any money to be after. I told him he wasn't getting a penny from me. Nor are they going to live here, which they seem to expect." Then began a terrible fit of coughing.

"Sam, are you all right?"

"Oh, I seem to have some bronchial thing. Ralph

Battaglia says there's a lot of it going around.'' He could
hardly get the words out.

"How are Stu and Shelli?"

"Oh, the same as usual. School starts in a couple of
days, and I suppose that'll straighten them out.''

After this depressing conversation, I suggested to Mother
that perhaps I should go home, at least for a while, because I felt my family needed me. But Mother burst into
tears.

"Oh, Cassie. I need you so. You're the only one who
really understands. I feel so selfish asking you to give up
your life for me, but it's just for a little while.''

"But Celia is here, Mama.''

"Well. You know how she is, with her wisecracks. And
she isn't here all that much; she's with that married man
she's carrying on with.''

Honestly, I didn't know what to do. Then when I called
back a day or two later, things sounded strange, but I
suppose a little better. Sammy Junior and Eleanor had
arrived, and Sam had weakened and said they could stay
for a while, just till they got on their feet. Actually,
Eleanor wasn't so bad, he said. Being married was part of
a general project to become straight—she was sick of the
gay life and its complications. He was sure she hadn't
married Sammy for his money, because she sure as hell
didn't seem materialistic; in fact, she was one of those
hippie types with bare feet, Indian dresses, beads and hair
down to her waist.

I said, "I can't believe you're actually welcoming her
into our home. She sounds perfectly awful. If I were there
I'd throw them both out.''

"But you're not here, Cassie.'' A little nastily, I thought.
"Anyway, maybe you wouldn't. She's kind of maternal,
actually, and she's trying to fit in. She was helping Shelli
with her homework. And Stu, for some reason, is crazy
about her.''

Sam had another piece of bad news: the deal for reruns
of *The Wimples* had fallen through. We were not as rich as
we had assumed we were going to be. Of course, Sam has
made sensible investments, and he has other irons in the
fire, so we are perfectly comfortable. But he asked me,

which he never has before, to "take it easy about spending money." I was amazed to hear him say such a thing, and of course glad that I had already done most of the necessary shopping to see me through a New England fall—wool skirts, pants, sweaters, shirts, a raincoat, boots, good walking shoes and so forth—at the nearby shopping center, which conveniently has Lord & Taylor, Saks, Bloomingdale's, Bergdorf Goodman and Neiman-Marcus. I still need scarves, gloves and heavy stockings, but those I can pick up anytime. I must say I've enjoyed buying this cold-weather clothing, which I have hardly ever had in my life because we don't need such things in the balmy climate of Santa Barbara, nor have I ever seen it in the stores there. Some things I liked so much I got two of them because I knew this would be my one chance to get them, besides which they were on sale, which is important now that we are in a period of economizing.

After hearing the news from home, I went to church to take my difficult decision before God. I sat in the back pew of St. Anthony's Church which I remember so well from my early years and asked God for His help and guidance. How soothing it was to sit there with the afternoon light coming through the stained-glass window in lovely colors, and to see the shadows of the trees moving outside. The organist was playing a simple old-fashioned hymn, and the air was faintly fragrant with candles. When I asked God what to do, His answer was clear and strong: Your Mother Needs You More. Children Must Make Their Own Way.

As I left the church and walked home through the sea of golden leaves, I felt more peace of mind than I had in weeks. I felt my heart lift up with joy as I came up onto the porch and went inside to start our dinner, peeling the potatoes and putting them on to boil. As I went out into the neglected vegetable garden to pick some tomatoes and squashes, I felt truly happy as I pulled up weeds and loosened the soil around the base of the plants. As I thought it over, it made perfect sense—they were all working out a *modus vivendi* without me back home, which would be better for them in the long run. Staying here would tell Eleanor better than words ever could how I felt about her. Not that there was anything to do about her anyway, for Sammy was twenty-three and could do whatever he wanted. I have even managed to talk to her on the phone, but had trouble not screaming when she rumbled, "Hi, Mom. I'm your new daughter."

I felt so serene, and so restored by being in church, that I knew I must try to love Celia, whom, I must admit, I have been a little short with at times. She is certainly not very lovable, but if Christ could love the leper I can try to at least be charitable and understanding with my own sister. So when she came in looking sulky and glum, I sat down with her at the kitchen table and asked her if there was anything she'd like to talk about.

She looked a little surprised. Then she said, "Oh, well, I'm involved in this affair that doesn't seem to be going anywhere." And she told me about Bernard and his endless divorce, which has been going on for three years and never becomes final.

Well, I've heard the same story before from other women, and there is always the same answer. So I said, "Celia, I truly hope that you aren't too much in love with this man, because I have a feeling that his divorce *never will become final*. Men like that are irresponsible in a basic way and use their so-called divorce, which probably doesn't even exist, to play on the affections of women."

"Oh, Bernard's not like that. No, he's a good, gentle man. But *very* family-oriented, and guilty about his two kids. Oh, the divorce exists, all right; I've seen some of the endless papers. They've gone too far to go back." She looked annoyed.

"I'm only saying this to help you, Celia. I've known too many women who believed men who told them they were going to get divorced. It almost never happens. Usually the man goes back to his wife for a second honeymoon, and the marriage is the better for having been shaken up a little, and the poor woman is left—"

"He *will* get divorced!" Celia screamed. "He will. He will." She covered her face with her hands. "I know he will. This is different. Damn it, what do you know about it?" She took her hands down, and there were tears of anger in her eyes. "Thanks, Cassie. You're a big help.

You're all heart. Remind me not to have anything to do with you.''

I reminded myself of Christ and Mary Magdalene. ''I'm sorry, Celia. Of course Bernard may be the exception to the rule. I sincerely hope it works out.''

''Shit,'' said my charming sister. ''Shit, piss and corruption'' resorting to infantile high school language. And she got up and ran up the stairs to her room. Celia's supposed help in this trying situation is like that of a small child. Honestly, she isn't much better than Mother, though Mother does seem to have improved slightly now that she has an attorney.

I haven't mentioned it, but the truth is I get very lonely here. I called Angela the other night, but all I heard about was how broke she was and how she couldn't pay the bills and had to go back to work, though nobody would hire a woman her age. Plus how Eleanor puts on Indian sitar records at night and lights hurricane candles and they all do strange dances on the patio, Sam included. It sounds as if they've gone out of their fucking minds, if I may use that word just once, and I think I'd be just as lonely back there as I am here, except that here at least I'm doing God's will. Mother is now involved in her affidavits, which keep her busy, and I truly wish I could get along with Celia, but oh, how difficult it is! I keep reminding myself that Celia is more to be pitied than scorned, as the old saying goes. She is well on her way to being a dried-up old crone. No matter how many men she has been to bed with in her life, she is now divorced, childless and in love with this hopeless Bernard. I will persist in trying to be friendly, for at this time in her life she needs the support of her family, which is all she has.

Now I must tell about last night, though I would rather not even think about it. Celia and I went to dinner at Daddy and Yo's. When Celia first told me of this idea I said I would die first, rather than spend the evening at That Woman's house, the scene of our father's adultery. But Celia insisted, saying I should ''stop moralizing'' and face the inevitable. She pointed out that most of the people she knows are divorced, including their parents, and the sooner everybody accepts it, the easier it is all around. Well, probably she's right, but it's still hard to accept the things in one's parents that one does in one's friends.

The whole arrangement had a sordid air, which was necessary to avoid letting Mother know where we were going. Celia told her we were going to meet friends in the city.

"I'm surprised you girls are going out together. Of course you can go where you want—you aren't prisoners. But you look tired, Cassie. I should think you'd want to go to bed early tonight. I know you didn't sleep well last night, I heard you go down to the kitchen around midnight."

"I'm not tired, Mama," I said.

"And Celia, aren't you seeing Bernard tonight? I thought he called before."

"He did. I'm not," Celia said in that hard way of hers.

"Well, I was just curious as to where you're going together. It just seems funny is all. There's a good movie here in town; maybe the three of us could go."

"We'll go tomorrow," Celia said. "Dorothy, Cassie and I are forty-three years old and where we go is none of your business."

At that Mother started whimpering and fussing, and after a half-hour or so of carrying on, she was back in the pink quilted bathrobe which she had not worn in days, with the flask in her pocket. I didn't understand her behavior at all, for our destination had been kept strictly a secret.

"Mama, we'll be back around ten. Honestly, you're being very difficult, and considering the fact that I left my family to come here and be with you in your hour of need and have been waiting on you for two weeks and being at your beck and call, I think it's a little ungrateful of you to behave this way just because I want to go out for a while. And Celia too."

"Well, it's just funny, that's all. I mean your lives have always been separate, and now this. I'm terribly nervous and I don't want to be left alone. When I'm alone, I start thinking about my forty sleeping pills. I should think one of you would have the decency to stay here—I don't care which."

Well, she was so impossible we ended up calling Ol'

Doc Schroeder, who was just sitting down to his dinner, which made him so furious that he was bright red by the time he arrived at the house.

"Dorothy," he bellowed, "I want you to stop this dad-blasted nonsense and let those girls go out and have a good time! By gum, I saw you downtown yesterday all dolled up coming out of Jack Brodsky's office, so don't tell me how miserable you are. Now pull yourself together and look at TV or do some sewing or read the paper and stop feelin' so sorry for yourself. If I hear any more of this goldarn snivelin', I'll come over and whale the tar out of you." This cost twenty dollars, but as always, Mother calmed down immediately, and as we left all she said was "Well, after all this time, I must say."

In the car, Celia said mysteriously, "We should have left the house separately."

We were half an hour late meeting Dad at The Bower of Flowers, which had been our arrangement so that Mother wouldn't know where we were going. We all got into an unfamiliar car, a dented black Volkswagen with a ripped and filthy interior, which Daddy drove to the end of town and up a small country road, then pulled up in front of a small, dark house huddled in the woods, so buried behind shrubbery it could hardly be seen. I've often noticed that people's houses resemble those who live in them, and Yo's was no exception. We followed Daddy up a short front walk and waited as he took out a key and opened the front door. How strange it was to see his easy familiarity with this peculiar and slightly revolting place, which reminded me of an illustration of the Witch's house in "Hansel and Gretel," even including the thin trail of smoke that rose from the chimney. When the door opened, I half-expected to see a cackling old crone in black, stirring her pot, while above a male child hung in a birdcage.

Inside was a large room notable mainly for its lack of taste. On the floor was one of those cheap shag rugs in red and orange, and the furniture looked as though it had come from Triple S Blue Stamps. On the wall hung those awful pictures of deformed children with huge Bambi eyes, and the few lamps were so spindly they looked as though they would fall over if anybody exhaled. There was a lighted tank full of fish, which I personally consider a repulsive sight, and an awful motel smell of stale cigarette smoke. And a flickering television screen in garish color, and slouching in front of it a male child smoking and piling cigarette butts in an overflowing ashtray.

"Pierre," Daddy said. His voice sounded odd, and I realized he was extremely nervous. I saw his bald head glistening with perspiration and his glasses steaming. Pierre stood up and stared at us. He was an ordinary young male of about eighteen in the usual jeans and rock-music T-shirt.

"This is Pierre Dev-row," said Daddy. "Pierre, these are my girls, Cassie and Celia."

We all said hello, Pierre smirking slightly, probably at the word "girls." I couldn't help darting glances around the place in search of Yo, meanwhile feeling myself becoming more and more depressed that my father had chosen to live in this place rather than our simple but comfortable home on Maple. I doubt if Celia responded as I did, for she was probably used to shabby surroundings, but beautiful things are extremely important to me, and this place was so unattractive I longed to go out, get into the car and go.

Then out of a gloomy corner came Yo. Perhaps she had been there all the time, but invisible, and now she moved forward like a small dark ghost. She is a small person, and even her black hair, which stands up all over her head in little kinks, doesn't make her seem taller. She was wearing some shapeless dark garment that gave her the contours of a mushroom, and she has a face that I personally wouldn't notice in a hundred years—a rather ordinary round white face with glasses. I usually dislike short women, who are often so controlling, and it was with some effort that I attempted to hide my natural reaction to my future stepmother, which thought brought me near tears, and tried to find something to admire about her. She did seem to have rather nice, if large teeth.

"I am zo very glad to meet you," said Yo in a thick French accent. "I hope we get along, yes?" Celia and I mumbled "Hello" and "How do you do?" at the same

time. "Caz-par, zey zertainly look alike. It iz remarkable.
But not like you—zey must rezemble zair muzzer."

Of all the annoying things she could have picked to say,
she could hardly have done worse. Celia and I glanced at
each other with hatred as Dad and Yo embraced and kissed
tenderly—a sight neither of us wanted to see. But the
curious thing was that in a way, we did look alike. Just by
chance we'd both worn gray skirts, and I wore a white
sweater while Celia wore a tan one, but of a similar
cowl-neck style which, of course, was nothing, because
half the sweaters in the stores are exactly that style. But
Celia does nothing to her hair, just lets the gray streaks
appear, and as for makeup, she just hastily puts on some
lipstick, if she happens to remember, and nothing else
(though since I've been here I've been wearing less makeup
than usual—When in Rome, as Sam says). And of course
there was a very obvious difference in the quality of our
clothes. Mine were cashmere, which is the only thing I can
bear against my skin, and Celia's were of some cheap
synthetic.

We all sat down for fifteen dreadful minutes and had
small glasses of *"apéritif"*—a brownish sweet wine very
unlike Cinzano or Boissière; then we went into the kitchen
and sat down at an oilcloth-covered table, which I assume
is where they eat. Yo was trying to be a good hostess—
"Caz-par, you sit here. Cassie, you zit zaire. Pierre, *le
vin, s'il vous plaît.*" Pierre rather clumsily poured the
wine, and Yo put dinner on the table—a dreadful slimy
mess she said was "tripe."

"Just wait till you try this. Yo is some cook. I never
really realized how good food could be till I had her
cooking." Which I thought was in bad taste (no pun
intended), an unfair slur against Mother's simple but delicious home-cooked food. "The French consider food an
art, you know. Yo learned it at her mother's knee."

Though the tripe was perfectly vile, and reminded me of
someone's intestines, I had to admit that the vegetables
were quite well cooked, and so was her dessert *"gâteau."*
As for conversation, Pierre turned out to be one of those
offensive, insecure children who have to dominate the
conversation, and he talked unceasingly for fifteen minutes

about computers and what they implied about the future, which I have no interest in at all. Apparently he is a mathematical genius of some sort, and we were all supposed to admire him and admire Yo for having brought him up alone.

After dinner, Pierre went into his room to solve calculus problems and the four of us remained at the table with our coffee. After some sighs, glances and nudges between Dad and Yo, they started their inevitable speeches, which turned out to be as difficult to listen to as I had expected.

"Now, girls, I know this situation is hard on both of you. And I know Dorothy isn't taking it well, though I'm convinced she'll be all right in time. I've talked to Ol' Doc Schroeder, and he agrees your mother's tough as nails."

I said, "Dad, I honestly don't think it's right to sit here and talk about Mother's suffering, since you are the one who has caused it, and Celia and I are the ones who have to pick up the pieces." Celia smiled, looking down at her plate. "Personally, I have sympathy for any woman who is mistreated by a man no matter who she is."

Yo and Dad began talking at once—"But she has not been miztreated" and "Now, there's two sides to every story," which Yo eventually won. "But Cazzie and Zelia, your parents' *mariage* has been *très difficile* for many years. You are adult women, and you must know a man cannot live wizzout zertain privileges of *mariage*—"

"*Please,*" Celia said. "Spare the details. Honestly, Yo, I'm perfectly willing to try to be friends. But for God's sake, don't *explain.*"

Dad looked miserable. "I've never been in this situation before. Neither has Yo. It's hard to know what to say."

Yo got up and began clearing the table, and I noticed that she picked up the enormous cast-iron casserole in which the tripe had been served as though it were light as a feather. She whipped it into the sink, washed it and dried it and flicked it back onto a shelf.

"Well," I said, "possibly it's too soon to say anything. I imagine this situation is one in which time must heal the wounds. If Celia is willing to be friends, I honestly don't think I am ready yet to forgive and forget, though in time I might be. To be absolutely frank, I have found this evening extremely difficult.''

Yo gave a ''Gallic shrug.'' ''In *la France* we are much more *philosophique* about zeze things.''

''Not true,'' Celia said. ''In *la France* you're Catholic and there isn't any divorce. If this were *la France*, Caz-par would never be your husband at all, which I presume is what he intends.''

''As soon as the law allows,'' Dad said fervently, taking Yo's dark square little hand. ''And Celia, I don't like your sarcastic tone.''

''I'm sorry, Dad. This is all a little sudden.''

''Sudden,'' said Daddy. ''Sudden. Now, you listen to me, you two. I have known Yo for twenty years—twenty years, do you hear? We became intimate much more recently, but that is how long ago we met. Sudden is hardly the word.''

''Okay. But it is to us,'' Celia said. She looked very sad, and I knew exactly how she felt. It was the end of our family and our home. I had not really realized until that moment how important that old home had been. No matter what happened with Sam and me and the children or anything else, that image of warmth, love and sweet security had always been in my mind, and the firm belief in my parents' love had given me strength to handle my problems. Now it was gone and I felt frightened, as though the floor were going out from under me.

It was obviously time to leave, and Daddy was to drive us back in the battered Volkswagen. Celia and I thanked Yo as politely as we could, and on the way out Celia stuck her head into the back bedroom and said good night to Pierre, which was thoughtful of her considering how tiresome he was. On the way home, none of us said anything as we bumped over the ruts in the road that went past the row of tall trees that led down to the highway. The night air smelled fresh and sharp, and it was definitely chilly. I would have to get a winter coat in the next day or two or else I would freeze to death, owing to my ''thin'' California blood.

Daddy dropped us off at The Bower of Flowers.

''I'm sorry it wasn't a happier occasion, Casselia.''

"Come on, Dad," Celia said. "You've made your choice. You can't expect us to jump up and down and applaud."

"I suppose it's hard for me to accept that, because that's exactly what I feel like doing in my heart."

He drove off, and Celia and I walked slowly home. It was strange, and a little upsetting, how close we felt—or I did, and I was almost sure she did too. After all, we were sisters.

As we walked up on the porch, Celia said, "But we did get along once, Cassie. You've just forgotten."

How strange was the impression of her words, almost as though they had come from my own mind. I stood there in the hall for a moment, confused, as though I had stepped briefly into a dream.

Then from upstairs, Mother's voice called, "Well, it's time you two were back. Do you realize how late it is? It's almost ten o'clock. Five more minutes and I was going to call the police. Honestly, I'm so upset and nervous I think I'm going to die. Where on earth have you been?"

CELIA

Bernard and I had a fight—something I usually try to avoid, because I'm afraid of driving him away. Dangerous ground. He said he was sick of hearing me talk about Cassie. I said now he knew how I felt about Maria. He said I should get another shrink; I said I couldn't afford it and he should mind his own business. We both got mad and yelled. After the fight, which took place at the Hunan Szechuan Wok on Third Avenue, we came back to my apartment and made love, better than in ages. Maybe we thrive on war, or else I do. I was excited even over the green tea while Bernard was lecturing me on the nature of parental love. And then scolding me because he and Maria had had a court appearance that day and he hadn't done well. (She had played poor little immigrant girl, dopey clothes and thick accent, one of her spies having told her that the judge was Hispanic.) How could I bother him with my so-called troubles? I should have been holding his hand. I said, Come back to my apartment and I'll hold more than that. He said I was perverted, but he was excited when he said it, I could tell. So we came back and made love in the dark, except for the violet light outside. We did all sorts of dirty things. But he wouldn't stay the night, and I ended up begging again, which I always do. Please, Bernard. Talk to me on the phone. Spend the night. Love me. I don't even care anymore if he understands me. Oh, please, let me count on you forever.

Most women are obsessed by the future. Poor Dorothy is. How will she survive, how will she keep up the house, how will she face the world? She ruins today grieving about yesterday and tomorrow. I do the same thing. In worrying about what will become of me I damage my own future—if Bernard is my future. I cling to him, pick on him, want promises from him he can't make. Swear you love me, you'll marry me, that I'll die in your arms. That's how I tortured Richard and that's what I'm doing to Bernard. Though Bernard takes it better, because he has experienced only possessive women and doesn't know there's any other kind. I live in dread of the blinders dropping from his eyes, and stand poised to change my nature completely the minute they do. I'll be whatever he wants—I don't care.

Cassie went back to California, leaving most of her clothes here. "Most" of Cassie's clothes is three times anybody else's. She has a hunger for shopping that borders on addiction. She has to do it every day, even if it's for something small, tweezers or a new lipstick. Once I shamed her about it and she tried to get through one day without going to a store. She ended up yelling at Dorothy when Dorothy was down, sending her back to pink-bathrobe-and-flask.

When she first arrived she looked like Judy Holliday in *Born Yesterday*. Betty Grable or Ginger Rogers updated. Lorelei Lee circa 1982. And oh, so queenly, such a royal pain in the ass. *Oh, I can't carry all my luggage. Aren't there any porters? Can't you bring the car closer? Can't you transform the car into a coach-and-four? Oh, dear, it's so dirty. The roads are so bad. How do you stand this, that and the other? In California we-have, at home we-always . . . .* And does Dorothy lap it up! My daughter the producer's wife. My daughter the arbiter of good taste. Cassie the wise and sweet. It was so hard at first. I had sworn to myself, promised myself I would die rather than fight with her.

Possibly the most surprising thing is that I like Cassie. Not love her—I know I love her. But for some reason that still eludes me, I like her, even though I disapprove of her life, her ridiculous hokey religion, her cliché approach to complicated human problems. Sometimes, possibly by accident, she's right about things. I suppose she's decided I'm not quite so bad, since she left me here with Dorothy. So now I stay here weekends and Wednesday nights, and have neighbors and Ol' Doc Schroeder lined up. Sometimes Bernard comes out with me.

I took Bernard to Caspar and Yo's one night, on the supposition that exposure would bring immunity, and I'm determined to get used to Yo. To my amazement, Bernard told me afterward he could see why Caspar found her so attractive.

"But she looks like a dark little mole."

"She's exotic, Celia. She has charm. Men know."

"Anybody with a French accent people think has charm."

I'll have to admit I like Yo for not knocking herself out to be ingratiating. She keeps her distance with me, and probably with everybody. She waits on Caspar, but she doesn't smother him. But then, neither did Dorothy, who was ever so cool till the shit hit the fan. Caspar likes his space, and Yo knows it. He does seem happy, and his rather stunned expression now seems to reflect wonder at his own happiness. Bit by bit, little things have come out, things I do and don't want to hear. Dorothy hardly ever slept with him for years, maybe only as a reward on Christmas or his birthday or something, gritting her teeth and thinking of England. So he wasn't getting his rights of *mariage*. And of course, she was always putting him down.

"A man needs a little praise," he told me. "Just every once in a while."

"What about a woman?" I asked.

"Sure, Cece. And your mother needs particular amounts."

I had known their marriage wasn't very good while not knowing it. Each transgression had led to another on the part of the other one. She was this way because he was that way, and vice versa. And on and on like those sets of Chinese boxes getting smaller and smaller inside one another. But it had to stop somewhere. What was the nature of the one in the middle—or was there one?

For some reason I don't really understand, I like Pierre Dev-row. He's a fierce, tough-minded little bastard, like his mother. If only he weren't so bloodthirsty and competitive, which is how those math geniuses always are. He says he's going to Harvard on a collection of loans, grants and scholarships. When isn't clear, probably January. He wants to be around for his mother's wedding. I told him not to hold his breath about that, because Dorothy was having too much fun going through the crazy gates, which I explained to him, making him laugh. I felt a little disloyal saying it, but on the other hand, in this situation a kid needs a friend. He asked me which side I was on, Dorothy's or Caspar's, and I said with your parents you couldn't really take sides, but it was okay with me about Caspar and his mother. He said if it wasn't, it wouldn't make any difference—which is true, the little prick. Anyway, I suppose we're friends, though from what I've seen of situations like this, it can't last. Somehow, usually blood gets in the way and the lineups take place according to tribe.

Before Cassie left, I asked her why she was going, and she said Sammy Junior, the oldest one, had suddenly gotten married to "an unsuitable person," about whom she would not elaborate. Said maybe she'd tell me another time. Cassie's a tease—another reason I frequently feel like killing her. Or maybe it just makes me mad that she won't open her heart—which she has no particular reason to do when she doesn't like me much. Anyway, Dorothy is on an evener keel, and Cassie felt she should look in on things at home. If she was needed, I should call her and she'd come back.

It's funny how different she looked when she left, though maybe not really funny. Her hair was much darker, and she wore much less makeup; no longer did she appear every moring with ten dollars' worth of Clinique on her face. And country tweeds and cashmere sweaters. Very Greenwich, I'd say. No, wrong. Greenwich would be a twenty-year-old Shetland sweater with a hole in it. She looked like a Hollywood producer's concept of Greenwich. And she'd gotten a pair of large round bifocals. The Hollywood producer's concept of the bespectacled wallflower off whose face William Holden would remove the glasses, then saying, "Why, Billie, you're beautiful."

So Dorothy and I took her to the airport. This time she lugged her own bag. She said, "Sometimes I feel so lost." At first I thought she meant lost in the confusion of JFK—ticket, boarding pass, gate, baggage and so on. But later I suspected it had nothing to do with the airport at all. Now that she's gone, everything here seems duller and more difficult. I find myself wondering why I'm doing anything.

Dorothy is making an astonishing recovery. She has her bad days, but the direction is generally up. I had expected her divorce to run on for years—like mine, like Bernard's, like *Jarndyce v. Jarndyce*, suits and countersuits, plaintiff says this and defendant replies so-and-so. But instead, it is snapping along briskly. Jack Brodsky, it seems, doesn't want to dillydally, has talked to Caspar's lawyer and established that there is no chance of a reconciliation. And he gives her plenty of homework. She is forever totting up expenses, Xeroxing income-tax returns from ten years ago and revising her projected budget. She works at the desk in the living room over by the window and is busy by 8:30 A.M., hair neatly combed and dressed in a businesslike skirt and blouse. As I come down I hear the tick-tick of the typewriter, and then I see her looking over her reading glasses and pushing buttons on her little calculator.

"Celia, how much do you spend a year on clothes?"

"I don't know. Less than a thousand. Sometimes almost nothing."

"Where do you shop?"

"Discount places. The thieves on the street."

"Well, I'm not about to start that at my age. I'll make it two thousand." Clickety click. "Now food. It's so hard to tell. I've been writing down every single food expense for a week, but sometimes you're here, so I can't tell."

"Sorry to throw off your calculations. Sorry to exist."

"Please, Celia. It's not that. Oh, I'm so poor at mathematics. It's just that if you're here for four meals a week, for instance, I don't know how to figure it."

"Do it by the cost of each meal. Anyway, maybe I'll always be here for four meals a week."

"Well, yes, but probably the judge would consider that irrelevant and immaterial."

"Dorothy, I think you've found your true *métier*. Why don't you train to be a paralegal?"

"Oh, you sound like Jack. I'm too old."

Jack. "Has he told you what his fee is?"

"He'll ask the judge to charge the court fees to Caspar."

I sighed. "But Mother, Daddy doesn't *have* that much money. He can't give you what he doesn't have."

Dorothy's eyes hardened—or toughened, which sounds a little better. "Jack pointed out that we don't know what Caspar has. Don't forget I never saw those account books."

"I thought all those nights with the account books turned out to be nights with Yo."

"Please don't mention her name in this house. There are still account books and ledgers which will have to be subpoenaed. For all know, Caspar has many secret investments."

"I doubt it."

"But Celia, you don't *know*. And neither do I."

Would that I had inherited some of this financial shrewdness, as Cassie obviously had. During my own divorce I did everything wrong. I kept no records, and I failed at my first assignment as plaintiff—to Xerox Richard's income-tax returns for the past five years. By the time I got to the file, he'd whisked them off to his office. That set us back considerably. It sounded as if Jack were doing his job, but how sad it was to see this legal distrust being fanned between my parents, who as far as I knew had never had any trouble about money.

There were frequent appointments with Jack—a couple of times a week. Off she would go all dressed up in her good suit, heels clicking along the sidewalk. Jack's office was on Main Street near The Bower of Flowers. Morning appointments sometimes turned into lunches at The Carriage House or the Holiday Inn on the other side of town, from which Dorothy would return at about three in high spirits.

"Oh, Lord," she'd say, collapsing on the living-room sofa and kicking off her shoes. "I really shouldn't drink those Bloody Marys."

"If he charges for his time, does lunch count?" I asked.

"Of course not, Celia. Anyway, he's giving me a dis-count. Oh, what a lovely afternoon it is. Did you notice? Jack and I took a little walk after lunch through the woods behind the library. The leaves are falling in golden show-ers." It had been a month since Caspar moved out, and now leaves were falling in golden showers. "I'm not too hungry, Celia. Let's just have some soup or something for supper."

God, this was depressing. I couldn't even blame Doro-thy for guilting me into coming up here and then deserting me for Jack, because the truth was I didn't have anything better to do in New York. Bernard was evasive these days—people coming from out of town or something, the kind I wasn't allowed to meet. I didn't feel like hanging around The Gibbon's Head on a Saturday night. Nor around my own apartment. New York, once the magnet, had lost its pull. Now the core of my existence was in Rivertown. So Dorothy and I would watch TV together, and I would listen to Jack's latest brilliant pincer movement designed to bring Caspar to his knees. Well, I didn't really listen; this dread enemy was my father. Actually, I couldn't stand it.

"Jack is going to try for half the business."

"Dorothy, don't tell me any more. It makes me sick."

One Saturday I went down to the shop and arrived just as Dorothy and Jack were coming back from one of their bacchanalian lunches. Dorothy was wearing her green tweeds and boots, and she held on to his arm. Jack was large and red-faced, with grayish-black styled hair neatly parted on the side and sprayed into place. He wore a suit of what I think is called Windowpane Plaid and a huge golden wrist-watch. He looked like what used to be called "a sport."

"Dad, does Jack Brodsky have a wife?"

"Millie Brodsky died of cancer a few months ago."

"I see."

"He sure drives a hard bargain."

"But Dad, you'd support her, wouldn't you? Why do you have to go through all this?"

Caspar shrugged. "I left Dorothy for another woman and made no secret of it. A man has to pay for that. She has to be protected. I don't resent that."

"You are much too nice. You're driving Mother crazy; she's dying for a good fight."

"Well, she has something to seek revenge for. I don't."

"But you must be angry at her for bugging the hell out of you for all those years."

Another shrug, this one Gallic, like Yo's. "I wasn't perfect. And a good part of the time we were content."

"When are you going to get mad?"

"I guess when she pushes me too far."

"When that happens I don't want to be around."

If my father seemed unduly passive, he was turning out to be wiser than I had ever thought. I had picked up some of Dorothy's opinion over the years, which was that he was something of a dimwit. But now that they had been peeled apart—that I could see one without the other—I knew it wasn't true. I loved him more for having been more than I had known. I was angry at myself for having underestimated him, and for not having gotten what he had to offer, and I forgot that he had not really offered it.

One night in Manhattan, Meg, the psychologist, phoned and said, "Let's go to The Gibbon's Head."

At the bar, she said, "I hear your ex is happily married."

"So what?"

"Come on, Celia. Everybody's interested in what their ex is doing."

"I don't believe most people hate as deeply as I do."

"You think not? Listen, I could tell you stories. She's a model with a business degree. She's one of those very tall, extremely skinny women with burned-out eyes."

"Have you met her?"

"I have, and she wanted to know about you. So I told her you were perfect. And that you had left him—not the other way around, as he had told her."

I was annoyed. "Why did you do that?"

"I was drunk," Meg said, "and she was pregnant."

The Gibbon's Head was its usual dark, dirty self—but pleasant. The stuffed monkey's head mounted on the wall, its puckered furry little face grimacing down on us. The sharp, cool smell of gin. The thump-thump of the jukebox playing fifties music. But mostly the people, who had graying heads and what might be called lived-in faces.

"I suppose it was a lousy thing to do," Meg said.

"Probably she didn't pay any attention to you. It's amazing how little attention anybody pays to anybody else."

"Not when they're paid for it. When people pay my hourly fee they get my complete attention. Otherwise I don't listen."

I said, "I suppose you envied her being pregnant."

"Well, we're old, Celia. It's more that than what you said. I'm almost forty."

I said, "Meg, I don't feel like getting into some shitty depressing conversation about how rotten life is. I have enough going on at home."

"I thought everybody was doing fine."

"Well, they're not. Dorothy either lies around with her flask or skips around town with Jack the legal eagle, running up bills."

"So what?" asked Meg the ever-sympathetic. "She wants a divorce. She's getting one. Everybody's happy, except Celia. Listen, I could tell you stories about mothers that would curl your ears. And fathers who run out and the wives have to go on Welfare."

I ordered us each another drink, vodka-on-the-rocks. "I think I'm probably going to get drunk."

"Well, meanwhile you can listen to *my* problems for a change." She then launched into a truly terrifying narrative of some distant cousin who she said was plotting to kill her so she (Cousine) would get all Grandpa's money. The fact that Grandpa didn't have any, nor if he had would Meg get it, was only the beginning of Cousine's delusion. Even though Grandpa had been dead for twenty years and it was too late anyway, Cousine turned up everywhere, at cocktail parties and on the street, and had once made an appointment with Meg under an assumed name and arrived as a patient, fingering a knife. When Meg had started to dial the police, she had fled. And on top of this, the only man in Meg's life was manic-depressive and lithium didn't work on him, nor did anything else, so he was always either out spending all his money or else sitting on the toilet crying. "I'm thinking of moving to the country," she said, "The *real* country—Vermont or Iowa or some-where. Get my hands into the earth. Maybe I could live off the land. Want to come?"

More drinks and then both of us in tears. What a pair of sots we were—everybody avoided us. Except that Meg, at least, had some decent problems and I didn't, or I didn't think I did. "I get frightened," she said. "I have enough money. I lead a pretty comfortable life in this town."

"That's it," I said. "Cousine wants your apartment."

"Fuck her. I'll kill *her*. How dare she do this to me? I lie in my bed and shiver. I can't sleep. I'm getting as crazy as she is."

There were two little girls sitting at a table nearby drinking Cokes. About eight and six. It was the kind of place where the divorced Daddies brought their kids. Or dumped them. When I asked who had brought them, the older one said, "Daddy said to wait here, he'll be back in a little while. He just had to take the lady home. We can have as many Cokes as we want, and he left quarters for the jukebox." She had a thin, pale face and dark straight hair.

"Would you like to come home with me and wait for Daddy?" I asked. "You can sleep on the sofa bed. We'll leave my phone number with the bartender."

"You can't do that," Meg said. "That's kidnapping."

"*He* can't do that. I can't stand it. I'll have him arrested whoever he is. How dare he leave his kids here while he goes and fucks? I'll tell Mom, that's what I'll do." I was absolutely enraged, partly by the vodka, partly by our terrible lives. The smaller child was sleeping at the table. "Where's your Mommy, dear?"

"In London."

"Who are you, the Morals Squad?" Meg asked. "It could be worse. Let me tell you I've seen worse. Anyway, this is a pretty nice bar; if I had kids I wouldn't mind bringing them here."

I was in tears again. "This city is rotten. Our lives are rotten, terrible. Bernard would never bring his kids to a bar. Look at her—she can't be more than eight. She should be home in bed."

"Daddy will be back in a little while," the child said.

"Meg," I said, "either I rescue these kids, or I kill somebody. Or I leave. There are only those three choices, no others."

"Leave, then," said Meg. "I'll sit here with them. Shortly Cousine will come and kill all of us."

I screamed, "You think you've got problems! My whole life is falling apart. My home. My past. Everything." People began to stare. "It's the loneliness," I explained. "Everybody's floating away. I'm left on the iceberg. Come on, little girls. Come back with me. I'll make up the bed for you."

Through the drunken haze a man appeared, one of those bearded clones that inhabit the East Side. "You'll make up nothing, you old dyke. Keep away from my kids."

"Hey, cool it," Meg said. "You're the one who dumped them here. You're lucky they're still alive, you bastard."

"Well, Christ. Some nerve. Are you all right, Susie and Janie?"

"Can we have another Coke?" Susie asked.

I snarled, "It's midnight. You should be garroted. Reamed. Drawn and quartered. Can't you keep your cock down for one evening?"

"Why, you bitch." He would have swung at me, or that's the impression I had, if Meg hadn't dragged me out of the place, throwing a bill at the bartender.

"Celia, Celia. What am I going to do with you—always getting into fights in bars?"

"I'm going to see Bernard," I sniffled. "I need him. I'm sorry I made a scene. But how did that creep get custody?"

"I wouldn't go see Bernard."

"Why not?"

"Because you're drunk."

"Well, what are friends for? He gets drunk. I listen to him. I've dragged him home. I need to be close to him. Not for sex—just close."

"Come on home with me. Please don't."

"Let him listen to me for a change."

Weaving around the street, I shortly found a taxi and got in, blowing kisses at Meg as she stood there on the sidewalk watching me. We rolled across town while I combed my hair and tried to collect my wits. I had never done this before, but never mind. My mind had a drunken fixity: Any good relationship has a few obligations. This is his. In the small mirror I looked a trifle mad, wild-eyed and disarrayed.

At Bernard's I pressed a five into the driver's hand and climbed the front steps of the brownstone, pausing to sit down and dig for the key, which was buried in the bottom of my handbag. Only the vodka would have allowed me to sit on the steps of a West Side brownstone on a lonely block at midnight, methodically removing and lining up wallet, credit cards, checkbook, letters and keys in a neat row as I tried to focus on what I was doing. Bernard. His house. I would explain why I had come. Now the key, which he gave me from time to time and then asked for back, according to how smothered he was feeling or how his divorce was going. It had never occurred to the trusting man that I'd have copies made, which of course I had. It was elementary—once you gave somebody a key, the only way back was to have the lock changed. Key was found. I put everything back, and nobody had walked by but a man with a poodle.

Crunch, the downstairs door opened, and I closed it behind me and started up the stairs, feeling a touch more sober, but still unnaturally brave. It was quiet and very dark, lit only by a murky light on the ceiling. If he wasn't at home, I would wait for him; it would be almost as good to curl up in his bed, where his smell was. In the second-floor hall I slowly opened the door. Inside, Bernard's living room was dark and still. No hall light, which meant he was home. The room was a mess of dark furniture forms in the pink light from the night sky. I tiptoed toward the bedroom.

Did nothing warn me? No, the vodka had turned off my usual wealth of wild speculation. I, whose mind was hardly ever free of terrible visions of robbers, rapists, vandals, maniacs of all kinds; I, whose radar worked overtime: not once, not for a single second did it occur to me that he might not be alone. There on the queen bed (the new one; she had the old one) lay Bernard and Maria. The blind was up, and they were lit by the rosy sky of late-night Manhattan. Naked and obscene, Maria lay sprawled on her back, dark furry cunt in my direction as though on exhibit. In its center her pale innards. Big tits flattened out, chest rising and falling. She looked pretty and Rubensesque, the bitch. And next to her Bernard face-down, half-tangled in a sheet. The two white globes of his behind shining forth, his face turned in my direction, mustache crushed. His big shoulders and broad back outlined against the far wall.

I was indeed very drunk, and it took a moment. Then I began to scream—what I'm not sure. Every obscenity that came to mind. Cunt. Prick. Twat. Bernard woke up instantly, sat up with wits collected. "Celia! For God's sake. How did you get in here?"

"Oh, God. Is that all you can ask? Who cares? You're a fucking psychopath. I came down the chimney like Santa Claus."

It took Maria longer. "What is it? Who's there? Who's that?"

"You know damn well who it is," I yelled. "How dare you? How can you fuck with people's lives like this?" I leaped over toward her—I think I was going to hit her; but my aim was bad, and Bernard grabbed my arm.

"Is this Celia?" Maria asked Bernard.

"Yes, it certainly is. Celia, pull yourself together."

"How dare you say that to me? Oh, how rotten you are. How low. How vile. I thought you were better. I could take every bit of the understanding I've given you and shove it up your ass."

"You forget Maria is still my wife. And obviously we've had a reconciliation."

Briefly the room spun. Cassie was right. The shock was sobering me up fast. "Oh, obviously. What a pitifully tiny mind you have, Bernard. Only the piece of paper makes for real obligations. Oh, how you fooled me, you bastard."

Maria looked at him and said, "You mean you didn't tell her that we'd gotten back together?" She'd managed to get herself into a slithery white peignoir.

"For God's sake, we only got together day before yesterday. And in case you've forgotten, I've been busy, and frankly, I forgot."

That was a mistake. Maria and I screamed simultaneously:

Me: "Oh, you forgot, did you? You've been too busy fucking — right? Well, it won't last, any more than it ever did, you fool. In a week you'll be back on my doorstep."	*Maria:* "Oh, too busy to get rid of your mistress! You know damn well you forgot because you didn't want to get rid of her—because you were going to string both of us along, you prick!"

Maria came out rather well, better than I'd thought. Standing there in her shimmery white gown in the pink light, lighting a cigarette, she had real dignity. Bernard, on the other hand, was pathetic, his limp cock cringing between his legs like a frightened little worm. He snatched the sheet over himself as I stared at him scornfully, then reached for his jockey shorts and put them on under the covers. Maria and I looked at each other with an understanding terrible in its profundity. So often the woman seemed to come out stronger.

Maria turned on the bedside lamp and sat on the edge of the bed, looking at her husband. "I no longer trust you," she said. She didn't have an accent really, just a charming inflection like Yo's but much slighter. And God, was she cool. "Not that I ever have, really," she continued. "I have made the mistake of thinking I could live with a man I don't trust. Truly it isn't worth it."

This interested me. "It isn't?"

Bernard said, "I've heard this speech before. It's irrelevant. It isn't trust, it's money you can't decide whether you can live without."

"There is no possibility that I will ever have to, Bernard," Maria said. "As usual, you reduce every subtle and sensitive thing to dollars and cents. Oh, it is hopeless. I try and try for the sake of the children. For twenty years of my life. I came back this time determined to make it work. And in comes this woman."

"I am not 'this woman.' My name is Celia—Celia Armstrong. Come on, Maria. You were doing fine till you started lying. I was even beginning to be on your side." I looked at Bernard, who was groping around in the dark for cigarettes. "You're cruel to goad her about money. She has to take from you."

Bernard stood up. "Celia, will you please leave. And stop with the sisterhood." Actually, it was a sensible idea. I looked at Maria. Her eyes were focused on me, but her expression was unfathomable.

"Oh, shit," she said, jamming out her cigarette. "I am going to be forty-nine next week. I'm tired. I'm sick of this legal shit. All I ever wanted was to be a wife and mother. So simple. I still hardly understand how difficult it has all gotten. I just want it settled, Bernard. I just want some peace—with you or without you."

"There," I said to Bernard. "You can't argue with that. She doesn't care if she's married to you or not. How could you have told me this girl is hard to please?"

Maria froze. "So you have talked to her about me. How could you? Though I don't know why I'm surprised."

"Celia, get the hell out of here. And give me the key."

"Sure." I started digging in my handbag again, this time lining up the contents on the foot of the bed while Maria and Bernard watched as though hypnotized. Wallet, sunglasses, checkbook, credit cards, address book, comb, Tampax. Matches and Sen-Sen. "It's here somewhere, I promise." I finally found it and gave it to him. I had another at home.

Maria said, "You are a strange person, Celia. Usually I get a distinct feeling about people the moment I meet them. But with you I feel confused."

"A lot of people feel the same way." I tried a smile— probably a pretty weird one. "Goodbye, Maria. Goodbye, Bernard. Sorry to disturb your sleep. Sorry to exist. Goodbye."

What a long way home it was. Particularly since I got there by walking across the park. In my drunken, charmed state no one threatened me. When I woke in the morning and remembered what I had done, I was amazed to be still alive. I was repellent, bulletproof and broke. Even the rapists didn't want me.

CASSIE

Well, I decided to go back to Santa Barbara after all.

Even though God had told me that Mother needed me more, I couldn't help worrying about the condition of my family, who from all reports seemed to have gone off the deep end, mainly because of my new daughter-in-law Eleanor. Mother's spirits certainly had improved since she had gotten an attorney, and Celia, though certainly peculiar, has apparently changed somewhat from the evil and suspicious person she once was. However, she still has her sarcastic sense of humor (if it can be called that) and her habit of picking on poor Mother. But I can't be responsible for everything, for God's sake, and so I told God that if He thought about it just a little more, He probably would see it my way, and so I packed up a few things and left.

I took the "Red-Eye" and arrived home unannounced early in the morning. The taxi brought me up our long driveway and dropped me at the front door. Nobody seemed to be around, and I went into the house. The lights were off; but when I turned on the switch, I was horrified.

Never had my tastefully decorated and impeccably clean house looked this way. Dirty clothes on the floor. Dried-out TV-dinner trays with remnants of old food stuck on them. Glasses and dirty ashtrays everywhere. A disgusting smell of rotten garbage, marijuana and the vile odor of unclean bathrooms. Dog shit on the hall rug, as though nobody had bothered to walk the poor thing. One of the lamps had fallen over and broken, and nobody had cleaned up the broken glass. In shock I walked through the living room, the dining room and the kitchen, where I found the same terrible disorder.

I went down the hall to the bedrooms. Stuart and Shelli were both in their beds asleep. I won't even attempt to describe their bedrooms. In fact, I could hardly find Stu amid the clutter and knew he was there only when one of his limbs twitched. In the guest room lay Sammy Junior and Eleanor, his bride, on a "futon." Both were stark naked, and I could not help noticing the contrast between them. Sammy has an excellent physique. He is tanned and muscular and perfectly proportioned. But Eleanor looked every day of her forty years, and besides that had obviously never been very attractive to begin with. Scrawny, with ribs sticking out and big hands and feet. Mottled, freckled skin. Stringy breasts and a small saggy behind. Long, unkempt hair that looked dirty and a large nose. This was the creature that called me "Mom."

Then down the hall to our bedroom, where Sam lay snoring. He was unshaven, and one red-rimmed eye was half-open in his sleep, staring at me with an idiotic blind expression. I can honestly say I had never been so depressed in my life. I sat down and let the tears come. When I saw that Christ and Mary Magdalene had been taken down from the wall, and that the breast rug was on the floor of the bathroom, I cried even harder.

In a few minutes Sam heard me and woke up, staring at me as though I were a ghost. "Cassie! What are you doing here?"

"I live here, you bastard." Suddenly I was so furious that I could have walked over, picked up that sagging penis in my hand and cut it off with the desk scissors. Probably the only reason I didn't was that this organ has fathered my children, though at the moment that didn't seem like much of an accomplishment. "What's been going on here?"

Sam struggled to a sitting position and rubbed his eyes. "Christ, my head hurts. We had a little party last night."

"Where is Concepción?"

"Oh, God, she left days ago. And I was glad to see her go—she was driving me crazy." He looked at me and attempted a smile. "You should have let me know you were coming, honey."

"Don't you 'honey' me. I hate you, Sam Coopersmith. I've never been so disgusted in my life. Obviously nobody has picked up a thing or washed anything since I left. This kind of disorder is a sign of a person's character. Yours is obviously weak to the core, besides which you are a complete pig." My voice must have been rather loud, because Shelli appeared in the doorway, and her face broke into a smile.

"Mom! You're back!"

"Shelli, you will not get around me for your part in this horrible scene. I simply cannot believe the things that have apparently been going on here in the last three weeks. While I have been at my poor mother's side, carrying out a family obligation, you people have been living here like animals. I'm ashamed of all of you."

Shelli's face sagged. "I'm sorry. It's just that Eleanor—"

"I'll deal with her in a minute. Where is Stuart?"

"I guess he's asleep still," Shelli said. "He sleeps a lot."

"What do you mean? Hasn't he been going to school?"

"Of course," Sam said. "Actually, he's been working harder this term. He's always in his room studying."

"Well, that's the only good thing I've heard since I walked into this house."

"Are you staying, Mom?" Shelli asked.

"I am certainly staying until I get this house and all of you people in order. After that, I will have to see how Mother is doing with her divorce."

"I hope you stay."

"Well, that depends on many things. In the meantime, I want you to go in and start cleaning your room. And I hope you have attended to your horse."

I knew that this stay at home was going to be difficult, and so it turned out to be. I have long had a motto "Start with the hardest job," and so I went immediately into the guest room and told Eleanor and Sammy Junior that they would have to leave and I didn't care if they slept on the beach. As I stood there talking, Sammy yelled, "For Christ's sake, Ma, let us get dressed, will you?"

"Then put your clothes on immediately and I'll talk to you downstairs."

I went down to the disreputable kitchen, with its over-flowing trash basket and piles of sticky dishes, where I managed to find the electric coffeemaker, wash it and refill it. I was plugging it in when Sam shambled in, more or less dressed.

"Cassie, I'm really sorry about this. That fucking maid quit last week and I haven't been able to get another. The agencies are loaded with requests. And you know how the kids are. I've tried to keep after them, but, well, they'll do anything to get out of it."

"Sam, to tell the truth, nothing you say is making any particular impression on me. I've been among real people with real problems, and frankly, the contrast between my poor parents' misery and the pathetic incompetence of you people can't be avoided. You have no right to blame Concepción or the agencies or anybody but yourself."

As I stood there giving Sam a piece of my mind, in came Sammy and Eleanor, both looking extremely cheer-ful, though God knows why. Eleanor is extremely tall, probably about five feet ten, and she was wearing one of those Indian dresses that you buy on the street for about five dollars. She has huge teeth, and she was grinning, and before I could stop her or move aside, or fend her off, she had come over and thrown her arms around me and said in her deep rumble,

"Mom. We're so glad you're home. Everybody's missed you." She smelled of stale incense and sweat, and in this endless embrace my nose was forced into her greasy hair and I had a close look at her yellow, waxy ear.

When I finally struggled out of her perverted grasp, I said, "Don't you dare call me Mom. And keep your hands off me or I'll call the police. The welcome given you by this family does not include me, and as I said before, I want you and Sammy to leave immediately."

"Oh, come on, Mom," Sammy said, trying to be charm-ing. "We have no place to go. And you'll love Eleanor when you get to know her."

A long, stupid argument ensued which ended in a draw. They could stay temporarily if they started looking for jobs immediately, or else if Sammy Junior enrolled somewhere for some courses in something that would equip him to function in the commercial world. And if she would never call me "Mom" again, though I would permit "Cassie." And if everybody started cleaning up the house *immediately*.

While they started on the kitchen, and Sam started off to work, I went back to Stu's room. He looked dead to the world, and I wondered if he had been "tripping" again. I shook him and shook him, and finally he woke up and looked at me in a dim, dazed way. When I questioned him, he said that he had been taking something, but he didn't even seem to know what. When I asked if he had been going to school, he said sometimes he was so tired he just stayed in his room and listened to music.

For the first time it occurred to me that there might be something seriously wrong with him, so on the new list I was making, which was already getting very long, I wrote down *"Appointment with Dr. Battaglia"* to get him a general checkup and possibly some injections of vitamin B_{12}. He did not look well, though when I felt his forehead he didn't seem to have any fever. He said he was glad I was back, because everything at home had been "weird"—a word he uses to describe almost everything. If it sounds as though his problems were mental and that he should be going to a psychiatrist, well, he was already going to a psychiatrist, though he hadn't been there since I had left. I wrote on my list to make sure Stu went to his regular appointments.

I called a cleaning service, which said it would do the place from stem to stern for a thousand dollars—which seemed like a lot until I saw the wonders the workers did. How my spirits improved as they washed windows, shampooed rugs, polished furniture and brass. Soon the house was in good shape except for the permanent damage that had been done to certain pieces—the lipstick marks on my white velvet chaise lounge and cigarette burns on the Naugahyde playpen. I took the breast rug and threw it out, and knew Sam was so guilty he wouldn't dare say a word.

When I went to look for Angela, whom I had asked to

keep an eye on things and who had obviously failed in her duty, I found a strange woman in the front hall who said she was a real estate agent. She said the bank had fore-closed Angela's mortgage and that Angela had moved into one of those cheesy little apartments down near the beach and was working as a waitress at El Paseo. The house was now on the market, and somehow because of Angela's horrible settlement Paul would get the money, even though he was already loaded with it. I wrote on my list, *"See Angela—speak to her about taking prick back to court."*

I sighed at the realization of how much divorce there was among my friends and family, that terrible catastrophe which even I might someday have to face, for it lurked below the surface of every marriage. How sad it was that marriage was no longer the sacred institution it once was, a haven of joy and peace and security where children were raised with good discipline and solid Christian values. Now it seemed to have become just the opposite, an exhausting "maelstrom" and battleground for struggles about drugs, money and sex.

As I looked at the troubled people who surrounded me in my own home, I felt more than ever that I was the only one who had decent and clear-sighted Christian beliefs, besides being willing to take some trouble to carry them out, and it brought back a feeling of loneliness that came upon me more and more frequently, probably similar to the feelings Christ must have had when He was among the lepers, thieves and sinners. I don't mean to be so conceited as to compare myself to Christ, because I am nowhere near as good, and I am, of course, a woman. But possibly there are some half-Christs who have been chosen to try to keep God's Word in a smaller way, and if so, I'm sure I'm one of them. Anyway, even if I'm not, I still feel the impor-tance of God's Word and the strong will to carry it out, even if those around me are falling by the side of the road, floundering in their own weakness and corruption. I know I am obligated to help those who need me in any way that I can.

When I came back from Angela's house, I found Elea-nor on the patio, pushing a broom around in what I thought was a rather inefficient way. She rushed at me as I

appeared—obviously the creature refused to let me alone—
though thanks to the stern and forbidding expression on
my face, she didn't try to embrace me. Instead, she crossed
her arms and said, "Cass, I know it's tough having us
here, and the marriage and all. But man, that kid swept me
off my feet." She grinned. I assumed "that kid" was my
son. "I mean, maybe you can remember what it's like to
be really zapped by somebody."

"If I do, Eleanor, I have no desire to discuss it with
you. And don't call me Cass."

"You know, I really hope we can get to know each
other. I'm a very warm and demonstrative person. I'm into
the laying on of hands."

"Look here, Eleanor. Whatever you're into is no concern of mine. I'm putting up with you until you and
Sammy Junior can get yourselves gainful employment and
get the hell out of here into your own home. I make no
secret of the fact that I disapprove of your hasty marriage
and am suspicious of your motives. And please don't lay
your hands on anybody but your husband. From what
Sammy mentioned to me about your past sexual life I
wonder what you're doing with a husband anyway."

Oh, why did I say it? Eleanor then talked for fully
fifteen minutes about her newest "breakthroughs" and
"realizations." In short, she had decided that a person's
sexuality was "irrelevant" and it was only physical love
that counted.

"Look at it this way, Cassie. I think that people being
two different sexes is God's joke. He did it on purpose to
see if we could rise above the ridiculousness of being male
and female onto higher planes of human love. Which is
best expressed by physicality, because words are only a
metaphor to pacify the intellect. Only bodies speak"—and
on and on she went. My God, the woman was long-
winded. Then she said, "I groove on you, Cassie. I didn't
know whether I'd like you or not. But you're a very honest
person. You don't have a problem with your anger."

"Well, *you'll* have a problem with it if you think you've
moved in here."

"That's another thing, Mo . . . Cassie. I think I can be
a help to you. We all get along real well here. And I've

gotten everybody into Hindu metaphysics. We'll try some expression dancing tonight. You'll see how fabulous it is.''

"We will not."

"Well, maybe another time." She was determined to be ingratiating. "But anyway, I thought I might be a little help to you if you have to go Back East again to your Mom's crisis. And even if you don't. The nuke family is hard on the female."

How I longed to get away from this tiresome woman by simply diving into the pool—but the pool was a stagnant and slimy broth. The thing to do was shut her up by keeping her busy, so I gave her several jobs to do, such as the laundry and taking Stu to the doctor, while I continued to phone the maintenance people who kept us from descending into savagery: the pool man, the vet, the dry cleaner and so forth. Then, because I deserved a treat, I went to Elizabeth Arden's and had a shampoo and set, a manicure, a pedicure, a massage, a facial and a leg waxing—in short, "the works"—and emerged several hours later feeling much better. I left my hair the slightly darker shade that I had had done in Rivertown just for a change.

It took a while to get Stuart to a doctor, because Dr. Battaglia was scuba-diving off Catalina and his partner was up on the mountain in a think tank. Finally Eleanor found somebody to take him to, and reported afterward that there was nothing very wrong with Stu except the usual adolescent problems, and he should be encouraged to take on more physical activity and to be more a part of the family. I have to admit that Eleanor was helpful with him, and she dragged him out of his room and took him on hikes and down to the beach. He didn't seem to have too many friends, so in that sense, though I hate to admit it, she was a good influence. It occurred to me that she might be laying her hands on him, but possibly that wouldn't have been a bad thing. It was true that people needed physical affection.

Then suddenly, when things seemed to be back in order again, the most terrible thing happened: Ginger, Shelli's horse, died of neglect. I had forgotten all about the animal, and so, apparently, had everybody else, Shelli included.

Nobody knew about it until the neighbors began to notice the smell and went to investigate, and there was poor Ginger lying dead on her straw. A small group of them came to the door one night along with a representative from the SPCA. They were all very angry and charged us with negligence and Lord knows what else, and poor Ginger was taken away and buried.

But the worst part of it was that Shelli didn't even seem to care. I was deeply shocked when I talked to her and she only said unpleasant things like "Oh, she was old anyway. She's better off dead." I was appalled at my daughter, who had always been a perfectly normal child, free of some of the more disagreeable characteristics that seemed to surface in the rest of the family. But now she showed a coldness and cruelty that I had never suspected.

That night, I gave in on the Hindu expressionist dancing, because it seemed like a good way for all of us to purge our feelings about poor Ginger. So after dinner we lit candles on the terrace and put on some sitar records and did a slow, soothing and graceful dance led by Eleanor, which was good for all of us, though in the middle I burst into tears and wept for the poor dead horse, of whom I had been quite fond. The strange thing was that I was more upset about it than anybody else in the family, and it took me several weeks, even months, to get over it. I even had dreams about Ginger and couldn't get rid of the idea that we had killed her. Sam got impatient with me and said, "For Christ's sake, Cassie, it's just a fucking horse" and made other supposedly comforting statements. But I still had terrible nightmares of horses jumping over fences and falling, or crashing into cliffs and breaking into pieces, or just of broken and bleeding horses lying crushed on a bright green lawn with the blood soaking in. I'd wake Sam, and we'd hug each other, and if he was dying to, we'd make love, though what I really wanted was just to be held close.

Sam seemed glad that I was back, and there was no talk of divorce, for which I was grateful. In fact, he was quite affectionate, and we even went out to dinner alone together a couple of times and for a drive up the coast while Eleanor entertained the children. It was true that it was helpful to have another woman around, even if she wasn't exactly the one I would have chosen. She became especially close to Shelli and continued to pay attention to her in spite of the dreadful thing the girl had done, which made it difficult for me to treat her with my usual affection.

Then one night Sam said he wanted to talk to me about something, and he would rather not go to El Paseo, where I wanted to go for old times' sake and also to give a tip to Angela. I didn't like the way he said it, which meant he was going to confess to some affair—not for the first time in our marriage—all in the name of "honesty," which is a word I sometimes wish had never been invented. So we went to one of those steak places with a huge fire where they do the charcoal broiling, and sure enough, I was right, and this time it was Angela.

Oh, I can't begin to say how dreadful I felt, as though my whole world had fallen apart. Sam was blubbering with guilt, the bastard, which was why he was telling me about it, and went on and on about how the poor woman was so broke and losing her house and how her life was so terrible that he'd done it only to comfort her. Well, I think I would have killed him if we hadn't been in a public place. Somehow I could live with Sam's sleazy affairs if they were with women I didn't know. But this cruel deed was aimed directly at me. Now I knew why I had been unable to get Angela on the phone even though I had left messages for her and even stuck a note under the door of her apartment. The worst part was hearing this about the person who had been my best friend for so many years and now would never be again because there would always be this thing between us. As for Sam, it was just one more pinprick where he'd already stuck about a thousand, and by this time I was getting numb.

Then Sam tried to tell me exactly what had happened, and I said if he did I would kill him. I asked why, if he felt so fucking sorry for her, he didn't just give her some money, which she could have used better than a few nights with him ("Only three times, Cassie, that's all") which probably left her feeling worse than ever. Even though I was furious at her, I still couldn't help feeling sorry for her as one more woman who had been ill-used by a man. Then to make things worse, Sam said, "Because we haven't *got* as much money as I told you before. Not only did the reruns of *The Wimples* fall through, but so did two other deals. So I'm working, but barely, and we're going to have to *cut down*. I've put the condo in Acapulco on the market, and we can go awhile on that. But unless something pretty hot comes along, Cassie, *we're in trouble*."

I said, "Sam Coopersmith, you are a rotten son-of-a-bitch to tell me all this in a public place where you know I can't yell, which is what I'm dying to do." It was hard to keep my voice low so people wouldn't stare at us. "Not only have you screwed my best friend, but you have the nerve to tell me to cut down at this time when our whole family is in a state of crisis. I simply refuse to sit there as Angela did among the dead plants and falling masonry squeezing out a living among broken appliances. Nor am I about to let my looks go or creep around in old clothes, worn-out shoes or other signs of deterioration, because to me, Sam, my appearance is my self-respect, and I will never, never compromise on it. If I were going in front of a firing squad I assure you I would spend my last hours setting my hair, making up my face and choosing the best-looking outfit I owned."

"I believe it," Sam said, puffing furiously on a cigarette even though he hadn't finished his steak.

"Besides, none of this is my fault, Sam. No matter how you try to get around it, I don't believe any man can be at his best in his work if he drinks and takes drugs the way you do. There have been many, many days when you simply didn't go to work, for instance."

He stabbed out the cigarette. "I've explained at least a hundred times that being a film producer is not like working at a shoe factory. I don't punch a time clock, for Christ's sake."

"I'm aware of that, but I do know successful men never stop thinking of their work day or night. Look at the ones in that Bache commercial. They're always getting up from dinner to go to the phone, which you have never done in your life."

Sam looked so angry I decided to stop. "Cassie, keep your fucking opinions about my work to yourself. You

don't know *shit*. The industry has hit hard times. None of
this is my fault—except possibly that because you weren't
here on the seventeenth, I took the Top Enchiladas to El
Paseo and it wasn't such a terrific evening, and that might
have had something to do with the *Wimples* reruns not
coming through.''

"That is so ridiculous I can't even get angry. In fact,
I'm amazed, Sam. As long as I've known you, you still
manage to surprise me from time to time. You tell me
you're 'self-destructive,' and by God, it's true. You should
have taken them to a fancy French place and ordered
everything ahead of time, using the suggestions of the
maître d'. What did you feed them—tacos?''

"Well, Angela said she'd serve us, and—''

"Stop.'' I put my elbows on the table and leaned my
face in my hands. "Angela can't even get breakfast on the
table.''

"Well, shit. I felt sorry for her. I left her a big tip.''

There is no point in going on with Sam's and my
conversation. All I can say is, after all these years I finally
understand this self-destructiveness he's always talking about.
Sam has, or had, many good qualities, which he constantly
tries to undermine. It's as though Renoir or Picasso or
somebody created a beautiful painting and then destroyed
it. Not that Sam is any genius, but he is, or was, a very
talented man, and as far as I can see, he hasn't accomplished much in his fifty-one years, unless you count
dog-food commercials and those stupid *Wimples*.

Anyway, of course I didn't agree to cut down right after
he'd told me about himself and Angela, the fool. When he
threatened to cancel all the charge accounts, I told him if he
did I'd go straight to a lawyer. Then he said, with a
strange look, if that was the way I wanted to do it, we'd
just go along the way we were until the money was gone
and then declare bankruptcy. If I wouldn't stop spending,
the stores would stop extending credit when the bills weren't
paid, and there I'd be in Gucci or somewhere, and they'd
call me discreetly aside and say, "Mrs. Coopersmith, I'm
afraid we can't charge this item until your account has
been settled.'' So maybe if I didn't believe him I'd believe
Gucci.

The next morning Sam called the whole family together and said that we had to cut back on expenses, and everything that wasn't necessary would have to go—for instance, psychiatrists, because it would be better for us all to solve our own problems anyway. Nobody really paid much attention to him except Eleanor, who said she welcomed the new regimen—I don't know what regimen she was talking about—and we would start by tearing out the roses in the rose garden (varietals I have collected for years) and putting in carrots, tomatoes, broccoli and herbs. We would have a farm co-op and live off the land. We could even get a few chickens and a cow and put it in Ginger's old stall, using that tennis-court space for a pasture. I said if this family had been incapable of keeping a horse alive, we wouldn't do any better with a cow.

On the heels of this depressing discussion, Angela came to pay me a visit, cleverly picking a time when Sam wasn't there. Of course she wept and cried and apologized, which meant they'd talked and he'd told her when he was telling me. She really looked like shit and about eighty years old, though in fact she is two years younger than I. I sat through her tiresome explanations of having been drunk and down in the dumps anyway, and how Sam was comforting her and it just sort of happened one night after the Hindu dancing when everybody was smoking a lot of grass.

I hadn't heard much about drugs since I got back, but after listening to Angela I realized that all the members of my family had been taking anything they could get their hands on, mainly because of Eleanor, who had connections all over the place and believed that not being stoned was God's joke and drugs were the way to higher planes of human love. Obviously they'd told her to cool it with me, but now I realized that the woman was turning my family into a bunch of addicts.

Anyway, Angela's brain had really rotted if she thought telling me about being stoned was any sort of explanation, and I told her so. I said I didn't care anymore whom Sam fucked or whom she did, but why, with all the sex available in Southern California, had they had to pick each other? Angela said it was because they both loved me and it was a way of pretending I was back, which was so ridiculous I almost threw her out of the house, except that I felt sorry for her, so I wrote her out a check for $250 for her rent and a few groceries. I honestly feel that a lot of what people do has to do with how much money they have, though I didn't tell Angela this, and I don't think she would have slept with Sam if she hadn't been so broke and thought he was rich. Of course, I didn't tell her she'd been barking up the wrong tree and just hoped the check went through. As I watched her drive away in her old wreck of a car, clutching the check greedily, I felt dreadfully sad at losing my best friend, and lonelier than I had ever felt in my life.

It turned out I was right about the drugs. I soon found out that they were all smoking, popping pills and snorting whenever they had a chance, which certainly helped use up the available cash. Sam went back to his old "anxiety attacks" when he lay on the bed looking peculiar and talking about how his impending bankruptcy was a metaphor of his relationship with his father. In fact, things suddenly started to get worse all around. One night I woke up to hear a kind of whimpering out in the hall, and I went out and found Stu crouching on the floor saying snakes were after him. He seemed too enormous to cuddle the way I once did, so I sat down near him and told him he was only having a nightmare, the way he had when he was a child. He said he wasn't having a nightmare, he was wide awake and the snakes were still coming, along with bats and scorpions. I said, "No, Stu, they aren't real; it's just your imagination." Then he broke out in perspiration and began shivering as though he were ill. He told me he'd been "tripping," which I had guessed. Then he began to cry—which amazed me, because he'd always tried so hard to be "*macho*." "Mom, everything is shit," he said. "I can't take it."

I said, "Stu, every family has difficulties, and ours is no exception. Your father and I are still together, which isn't true of many of your friends. If we are having financial reverses, it just means we have to cut back from luxury to affluence—which isn't so bad; in fact, it might be good for all of us. In fact, I haven't bought any clothes for a month and have resolved not to do so till next year''—which I hadn't told Sam because I didn't want to appear to capitulate to him—"nor will we hire another maid. You must do your best at school and the chores at home which Eleanor and I will assign to you."

"But I can't keep my mind on my work," he said. "I can't even think straight."

"I'm sorry not to be more sympathetic, Stuart, but if you persist in taking drugs your brain will continue to decay. If you really can't stop, maybe you should go to one of those places where they get you off them—Silicone, or whatever it's called."

All of a sudden I thought of Ginger again, this time with blood gushing out of her ears and mouth and bits of gray livery-looking stuff which I knew to be decayed brain. I began to shake just like Stuart, who looked at me in an alarmed way, or as alarmed as he could get considering his general condition. The truth was I didn't feel right at all, particularly since the business about Angela. I wondered if I were taking the family's problems too hard, for I seemed to be under an unusual amount of "stress." It was frightening, because I knew I was the only strong one around, and if I collapsed from illness or nervous exhaustion, they would all go down the drain.

Then as if that weren't enough, I was sitting out by the pool the next afternoon, trying to summon up some pleasant and relaxing thoughts, and a voice came out of the lemon tree, clear as a bell: Your Mother Needs You More. I knew it was God speaking, and I knew there was some crisis at home, for He hadn't even waited till Sunday to tell me in church. I said, "Oh, God, can't she wait?" But there was no more sound, only the rustle of the leaves, and I should have known better than to try to argue with Him. It was a very difficult time to leave, to say the least, but there was Eleanor, which made the whole thing a possibility.

I went inside and called Celia at her apartment in New York.

"Celia, is Mother all right?"

"Well, it depends on how you define 'all right.' I'd say

she's swinging right along. She's tripping the light fantastic. She and Jack Brodsky are out every night together dancing, drinking and God knows what else.''

I was stunned. "Do you mean that lawyer?"

"I do. I do I do I do I do."

She sounded very strange. "What's the matter with you?"

"I'm drunk."

"Well, it seems too early to be drunk. It must be only seven o'clock there."

"I've been drunk since five."

"Have you been fired from your job?"

"Well, almost. Not quite, but almost."

I said, "So in other words, you aren't capable of helping our dear mother at the time when she needs it."

Silence. "Cassie, you have some nerve. And you don't make any sense. Needs it—I should be having the fun she is. She's never looked better. She's in love. Her court date is in a couple of weeks—"

"She's what?" I felt my whole insides collapse as though I were in an airplane.

"She's in love. She and Jack the Quack are being swept away in the tempests of passion. She even muttered about marriage."

"Celia," I said furiously, "are you doing anything about this?"

"Doing . . . What to do? Love will find a way."

"Have you even *considered* stopping her? Speaking to her? Sitting her down and pointing out the nonsense and folly of falling in love at her age? Do I have to do *everything?*" I was screaming. "Good God. Is there nobody on this earth or in this family who can do anything but me? Am I surrounded by idiots and incompetent people? *Can't anybody do anything?*" There was a silence during which I heard Celia take another gulp of whatever she was drinking. "All right. I'll be there tomorrow afternoon."

"Cassie, not that it isn't always a joy to see you. But I don't honestly think you're going to be able to stop young love. Let her alone. At least, she's given up the pink bathrobe, and she does her drinking in bars and nightclubs.''

"Don't bother to meet me," I said, "I'll rent a car. I refuse to ride in that revolting Ford."

I slammed down the phone and pressed my fingers to my temples, for a tension headache was starting. But headache or not, I went to my desk, took a large piece of yellow paper and began making a list. *"Stuart to Syllabub. Speak to Eleanor, Sam, etc. Call American Airlines and Hertz Rent-A-Car."* I started to write, *"Call pool man, gardener, etc.,"* but remembered they were all being fired and we were going to do our own work, so I sighed and wrote, *"Assign jobs to all members of family."* As I wrote it down my headache got worse, and I realized again what I had suspected before, which is how my good spirits and optimism depend on spending money, and how depressed I get when I must economize. It's been said that misfortune never strikes once, or something like that, and it was really a shame that I had to leave when everything was so difficult here.

Now I had to depend on Eleanor, so I went looking for her and found her washing clothes in the pool, which she said would save electricity. I must say she has a great deal of enthusiasm. She told me that she was planning a garden of medicinal herbs so we could save on medical bills, and how she was going to send for her loom so she could weave clothes for her new extended family so we would never have to go to stores. She was already knitting some lumpy gray garment out of what she said was "natural sheep's wool," and in fact she wondered what I thought of getting a few sheep for the tennis-court area instead of a cow. We would all save fortunes and rise above all God's jokes to higher planes of whatever the hell we were supposed to rise to.

I told her I had to go Back East again because of a new crisis with my family and I was forced to leave the household in her hands. I told her she could be as natural as she wanted, and of course Sam and I would be glad if she saved money, but I forbade her to bring drugs into the house. Of course, she gave the usual old arguments about how they'd get them anyway and so forth, but I told her that there would simply be *no discussion* about it and it was my house and I didn't believe in them, and besides, Stu had a serious drug problem that had to be taken care of. (I told Sam that he must be responsible for Stu's care, and he promised that he would.) I said if she didn't do what I said, I would throw her and Sammy Junior out immediately. I added that although she was entitled to her own ideas and beliefs, I had found in my experience that God didn't make jokes and that, in fact, He was quite a serious person and might actually be annoyed if somebody didn't think so and might even punish that person for having a depraved sense of humor. Which shut her up at least for the time being.

Finally, everything was more or less taken care of. But there was one last problem. As I was packing, Shelli came in, even though she should have been in school—and frankly, I had been hoping to leave before she came home. I had not gotten over the horse episode, and I couldn't help being rather short with her, but I did notice that she looked upset.

"Mom, please don't go."

"I have to, Shelli. My mother needs me."

"But everything's so lousy when you're not here." She looked as though she were going to cry. "And Mom, Stu's sick. I mean, his brain is really messed up."

"I know about Stu, and I've spoken to Sam about getting him help. He needs to get off drugs along with the rest of you. Then he'll be fine." I looked at her. At fourteen, she was not particularly pretty—she just looked like a sad little girl. I have never admitted this before, but the truth is I have always found my daughter a little depressing. She hasn't her brothers' good looks and sparkling personalities, and she has never had the usual feminine interest in her appearance. Her customary outfit is blue jeans with holes and horrible faded T-shirts, and she never combs her hair. She has always been too skinny, and no wonder, for she hardly eats anything.

"Mom, please take me with you." Her eyes lit up at this impossible idea. "Oh, please, let me go. I'll help you with

Grandma. I'll be nice to Aunt Celia. I'll do anything you want.''

"Shelli, dear. I can't. You belong here in school.''

"Oh, but Mom. Oh, please. It would be good for me to go Back East. I'll take my work with me and do it, I promise. I'd do more than I do here, I'll tell you that.''

"It's impossible, dear. Please don't keep asking. I need you here to help take care of the house while I'm gone, and to be supportive of your poor brother.'' Her face went into the sulky look that I hate. "Anyway, Eleanor will take care of things.''

"You don't understand,'' Shelli said. She had gotten quite pale. "Eleanor's a *dick*. She's crazy. She's always stoned and trying to get everybody else stoned. And besides that, she . . . '' She stopped and gulped. "She has this laying-on-of-hands crap, and I hate it.''

"Shelli, Eleanor is one of life's problems. I'm not crazy about her either, but now she's a member of the family. She seems to make Sammy Junior happy, and that's what counts.''

"Oh, he's always happy. He'd be happy in the middle of a fucking nuclear war.''

"Please don't use those words, Shelli. They sound terrible coming from a young girl. Now listen to me. If you want to help me, the best thing you can do is stay here and help Daddy and Stu and do your schoolwork so I'll be proud of you. I'll be back as soon as I get Grandma settled. Don't forget, she's a poor old lady and she's not well and she needs help.''

"What do you mean, not well?''

"Well, she's acting strangely. For all I know, she's going off the deep end. After all, if it were me, Shelli, I should hope you'd do the same. Aged parents deserve some care and attention. Senility comes on much earlier with lonely people.''

The last thing I saw when I left was her face as she stood in the driveway forlornly waving. For a moment I thought of changing my mind, but the thought was ridiculous. But as I drove to the airport I was in a very nervous state. My head was splitting, and I was seeing Ginger again, this time with her stomach gashed open and all her insides spilling out. Lying on a broad, green lawn under a bright blue sky with puffy white clouds. Her big, brown horse eyes were wide open and sad, and she was dying.

CELIA

Cassie arrived at the worst possible moment, just as Dorothy, all dressed up, was being picked up by Jack. Maybe she couldn't stand it that Dorothy looked so good. Brown silk dress and gold beads. White hair in a pretty chignon; some well-applied makeup, which had been increasing in quantity slowly but steadily. Her old fur coat had been restored and looked almost new. I was clucking approval, martini in hand. Our roles were reversed—a change that pleased Dorothy and was making me an alcoholic. Whoever didn't have the man had the booze.

"Celia, you're drinking entirely too much. I didn't notice how much I'd been drinking till after I stopped, and then I realized how bad it was making me feel. Please try to stop; you don't look at all well." She twirled in front of the mirror. "Is my skirt even?"

"It's perfect."

"I'm not sure my stockings are the right color. Are they too light for these shoes?"

"Never have stockings matched a dress better."

I had been fired. Laid off. Sacked. Horrible scene with *New Day* boss. I'd fucked up two assignments, one by doing it badly and the other by not doing it at all. Dorothy had been aghast, but I was rather pleased: Now I could collect unemployment. And hang around Rivertown. Give myself up to self-destruction slowly but surely. But I wasn't entirely useless: I cleaned the house and did the laundry, and cooked for Dorothy whenever she was there. I was mother of the prom queen. Steadily tanking away, I listened to Dorothy's late-night confessions—for this affair was, so far, according to her, still chaste.

"He wants to go all the way, Celia. But I'm not sure if it's right."

Twenty-five years peeled off my life. Thirty years—or had I ever even had such a problem? I suppose I did in the beginning, but it didn't last long. "But can't he be sued for malpractice, or something?"

"Of course not. We're going to court in two weeks. There's no contest from your father; it's all perfectly routine." She'd kicked off her high-heeled pumps cozily. "Oh, do my feet hurt! Jack is just crazy about dancing."

They'd found this Nostalgia-for-World War II place in a nearby town which was all done up like the old USO and where a crew-cut combo played songs like "When the Lights Go On Again" and "I Had the Craziest Dream" and "White Cliffs of Dover" and "Praise the Lord and Pass the Ammunition." They even had mock blackouts— without the bombs, of course. Jack too was crazy about the early forties—they had compatible nostalgias.

Now, as Dorothy twirled in the brown silk dress, a car drove up outside. Two cars—Jack tooting in his convertible and Cassie in a white rented Chevvy. She got out, staring at the tableau before her eyes: Jack tooting his horn, which played the theme from *The Godfather*, and flinging back his muffler and grinning, showing a row of perfect white teeth. Dorothy skipping down the walk—"I'm coming! I'm com-ing!" Drunken sister Celia, glass in hand, hanging on to a porch column. Cassie took it all in, fast. Slammed the car door. Marched over to Dorothy the Deb.

"Moth-er. What on earth is going on?"

"Cassie, what a surprise! Why didn't you *tell* me you were coming?" Hug—kiss, which Cassie accepted stonily. "Cassie, you remember Jack. Jack, this is Cassie."

"Well, hi, there, honey. Of course I remember you, you and your sister. My God, you two looked alike. And I

remember nobody could tell you apart but Dorothy."
Chuckle chuckle.

"Mr. Brodsky, I must say you seem to have gotten your functions mixed up. I thought you were my mother's attorney, whose sworn duty was to represent her adequately and keep her from rape, Welfare and social injustice. Now my sister tells me there is some kind of romance going on, and it sure as hell looks like it to me."

"Hey, there, honey. Your Mom and I—"

"Don't call me honey. Don't call her Mom. Obviously you are both adults and can do as you please. What I'm concerned about is Mother's welfare, and it doesn't look to me as though you can be even slightly objective about her. Let me tell you, if you don't get the best possible financial arrangement from my father, I'll have you disbarred." I clapped, dropping my glass, and they all ignored me.

"Now, see here, Cassie. We have Caspar by the short hairs, and he knows it. First there's adultery and then desertion—"

"Mr. Brodsky, nobody has my father by the *short hairs*. You are even crasser than I expected." She gave Jack a withering look, country tweeds, pinky ring and all. "Mother, I honestly think you are being led down some primrose path, and I beg you to reconsider your relationship with this man."

"Why, Cassie, I can't believe this is you talking," Dorothy said. "I swear you sound like your sister. You were always the peacemaker. I'm sure you'll see it my way when you understand. Jack is rescuing me, not endangering me. Celia will tell you all about it."

Jack snarled, "Dotty, get into the car and let's go."

Cassie shrieked, *"Dotty!"*

"You'll see that I'm lucky to have Jack represent me, and to give me affection and moral support besides. And this isn't any primrose path. This is a *very serious relationship*."

While Cassie practically frothed with rage, Dorothy got into the car and closed the door, and then Jack gunned his motor and off they went for another mad night. I weaved over to Cassie and the white Chevvy.

"It's hopeless," I said. As usual, she looked great, in a

burgundy suit, black boots and heathery-looking tweed cape. I gave her a peck on the cheek. "I'm glad you're here."

"God, Cece. You're drunk again."

"Oh, just a little. You probably will be too after a few days here."

Together we lugged in the suitcases, and while she went upstairs to change, or redo her face, or whatever, I collapsed into a chair at the kitchen table. She had called me Cece. Were we going to be friends? She came down shortly, having replaced the jacket with a black sweater.

"Well, I think I'll have something too. Just a little glass of wine to relax. Honestly, Celia, I can't believe you've been sitting here letting this go on. Our mother is old, despondent and getting addled. And this Jack person obviously wants to take advantage of her and get his hands on our father's fortune."

"What fortune?"

"You must realize that The Bower of Flowers is probably worth half a million dollars, which will someday be ours, but it never will if we don't stop this shyster from getting it in his name."

"God, Cassie. You should have been a lawyer." I tried to think my way through the drunken haze. "Maybe you have a point."

"Unfortunately, we don't have only him to worry about. It's also possible that Daddy's head will be turned by this middle-aged Frog of his and he'll leave it all to her and her genius son. And even though the idea of our parents' deaths may seem hard to believe, someday it will happen and you and I will be left in the poorhouse."

"Correction. *I'll* be in the poorhouse—you'll be in Malibu." I watched as she poured herself a hefty slug of vodka. If we didn't watch out, Cassie and I would end up sodden heaps on the floor and the money would all go to our rehabilitation.

"But I won't, Cece. We don't have that much money. In fact, we are in *dire straits*."

And that was the beginning. Then I heard all about Sam. And Angela. And the kids, and Eleanor. Her whole life, in fact. And I told her about Bernard and Maria, and about Richard, and a lot of other things that she had never had any interest in. We sat there for hours talking. We were both drinking at first; then at some point we stopped and switched to coffee and sent out for a pizza. We ate it, and we hugged each other and cried. Then we talked some more. I hadn't been so happy in weeks—maybe years. I don't know if the same was true of her, for parts of her are forever closed off, sealed up like uninhabited rooms. But that night was wonderful.

Part of it was twin talk—all the eerie coincidences that had occurred over the years. We had both had gallbladder attacks on the same day. We had had the same cavities in exactly the same teeth. We could wear each other's reading glasses, and we both got headaches when we felt frustrated, the kind that throbbed on the right side. Our periods came in identical cycles. When we got frightened, our fingers got numb. We were the same weight, 122. We were both allergic to cats and strawberries. It was typical of the delusion of twin-ness that we saw these things as miracles and forgot the perfectly obvious fact that two women's lives could hardly have been more different than ours. That night we were seeking similarities.

We began reminiscing about our childhood, but drew back when we found how differently we had seen everything and how we had disliked each other. It made us both feel bad—we cried some more and said how sorry we were. But the worst moment was when I said, "But don't you remember how close we were when we were little, before we started to separate?" And Cassie said she remembered nothing at all before six, and all she remembered about the sweaters was that she knew I had hated her for having the blue one, just as I had always hated her for having better things. "Which I *didn't*," she said. "You were the one who got to go to boarding school, and the fancy clothes to go in." Which drove us back to the vodka. I said, "Cassie, do you swear you remember nothing about when we were small? About how we thought the same thoughts, and cuddled together in bed, and didn't even know the difference between each other?" And she looked a little frightened and said, "I remember nothing."

Then I suggested we go upstairs and take off our clothes

and look at ourselves in the mirror, to see if we were really exactly alike from head to toe. But that was too scary for her—and probably for me too. When I asked her why she had put me out of her head for all those years, she couldn't answer that either.

Then we talked for a while about how we had tricked people in school by changing places and about Miss Larkin and how she had insisted on our different-ness to Dorothy, and Cassie said she hadn't known about that. What she remembered mostly was fighting to get away from me; what I remembered mostly was trying to keep us the same. So it was logical that I was the one who thought of dressing alike.

"Cece, you are out of your mind. I don't think God would approve."

"Who cares? Anyway, I know that you thought of it before, because when I went through your closet I found two of a lot of things."

"Well, that was because Sam said we had to economize and they were on sale."

I laughed. "Come on. God probably planned the whole thing."

So we went upstairs and Cassie dug out two skirts, two Irish sweaters she had been unable to resist, two-for-the-price-of-one suede walking shoes and two pairs of dark brown stockings. Our hair was still different, and we had the bright idea of dying mine (It must have been about midnight by this time) with some extra rinse she'd gotten when she'd had hers done the last time. So still slightly looped, we dyed my hair. She tried to make hers straight, which was impossible because she'd had it permanented. This was all done with a great deal of giggling and bickering of the sort that reminded me of, say, junior high. We had regressed to about age thirteen.

Finally we had made ourselves as alike as possible, and we stood in front of the big mirror in the upstairs hall. And what we saw was truly awesome—I suppose that's the word. We both caught our breaths, and I wondered if indeed God would approve or would unleash terrible revenge on us for parodying His works. If that was what we were doing, for by then I scarcely knew.

When I first looked, I had that disoriented feeling one gets when looking at a crowd in a mirror, or at one of those closed-circuit TVs in a store. Which one was I? Though we weren't absolutely alike—our hair was still different, and Cassie hadn't been able to get off all the mascara and eye glop which she probably hadn't completely removed in twenty years—we were close enough to be frightening. Our hands were the same, which I had noticed before. Our ankles, the curve of the calves. Even the way our bodies moved. Our faces . . . not quite. Very, very close, but something was different, what I didn't know. Maybe it was just the mirror effect.

Like two children in Halloween costumes we started downstairs just as Dorothy walked in the front door with her *innamorato*. Only the small lamp on the hall table was on. In came the happy couple a little unsteadily, Jack leering and grabbing, Dorothy ducking and giggling. "A little kiss, Dotty. Not a little one, a big one. Oh, you're my sweetheart. How much longer are you going to torture me?"

"Not torture, Jack. This should be the happiest time of our lives. I can't help it if I'm old-fashioned, but I'd rather wait till . . . well, till we're more committed."

"We are, baby love. Come here to Big Jack."

"I am here, sweetheart. Oh, you mustn't do that. Naughty naughty."

"Oh, God. I haven't had a woman since Millie died. And before that for six months."

"Now, Jack, Mama says no."

"Oh, Lord, Dotty. You're so beautiful. You're so—"

"Don't *call her Dotty!*" Cassie screamed.

Dorothy and Jack looked up, stunned, Jack panting slightly. Cassie and I slowly came downstairs into the light.

Every girl dreams of making an entrance, but few manage one like that. I can still see the two stunned faces—Jack's horrified, Dorothy's with a deeper, more reminiscent amazement. Almost awestruck. Ding, ding—we'd done it again. Her two matching girls. Almost a smile for a moment, then the old expression. I caught my breath: could she still do it? I prayed Cassie would be quiet, because the

one drastically different thing about us was the way we
talked. She looked rapidly back and forth at us, then
looked me straight in the face and said, "Celia." It was
quite a moment. Dorothy had that prideful old smile I
remembered so well. Oh, Dorothy, you're just wonderful.
She was ours again, if just for a moment. We had turned
back the clock.

Jack, however, was not so enchanted by our game,
though of course, we'd hardly gotten him at the right
moment.

"Do you girls do this often?"

"We never do it," I said.

"Well, frankly, it's a little creepy." From the turn of
his body it was obvious Jack was concentrating on willing
his erection to go down.

"I don't think that's very polite," Cassie said.

"Maybe it's because you sneaked up on us."

"You should have cleared your throats or something,"
Dorothy said. Her moment over, she was beginning to
look annoyed. Time ticked back to the present, never to
return. "In fact, this whole performance is silly. You
haven't dressed alike since you were six. Have you just
been sitting here all evening doing this? Good Lord, Celia,
you even dyed your hair."

"It's the mascara," I said to Cassie. "I'll bet when you
get the rest off she can't tell. Or your nails"—for Cassie's
nails were perfect ovals done in Caribbean Mango, and
mine were short and chewed.

"Dotty, I'm going along now," Jack said, scowling.
"It's late. We have to meet with the other side at ten."

"So we do." She kept looking at us. "My Lord, I can
hardly believe it. And it's so childish. You're grown
women."

"I'll—see—you—at—ten," Jack barked. "Good night,
Dot. Good night, twins." And he left, hardly noticed by
Dorothy.

"There's something about your mouth, Cassie. I can
tell," Dorothy said. "And the way the eyes move. You
can't fool me."

"Maybe we can," Cassie said.

"I wonder what was the matter with Jack," Dorothy said, as we went upstairs.

"Well, you know how it is," I said. "Nobody likes a couple."

What a grand game Cassie and I had discovered, apparently by accident. Though as always, it was I who wanted to do it and Cassie who hung back.

"It's not cute anymore, Cece. It's not natural."

"Then *we* aren't natural."

"And you may think it's stupid, but I'm worried about God."

So we got dressed alike and went to St. Anthony's Church to ask God. I hadn't been there since I was about fifteen, and as we sat there I thought how foolish I had been to turn my back on such a pleasant place, particularly as I was always seeking peace of mind. I can't say my troubles blew away, but there was certainly something soothing about sitting in the pew watching the shadows from the trees outside skitter through the stained-glass window, Rivertown's pride. And it had been fun to see the Reverend Mr. Bellwether start at the sight of us. *He* certainly couldn't tell us apart—though most people were easy; it was Dorothy we wanted to fool. Or I did, for there was a doubt, a negativeness about Cassie that I didn't remember from before. A cloudiness.

In the pew, her face grew worried, then startled. "God says, '*It's too late.*' "

"For what?"

"For being alike."

"Well, I'm not so sure He means that. He could mean anything." I privately thought that Cassie's God was like that ancient holy man in the old joke who, after people have traveled thousands of miles and scaled mountain pinnacles to hear his infinite wisdom, says Life is a rainbow or a fountain or something. "If you think about it, it's too late for a lot of things."

"But I don't see why we're doing it."

"Who cares?" I was annoyed. "I don't know. Just for fun. Because we can do something that nobody else can." It was funny—I'd always been the one who worried about *why* all the time. Now I didn't care and she did. "It makes us extraordinary for a change. I love it when people stare at us and can't tell us apart—it gives me goose bumps. Nobody has stared at me in years—and not even much before that.''

"Well, they have at me.''

"They've stared at your clothes and your makeup.''

That hit a nerve. "You bitch,'' she whispered. She got up and tore out of the church. I followed, showering apologies. Our customary postures. It's been said there's always one who loves more. "This is ridiculous, Celia,'' she said, half-running along the street. "I'm going back to Santa Barbara. I don't even know why I'm here. Certainly Mother seems deaf to anything we say to her. She is determined to destroy her life. And Daddy likewise.''

"Cassie, please stay. I need you. I don't believe you really want to go back yet anyway. I don't even believe you came here this time because of Dorothy. You came because your life at home is rotten and I'm all you've got.''

It was a mistake to be that direct with her, or maybe not, considering that I loved to see her get mad. Now I saw her eyes sparkle and the muscles of her neck tense, exactly the way mine must have. It was like living with a mirror.

"Celia, you are as nasty and cruel and dishonest as ever. You have nothing—no job, and not even that divorced one anymore if you stick to your resolution never to lay eyes on him again. No money—and not even a decent haircut. I have everything a woman could want—a devoted husband, three lovely children and a new daughter-in-law who at this very moment is watching over my household. I have closets full of designer clothes and a joint checking account, not to mention stocks, bonds and money-market funds in my name. I have a four-bedroom ranch on three acres of prime mountainside land which must be worth half a million dollars by now, and a BMW and a condo in Acapulco—''

"As always, you have everything and I have nothing. But I don't believe it makes you happy. You told me yourself—you feel lonely and different from everybody in your family. You haven't anybody to talk to. So stay here and talk to me for a while."

At the time, I didn't see why she shouldn't. Cassie's version of her life at home had been edited and a good deal prettied up. She had told me about Angela and Sam, but not about Sam's many other adulteries, nor did I know how bad her marriage really was. She had minimized her son's drug problem. I didn't know about the bad dreams, or that her daughter had begged to come along. I had the impression of a typical laid-back, go-with-the-flow California family who were a little faddy and crazy and who smoked a little grass but who were all right underneath, and probably sick to death of Cassie's fussing and preaching and compulsive cleanliness, and I thought it might be good for them to be without her for a while. In other words, I didn't see what was going on at all.

"Oh, Cassie, I don't know." We were back at the house, and I sat down on the porch steps. "I think something wrong happened to us somewhere. We used to love each other, but then I got envious of you and I was mean and nasty because you wouldn't have anything to do with me."

She softened. "But I wanted to be myself. Whenever you were around I felt as though I were only half of something. That's why I went to Hollywood, because I had to get as far away as I could, even if I had to be broke and work in those horrible places. That's why I put you out of my head."

Tears came into my eyes. "Isn't that. funny," I said. "All I ever thought of was that you were leaving me."

"Cece, don't cry. I don't understand any of this. I am lonely, it's perfectly true. I feel as though I'm the only person who has moral standards, which come from my religious beliefs which hardly anybody else seems to have. I have never had much interest in Freudian theory or the 'unconscious,' which is only a way to torment another person by making up things you want them to have in their head."

"Well." Sometimes she was hard to believe. "But sometimes people have to go back and finish their childhoods. That's what we're doing right now."

"Well, you may be right, I'll stay a while longer. The truth is I've been very nervous recently, and I have these terrible dreams which wake me in the middle of the night, and they seem a little better since I've been here. And certainly I want to be around for this ridiculous divorce. Though I'm not sure about playing twins all the time."

So she stayed. It turned out that one reason she had reservations about the twinning was that she was afraid she'd have to give up her makeup and manicure and hair and be dragged down to my ungroomed standard, which I suppose I had expected in the name of being "natural." But I agreed to meet her halfway—more than halfway, in fact, because I, as always, loved more, and was willing to give in more. So I had my hair done and learned to put on all the Clinique and whatever in the proper way, and let my nails grow and painted them with Caribbean Mango.

I photographed us—perhaps I would make my fortune yet. I did us with mirrors, and I did time exposures and silhouettes and color and grainy black-and-white and God knows what else. It had been years since I'd taken the pictures I really wanted to take, and I considered installing a darkroom in the basement. I took pictures as though one would show me why we were doing this, as though some ghost, invisible to the naked eye, would appear in a photograph. I took pictures to help myself see what seemed mysterious and veiled.

One night when Dorothy and Jack were out at the Sirloin Saloon, I took Cassie into the city to The Gibbon's Head. After all, it was time she saw something of Manhattan. We both wore black sweaters and identical skirts, and we were about as indistinguishable as we could get.

"Celia, I don't feel right going to a singles bar."

"It's not what you think. In fact, it's more like a nursing home."

The first person we saw when we walked in was Bernard. I was amazed—I didn't know he went there any longer. Cassie walked in first and stared at him blankly. He began talking to her because he thought she was I, and I hid behind the coats that hung on a row of hooks near the front door.

"Celia, we have to talk. I've felt terrible about that

night, but when I explain I'm sure you'll understand. Maria and I were celebrating our divorce becoming final. A lot of couples do it for old times' sake. She left the next day, and I haven't seen her since."

"Lies, lies, Bernard," I said, skipping out of the coats. "That wasn't what you told me. How false you've become; you never used to be."

Bernard's reaction was a marvel. Before that moment Cassie had been a theory. Now his mouth dropped open beneath his mustache, and his normally gloomy eyes darted back and forth between us. "Oh, my God," he said in a soft croak, "I can't tell you apart. Celia, which are you?"

"I'd love to make you guess, but I can't keep my mouth shut."

"Oy vay." Bernard got more Jewish as he got more anxious. "And you're different. You've fixed your hair. Celia, you have *makeup* on."

"Right. In case you haven't guessed, this is my sister Cassie. Cassie, this is Bernard, the getting-divorced one."

"How do you do," Cassie said. "Well, I've heard a lot about *you.*"

By now, quite a crowd had gathered around to stare at us. Never had I attracted so much attention at The Gibbon's Head—or anywhere, as a matter of fact. Not that it was all complimentary. There was one of those so-called anthropologists who said that in certain tribes or ancient times or something, identical twins were killed at birth and their mothers stoned as witches. They were thought to be evil, and of course in mythology, Castor and Pollux had to spend one day in Hades and one with the Gods. And everybody knew how maladjusted they were. And Meg, a little drunk: "I can tell, you're Celia" (to Cassie). There were several there who wanted to do something with us— put us in a commercial; ship us off to some psychologists who were doing studies of twins; stuff us and put us in the Hollywood Wax Museum. And the inevitable creep who sidled up to Cassie and suggested a "threesome." Cassie said that was the most disgusting thing she had ever heard in her life, and if he didn't have some kind of moral standards about his sexual life, she did, and if he didn't get lost fast she'd . . . There was the one with the pale eyebrows who said he had a twin brother and he'd call him up, and we'd have a double date. No sex—just an exhibition waltz. I told him it was an adorable idea except we were old enough to be their Mommies.

What a funny, lovely evening it was. What attention. Lots of new friends, though Bernard left early.

"See," I said to Cassie after we got home. "We can go anywhere. Do anything. Conquer the world." Her smile was a little vague. "Did you have a good time?"

"Very nice."

"Do you want another drink?"

"Oh, well. I guess just one more."

She always got primmer when she drank. Did she ever unbend? "Cassie, what are you like at home?"

"I suppose a little different. To tell the truth, I'm not myself these days; I don't know why."

"Is it the twinning?"

"I don't know. I'm not sure. Maybe partly. But it began before we started doing this."

Like a loving groom with his innocent bride, I was afraid of hurting her. "Maybe it's me." I wanted badly to make her happy—which, in my vanity, I thought I could do by making her love me. If she didn't—which was hard to tell. "It was like a group therapy session this evening," I said. "One woman said she hated us out of envy. We would never be lonely."

"But Cece, that's what people think about marriage. And it isn't true."

"But we're different. We're part of each other; we come from the same egg."

She stood up and went over to the bureau—we were sitting in her room. "I don't like that idea. Anyway, I don't think it's so." She turned back to me. "Don't you remember what God said? 'It's too late.' "

"I don't agree with God."

"Celia, don't push me. I've agreed to play this game for a while, but frankly, it makes me extremely nervous to be too close to another person. At least in the way you mean."

I put out my hands, palms up. "What's it all about, Alfie? If you can't be close to somebody, what have you got? Jesus. Everybody needs a friend."

"I didn't mean that. I meant . . . in the way you're thinking of." She was looking at me levelly, with that profound look we didn't risk often.

"I don't know what you mean." But my heart was thudding against my ribs.

"You want us to sleep together," she said.

"You're nuts," I said, astonished. "It never entered my head." But even as I said it, I knew that I had been thinking of it all along. On that dark level. In that netherworld of thirty-five years before, or whenever it started. I couldn't look at her anymore. How strange that she had been the one to say it.

"I want you to know, Celia, that I will never do such a thing. Frankly, I consider it perverted in the worst way. Both homosexuality and incest are completely against—"

"—your moral standards." I was slowly starting to bite off one of my Caribbean Mango nails.

"If by any chance you think I'm prudish and unliberated or whatever, I can't help it. I feel very strongly that sex used for purposes other than affection or commitment between men and women defiles God's word. I have seen people who use sex for money, for power and for cruelty and aggression, and I consider it a sin of the highest order."

"Well . . . of course I agree." My heart was still beating, and now my head was full of pictures of the two of us making love together, our matching tongues, our cunts and our four breasts sending each other into matching transports of bliss.

'I'm surprised to hear you say that, Celia. You of all people, with your casual sex."

"Well, I don't. I mean I do." I couldn't even concentrate on whatever the hell we were talking about. "You're right." I covered my face with my hands. "I did think about it."

"I know when people are thinking about sex, Celia. I can always tell. And it really isn't difficult, because they almost always are. Sam never gets it out of his head."

"But don't *you* think about sex? Do you *like* sex?"

She looked at me coolly. "Since you ask so directly, I'm not crazy about it. I don't *hate* it. Usually I find it boring and rather pointless. You're ruining that nail. I'll fix it for you tomorrow."

"I feel terrible. I feel guilty." I didn't add that I still wanted to do it—ferociously.

"Well, you needn't. You're no different than anybody else, and I'm used to being different. I used to dislike people for their crude thoughts, but God has helped me be more forgiving. Anyway, Cece, you're my twin sister, and I love you. And we have been getting along much better than before." She loved me. Ah, she loved me. "I believe blood relatives have a sacred duty to each other, and our relationship is very special. Though certainly strange. Anyway, I need a friend."

I lay on the bed and listened to her as she modestly undressed behind the closet door, then emerged in her blue silk nightgown. How beautiful she was—and if she was, so was I. But not for too much longer. The line under her chin, once so clean and firm, had softened slightly. There were tiny wrinkles around her eyes, and the veins in her hand were heavy. Her breasts sagged a little. I was awed by the way she had handled this impossible subject—God knows what I would have done had she never mentioned it. Run off to the shrink. Attacked her. Burst into tears and fallen at her feet pleading, or slithered into her bed. Or never let myself realize it and broken out in hives or developed a major tic or something. God knew what I was going to do now that she had mentioned it. I had never wanted a woman in my life, and now the idea was magical, the only new thing in a tired world . . . but only this woman. Only our two faces close enough to breathe each other's breath. I remembered how delicately, how lovingly she had once spat into my mouth so I would catch her measles. Her lips on mine and the warm saliva running onto my tongue. The fragrance of her young body.

"I'm going to bed," I said. And jerk off, I added to myself. "Good night."

She came over and hugged me gently. "You see why it can't ever happen, Celia."

"Of course." I kissed her on the cheek, sweet and sisterly.

"I've discovered that people's minds can become truly

twisted by sex. They believe that the sexual act will make everything fine, and of course, it doesn't—it just makes everything different and sometimes worse. I've found on numerous occasions that it's better to just mention what I know is on the other person's mind anyway. It rescues them in a way, and is much better than resenting them for something that I lack."

"Very sensible."

"Good night, Cece. I do love you."

Now that you've flushed out my evil thoughts. Now that you've turned me down and put on your chastity belt. Drive me crazy. She had always had something I wanted, always. Even children. And now her body, which I wanted more strongly and more specifically than anything else.

As I went out of the room, she said, "Cece, I *know* if there was sex between us we would be punished in some terrible way. I know you may think it's silly, but sure as I'm standing here, we would be struck down."

"My Lord. Everybody screws everybody else and they aren't struck down."

"You aren't thinking straight because you're still thinking about it. I know we would suffer a dreadful punishment. Please trust me, because my head is clear and yours isn't. I can see things that you can't. I swear we're jinxed in some way. You heard the man at The Gibbon's Head who said twins were thought to be evil. It's wrong to be too close. And I, for, one have responsibilities to my husband and three wonderful—"

"Good night, Cassie," I said, and fled into my bedroom.

This extraordinary exchange put Cassie on top. While I was down below in the slime of my fantasies, she was cool and in control of us both, keeping our eyes on finer things. Neat, when you think of it. Probably she did something similar to poor Sam, whose numerous therapists still thought it had something to do with his parents. I could hear him now: "I don't know what's the matter with me, Dr. Whoever. I'm married to a perfect woman and I'm not contented"—listing five hundred anxiety symptoms. I had never had much sympathy for Sam until now.

Of course, it wouldn't have worked unless Sam, as well as I, had large reserves of basic guilt. No matter how I told myself that sex was the logical culmination of Cassie's and my relationship, philosophically and spiritually speaking, no matter that it seemed so fitting after a lifetime of masturbating in front of mirrors or how I tried to convince myself that sexual taboos were as passé as bustles, in some part of myself I agreed with Cassie that it was deeply wrong. In some way I hardly understood, it was like the twinning—tinkering around with nature's mistake. When God said that it was too late, maybe He meant that it was too late for Him to correct His own error. But we shouldn't screw around with it. Parody it. Point it out. Make fun of it or misuse it. Whatever the transaction was between Cassie and me—which I still didn't understand—it wasn't sex; and it wasn't playing look-alike, either, which seemed to upset people in some unexpected way, even more than when we were small. Look at Jack the Hack and the guy at The Gibbon's Head. And Bernard on the phone:

"Look here, Celia. I wasn't lying the other night. Or only partly. The divorce is final, although it is true that Maria's and my involvement is still on-and-off."

"Call me when it's off, Bernard. Honestly, I've had it."

"Well, of course, that's up to you. But what I really called about is this sister act. What's that supposed to prove?"

"I don't really know. It's a game, I suppose."

"Who wins what?"

"I'm not sure. We have each other, I guess. We sure don't have anybody else." Stick it to him.

"Well, Celia, there's something unhealthy and abnormal about the two of you running around town like the Doublemint twins. If you're interested in my response, I found it rather sickening. How would you like it if *I* had a twin?"

"We'd double-date. We'd do foursies."

"I'm very serious. Have you discussed this with your therapist?"

Dear God. No. I'd been fired, couldn't afford her. Fired! Cece, what happened? I don't know . . . et cetera et cetera. Are you looking for a new job? No—I'm sitting here going psychotic. Let me alone. Actually, I'm quite contented—Cassie and I do little dance routines in the town square.

"All right, you're determined to make jokes about the most serious matters. You probably didn't notice the way people were staring at you in that bar the other night. It might have been cute when you were five or six, but now it's just plain strange. I don't know if you realize that the effect is *torturous and tormenting* to others."

"That's not why we do it. We don't mean to be like that."

"Well, you are. In this case, your indomitable sense of humor is off. It just isn't funny."

Now that the rock of my unconscious had been turned over and all the worms exposed, Cassie was much more agreeable about the twinning—so perhaps her definition of the unconscious wasn't so bad. Now she had tormented me by telling me what she wanted to be in my head. Probably to get it out of her own head. How complicated it was— but it was a relief to let her lead for a while. My arm was tired from dragging her along.

Caspar and Yo loved our act, and Yo was able to tell us apart no matter how we tried to fool her. Caspar never had been able to and still couldn't, but he thought we were funny. "Casselia, Casselia. I can't believe it. My girls again." We were too big to sit one on each knee, but we sat one on each side while he beamed at us and tried to guess.

"You're Cece."

"*Non*—Caz-par. *C'est* Cassie. Look at the eyes, and *certainement* the line of the hair is different."

Only she could see it. And Pierre Dev-row came out of his lair, took one look at us and scowled.

"It's not funny. What a stupid joke. I thought I had one friend and all of a sudden she's two. Maybe next time you'll be four. Then eight. Then sixteen. Then thirty-two, sixty-four. . ."

"Come on, stop," I said. "I'm still here."

"You have goop on your face and your hair's all done. I liked the way you looked before better."

"Listen, Pierre. I'm not dressing for you. If I'd wanted your opinion I would have asked for it. Have you heard from Harvard?"

He gave me a lot of stuff about early admission, late admission and rolling applications, none of which I could follow. He and I were sitting over near the fish tank with its eerie green light. The living room seemed darker than ever, and to my amazement there seemed to be a male figure in the shadows near the door. I grabbed Pierre's arm, knocking a glowing ash off one of his endless succession of cigarettes.

"Who's that?" I whispered in fright.

"Oh, that's Tommy Triste."

"What?" Tommy Triste, large and stocky, moved into the back hall. He had a peculiarly short haircut and a roll of fat under it in back that went down to the top of his T-shirt. When he felt me looking at him he turned his face in my direction—a face only a mother could love, and a pretty saintly mother at that. A nose like a potato. Eyes like granite rocks. The red of broken blood vessels. A surly mouth. "Pierre, will you please explain—"

"Be quiet, Celia. You'll embarrass him." Tommy Triste picked up the trash and lumbered outside with it. "That's Mom's prisoner. You know, the two-hundred-pound one she subdued with karate. He works here sometimes."

"Pierre. Are you telling me your mother has a convicted murderer in her house?"

"Oh, come on. He loves us. He's glad to get out of the pen for a few hours a week. Lots of people have prisoners working for them."

"But my God. Maybe burglars or shoplifters or graffiti artists."

"Well, they all did something. Is murder worse than a mugging, say? Suppose the mugger doesn't mean to kill, but he's tripping or something and the knife slips. The bullet hits the mark. Who's to know? Tommy swears he didn't mean to kill those five women."

Tommy Triste came back into the room and fixed me with a stare that was not friendly, while I broke out in a cold sweat. Then he looked at Cassie. Back and forth.

Back and forth. Jesus. Was the world going crazy? There was my father smiling genially.

"These are my daughters, Tommy. Bet you can't tell 'em apart. Casselia, this is Tommy, our friend and helper."

Cassie and I mumbled hellos, while Yo beamed at all of us. She was a nice woman, if a little eccentric. While she put the wine on the table and stirred up the innards in her huge iron pot, Tommy looked long and hard at Cassie and me, then at Caspar. His mind didn't seem to work terribly fast. You Caz-par. You twins. You match. You evil. Unless, of course, I was reading him wrong. Then he nodded. "How do." With a contortion of the face that might have been a smile, he went out in back, from where we could hear heavy thump-thumps that Yo said were the sound of Tommy chopping wood with an axe.

"It may seem a little strange. But in *la France* everybody has a servant, and they are so *difficile* to find here. Here we are all so *occupés*—Cazpar at *la fleuriste* and Pierre with his studies and I at ze Correctional Institute. Tommy Triste is *très fort* and *très* loyal and helpful."

Cassie was staring at the casserole. "Yo, I don't mean to hurt your feelings, but I am simply unused to eating the insides of animals, whether because we don't have such things in Santa Barbara or because of . . . certain bad dreams I have been having recently which I think of every time I look at these . . . whatever they are."

"Kidneys," said Pierre.

"Oh, Cassie. *Je m'excuse.* If I had known, I would have gotten you one special small chop or a *poitrine* of *poulet*. Let me cook you an egg."

"Oh, please don't bother. I'll be just fine with the noodles and vegetables." She sounded a little strange. I knew she was trying to be polite, but she had gotten extremely pale and was staring fixedly at the kidneys. Kidneys. Dreams. Tommy Triste. Christ, what an evening. Then she closed her eyes and covered her face with her hands, rocking back and forth in her chair. "Oh, God. What's happening to me?"

I was next to her in a quarter of a second, my arm around her. She was stiff and sweaty, and she was moaning softly. "Cassie, tell me what's wrong."

"I can't. I'm sorry. I'll be all right."

"You aren't all right, you're terrible. What is it?"

I took her into the bedroom amid cries of consternation.

"I'll just lie down for a few minutes."

"You don't make it any better by bottling things up. What the hell is the matter?"

Well . . . all right. The kidneys looked like Ginger's insides coming out on the green grass, soaked with blood. It was horrible, she couldn't get the image out of her head. The horse dreams were getting worse—she'd mentioned them, but had never said how they tortured her. Sometimes Ginger looked at her with a terrible pleading expression, and she'd run around trying to help but didn't know what to do. If she sewed up the wound it came open again; if she mopped up the blood a new avalanche poured out. Once Ginger had looked at her pleadingly and said, "Help me." Was she going crazy?

"I've never known anybody less crazy," I said tenderly, stroking her hair. "Even though you're impossible."

"Go back and eat your . . . dinner. I'll just stay here."

"Maybe it wasn't the kidneys but Tommy Triste."

We got through the evening, and that night we lay together in her bed. No sex, just closeness. She said she'd done that with one of her roommates in Hollywood, they'd been so lonely. So I promised her that if she had the horse dream I'd be right next to her and would hold her tight in my arms. Now she could let it out; she knew I wouldn't dare start feeling around—she'd short-circuited me. It was incredible how she knew. Once I started to get a little excited, and she raised her head and said, "Oh, Celia, *don't*. I need you more for help." That ended that—you don't fool around with an invalid. We went to sleep that way, while I resolved to drag her off to Ol' Doc Schroeder. Later in the night, when she began to moan and cry out in her sleep, I held her tightly and said, "I'm right here, Cassie. It's all right."

"Cassie, I have a favor to ask of you—something absolutely rotten."

She looked depressed. "What is it?"

"I want to torture and torment Richard." The idea had

started to germinate the night we went to The Gibbon's Head.

"You mean your ex?"

"Right. I want us to turn up in our matching clothes and make him miserable."

"Well, Celia." She stirred her coffee listlessly. "I can certainly understand your wanting to do that, if he's as bad as you say. But frankly, I feel very confused and torn about the twinning. I'm sure God hates it, and as a matter of fact, I've been meaning to tell you I don't want to do it anymore."

"I promise—we'll never do it again. Just this one last time, so I can have a little divine revenge."

"I'm afraid we're going to be punished."

"*I'll* be punished, Cassie. God is listening to this whole conversation and He'll know I'm to blame. Anyway, the way I want to do it is cheerful and sort of funny. I don't want to spring out of his closet or anything. We'll dress up in cute costumes and go dancing."

This brilliant idea had jelled as I read an item in the local paper.

GATHERING OF THE CLANS IN CONNECTICUT WOODS" —the big annual fall Scottish wingding, where Richard was sure to be. The works—pipe bands, haggis hurl, sheepdog exhibition, caber toss, all on some local bonnie brae.

Cassie grudgingly agreed. "You swear it's the last time, Cece. Honest to God, I'm only doing this for you."

I hugged her. "Thank you, darling. I'll do something just as lousy for you whenever you want."

The Gathering took place in a big clearing in the woods an hour's drive away, chosen, according to the pamphlet, because of its uncanny resemblance to the Highlands. Indeed, it was misty, and in the gloaming when we arrived it bore a slight resemblance to Brigadoon, except for the New England late-fall leaves which covered the ground. There were Scotspeople, real and fake, as far as the eye could see, plus sheep dogs and even a few mangy-looking sheep. In the air was the vile smell of haggis (oatmeal cooked in the stomach of a sheep), which I didn't describe to Cassie for fear of upsetting her. We could hear the mournful tones of the bagpipes as we got out of the car.

"I don't see how we'll ever find Richard," Cassie said as we started pushing our way through the crowd.

"It's a question of patience and persistence. I can't wait to see the expression on his face."

We were dressed unauthentically—the best we could do on a couple of days' notice. The plaid skirts were not kilts, and the knee socks and little velvet jackets came from the Junior Department of Saks. We had added little Glengarry hats and white ruffled blouses. But as always, we attracted attention anyway, and the stares were gratifying as we marched along in step, left hand on hip, right hand swinging. Torches were lit, and groups had gathered in formation to do folk dances, a couple of which I had taught Cassie that morning, to the tunes of the pipe bands.

"But they'll know we're not really Scotch."

"Oh, half the people here aren't Scotch either. Look at that face—a Cohen if ever I saw one. And look at Rosie O'Grady over there. I've even seen three blacks."

After half an hour or so of wandering around I finally located the MacDougals, and Richard in their midst. I hadn't seen him for five years, in which time he had become a little grayer, fuller of face and of belly. But there were the amber eyes, the perfect ears that had haunted me, the neck, the classic nose—though now there were pouches under the eyes and the slightest sag to the cheeks. Very little considering he was fifty-one. "He's awfully good-looking," Cassie whispered. Indeed he was, and I found myself gazing at him through the torchlight, all the bad memories edited out. I had sometimes wondered why I had married this man, and at least, I now knew. I had married him because I was insanely in love with him. He had been my fate—my brother, my other half, my opposite number. My male counterpart. The Yang to my Yin. Bernard was something else, a stranger I loved because of his strangeness. But Richard, faults and all, was me, myself.

The bagpipes started playing a familiar dance, and I dragged Cassie into the formation, angling us along until we were near Richard and opposite him. We caused a stir of attention, and Richard looked over to see what everybody was staring at. It took him a moment to realize what he was seeing; and then when it penetrated, his expression was transformed. But, Lord forgive me, not in the way I had expected—not the good, healthy horror of Bernard or even of Jack Brodsky, but rather the transfixed stare of a deer caught in a headlight. He didn't stop dancing, only slowed down; but his mouth was open the slightest bit, and his eyes were clear to their depths—an expression that held mine for the entire dance. Mine—not Cassie's. He knew.

When the set was over, we approached him as planned and chorused. "Hello, Richard." Like the two children we became when we dressed up, we—or I—had envisioned comic-book horror, cries of "Oh God, she's come back to haunt me" and possibly a headlong dash for freedom. Later he would tell the story at parties: "You think *you've* got problems. My ex has *doubled*." We had no plans past watching Richard's reaction and then dashing off hilariously to the car and convulsing in giggles—a silly, glorious final twinning adventure before we went back to our separate selves forever.

But hark—Richard the ever-unpredictable found us enchanting. Had no trouble telling us apart. "Why, Cece. Of all things. What a surprise. How have you been?" (Kiss on the cheek.) "And Cassie—a pleasure to see you." Another kiss, but with his eyes on me. "God, what a delicious idea." He whisked us off to the bar in a nearby lodge for Scotches—of course. All charm, as usual. He was there alone; his new wife didn't go for this any more than I had. He stared musingly at us. What an incredible resemblance! He'd never dreamed we'd want to dress up like this; it was brilliant, a flight into fantasyland. What fun we must have had doing it—while Cassie went from amazed to doubtful to downright suspicious.

But on some dark level it made sense—as usual, I had underestimated Richard's demonic wisdom. If we were evil, of course he'd be able to tell, though this was Cassie-esque thinking. And I had forgotten how he loved fantasy; or had I?

As he chattered away, I saw Cassie's gaze dropping slowly from eye level to below waist level. And what do you know if Richard's kilt wasn't sticking out straight in front. Cassie's stunned glance moved from him to me again. Oh, gulp. A little miscalculation—my idea was truly rotten. Not that the world wasn't full of erections, but not ones that I responded to the way I was responding to this one. But Cassie began fuming—nothing stirred her up more than somebody else's lust.

"I must say this is ridiculous. I don't know you at all, Richard, but you seem to have very little control of yourself. And everybody here in these stupid skirts. Celia, if you don't mind, I'd like to go home."

Richard, smooth as silk: "Maybe Cece would like to stay a little longer, Cassie. I'm sure she wouldn't mind if you went along." His hand was on my back, shooting electricity through my entire body. "Did you drive here?"

Cassie: "We certainly did, and I'm sorry we ever came to this ridiculous gathering. Celia, are you coming?"

Me: "I . . . er . . . yes . . . I . . ."

Richard: "Do you have the car keys, Cece. You could give them to Cassie and she could go along home, if she's uncomfortable here. You and I might have another drink for old times' sake, and I'll take you home later."

Me: "Well, I. . ."—slowly reaching into my jacket pocket and pulling out the keys.

Cassie: "I certainly *will* go along. Whatever you do is of course up to you, Celia. But I must say I'm annoyed that you dragged me here under false pretenses. And I need hardly say again that we will never, never wear these stupid matching costumes again, because it is just—plain —*wrong.*"

Richard: "It's not, Cassie. It's just playing a game. You both look lovely."

Me (guiltily handing her the keys): "Cassie, I promise and swear on my life that I didn't mean this to happen. Not in a thousand years. I'm as surprised as you are."

Richard (all innocence): "You didn't mean *what* to happen? We just all ran into each other, that's all." As Cassie scowled—"Cassie, please don't go away angry. You both look charming; I'm tempted to try and make you stay."

This was too much for Cassie. "Never, never! Don't

touch me!''—as Richard tried to put his arm around her in a friendly way. She grabbed the car keys and took off, I shouting after her, "Two lefts to the Merritt, then south to Exit 34" as she ran back through the woods to the parking lot.

As soon as she was gone, Richard gently took my hand and led me out of the lodge and back into the dark deep woods. We were not alone, because between the booze, the dancing and the heather on the hill, a lot of couples had been moved to romance and were humping around in the dark. How happy I was, how I hated myself for being so happy, as I followed Richard's MacDougal kilt and Prince Albert Coatee into the darkness. His long legs in knee socks and the little garters called flashes. The proud column of his neck. His hair a little longer, his hand giving me an occasional encouraging squeeze.

Neither of us said anything until we reached a small grassy clearing, lit only by the moon and the faint flickering light from the torches, the music faint in the distance. Then he pulled me to him. "How do you want it, Cece?" he asked, in that familiar sexual voice of his. "This way?" He reached up under my skirt and with one graceful and practiced gesture pulled my pants down and off, and then slid his fingers into my warm, wet places while stars went off in my head. Then he slid that great Scottish penis inside me and picked me up from behind. I had never, in all my fantasies, felt like this—so hot and wet and open, so wild, so near to splitting in pieces, or so unstoppable as he marched slowly around the clearing, his hands on my bare behind. First he hummed with the music; then he said, "Cece, dear, try to be quiet or I'll come, and I don't want to yet; I'm an old man and it doesn't return so quickly." And so we crouched on the grass together, I on all fours; and then I turned over, and we twisted and turned and tangled; and we took off some of each other's clothes, so that my breasts were naked to his mouth. And finally he lay on top of me and exploded inside, our cries mingling with the distant skirl of the bagpipes.

I woke up in Rivertown the next morning—or rather noontime, for Richard and I had been at it in the woods, and then later at a motel, till four in the morning—and thought, *I'm pregnant.* A dream to that effect: My belly opened up and out marched three small children in kilts. Then I zipped myself up and we all played on the grass. Sure sign of pregnancy.

I put on some jeans and an old sweat shirt and staggered downstairs, stiff as a bride. It had been a while since I had been so athletic. I poured myself a cup of coffee and went out onto the porch, where Cassie sat on the swing under a lap robe, rocking slowly and staring into space.

"Hi." Silence. "I'm sorry." More silence. "I'm *not* sorry, for God's sake. Just because you're hung up about sex doesn't mean I am. Yes, I spent the night with Richard. So what? I had a great time."

She turned and looked at me. She looked tired and a little unkempt—which for Cassie meant six hairs were out of place and she had no mascara on. "Do you have any standards at all?"

"Christ, am I tired of that word."

"I thought you hated him."

"Oh, I guess I do. It's all mixed up together—don't you know that?"

"Are you going to marry him again?"

"Richard?" I laughed in amazement. "I'd die first."

"I don't understand a lot of things," she said. "Sometimes I feel terribly confused. I don't know where I belong. I feel different from everybody else—as though I can see farther, or something. Please don't laugh, Cece. You're the only one I can say these things to. I know it was stupid of me to get angry last night, but I couldn't help it. I honestly feel I can see wrong in places other people can't. I shouldn't blame you when it's me that's different."

"It's all right," I said.

"When I was driving home, I missed the exit and I found myself at a place called the Mountaintop Priory. It's in the Berkshires, overlooking a river. I found myself on this dead-end road going nowhere, and I looked down and there were nuns praying in the moonlight, chanting old hymns."

I sipped my coffee. "You did get lost."

"The strange thing is, I dreamed about exactly the same place a long time ago when I was still at home. Every detail was the same."

"Well, you might have seen it once and forgotten."

"But three nights ago I had the dream about Ginger again, and this time there was a nun in a black gown and white wimple. She was chanting and holding a prayer book."

"I think it's called a habit." God, did I have a headache! "Cassie, let's talk about something else. I don't give a shit about nuns this morning."

She ignored me. "She came over to the poor, bleeding horse and said, 'It isn't too late.' And she sang a little song over Ginger, and her wound was healed, and she got up and smiled and trotted away." She had that cloudy, dissolved look she had more and more often. "So this morning I said a special prayer of thanks. I can't tell you how relieved I am, Cece. Now I know exactly what I'm going to do. As you have probably guessed, I've been at a crossroads. And Sam's phone call when I got home last night, and the news about Stuart, has decided me."

"Stuart?" It was cold, and as I got up to go inside for a jacket, which would also get me out of earshot of Cassie, Dorothy and Jack drove up in the convertible. Somewhere in my muddled head emerged a memory: it was the day we'd all been waiting for, the day of the divorce. An event that had obviously waned in importance in the wake of Cassie's and my family romance, if that's what it was, plus last night's highlands gala.

"So what happened?" I called, bounding down the steps, or trying to on my stiff legs.

Dorothy and Jack, still in the car, had their heads together in frantic inaudible conversation. When Dorothy saw me, she immediately burst into tears, groping in her handbag for Kleenex. She was wearing Jack's prescribed divorce outfit, a plain navy blue suit and demure little hat, simple and deserving.

"Oh, dear. We lost."

"Lost *what?*" I asked, astounded.

"We didn't lose, Dotty," Jack snarled. "You got the

divorce. And I told you all along you'd never get half the business."

"What about the house?" I demanded.

Jack dropped his eyes and gritted his teeth. "Caspar got it."

"I'll starve," Dorothy wailed. "I'll have to go on Welfare."

"Oh, for Christ's sake," said Jack. "Stop blubbering, Dot. You get to live in the goddamn house, and you get a hundred and fifty a week. It could be a lot worse. Anyway, I told you we'll appeal."

"Terrific," I said to Jack. "Good work."

"All right, Missy Whichever-you-are. Celia. Cassie." He glared at me. "The judge was with Caspar all the way. He had a problem, see. He saw you and your cute matching sister running around town and knew who you were. Seems *he* had twin sisters, and he hated the sight of them because they got all the attention. Plus he never forgave his mother for having them."

"I don't believe it," I said. "Judges are supposed to be fair."

"Judges are human, sis. All this I got from the court clerk only when it was too late. If I'd known, I would have locked you two in the basement till today. On bread and water."

"But he can't make a decision based on that. He could get dis-judged."

Jack gave a hollow laugh. "What she got was bare-minimum fair. Everything is in Caspar's name, which counts in this state. If Dotty's careful, she can live on a hundred and fifty a week—Caspar's responsible for house maintenance, and in two years she'll be eligible for Social Security."

I looked at my poor mother, blowing her nose. "Oh, Dorothy. I'm sorry. It'll be all right."

She opened the door and slowly got out as I held the door for her. "Thank you, Cassie."

"I'm Celia."

"Oh, so you are. How silly of me; it's the shock. I'm going in and lie down." She looked at Jack. "We'll talk later, and make plans for the evening."

"Well, I might be busy," said Jack, avoiding her eye and mine too. "We said we'd have dinner to celebrate, and to tell the truth, I don't feel much like celebrating. I have to think a lot of things over, Dotty—a lot of things."

And with that the cad drove off, leaving Dorothy to burst into tears afresh and run inside, slamming the screen door. I should have followed her in to be supportive, but the thought of the flask and the pink bathrobe, now inevitable, was so depressing that I sat down on an old tree stump by the sidewalk to hold my head for a minute and to try to work up the courage to go inside. How fragile our hopes at any age.

As I sat there in my old spot—for this was a place where, many years before, I had spent hours brooding and dreaming—a skinny little girl in jeans came around the corner, a heavy knapsack on her back. She looked tired and weighed down and, when she got closer, about as unhappy as any kid I'd ever seen. She had big, sad eyes and long dark hair, and she looked so much the way I must have looked at the same age that I wondered if I was making her up. She dragged her scuffed Nike running shoes along the ground, and her jacket was dirty and had a couple of holes in it.

She looked like a hundred other kids in Rivertown, and I would have accepted her as such; but when she saw me she began running toward me, saying, "Mom, oh, Mom! Oh, Christ, I'm so glad to see you!" and then she flung herself into my lap sobbing. "Oh, Mom, I've missed you. I couldn't stand it another fucking minute in that crazy house, and especially after Stuart—"

Things started clicking into place. "You're Shelli. I'm your Aunt Celia."

She started and stared at me. "Oh, shit, I forgot that twin business. Is my Mom here?"

"Yes, she's right on the porch."

As I recount all this, it's obvious that my mind was working slowly that morning, I having had no breakfast and being freezing cold besides, and probably because the Scottish interlude had confused my normally brilliant deductive powers. For whatever reasons, not only had I not noticed that Cassie didn't follow me to the car when

Dorothy drove up in her new destitution, but I had also not noticed what Shelli now pointed out, that she was no longer on the porch under her lap robe. Taking my niece's hand, I led her up the path and into the house, where I yelled for Cassie but heard no sound except the predictable sobbing from Dorothy's room.

"Is that her?" Shelli asked, alarmed.

"No, that's Grandma."

"What's wrong with Grandma?"

"Oh, nothing really bad. She didn't get Grandpa's money is all. Here, sit here." I took the knapsack off her back, and she sat by the cold fireplace while I searched the house from stem to stern for Cassie.

When I came back, the child was sobbing again.

"What is it, darling?" I hadn't seen her in five years.

"Where did she go?"

"I don't know. All her things are here. Maybe she went for a walk or something. Or to Neiman-Marcus, which she loves." (But she hadn't taken the car.) "Shelli, what's the matter?" Then, as red and green lights started going off in my head, "What happened to Stuart?"

"Didn't Mommy tell you?"

"No." I began to go cold with fear.

"But Daddy told her. He called her just before I left for the airport. But Christ, he's such a jerk. I mean he just let her have it like that: 'Cassie, Stuart is dead.' And he sounded angry and cruel, and I couldn't stand the fucking place another minute. Or him. Or that goddamn Eleanor, who was always telling me how in love with me she was. Honestly, she's crazy. And all the drugs—"

"Shelli, you're going too fast for me. What happened to your brother?" I was afraid to hear it.

"He just *died*." Tears flooded her eyes. "He was always lying around his room stoned, and nobody noticed much when he didn't appear for a long time. And he'd been sleeping a lot, because sometimes sleeping helped him think straight. His head was really messed up from drugs. He said he didn't think his brain would ever work right again." The horror of what she was saying filled me with a cold, sick feeling. "Then last night I went in to see him, just to check up on him. I was always the one who did it. He looked funny, and I shook him. I couldn't get him to move. Then I got the rest of them to come in, and Sammy looked at me in a funny way and said, 'He's dead. Shit, he's dead.' Like Ginger.''

Together we wept. I was chilled to the marrow with horror. I held her against me half to comfort her and half so she wouldn't see my face. This was my sister's house, where a child had died of neglect and another had run for her life. A California bedlam, this perfectly run home of Cassie's. I had never, never understood.

"Shelli, does your father know you're here?" I asked when we had recovered somewhat.

"Well, I left a note saying I was going to Mom. And I took two hundred dollars from his wallet and I told him I was going to get a job and pay him back.''

I looked at her tear-stained face and stringy hair, and I had never felt so helpless.

"Are you hungry?" I asked.

"I don't know." She wiped her nose on her sleeve. "Is there a McDonald's around here?''

"No, but there's a lot of food here." I led her into the kitchen and opened the refrigerator. "Cold roast beef. Chocolate cake. Apples. Bread. Cheese." I put it all on the kitchen table. "Now, listen, Shelli. I want you to sit here and eat. Then go over to that little room there—the study—and sleep.''

"Where are *you* going?" Slight alarm.

"I'm going to look for your mother.''

"Okay." She gave me a long look, which turned surly at the end. "I hate it that you guys look alike.''

"Well, we can't help it. Anyway, soon we won't as much.'' Three of my Caribbean Mango nails had broken off, and my hair was getting as wild as ever, because I'd given up the hairdresser a few days before. She looked around and glanced at the door. "Promise me you won't leave," I said.

Her eyes dropped. "Okay. I haven't any place to go anyway.''

"If you want, you can go up and see Grandma. It would be a nice surprise for her. But try not to cry anymore, because one weeper at a time is all I can cope with.''

I left her with a roast-beef sandwich in one hand and a piece of chocolate cake in the other, her eyelids already drooping. I ran into Caspar's old bedroom and whisked off the bed cover and turned down the sheets, then turned on the bedside light and pulled down the blind. Then I ran out the back door and got into the car.

I had no idea where Cassie had gone. First I drove around the block a couple of times, then went slowly toward the center of town—in which direction she could have gone without my having seen her from the front walk. My mind was going pretty fast, but not fast enough, because I hadn't the slightest idea why she had left, and I tried to remember what she had said before on the porch. I was bad. I had no standards. She was confused. She was different. Crossroads. Decision. Nuns in the moonlight. Ginger dream this time with optimistic nun who saves the day.

The dreadful logic that presented itself to me would have been almost funny if it hadn't been built on tragedy, or if it hadn't suggested, in the most frightening way, the destruction of the person I loved most in the world.

I swung onto the parkway to go northwest toward the foothills of the Berkshires.

CASSIE
(At the Mountaintop Priory)

Well, it seems I've made it. The obstacles have been overcome and I am at peace with myself at last. Certainly I never expected it to be easy, because following God's Word has always been extremely difficult throughout history. Only knowing what I had to do has made it possible; and still, all those I love—Cece, Mother, Sam, Sammy, even little Shelli—have tried to make me leave, because no matter how carefully I try to explain, they still don't understand. I'm sure now that all the events of my life have led me here, culminating in the tragic death of my younger son, which God sent as a final convincing sign that He wants me to be His daughter—or something like that. There are still details I haven't figured out, but now I have plenty of time to look back over the past.

You may think it's strange that I, who was so involved in the hurlyburly of a growing family, a successful husband and a busy household have chosen the contemplative life. Well, all along the way were signs which passed almost unnoticed at the time but which I now know were flagstones on the path that led me here, culminating in my dream about Ginger and the nun. You may remember the two times God spoke to me, saying "Your Mother Needs You More." Though God certainly must have had Dorothy partly in mind, now I'm almost sure He was also referring to another, more divine Mother—either the Mother

Superior of the Priory, Mother Gregory, or else even God *Her*self. This may seem like a strange idea at first. But one of my scholarly projects while I am here is to pursue the possibility that God is actually a woman—for I'm sure there's a strong case to be made for such a thing. And since I know that truth can come from unlikely mouths, I think even Eleanor's babble about the sexes being "God's joke" hinted at this, especially since she added that we "must all *rise above*" whatever it was we were supposed to rise above—our bodies, I think. And in coming to this lovely place on top of the mountain, I have certainly risen above my entire previous life. So you can see how the way was pointed out to me.

It wasn't so easy to be accepted here, even after I explained all this to Mother Gregory. When I first drove up in the Rivertown taxi, she was extremely doubtful about whether I'd fit into the monastic life, because I was "so much of the world" plus being a little on the old side. But I explained that this was exactly why my decision to give my life to God was so much deeper and truer, knowing so well what the world was like, and having been called so loudly and clearly. I added that I was sure I'd be an asset to the Mountaintop Priory. I have a good mezzo-soprano voice, which, I said, needed only a little training to make a striking addition to the chants I had been hearing in my dreams. I was skilled in tasks such as gardening and cooking, as well as being experienced in the organization of community life and having the ability to delegate work, if I ever rose to such a position of responsibility. I added that I had been attracted to convent life ever since seeing *The Sound of Music*, which made a deep impression on me many years ago when I first saw it.

The Reverend Mother sat and listened to me with her mouth slightly open and that same expression I have seen so often on people's faces when I try very hard to speak the truth in a direct way. Then she said, "Wait here, Mrs. Coopersmith," and she went off to confer with some of the other Mothers or Sisters or whatever, and as I sat waiting in that simple office, where a picture of Mary Magdalene hung on the wall, I knew I had found my true home at last.

I'd talked fast, because I knew it wouldn't be long before Cece found me, and sure enough, I had been there for only an hour or so when I saw that miserable Ford roaring up the mountain road, clattering and clanking. I did something I almost never do, which is ask God for his help to get me through a trying situation. Usually I consider it a cowardly thing to do, but this time, since I was carrying out His Word, I didn't think He would mind. I hoped that Cece wouldn't be wearing those stupid twin clothes—namely, the same gabardine pants, cream silk shirt and Perry Ellis sweater that I had put on that morning and was still wearing, along with my new ombré calf ankle boots from Susan Bennis/ Warren Edwards, tweed cloak and coral alpaca muffler. But she got out of the car and I saw that she was already starting to forget the good grooming I'd taught her, and had reverted to an old sweat-shirt with CONNECTICUT STATE U. on it and old jeans and her dirty U.S. Keds. Plus half-combed hair and no makeup.

Cece has been at the root of my conflict all along, or at least been a very important part of it. I love her dearly and always will, which is the only reason I ever did this stupid twin-playing, even though she is perverted and has a peculiar sense of humor and screws everybody in sight and has not led a normal life like mine. I swear I still don't understand why she wanted to do it, and I pointed out from the beginning that there was something evil about it, which was one reason I had to leave and come here. I knew all along we were doing something bad, and when I heard what the judge had done to Mother because of our twinning, that confirmed it in my mind, and I quietly got up and left, walked quickly downtown and got a taxi at the train station. Innocent people were paying for our foolish game, and more are yet to come. Possibly even the death of Stuart was punishment for it too—I'm not sure. Certainly God had told me that it was too late to try to be children again, though Cece could never see anything wrong with it. The only good thing that came of it was that the horrible Scotch business led me here that night, which was another sign. While Cece gave herself up to her bodily lusts, I was chosen for higher things.

Anyway, because of the evil lure of the twinning I knew

I must stay away from Cece until I was stronger, so I went and hid in the closet of Mother Gregory's office, leaving the door open the slightest crack so I could hear what was going on. As Mother Gregory came back into the room, in stormed Cece. She explained who she was, talking a mile a minute the way she always does, and asked if I had come. "Why, she was just here a minute ago, Miss Armstrong. I can't imagine where she went." "Well, we'd better find her," Cece said in her impatient way, "because we're both going to have a big problem on our hands. She's mentally ill, you know."

Oh, the bitch! I never cease to be amazed at the way she lies.

The Reverend Mother Gregory is a wise and sensible woman, which she has to be to run this place, and she took a long look at Cece and said, "Oh, you say she's crazy, do you?" I almost laughed out loud, because Cece looked like an inmate from Bedlam herself.

"You've got to listen," she said. "She's having a psychotic episode brought on by the death of her son."

"Are you a doctor or a psychiatrist?" she asked.

"No, I'm her twin sister."

"I appreciate your concern, Miss Armstrong, but twenty years as head of this Priory has made me quite a good judge of people. This is a serious and hardworking place, and Mrs. Coopersmith strikes me as a stable, mature person, as well as intelligent and unusually devout."

Cece screamed, "Don't tell me you're going to take her in!"

"Calm down, please. It's being seriously considered. Of course, there's always a trial period."

Cece closed her eyes and said melodramatically, "I don't believe it. I just don't."

"It's your word against hers, Miss Armstrong. I have to go on my own instincts. Of course we have to find her, but as far as I'm concerned, right now she's under the jurisdiction of this abbey."

Celia argued some more, but Mother Gregory won. Cece left in a huff, saying she'd be back with psychiatrists, commitment papers and subpoenas. I hoped she wouldn't waste her time.

So I came out of the closet, and Mother Gregory said, "It's not unusual to have members of the family coming to say our novitiates are mentally disturbed. It's hard for them to accept God's Word when it comes so suddenly and strongly." So with that she gave me the Blessing of the Mountaintop, a kiss on each hand, and then scurried around and got me the white novitiate's robe and led me to a small dressing room, telling me to put it on and give my worldly possessions to her in case I changed my mind during the trial period. Well, that was the hardest part—giving up my lovely clothes for this plain unbleached linen robe. But by then I knew this was part of the whole plan, and there had been something bad about my unusual love of "stuff" if God was taking it away from me and leading me into this simple life. Then when I had changed (I was dying to see how I looked, but there are no mirrors here), Mother Gregory showed me to a small bare cell with cot and desk, where I would live for the next few months as a "Bride of Christ."

Fortunately, during the trial period novitiates are not allowed to see anybody from the outside world; and I will always be grateful for the way Mother Gregory fended off Cece, who came back dragging Jack Brodsky and Mother and Shelli, who seems to be living with them, and then Sam, who I was told made a dreadful, embarrassing scene, saying that he wanted his wife back, his life was useless without me and so on. I only heard it later from the Reverend Mother and know that she handled the situation in a kind, sympathetic but firm way. Father and Yo came too, and of all of them, Yo was the only one who approved of what I had done, probably because of her Catholic background. I believe she is a good woman in spite of her strange job, her peculiar employee and her hideous house. But I have a dreadful premonition about her, which appeared in another Ginger dream the night before she came, and this time Ginger had Yo's face and she was crying "Help me," and again I couldn't help. I was so worried about it that I told Mother Gregory and asked if I, or someone, could just tell her to be careful; but she kindly but firmly refused, saying I was in seclusion for my own good, and I should just pray for Yo an hour a day, which I did. I deeply hoped that I was wrong and that she and Daddy would have a long and happy marriage, for in this tranquil place I have lost all bitterness about my parents' divorce and firmly believe that it was all for the best.

Now I've been here six months and have safely passed through the dangers of the earlier stormy seas—the fear that my faith might prove too weak, that I could not give up the material world, that I could not fit into life at the Priory or that the members of my beloved but misled family would succeed in taking me away from here and putting me in a mental hospital. Certainly they tried hard, though recently their efforts seem to have abated as they have run out of ideas. Cece brought a psychiatrist named Edith, whom I talked to after the trial period was over when I felt strong enough to deal with difficult things, and Edith said I was definitely psychotic. Then Cece brought a psychologist named Meg who said I was schizophrenic. They brought Ol' Doc Schroeder, who said, "She's nutty as a fruitcake. Lock 'er up." Jack Brodsky started out by making a lot of threats to Mother Gregory about the harboring of the insane, but he ran out of steam because he's basically not interested, since he's decided to retire with Mother to his Florida condo. And I don't believe he was really interested in getting me out. I heard him say to Mother, "Oh, hell, Dot. She's better off here," which was the first sensible thing I've ever heard him say. Even Sam has given up, though it was very hard for me not to help him or go back to my old habits as his wife. He has had a great deal on his mind, selling the house and the condo in Acapulco to pay his debts, and then he spent some time at Saracen—where, incidentally, he never sent Stuart because he couldn't find it in the phone book.

He told me he will never get over his guilt about Stuart and feels personally responsible for his death. I comforted him as well as I could and said there was no doubt in my mind that Stuart had had to be sacrificed for me to understand that God wanted me in His (Her) service, and though it was a terrible thing, it was the price I had to pay for my State of Grace.

And Sam listened and said, "Oh, Cassie, I've loved you so. I've been weak and I'm a failure and I've made a lot of mistakes, and you're still the best thing that ever happened to me. And you've never been more beautiful.'' And to my disbelief, he actually started to get sexually excited as we sat there under the rose arbor in the little Priory garden.

I haven't seen myself in a mirror since I've been here, and I'm not supposed to think about it, but I can't help thinking how flattering the cream-colored habit is, and I've always looked well with my hair—which is now back to its original chestnut color—pulled back in a tight knot. After a good deal of discussion I've persuaded the Reverend Mother that head-shaving is not only absurd, but a direct contradiction of God's feminism—which subject she has suggested I use for my first Philosophical Discourse.

So bit by bit, they all seem to have accepted the idea of my being here, particularly since their efforts to get me out have been to no avail, because basically it is up to Mother Gregory. She has allowed me to see only as many of them as she thinks my strength permits, and a great deal of what I tell now I learned only long afterward.

The truth is that what happens in the outside world seems increasingly unimportant. My life is full and rewarding. I bake bread which is sold commercially. I have learned to tend the beehives and cultivate the herb garden, where my specialties are rosemary and thyme. And I have worked hard to master the Gregorian chants we sing in the moonlight, just as I saw on that night after I left Cece in Brigadoon—a night that now seems to have taken place a hundred years ago.

How important and meaningful these things seem compared with the sad lives of my dear ones, their worries and miseries and disappointments. Instead of anguish I have a life of contemplation; instead of frustration and emptiness I have the greatest contentment and sense of fulfillment. I have suggested to Cece that she join me here, but she is obviously not ready yet, and probably won't ever be, though I know I am at last strong enough to be with her without the evil returning.

Dear Cece. I am with her in spirit all the time, and in a sense we are closer than we have ever been, particularly since I no longer have to live with her. But it has always been better when we were apart, which she never understood. She seems contented with her life, which she now understands she must live without me. So she's learned at forty-four what I have known since we were six, but that's better than never learning it at all. I'm grateful for her good qualities and pray to God to help get rid of her bad ones, though He hasn't made much progress. And I bless her for being different.

CELIA

I still don't know, perhaps I'll never know, if I drove Cassie crazy. I always envied her. I always wanted whatever she had. I was always pushing, and she was always pulling back. Maybe I made her nuts—but if so, I did because I love her. Is that any excuse? Oh, the things we do in the name of love.

I'm even beginning to wonder if she's crazy at all. She's the pride of the Priory and is already reorganizing the nuns along the lines of higher standards and greater efficiency. Her Discourse "God Is a Woman" has galvanized canonical law. It's possible that all the months we spent with shrinks and lawyers, trying to get her out of there, were wasted. As always, it looks as if Cassie has the last word.

And what is Sister Celia doing? Picking up the pieces— but that's all right. They are pieces I love, and even if they don't fit together too well sometimes, I will never stop trying to make them work. Here is our curious Rivertown household: Me. Shelli Coopersmith. Pierre Devereaux. Caspar, a sad old man. Bernard on a part-time basis, just as before. Did I relent? Finally—when Maria left him for a better, richer guy. He comes for weekends and when the rock music gets deafening, wonders why he left his quiet apartment. And what does he hear at his quiet apartment, every other weekend? The rock music of his own kids.

We are truly an odd group.

One of the reasons I take Cassie more seriously is that she knew something was going to happen to Yo. They didn't want her to communicate with anybody during that time, but she sneaked a note to me via the truck driver who takes the Priory bread, honey, herbs and such to the distributor. The note said, *"Cece, please tell Yo to be very careful. I've had a premonition of great danger. If you love me, swear never to tell about this note."* The note came when Caspar and Yo were on their honeymoon at the Delaware Water Gap—having survived their wedding, during which Dorothy, on the outs with Jack, turned up and made a big hoopla when the minister asked if anybody saw any reason and so forth. Dorothy—wonderful as ever, it was her finest hour—rose to her feet and announced in stirring tones that she saw plenty of reason, because Caspar had carried on with That Woman for years and in fact, the two *had a child together.* And in the stunned silence that followed, I looked around the church and there was Caspar standing with that tilt he has and his glittering glasses and his amazed expression, and there was Pierre (who was best man—or rather, best boy) standing in exactly the same way tilting and glittering and so on. And I knew I had known without knowing. Pierre Dev-row is my half-brother—the little bastard. No wonder I can't resist pestering him. Anyway, the wedding went on *malgré tout* . . . but I'm avoiding telling the unbearable story.

Since I've always believed that it's better to do things than not do them, I called Caspar and Yo at the Water Gap Inn.

"It probably sounds stupid," I said, "but Cassie thinks something awful is going to happen to Yo. Please tell her to be careful."

Then Yo gets on the phone. "But Celia, I do not believe in premonitions. I am very very practical. Sometimes I think Cassie has some strange *idées religieuses,* and I must speak to her about zem."

"Sometimes she's right. Please, Yo. Just be alert for trouble."

"Well, *bien sûr.* Anyway, I am extremely strong and able to defend myself, as you know. Caz-par depends on me for my physical strength."

She wouldn't listen. And when they got home, Tommy Triste came up behind her outside the back door and hit her on the head with his hatchet and split her skull open and killed her.

Poor Caspar collapsed completely, and Pierre instigated and joined the search party to find Tommy. He forgot about Harvard—not that Harvard had ever been a possibility anyway. The poor kid had made it all up, because he was just an average kid and an average student and he wanted to be special. Well, now he's at State U., where I went, and he's special to me. But inside, he's in pieces.

They caught Tommy, who confessed that he'd loved Yo and had been miserable ever since she'd gotten mixed up with "those cruddy people"—Caspar and Cassie and me. He was jealous, and he didn't trust Caspar somehow (which shows what sterling judgment he has), and particularly after he saw "those fuckin' twins." We made him crazy, because he knew twins were evil; the guy in the next cell had told him. He knew Yo wouldn't listen if he told her what he thought, and he knew that if he killed Caspar or us, she'd hate him and back he'd go into the pen and would never see her again. So therefore, he had to kill Yo. Of course—what other choice did he have? For his impeccable reasoning and forthright action, Tommy is now back in Solitary with about five life sentences to serve.

I've lived with that one alone, because I haven't been able to bring myself to tell Cassie. Though she'd probably take it a lot better than I, because she's got God. It's simple cowardice—I can't bear the thought of sitting there in the garden under the rose trellis and telling her. I know. I'd start saying this was proof that God was no good, and then we'd get in some long, convoluted argument. But I have to tell her. Every week I promise myself to do it; every week I put it off again.

Does it help Pierre to know that Caz-par is his real father, rather than that made-up man on the bicycle? They're cautious with each other, those two, approaching slowly, warily. I'm biding my time, trying to get Caspar to cheer up a little. He just sits and stares into space. He only half-runs The Bower of Flowers, though we all pitch in and help as much as we can.

Meg thinks I'm out of my mind.

"God, Celia. The pathology. Who do you think you are—Saint Francis? Even normal teen-agers are impossible, and the ones with deep psychic scars like your two are powder kegs. Drugs. Sex. Violence. Antisocial behavior and inappropriate acting-out. And poor Caspar with his senile depression."

"He's grieving, you nerd. He'll be all right."

"How do you know, Cece? He might need shock treatments or at least go on Elavil."

"No, he has a son. He has hope. He'll get over it."

But how do I know she isn't right? Only time will tell. Around here it's one day at a time. If I can't stand it, I'll join Cassie at the Priory.

Lest we forget her mother—an unlikely possibility—Shelli Coopersmith is resident moralist. Like Mother and Grandmother, she has *standards*. She won't even touch pot, and even though her fifteen-year-old friends apparently fuck their brains out, she remains chaste. Her interests are cheerleading and horticulture: not the most intellectual kid I've ever seen. She loves to help Grandpa at the store, where she is in charge of arranging the window, just as Cassie and I used to be. Nor will she let us forget Stuart, whom she loved deeply. She's trying not to blame anybody for his death, but it's hard. Particularly when all the adults blame themselves—me included, for not seeing what now seems obvious. She has bad dreams like the rest of us, and when she finally told me about how Eleanor was always following her around and trying to get into bed with her, I remembered Meg's dire words. What am I doing here? It all fell in my lap—that's what happened. No more or less than that.

Sam stays in touch with her and comes to visit every few months. For a while he was living with Sammy Junior and Eleanor in their newlywed pad in Venice; then he got his own apartment in Marina Del Rey. Though he's lowest of the low in Hollywood, he's still trying to sell rerun rights to *The Wimples,* and who knows? Stranger things have happened—and as he says, it only takes one deal. I've gotten to like him, and the way he looks at me breaks my heart. I always catch him at it, and then he drops his

eyes. "Sorry, Celia. I just can't help it." No more the
white jeans and gold chains of yesteryear. Now he wears a
three-piece dark suit, which is what all the L.A. enchiladas
are wearing now. And twenty extra pounds.

Dorothy and Jack love Miami Beach. Endless sun, endless bridge. Endless love. Endless fights.

When Jack went off to think everything over the day of
the divorce trial, it wasn't so much about Dot, it turned
out, as about his career. He'd never before lost a case, he
said, and maybe it was time to quit. He had never been
interested in Dorothy's so-called fortune, because she didn't
have one, and he didn't need it anyway. So his love was
true. Nor was he very much interested in Cassie's situation, though Dorothy dragged him over to the Priory during our initial panic. Basically, he liked the idea of one of
us being locked up somewhere so much that he couldn't
get into it. And since that wasn't how an attorney should
think, Jack decided to pack it in. Dorothy cried before she
left, and I cried too. And not a day passes without my
thinking how I could use her around here, for veal casserole, raking leaves and general kvetching. But she's gone
off to her second life.

Cassie didn't cry, because one of the things she left
behind in the outside world was emotion. Very, very
rarely does a flash of the old Cassie come through the
spaced-out manner that now expresses her madness/religion.
No matter how much I pick on her, she retains the disgusting tranquillity she had when she was a kid.

Neat, Sister Cassie—I end up with the kids and the
guilt that you don't have. The blame, which infests this
house like a plague, which we all try to fight; and who can
blame us for our blame? Shelli blames Sam and you.
Pierre blames not only Tommy Triste but Caspar and you
and me for upsetting the applecart of his life, and even Yo
for being so brave and so blind. And we blame ourselves
too. Caspar for giving in to Yo about Tommy and not
getting rid of him right in the beginning. For being too
distant from you and his grandchildren. The kids because
kids always blame themselves, which Meg says is a healthy
sign. And would you believe that Dorothy wrote that now
that her sex life is so terrific, she blames herself for

holding out on Caspar for all those years. No wonder Bernard likes it here—the place is *loaded* with Jewish guilt. He sits by the fire, smiles, reads the paper and tries to get me to wait on him. It's just like home.

And I, Sister Cassie? You already know, unless those veils you've drawn over you prevent you from seeing. I blame myself for loving you too much and not in the unselfish way we are all supposed to love each other. I picked and I nagged; I envied you, I was jealous, I wanted to change you. What I really wanted was for you to love me back even more, so you'd know how it felt to be the one with the ragged edges for a change. There was always something serene and secret about you that I couldn't get at, and I wanted us to merge so I could share what I thought was your peace of mind. And sometimes you were so special, so wise—much wiser than I ever was—and I wanted that too. But you simply turned your back and left me, and everybody else too. I still don't know who won and who lost, and that I even think in such terms is proof of my own earthbound mind. But we never forget you.

Now that Pierre is at State U. most of the time and Shelli is settling in at Rivertown High, I'm getting back to my so-called career. I do some free-lance work and have finally finished that darkroom in the basement. I earn a few bucks that we can certainly use, though I'm haunted by self-doubt. If I haven't achieved fame and fortune by this time, it's doubtful I ever will.

But something new is going on—grief, or else life, has cleared my eyes. I see through the camera as I never did before. I finally know what I want to show and how I want to show it. I used to have trouble finding things to take pictures of, because everything seemed like everything else. But now life is everywhere. It shimmers, it beckons as I walk down the street. It calls out to be preserved on film. All the details in this old neighborhood I've returned to have a sparkle and evanescence they never did before. I feel as though I'd never really looked—and seen—in my life.

In our house, everything counts, everything says something. My father's white-rimmed head as he sits on the porch rocker looking off down the street for his memories.

And the way he and Pierre looked the other day when they went for a walk together. I snapped them as they left and will show them my picture sometime as proof of genetic heritage. Shelli in the garden as she picks slugs off tomatoes. She looks like you and me. She looks at those rotten tomatoes with that cool look you used to have when you were telling me to get lost. Snap, snap, snap. And she turns and says, like her mother, "Oh, Aunt Cece, for God's sake. Not again." Yes, again. Even Bernard and the two tarts, Joanne and Sarah, when at my insistence he brought them for Sunday dinner, he making the salad and the two girls staring off into the distance. The same heads, the same necks. If I sound preoccupied with family resemblances, well, it follows. It's been a force in my life.

Even the dullest, homeliest objects have an excitement for me now. The light on the kitchen table in the morning and Dorothy's old china bowl she used to mix cakes in. Your room—now Shelli's—and those filthy old stuffed animals of yours she sleeps with. The garden at dusk. The empty porch swing where you sat that last morning; the unexpected sight of our two Glengarry hats on the closet shelf, dusty and forgotten. The spring-green maple, the fire dying in the evening.

It's all there. All I have to do is look.

About the Author

When Nora Johnson wrote THE WORLD OF HENRY ORIENT, the literary community witnessed the emergence of a fresh new voice. Since then she's gone on to become a frequent contributor to *The New Yorker* and *The Atlantic* and the author of the critically acclaimed FLASHBACK: NORA JOHNSON ON NUNNALLY JOHNSON and YOU CAN GO HOME AGAIN, named by the *New York Times* as one of the best books of 1982. THE TWO OF US goes to the heart of the myriad dilemmas of the '80s woman with the insight Nora Johnson's readers have come to expect. The author lives in New York City, where she is at work on a new novel.

Signet will sweep you off your feet . . .

(0451)

☐ **RANDOM HEARTS by Warren Adler.** Vivien Simpson assured herself that she had a perfect husband, but then, suddenly, shatteringly, he vanished. And Vivien was left with a mystery she had to solve even if it destroyed the only remnant of her marriage she had left to treasure. "Sensitive, ironic, very readable."—*New York Times Book Review*
(133951—$3.95)

☐ **WILD ROSE by Mary Canon.** Among the lavish plantations of the Carolinas, no other belle could rival Rose Marie Jacquard's beauty; no elegant gentleman could tame her rebellious ways. But when the fires of Civil War raged across the land, the wildness in her nature drove her to a reckless rendezvous with espionage and betrayal . . . (131010—$3.50)

☐ **ORIGINAL SINS by Lisa Alther.** Five kids spend their Tennessee childhood trading dreams of adulthood and they are certain that they are all destined for greatness. But what actually happens to them through twenty years of growing up is just about everything they had and had not dreamed of . . . in the sexiest, most searingly honest novel ever to glue you to every page, reading and remembering . . . (139666—$4.50)

☐ **RULES OF THE HEART by Gimone Hall.** Nora Jarret and Zan Scarborough were the best of friends growing up in the Depression-blighted small Texas town of Ganado. Then they met the Howland brothers and again their destinies were linked—in the men they loved . . . in the world they built and ruled . . . and in the destinies of their golden children . . .
(128605—$3.50)

Prices slightly higher in Canada

Buy them at your local

bookstore or use coupon

on next page for ordering.

FROM THE BESTSELLING AUTHOR OF *FAME AND FOR-TUNE*—A NOVEL OF THREE BEAUTIFUL WOMEN, RISKING EVERYTHING TO HAVE IT ALL . . .

PERFECT ORDER

Kate Coscarelli

A fast-paced luscious page turner that pulls out all the stops to tell it as it really is for the super-rich, the super-powerful, and the super-sexy. Glamorous Manhattan, with its whirlwind of social, political, and romantic intrigues, sets the stage for the story of Trish, Ann, and Millie—three women who share a passionate interest in the handsome senator and presidential hopeful Red O'Shea, and are soon swept into the exciting millionaire's world of Fifth Avenue condos, appointment-only luxury shopping, and high-level political game playing.